Devour Me

Books by Lydia Parks

ADDICTED

DEVOUR ME

SEXY BEAST VI
(with Kate Douglas and Anya Howard)

Published by Kensington Publishing Corporation

Devour Me

LYDIA PARKS

APHRODISIA

KENSINGTON BOOKS
http://www.kensingtonbooks.com

APHRODISIA BOOKS are published by

Kensington Publishing Corp.
119 West 40th Street
New York, NY 10018

ISBN-13: 978-0-7582-3800-9
ISBN-10: 0-7582-3800-2

First Kensington Trade Paperback Printing: September 2009

10 9 8 7 6 5 4 3 2 1

Printed in the United States of America

Contents

Dark Obsession

1

When Benjamin strode into the Tangled Net, letting the heavy wooden door slam behind him, his appearance quieted the dozen or so voices around the small bar.

"Welcome back, Captain," Rick said, pouring a double shot before it was ordered. After twenty years, he knew what everyone drank. "Hell of a storm brewing out there."

"Aye, that it is." Benjamin settled into his usual chair at the table in the corner. "Nothing like a good storm to stir the blood."

"And wake ghosts," a white-haired fisherman added from his seat at the bar.

"Oh, hush that kind of talk." Abby shoved the old man's shoulder good-naturedly as she passed behind him. "We don't need ghosts in here." She grabbed the glass from the bar and carried it ceremoniously across the room.

Abby wore a skirt so short, it barely covered her very round bottom, and a blouse cut low enough to draw stares. Flaming red curls encircled her face and played at her shoulders as she sauntered, head lowered seductively, placing one foot directly in front of the other so that her hips swayed hypnotically.

Benjamin took in every movement. Her full breasts rose and fell with each step, and the fabric of her skirt swished against her thighs. The tip of her tongue slid across her bottom lip and her green eyes flashed excitement.

She deposited the drink on the table with a thud. "Well, now, look what the cat dragged in."

Benjamin emptied half the glass and wiped his mouth with the back of his hand. Then he leaned back and smiled up at her. "I do believe you're lovelier tonight than you were last month."

"Three months ago," she said.

"Three? You must be mistaken."

She dropped one fist to her hip. "Three months and two days."

"I can't imagine where the time goes." He shook his head slowly.

"I bet you can't," she said quietly. She leaned forward, flattening her palms on his table, exposing every bit of her cleavage to his hungry gaze. "And I suppose you expect me to drop everything just because you happened to wander in."

She straightened and spun around to leave.

He caught her hand and tugged, and she tumbled into his lap with a squeal and a laugh.

Her familiar scent filled his head with memories of pleasure-filled hours, and he nuzzled her soft hair to pick up more as he tuned into the steady beat of her heart.

"I do expect you to drop everything," he said.

She wrapped her arm around his shoulders and made herself more comfortable. "Ah, what the hell?" Holding his gaze, she downed the rest of his whiskey, plopped the glass back onto the table, and then kissed him.

It wasn't a deep, meaningful kiss, but an invitation. Her warm lips paused against his for a moment, promising more when there weren't so many witnesses.

His cock began to harden beneath her rump and she grinned. "Missed me, did you?"

"I always do."

"And whose fault is that?" She raked her fingers through his hair. "You know where I am."

He slid his hand up the inside of her luscious thigh. "That's why I'm here."

"Then why are we sitting at this table?"

Benjamin rose and placed Abby on her feet. He offered her his arm, and she looped hers through it.

A bottle crashed to the floor in front of them and shattered.

"She's having a drink with me!"

"Bullshit! I asked her first!"

Two men squared off in the middle of the dimly lit bar, both raising fists and hunching defensively. Glass crunched beneath their boots as they circled. Judging by their ragged clothing and the smell of them, they were fishermen freshly returned from the sea and already well on the road to inebriation.

A wide-eyed mousy waitress stood against the bar behind them, clutching a tray to her chest. "Please, don't fight. Please."

"Aw, crap, not again." Abby released Benjamin's arm and stepped forward. "What do you two think you're doing?"

Benjamin drew her out of harm's way and moved around her. "Gentlemen, this is no way to behave."

"Fuck off, old man," the taller of the two said. "This is between him and me."

The shorter one took the opportunity to connect a fist with his opponent's jaw, and the taller man staggered back a step. Then, growling with anger, he swung wildly at the shorter man's head.

The mousy waitress stepped forward, pleading. "Please!"

One of the combatant's elbows sent her reeling against the bar. Her tray fell to the floor and rolled away.

Benjamin grabbed the two men by the fronts of their shirts, and raised them into the air. They flailed and tried to break free.

"Enough!" He brought their heads together in midair with a crack and then tossed them in opposite directions. The two men skidded across the floor, bumping into tables and chairs, until they came to rest against opposite walls.

The smaller one rose first, rubbing his head and glaring at Benjamin.

Benjamin took a step in his direction and the man staggered out the front door. The taller man followed, half running and half crawling, and the door swung shut behind him.

After a moment, applause rose from the remaining customers. Benjamin bowed formally, then turned toward Abby and offered his arm again, which she took.

As they passed the younger waitress, who swiped at tears as she retrieved her tray, Abby stopped. "Poor Tess. I'm not sure she's really suited to this job." She looked up at Benjamin with eyebrows arched. "Maybe she needs a little boost in self-confidence?"

"As you wish."

Abby whispered something to Tess; Benjamin purposely didn't listen. Then she waved to Rick, who nodded, and the two women started toward the back of the building arm-in-arm.

Benjamin followed. As they climbed the old staircase, constructed at least two hundred years ago, he studied the women, so dissimilar in their matching outfits. Where Abby was round and soft with curves he knew well, this new woman, Tess, was angular and tight—not unattractive, but very different. She was quite a bit shorter than Abby, who was fairly tall for a woman.

Both had strong, steady heartbeats.

At the top of the stairs they turned to the right and continued to the last room, which Abby unlocked with a key hidden on top of the doorframe. She called this her resting room, although as far as he could see she rarely rested here. The Tangled

Net had once been an active brothel. Now it was a nice, generally quiet place to drink a beer or two, and Abby, as part owner, did as she wished. She was, however, no whore, simply an enthusiastic partner for one or two men. And Benjamin.

"I'm really sorry," Tess said, wiping fresh tears with the back of her hand.

"For what?" Abby sat on the edge of a quilt-covered bed and drew the smaller woman down beside her.

Benjamin unbuttoned his cloak, hung it on a hook by the door, and settled into one of the upholstered chairs facing the bed where he could continue to study the two women. Wind rattled upstairs windows and drove occasional drops of rain against the ancient glass where they pinged like pebbles.

"They were fighting because of me," Tess sniffed. "And I dropped a bottle."

Abby patted her hand in motherly fashion. "They were fighting *over* you. A different matter altogether. And we all drop drinks now and then. No big deal, as long as you don't make a habit of it."

She nodded, but didn't look convinced.

Abby glanced at Benjamin.

"Tess, is it?" Benjamin rose and extended one hand, palm up.

The woman nodded again. After a moment's hesitation, she placed her hand in his. He drew her to her feet and gazed down into her hazel eyes. She couldn't be much more than five foot two, so barely reached his chest.

"My name is Benjamin," he said, softening his voice. "Are you from Black Cove?"

Her hand trembled in his, and she shook her head. "Gloucester."

He smiled. "Daughter of the sea, then."

She nodded.

He pictured heavy rock buildings and grey boulders rising from green hills leading down to the water's edge. He smelled salt and rotting fish warming in the sun, and heard water slapping against wooden hulls. He felt the steady rise and fall of the tides like the breath of the Earth itself. And he listened to her heartbeat.

Tess's hand stilled.

He rolled the sensations together into a bundle and let them radiate from his fingers as he reached up and stroked her cheek. "You are part of all this," he whispered, "reaching back through time. Take it into your heart." He cupped her jaw. "Draw strength from it."

He felt the line connect at that point, and Tess's eyes widened. She saw the glory of the past and the strength of the sea. He had a clear path into her thoughts. "What passes here tonight you won't remember as anything unusual," he said.

Her eyelids fluttered and he caught her as she collapsed. Gently, he returned her to her seat on the bed and plopped back into his chair.

Abby held the younger woman's hand. "Is she okay?"

Benjamin nodded. "Easier to influence than some."

"Like me, you mean?"

He raised his foot. "Perhaps."

Abby tugged off one boot and then the other, dropping them to the floor. "Come on, tell me. Did you do this voodoo stuff on me when we first met?"

He grinned, his mouth firmly shut.

In fact, he'd spent a full year visiting Abby every few months before she realized what was going on. But she was stronger-willed than most mortals he'd known, and he'd finally been unable to remove the memory. Fortunately, she'd remembered with acceptance.

Taking his hand, she drew him to his feet and toward the bed. "You don't plan to make me wait all night, do you? I have customers downstairs."

He had absolutely no desire to make her wait. In fact, he was doing his best not to think about the upcoming activities to maintain his appearance. But the sound of her heartbeat continued to strengthen in his head, reminding him of the beauty of her face in the throes of passion. His mouth ached and his vision began to take on a tinge of red.

Judging by her smile, his appearance had already changed. He ran his tongue across one enlarging fang.

Abby drew her blouse off over her head and then wriggled out of her skirt and underclothes and kicked off her shoes. In spite of the ten years she'd aged since he'd started visiting her, she was still an attractive woman. She had full breasts he loved to caress, and his palms felt empty as he admired them. Her red hair framed her face with a glow reminiscent of sunrise.

He unbuttoned his shirt, shrugged it off, and shed his stockings. Although his pants felt tight, he kept them on for the moment.

Abby laughed and dropped back on the bed with a bounce, raising one knee suggestively.

"What about Tess?" she asked.

Benjamin ran his hand down the side of the younger woman's face. She opened her eyes and looked up at him.

Her eyes widened as she found Abby lying naked beside her, and her gaze jumped back up to Benjamin. He watched as she took in his partial nudity, and her admiration flamed his already rising hunger. "Please, my dear, join us," he said.

She nodded slowly, suggesting his invasion of her thoughts hadn't yet worn off. No matter. She wouldn't do anything she didn't want to do. He hadn't planted those kinds of thoughts in her head.

Tess rose and took off her clothes as she held his gaze.

She was more attractive than he would have guessed. Her brown shoulder-length hair had little body, but was smooth. And the angles of her hips and limbs were softened just enough to keep her from being too thin, although she certainly looked more fragile than Abby. Her breasts were small, but not undeveloped, and her eyes flashed emotions he couldn't begin to keep track of.

He leaned down and kissed her lips, experimenting with the feel of them under his. They were tight and thin at first, but as she relaxed her lips parted. Benjamin slid his hand behind her neck and drew her up for more. He tasted no hint of alcohol or tobacco, only simple feminine sweetness. Her tongue met his tentatively, and her small hands warmed his chest. Intrigued, he searched farther, circling her mouth, enjoying the way she responded by drawing him in deeper. She gripped his shoulders.

He jerked at the sudden appearance of a hand at the front of his pants, sliding down the length of his concealed shaft, but realized at once it was Abby. She had a habit of getting straight to the heart of the matter.

Abby unbuttoned his pants, relieving the pressure on his swollen cock and he sighed into Tess's mouth. Then Abby began to stroke him, using both hands.

He tore his mouth from Tess's and watched as Abby licked the length of his cock, coating it with wet warmth, drawing it to its full size. She closed her lips around the head, and his fangs descended in a rush.

"Wait," he breathed. Things were moving too fast. He hadn't had two women at once in many years. Perhaps decades. The hunger would take over if he wasn't careful.

Abby sat up, pouting, her hands still sliding up and down his length. He backed out of her grip.

"Hey, what—?"

Benjamin leaned over and stopped Abby's question with a kiss, drawing Tess down beside her as he did. Once he had them sitting together, he stepped back and grinned. "Now, that's what I like to see. Two beautiful lasses disrobed and waiting."

Abby raised one eyebrow. "Make us wait too long and we may lose interest."

"I hope not." He laughed. The fire in Abby's eye was a long way from burning out.

He knelt in front of them, enjoying their contrasts. Tess still looked hesitant where Abby was sure of what she wanted. Of course, Abby knew exactly what was to come. Tess had no idea.

He nipped Abby's thigh, careful not to actually bite, and she laughed. Then he reached up and drew her mouth down to his.

He enjoyed her taste, as familiar as his warm study on a cold night, and more enticing than good scotch. Her tongue met his as she invited him in, and she buried her fingers in his hair.

Tess caressed his shoulder and back, and he turned his attention to her, first kissing her sweet mouth, then moving down to the side of her neck. He held his lips over her pulse and enjoyed the steady feel of it moving just out of his reach.

Abby groaned softly, and drew him back to her for the same treatment. He kissed her salty neck and playfully nipped her flesh, then stopped to enjoy her pounding heartbeat.

Yes, either would have been a wonderful partner for the evening. Together, they promised a symphony of pleasure.

He moved his mouth down to Abby's marvelous breasts, circling her large areolas one at a time and purposely avoiding her hardening nipples. She groaned in protest.

Turning his head, he attended Tess's taut little breasts and quickly realized how sensitive she was. Her scent of arousal peppered the air as he sipped at her nipples and suckled gently.

"Oh, god," she breathed, her hand curling into a fist against his shoulder.

He withdrew before he lost her and glanced up to find her eyes glazed over with lust. This maiden voyage was one he must handle with care. The thought kicked his own desire up a notch.

Gripping Abby's knee, he raised her leg, urged her to her back, and moved to kneel between her sumptuous thighs.

Tess turned to watch, one hand fondling her own breast. He

winked at her before turning his attention to Abby's hungry cunt.

A drop of rich cream already clung to her labia, and he lapped it up, savoring the thick saltiness. Her hips rose as he licked, and her rounded buttocks quivered in his hands.

"Christ, Benjamin, that's too good."

He sucked her hard clit between his teeth and squeezed.

"Oh, oh, oh!"

With two fingers, he drew slick cream from her twitching cunt and bathed her in it, preparing her. She spread her legs wide for him, angling her hips up, waiting.

Ready to feel warm flesh against his, he stepped out of his pants as he rose and stretched out on top of her. She wrapped her arms around his chest and covered his neck and shoulders with sizzling kisses.

The air in the room vibrated with his growl of delight as he centered his cock at her opening, anxious to bury himself but just as anxious to enjoy a few more moments of anticipation. He knew how well they fit together, and how her heart pounded against him when she came. He knew how pliant her flesh was under his mouth, and how powerful her emotions were when they exploded in his brain.

Her heels dug into his buttocks, urging him on, and he entered her, easing into her heat, sheathing himself. She rose up to him, her back arched, her head back, baring her throat.

He withdrew and thrust again, and again. Her clit swelled and hardened against his cock as the rest of her body stiffened.

"Now," he whispered in her ear, and he withdrew once more and started in slowly.

At the first hard spasm, he penetrated her neck and filled himself with her nectar as he filled her with his cock. Searing joy, pleasure, happiness, sunshine—all appeared at once in his head to fill the darkness with light. He sucked, tasting the ecstasy biting at his cock. The bliss rolled over both of them in pounding waves, and he fucked her harder until it eased.

Her cries softened, and he withdrew from her neck and held her as they rocked together. When her hands slid from his back to the bed, he rose up and kissed her mouth.

She smiled. "Damn, that's good."

Still enjoying Abby's warmth and emotions, he looked over at Tess. She sat with one hand at her crotch and the other on her breast as she met his gaze.

He eased away from Abby and moved to the smaller woman, carefully kissing her lips so as not to knick the tender tissue.

"You are a treat," he said softly.

She spread her legs a little, blushing, and he smiled at her. Her eyes widened at the sight of his fangs, but she didn't recoil.

He drew her to her feet and turned her around, encircling her so he could caress one breast as he kissed the top of her shoulder.

She stood on her toes and reached back to grab his neck, stretching her slight body against him.

He eased one finger between her pussy lips, sliding in her juices, and found her clit hard and swollen. She writhed against him and groaned softly as he stroked her.

"A very tempting treat," he whispered.

She arched her back, raising her ass against him, and he easily found her cunt with the head of his prick. Holding her around the waist he lifted her body against his.

Abby's body he knew; this one he did not. The thrill of newness summoned the hunger forward again, and he pressed his mouth to her neck. Her pulse pumped steadily, whispering.

Fighting to maintain control, he eased his cock into her tight cunt. She shook against him, grabbing a handful of his hair as her head went back to his chest, and then she cried out. Her cunt gripped him with the force of a noose, and he pierced her flesh.

Her body undulated against him as he fed on her, taking all she had to give. He saw her life in flashes of emotion: love for her hard-working parents, hatred for her cruel brother, joy at being out on her own, heartache as she stood beside her grandmother's grave. He tasted her surprise at his attention, and tumbled headlong into the pure ecstatic bliss she'd given herself over to.

His own seed erupted then, and he drew harder.

She cried out again.

Realizing he neared her limit, he quickly withdrew his fangs and held her as she continued to writhe. Finally, she slowed and stopped, and he eased her down until her feet touched the floor.

He pressed his lips to her ear. "Any man is lucky to win your favor."

She turned a tired smile up at him. When he released her, she dropped onto the edge of the bed.

Benjamin leaned forward with his hands on his knees, gathering his wits as he delighted in the view of two women so different, both smiling with satisfaction. Then he snatched his clothes from the floor and put them on, relishing the feeling of life still racing through his body.

It would last for a good hour or more before fading away. Normally, he would have wrapped Abby in his arms and enjoyed the time with her. But not tonight.

Something strange tugged at his gut, a feeling of unease. He'd hoped to stave it off by visiting Abby, but it hadn't worked. Not that he regretted his visit, of course.

Windows rattled under a gale-force gust.

He leaned over Abby, who still lay on her back, and planted a kiss on her mouth.

"You sure she won't remember . . . you know?"

"Quite certain," he said.

Then he straightened, smoothed Tess's silky hair, and kissed the top of her head before grabbing his cloak and strolling from the room.

Voices indicated a crowd gathering downstairs, probably anxious to get out of the storm. He, on the other hand, felt the need to be in it.

Benjamin dropped a few bills on the bar as he passed it, waved to Rick, swung his cloak over his shoulders, and left.

As soon as he stepped through the door he was assaulted by driven rain pricking his skin like cold needles. Squinting to see, he headed straight into it, crossing the parking lot and road, until he stood at the edge of the water. Waves splashed up, soaking his clothing and chilling his freshly warmed skin.

He stared out into the darkness, watching white caps form and tear apart in the force of the wind, and remembered a night not so terribly different many years ago when he'd suffered his last brush with death at the hands of Poseidon.

2

"We're breaking up, Captain!" The first lieutenant's words reached Benjamin as little more than a whisper over the force of the wind.

Men screamed as the *Spencer*, rolling hard, sent them overboard.

"All hands abandon ship!" Benjamin righted a midshipman, Jeffery Veech, by the scruff of his neck. "Abandon ship!"

"Sir, the prisoners," Jeffery yelled, holding a lantern high and clutching Benjamin's sleeve. In spite of the driving rain, lantern light twinkled in the boy's blue eyes and off the silver crucifix at his neck.

"I'll get them, lad. Away with you!" He gave the boy a shove in the direction of the first lieutenant's voice, and the young man and his lantern disappeared into the storm.

Fighting to maintain footing, Benjamin found the ladder and stumbled below into thickening darkness.

"Mercy! Release us!" the prisoners called from the bowels of the ship.

Rock splintered wood at a deafening volume with each wave, and the ship rolled harder to port.

Grappling with timbers he couldn't see and wading through knee-deep water, he followed the cries until he'd located the hold and the latch held in place by a wooden pin. The pin had swollen tight.

"Have mercy on us!"

"Black-hearted villains," Benjamin muttered, struggling with the pin. "I should let you drown."

"Please," one of the pirates wailed. "Take pity!"

The pin finally slid free and the door swung open. The prisoners charged through the doorway, sending Benjamin staggering back into a crate, which took exception to his head.

The hull heaved under a monster swell and he tumbled head over heels, smashing into immovable objects and splintered timbers, and splashing into cold, salty water. Sputtering, he managed to get to his feet, and tried to wipe the stinging water from his eyes. It didn't matter; he couldn't see anything.

Working from memory, he staggered and tripped back to the ladder where he climbed out hand over hand until he felt the Atlantic spray. Cold wind whipped him around, stealing air from his lungs.

"Abandon ship," he yelled, not knowing if anyone was even left to hear. "Abandon—"

The cold, black wall of water that struck him full force lifted him completely from the deck and tossed him into the air like a loose main sail. He landed not on a wooden surface, but submerged in death's seawater bath, sinking.

He noticed first the relative quiet. Water churned, but he heard no wind. And he saw nothing at all. Only blackness. His body ached from the battering, and then everything began to numb.

Everything but his lungs. They burned with need as he held his breath and his heart hammered against his ribs.

There was no way out, no way up or down.

Hell yawned around him as he opened his mouth to breathe.

For a moment, there was light. Something bright blue, like sun shining through packed snow. And then it was gone.

Benjamin gasped as air drove the water from his lungs in a gush. He retched and gulped again. Air, sweet and pure.

And then pain.

Pain burned through from his head to his toes and he realized he'd been battered beyond repair. The sea had not swallowed him but bashed him against rocks somewhere and spit him back out only to die on dry land.

He should have gone down with the *Spencer*.

And where were his men?

He opened his eyes to a night as dark as any he'd ever seen. Oddly enough, he'd landed under shelter of some kind, out of the rain. He felt mist in the air, and heard the thunder of great waves crashing against the shore, but the ground around him was dry.

He tried to roll to his side. Searing pain like a red-hot iron pierced his chest and drew a cry from his throat that he could not suppress. He remained still and waited for the pain to ease, but it didn't.

"Damn you, Satan," he said through gritted teeth. "Take me now."

Suddenly, a figure appeared above him.

An angel? He wouldn't have expected such an escort into the afterlife. Not that he'd done such horrible things as to warrant eternal damnation, but he'd never been one to follow the ways of the Good Book.

She must be an angel. Against the night, she was as white as new snow with golden hair that hung well past her shoulders.

Her eyes glowed in the darkness like quicksilver, and she wore a white robe.

He wanted to ask her name, but he couldn't find his voice. Perhaps he wasn't supposed to speak.

She leaned close, her lips parted slightly, and his pain began to fade. Her silver eyes studied his face as if looking for redemption.

If only he could reach for her, his angel. He would gladly forfeit his life to wrap her in his arms.

A blaring horn startled Benjamin from the past.

He whirled around and watched a rusted blue and brown van swerve to barely miss a vehicle pulling out of the Tangled Net's parking lot. The driver of the car gestured with his middle finger, and then sped away. The van slowed and turned at the next corner.

Benjamin glanced back at the angry sea where the bones of his crew had long ago dissolved. Good men, most of them. He still felt the loss of them like an ancient break that hadn't knitted well.

Why had Cassandra appeared in his thoughts tonight? How long had it been since he'd seen her last? Five years? Ten?

Perhaps more.

He hadn't thought much about her lately, which probably meant she was due to turn up. She had a way of appearing to stir up his existence just when things were pleasantly quiet. He always spent a year or two longing for her after she left.

And she would leave, just as she always had before. Ironic that he was the one who waited on the shore like a sailor's wife.

With a sigh, Benjamin drew his cloak around him against the rain and started up the road toward his house.

"Come on, dammit." Star pumped the accelerator twice and turned the key. The old van cranked and cranked, but didn't catch.

"You flooded it," Jack said.

"No shit." She turned the key again, and the engine cranked slower.

And then it stopped.

"Oh, this is great," Kyle said from the back. "Just fucking great."

"Shut up," Star said.

"We're on a road in the middle of fucking nowhere, the battery's dead, and it's raining so hard I can't see out the window." Kyle's voice rose in pitch. "Just fucking great!"

"I'm starved," Wendy said. "We should have stopped at that bar."

Star glanced at the woman in the rearview mirror. How could she think about food at a time like this?

Without the van's knocking engine, the storm sounded even more savage. An especially nasty gust of wind sucked out the piece of cardboard covering a missing back window, and the vehicle suddenly filled with swirling wet air.

Kyle shoved Wendy aside and scrambled around, looking for something to cover the hole. All he found was a dirty towel. Holding it in place, he frowned over his shoulder. "Now what? We can't sleep in this shit can."

"Maybe there's a motel back near that bar," Jack said.

Star cupped her eyes to the driver's side window trying to see something past the pounding rain, but could make out nothing in the darkness. "I don't really want to walk around in this crap unless we're sure." She wished for the hundredth time they had a cell phone that worked.

Her pulse pounded as she looked into the night, half expecting a car to pull up at any moment. She could have sworn they'd been followed since they left Atlanta, but figured it was just paranoia. Still, she felt like a sitting duck in a van that wouldn't start.

"Look," Jack said. "Some guy just walked by."

Star looked in the direction Jack pointed and thought she saw a shadow disappearing into the storm, but she couldn't be certain. "You sure?"

"Yeah."

If they were being followed, it wouldn't be by someone on foot.

"Maybe he's got a phone we can use," she said.

"Maybe." Jack opened the van door and a gust of cold, wet wind whipped his blond hair across his face.

After the van door slammed, Star watched Jack fade from sight.

"Shit." She took a deep breath, opened the driver's side door, and dashed out. Cold sucked her breath away, and wind-driven rain stung her face.

She caught up with Jack where he stood at a gate nearly hidden by overgrown hedges.

"Jesus Christ!" Wendy ran up and grabbed Jack's arm to use him as a shield against the weather. "This must be a hurricane."

"Hardly." Star squinted against the darkness, trying to make out the silhouette of the house before them. It looked like a mansion, but she couldn't really tell where the building ended and the trees began. She saw no sign of life. "He went in here?"

"He must have." Jack opened the gate and started up the walk.

"What are you going to do?" Star called after him.

"Ring the doorbell," he said over his shoulder.

Wendy kept her grip on Jack's arm, and Kyle hurried after them.

Star glanced back toward the van parked across the street, which she could barely see now. If they were in the middle of a neighborhood, the houses must be spaced really far apart. And there certainly wasn't any traffic on the road.

"What the hell," she muttered, pulling the gate closed behind her, and hurrying up the walk, head down against the rain.

They huddled together on the front stoop, barely sheltered, and Jack pulled a knob beside the door. A bell rang. Not an electric doorbell, but a real bell.

"This place must be a hundred years old," Jack said. He pulled the knob again.

They heard nothing from inside except the bell, but the storm would have drowned out most noise. Still, no one opened the door or turned on a light.

"Maybe he went farther down the street," Star said. She scrunched her shoulders against the cold water dribbling down her back and wrapped herself in her arms.

"He couldn't have." Jack yanked the bell twice more, then pounded on the door with his fist. "Hey! Open up!"

The door creaked slowly open under the force of Jack's knock.

"It's unlocked?" Wendy said.

A particularly nasty gust urged the four of them through the doorway.

The only thing Star could see for sure in a sudden flash of lightning was a tile floor, glistening with water. "Where are the lights?"

"Here." Jack must have flipped a switch because light suddenly filled the room, sparkling from overhead.

Star looked up at a chandelier dripping with gold-tipped crystals as she pushed wet hair back from her face.

At a sudden yelp, she spun around and found a monstrous man, dressed in black, pinning Kyle against the wall by his throat. Kyle's feet flailed a foot off the ground.

"What are you doing in my house?" The man's voice rolled across them louder than thunder, vibrating through Star's bones. She swallowed hard.

"We didn't mean any harm," Jack said. He started toward Kyle, but stopped when the man glared at him.

Star stepped forward. "Hey, you didn't answer the door. Don't get all bent out of shape. We're just looking for a phone."

The man turned sideways to fix her in a menacing stare. "Why?"

"We broke down." She motioned over her shoulder with her thumb. "We want to call a motel, that's all."

The man had long black hair, blown wild by the storm, and fierce black eyes to match, and he glared at her from under heavy brows. A cloak draped across his massive shoulders hung past his knees, below which black boots glistened with water.

Kyle clawed at the stranger's hand and made gurgling noises.

"You're hurting him," Star said.

The man glanced at his captive and eased him down the wall until his toes touched the floor, then released him.

Kyle stumbled away and fell. He sat staring up at the stranger, coughing, and rubbing his throat.

"Can we use your phone?" Star asked.

"No." As if suddenly deciding they weren't much of a threat, he turned his back on them to close the front door, then swung the cloak from his shoulders and hung it on hook. "I have no telephone."

"No phone?" Wendy asked.

He looked her over from head to toe. "No. And it would do you no good. There's no lodging in Black Cove."

"Well, crap," Star muttered.

He turned his black-eyed gaze on her.

She found herself standing as straight as possible to compensate for the foot difference in their heights. The man was no less intimidating without the cloak. His wet, black shirt clung to him, hinting at massive muscles to fit his tremendous frame. He'd make one hell of a bouncer.

He seemed to be waiting for some explanation.

"One of the windows in the van's missing and everything's wet. Not the ideal place to crash."

He looked from her to the others, one at a time, and then returned his attention to her. His gaze drilled into her head, and her chest tightened, but she knew her discomfort didn't show. She'd perfected looking frosty.

He stepped closer, towering over them all. "Who are you?"

The other three answered in unison. "Jack." "Wendy." "Kyle."

Star felt the others backing away, but she held her ground. She hadn't let a man use his size to intimidate her since she was twelve. She could take a hit, and give as good as she got. She curled her hands into fists at her side.

"Star Reid."

"Star? What kind of name is that?"

"It's *my* name." Angry heat rose in her cheeks, but he didn't seem to notice.

"What are you doing here?"

"Passing through," Jack said.

He stared at them for a long moment, then, muttering, he strode past them into the middle of a large living room filled with antique furniture spread across a dark oval rug. On the far wall, a giant painting, at least a dozen feet wide and nearly as high, portrayed an old-time sailing ship on a wild sea passing in front of a rock cliff. The sky above the cliff was deep blue and green with a hint of red, like a sunset at the edge of a storm. Every detail was so perfect, Star wouldn't have been surprised if the ship had started rocking.

Oddly, when the stranger stood in front of the painting, he looked as if he belonged in it.

"You may stay here for the night, as long as you keep to this floor. There are guest quarters at the end of the hall, and I believe you'll find what you need. I will be occupied until tomorrow night, and by then, I assume you will be gone."

"Wow. Thanks," Wendy said, using her bubbly voice.

The man turned to leave.

"What's *your* name?" Star asked.

He spun around, glowering.

She barely resisted flinching.

"Pardon me," he finally said, "Captain Benjamin Bartlett." He gave a slight bow, then marched across the room to a staircase and climbed it at a trot. His heavy footsteps thudded across the ceiling until they disappeared.

Star turned to find her traveling companions eyeing each other.

Kyle rose from the ground, still rubbing his throat. "Son of bitch," he whispered. "What was that?"

Jack whistled softly. "This place looks like a freakin' museum or something."

Lighting flashed and thunder rattled the windows.

Wendy laughed. "Can you believe this? What a place to break down!"

"I wonder what the rest of the house looks like," Jack said.

Star found herself drawn back to the painting and walked to the middle of the room to study it. She could almost taste salt in the air and hear the thunder of the surf against rocks. Men on the deck of the ship wore white shirts and bent over ropes. One man standing on a small piece of raised deck wore a dark coat, a strange pointed hat, and had long black hair. He must be the captain.

"Come on," Wendy said, tugging on her sleeve.

Dragging herself from the scene, Star turned and followed the group past a wide staircase and down a hall that led to a kitchen.

For such a big house, the kitchen wasn't much. Not that it was small; it was bigger than her last apartment in Atlanta. But she'd expected more.

"Jesus," Kyle said. "This refrigerator's older than my grandmother." He yanked the handle and the door creaked open. "And it's empty."

With her stomach growling, Star got into the swing of things and started opening cabinets. Inside them, she found a variety of what must be expensive china and antique pewter, all of it dusty. Captain Benjamin Bartlett didn't appear to have many formal dinners.

"Hey, over here." Wendy held open the door to a pantry.

"Not exactly overstocked." Star examined cans of soup that could have been left over from World War II.

"At least it's food." Wendy tore open a box of breakfast bars and passed them around. In a matter of minutes, the four of them had polished off the box.

"What else is in there?" Kyle pushed Wendy aside. She elbowed him playfully.

With her immediate hunger satisfied, Star wandered back down the hall. What kind of man lived in such a strange place?

Captain Benjamin Bartlett. His name bounced around in her head, spoken in his deep, commanding voice.

Jack slapped her ass as he passed her. "Let's check out the rooms. I want to get out of these wet clothes. And a hot shower doesn't sound too bad, either."

Star followed, agreeing with his assessment of a hot shower.

Benjamin stood in the tower at the casement windows facing west, searching the woods through the rain.

He thought about his unexpected guests. He'd considered tossing the troupe out. He should have. They were obviously vagabonds, and most likely thieves. But something about them, especially the smaller female, intrigued him. She'd stood up to him when the others backed down.

She reminded him of Jeffery Veech, his midshipman from long ago. Both were slight, both had startling blue eyes, and both were surprisingly fearless. She, however, was unmistakably female.

Star. Who named a child Star?

A fresh downpour blew in, blocking off his view from the tower and rattling the panes on all sides. Deciding the night called for a pipe by the fire, he started down the tower stairs.

But he didn't stop at his study. For whatever reason, he was drawn to the first floor, curious about how his guests fared. He still had another hour before dawn. Perhaps, if they were awake, he'd pass the time conversing with them. He rarely spoke with anyone these days besides Abby and, occasionally, Cassandra. He'd found his brief conversation with them somewhat confusing, and that bothered him. Cassandra constantly warned him about losing touch with the present.

Moving through the front hall, he doused lights left on and followed sounds of mortals to one of the guest rooms. He raised his hand to knock, but froze. Through the half-open door, he could see his visitors, and remained unnoticed because of their activity, no doubt.

The tall blonde, Wendy, lay on the canopied bed completely nude, stretched out between the two men, both also nude. With her back to the door, she kissed the fair-haired man, Jack. The redhead, Kyle, watched as he held his swelling phallus in his fist.

"What the hell are you doing?" Kyle asked over the top of his two bedmates.

Star rose across the room. "Hey, I don't know shit about these things." She motioned over her shoulder to the fireplace where crackling and dancing light indicated a small fire.

She wore a tight black shirt and pale blue underwear. Benjamin admired the slender sturdiness of her bare legs as she walked around the bed and stood with her back to the door. Her skin was darker than he'd realized, the color of smooth cherry wood, sanded and oiled. And her shoulder-length hair had dried to almost the same color.

Kyle put his hand on her thigh and drew her to him. "Come on, Star, we got some catching up to do."

She drew her shirt off over her head and tossed it to the floor. Her right shoulder blade sported a tattoo of a blue star. Muscular shoulders narrowed to a slim waist and then widened only slightly to her hips. She stepped out of her underwear to expose smooth, round buttocks to Benjamin's appreciative view.

He eased back into the shadows.

Besides being fearless, she was more attractive than he'd realized. His body reacted to the sight of her in spite of his recent activities at the Tangled Net.

"Don't get all bent out of shape," she said, climbing onto the bed to straddle the man's legs. "We'll get there."

Kyle's cock rose from between Star's thighs and she gripped it in one hand. Holding her arm steady against her leg, she rose slowly and eased back down.

Her partner's head went back and his chest rose. "Shit, that's good."

As she continued the slow, deliberate rhythm, the couple behind her moved so that Jack rose up above Wendy on straight arms. Once he'd mounted his partner, Jack leaned over and kissed Star.

The intimacy of this strange encounter drew Benjamin in. He heard the wet sound of mouth on mouth, and almost felt the warmth of Star's thighs hugging Kyle's hips. When she guided his stiff cock into the depths of her cunt, Benjamin barely bit back a groan.

Star arched her back as she slid down the full length of Kyle's cock.

Rolling back around to the empty, dark hallway, Benjamin closed his eyes and released his being, letting his senses float into the room and across the bed like an invisible fog.

The scent of sex coiled through him, inviting him in. Star's body heated as she rode Kyle's hardening phallus, drawing the young man to the edge of control. Kyle's fingers dented the flesh on her hips. Beside her, muscles in Jack's shoulders and back roped as he pounded harder, pushing Wendy up against the headboard.

Raw, animal need charged the air with energy that Benjamin sipped like fine brandy.

Wendy grunted her release as Jack pushed her to a climax with a half dozen long, hard strokes, then he withdrew and rose to his knees, facing the remaining action. He stroked his glistening cock in one hand.

Star continued her steady rhythm. The heady scent of her juices made Benjamin's mouth water, and the beat of her heart tingled against his incisors. He wanted to taste her, the one thing he couldn't do from this distance.

Kyle arched his back. "Oh, fuck, I'm coming." He gripped Star harder, pushing and pulling in time with his own need, until he stilled.

Jack crawled around between Kyle's spread legs, grabbed Star's waist, and drew her up to him. "I knew you'd need help," he said to Kyle, laughing.

Star fell forward with her hands spread on Kyle's heaving chest and watched over her shoulder as Jack entered her from behind. Once buried, he leaned forward and wrapped an arm around her waist. With his forehead pressed between her shoulder blades, he started a slow, easy motion, withdrawing to only half his length. Kyle fondled Star's breasts.

Star's soft sounds of pleasure grew louder as the trio continued, Jack thrusting harder and drawing her up tighter, and Kyle pinching and twisting her beaded tits. Star's skin began to glisten in the firelight, and muscles tightened in her arms and legs.

"Oh . . . shit," Jack breathed, suddenly fucking her harder and then burying his cock in a final thrust.

Star grunted softly.

The couple remained joined for a moment, and then Jack collapsed onto his back.

Star crawled off the bed, raking her hair from her face as she walked to the fireplace.

Pulling back into his body, Benjamin opened his eyes and frowned into the darkness. Star had not reached a climax.

He barely fought the urge to run in and choke both men, the incompetent bastards, and had no idea why such anger welled up inside him. He had no reason to care about any of these mortals, no matter how much any of them reminded him of the past.

The scent and sight of Star's aroused, glistening body stayed with him as he silently climbed the stairs to his room.

Star enjoyed the warmth of the fire. She stabbed the largest log with the poker and watched sparks dance up the chimney. She'd never lived anywhere that had a fireplace, but vaguely remembered camping with one of her foster families once and enjoying the fire.

The desire in her body cooled as she stared at blue and yellow flames crawling up the smaller log. She wondered if Wendy ever faked orgasms. They certainly seemed real enough.

It wasn't that Star had no sex drive. She'd been masturbating since she was fifteen. All she had to do was picture Brad Pitt and she was off and running. It was just that no man had ever brought her to a climax. But they didn't seem to notice.

Maybe they didn't care.

It was time for her to strike out on her own. She could hitch a ride into Boston and find work somewhere; there wasn't much she hadn't done before to earn a living, short of selling drugs and prostitution. Boston was far enough away from Atlanta to be safe from Jones. She didn't need to go all the way to Maine just because the others wanted to. It wasn't like any of them had ever been there. Kyle idolized Stephen King. That was the only reason for their destination. Jack and Kyle were okay, but she had no desire to spend the rest of her life with either of them, and even Wendy's friendship wasn't enough to keep her with the group.

"Hey." Wendy sat on the floor next to Star, raising her palms to the fire's warmth.

A snore from behind them suggested at least one of the guys was already asleep. Probably both.

"This is a crazy place, isn't it?"

Star raised her gaze to where shadows slid across the high ceiling like cobwebs in a breeze. "Yeah."

"And the old man, what the hell is he?"

"He's not that old," Star said. Staring into the fire, she could picture the spark in Benjamin's dark eyes as he spoke. He was commanding, and kind of sexy in a weird sort of way. "He's probably in his late thirties."

"You got a thing for him?"

Star glanced at Wendy. "Are you nuts?"

Wendy chuckled. "Good. For a second there, you had me worried. Kyle figures the guy has millions in antiques in this place, and probably some cash stashed somewhere. If we can get the van running while he's not around, we could really make out. Maybe we'd even have enough to buy a place in Maine."

Star stiffened. "You think he'd just let us walk out of here with his stuff without calling the cops?"

Wendy shrugged. "Kyle thinks he must have something to hide, since he didn't throw us out."

Drawing one knee up and resting her chin on it, Star returned her attention to the crackling flames. For some reason, the idea of stealing from Captain Benjamin Bartlett didn't sit well with her. It wasn't that she had such high moral standards; she'd stolen food before when she was hungry, and smokes and booze when she couldn't afford them. It was just that the man trusted them in his home, even though they were total strangers. When had anyone ever really trusted her?

Maybe he did have something to hide.

But who didn't?

3

Benjamin took one last look out the window at storm clouds blowing past, then rose from his chair and ambled down the stairs. In his study, he drew the screen across the fireplace, turned out the reading light, and stopped a moment to listen. Rafters creaked under the wind's wrath and windows rattled, but all else was quiet.

With practiced ease, he drew out the top book in the corner of his bookshelf, pressed the button under the chair rail, and stepped through the hidden doorway when it swung open. It creaked shut behind him.

Although shrouded in darkness, he didn't slow. He knew exactly where every item in the room waited, could see the colors and textures in his mind, had long ago memorized the smells. This had been his sanctuary longer than he cared to consider.

Drawing a match across the striker, he raised the glass chimney and savored the tang of sulfur as he held the match to the lamp wick. His room took on a yellow-orange glow, and he unbuttoned his shirt as he watched the flame sway.

Cassandra gave him grief about his affinity for lamp and

candlelight, pointing out that fire was one thing he wouldn't survive. But he was willing to take the risk to enjoy flames that sometimes gave his quarters a dreamy quality, and other times cast a light of clarity into the darkest corners of his thoughts.

His mind turned to those darkest corners as he shed his clothing, stretched out on his bed, and folded his arms behind his head. Somewhere back there was the memory of sunshine and life, and of his last day pacing the shoreline, futilely searching for signs of his men. He remembered sitting on a boulder, shivering, watching the reflection of a red sun setting behind him until the sky grew too dark to see the divide between water and clouds. Thundering surf drowned out all but the inner voice that cursed his fate. How could he have survived when all others perished? It shouldn't have happened that way. He should have gone down with his ship.

"They're gone, Benjamin," Cassandra said. "Face the truth and release your sorrow." She slid her hands gently across the back of his shoulders as if smoothing creases from his coat.

"How can I? If not for me, they'd still be alive. Collingswood, Fox, Ashby, all of them. Young Jeffery Veech had barely reached his fifteenth year. How am I to tell his mother that her boy won't return?"

"You need not tell anyone anything. Stay here with me."

"I can't abandon my duty." He rose to face her. "I have responsibilities."

She tilted her head teasingly. "Such as?"

"I'm to lead an expedition against the French in a month. The *Spencer* is to be the flagship." He cut his gaze to the rocks barely visible in the evening light. "Or was to be."

Cassandra stepped toward him, her bare feet soundless on the sandy beach. "The *Spencer* is no more, and they wouldn't have you lead a prayer now. Why would you go back to a place where people will revile your name? They will blame you for the loss of your men, just as you blame yourself."

Her hand felt soothing and kind on his arm, and she slid it down to his hand. He closed his fingers around hers.

"Stay with me, Benjamin. I'll make you happy again."

They had never spoken specifics, but he knew that staying with her meant giving up hope of ever returning to the world. She wasn't mortal. He knew that. Exactly what she was he didn't know.

"Come," she said, her voice now low and seductive. "Give yourself to me, and I will make you a gift of eternal life."

"How can life be eternal?" He followed her up the slope and into the woods where she led him effortlessly through the shadows.

"It is eternal through death," she said.

A shiver ran through him. "You wish to kill me, then?"

"Am I dead?"

He shook his head and then realized she couldn't see him in the darkness. "No."

"You'll be like me. You are nearly that now."

"What do you mean?"

She opened the cabin door. "How is it you healed so quickly?"

In less than a week, she'd nursed him from the brink of death. He'd wondered about the thick, cold broth she forced him to drink, but it had performed miracles on his tattered body. He believed it to contain animal blood. She wouldn't tell him what kind.

"By your hand," he answered.

She led the way into the cabin where she drew a spill from the hearth and held it to a candle.

Even dim light always seemed to leave her radiant like a lone cloud above the setting sun. Her eyes were an impossible metallic color, shiny and silver. At times, they appeared almost gold, usually when she tended to him and touched him in intimate ways.

She moved to stand before the fireplace and held out her hand to him. "Will you stay?"

She was right. The whole town would hate him for losing the *Spencer* with all souls but his own. He'd never be allowed to lead the forces to Acadia now. In fact, he'd surely be unable to raise another crew, if he even had hope of a ship. No one back in Boston would care that he and his men had caught the pirate ship and recovered the gold, now that both lay somewhere at the bottom of the sea.

His life was over.

Resigned to his fate, he stepped forward and took her hand. Raising it to his lips, he pressed a kiss into her cool skin.

Cassandra smiled as she drew him to her. When they stood together, the top of her head barely touched his chin.

Glancing up at him demurely, she untied his kerchief and drew it slowly from around his neck. Her fingers grazed his chest as she worked, and he felt the magic of her womanly charms. In their short time together, he'd found himself dreaming of holding her nearly every time he closed his eyes. At the moment, he wanted much more.

She unbuttoned his coat, pushed it over his shoulders and tossed it to the closest chair without care. Cold air chilled his exposed neck and seeped across his chest and back, but he didn't mind. He'd strip bare to touch her, to kiss her tempting lips.

Holding his gaze, she raised her head to look at him openly, and the gold tint returned to her eyes. Her hands gripped his shoulders with a strength he hadn't guessed she had.

No longer caring how improper his desires were, he touched her waist and found firm flesh under flimsy cloth. Vaguely, he wondered how she handled the cold, but the question floated away as she closed the small distance between them.

She drew his face down to hers and offered her mouth, which he gladly took. Her lips parted under his willingly and without hesitation, and she drew his tongue into her mouth.

Until that moment, he had not realized just how much he needed her.

He'd found pleasure between the thighs of more women than was likely his share, but he'd never felt the burn of desire sizzle through his loins as it did now. And she did nothing but fan the flame.

Her arm slid around his neck as he embraced her, pulling her up against him, suddenly desperate. His cock swelled between them.

Gripping a handful of his hair, she pulled his mouth away from hers and stared at him with blood-red eyes glittering gold.

"Tell me you want me, Benjamin." When she spoke he saw fangs where her teeth should be, and knew he should fear her, but he couldn't.

"I want you," he croaked, his voice barely rising through his choking need.

His senses began to scramble, and he wasn't sure of his sight or hearing. She seemed to growl low and deep, and she slowly drew his head back, baring his throat to her. Was he a sheep walking willingly to the slaughter?

He didn't care. All he cared about was holding her, taking her, giving himself to her. He tried to whisper her name, but nothing came out.

"You will be mine," she said in a voice altered to something unmistakably evil. "Forever."

He closed his eyes, surrendering.

The pain ripped through him as she sank her fangs into his neck. Having forsaken self-preservation, he held her tighter instead of pushing her away.

She fed off him, sucking the blood from his body. Pain transformed into something else—pleasure, laced with desire.

He fell to his knees.

The pleasure chilled as his strength began to fade. Still, he could do nothing but accept her actions. Whatever she demanded, he would give.

Anything.

Everything.

His vision crackled with strange lights and then lightened until he seemed to be caught in a midday snowstorm. Disoriented, he felt damp ground beneath his hands, and then his face. And then the ground disappeared.

Lost in a blizzard of loneliness, he saw and felt nothing, but he heard her voice. "Drink."

When he did as commanded, the snowstorm exploded, sending him hurtling through the heavens and falling to earth at terrifying speeds. He would shatter like a glass bowl when he hit the ground.

If he hit the ground.

And then he slowed and began to float, and he felt her hands stroking the side of his face and his neck.

When he opened his eyes, he looked up into Cassandra's face, as perfect as porcelain. He saw her differently than he ever had before. He saw every smooth line, every eyelash clearly. Her eyes had lightened to silver with flecks of gold and blue, glistening fangs dented her bottom lip, and a smear of blood marred her chin.

Every thought focused on wanting her, but not in the way he had before. He craved her—*ached* for her.

"Welcome back to the world," she said. She ran her fingers across his forehead and he saw a gash in her wrist.

When he inhaled, the scent of blood in the air did strange and horrifying things to him. He began to shake all over, and a deep, terrifying hunger surged in his soul. He grabbed her arm and drew the wound to his mouth.

The taste, both foreign and wonderful, made him whimper, and he sucked to draw more.

"Enough," she said, jerking her arm away.

He tried to snatch it back, but she held him off with ease.
"Not like that." She helped him to his feet.

In spite of the shaking, he felt strength unlike anything he'd
known running through his arms and legs. He could have lifted
the *Spencer* off the rocks with one hand if he'd had this strength
during the storm.

Yet, Cassandra guided him with ease. He knew, somehow,
that her strength was greater than his. He felt the power in her
slender fingers as she unbuttoned his breeches and drew them
down, kneeling before him to help him out of his boots and
clothing. She raised his shirt off over his head. Cold air drifted
past his bare skin, but he felt no sensation of discomfort.

She led him to the bed he'd occupied for the past week, a
small bunk against the wall. As he sat watching, she drew her
shift over her head and discarded it.

Her body was womanly, smooth, and pale—as perfect as her
face. His fingers itched for the feel of her flesh.

Teasing him by running her hands over her breasts and down
to her hips, she crept silently forward, her steps fluid and grace-
ful. By the time she stood within arm's reach, his cock had hardened to its full size. He gripped the blanket beneath him in his
fists.

Cassandra cooed as she straddled his legs and positioned
herself in his lap facing him, combing his hair back and then
feathering her fingers across his shoulders. She reached between them to aim his swollen cock into her. He barely bit back
a groan.

As her cunt worked its way possessively down his shaft, he
touched her thighs, and then her hips, thrilling to the feel of her
soft skin. He caressed her breasts and watched her face for approval. Her luscious lips curved into a smile.

A throb in his gums accompanied his growing desire. His
probing tongue found fangs to match hers with points as sharp
as needles.

When his cock was sheathed, ready to erupt inside her, she held his gaze with her own and his thoughts suddenly scrambled into an incoherent mass. He felt, and sensed, and knew, but couldn't think. Urges tugged at his gut, primal and base. He didn't understand, and didn't want to.

Giving permission, she raised her chin, baring her throat.

He wrapped his arms around her, cocked his head, and, with a beastly growl, buried his fangs in her neck.

He didn't actually taste her blood, but experienced it as if drawing in her soul and heart and making them his own. He felt her fondness for him, her arousal at their joining, and her satisfaction from drinking her fill of him. He knew the darkness of her beast, part of which he now carried. He sensed eternity.

She drew him away by a handful of hair.

He licked the last precious drops of her blood from his lips.

"Now you belong to me," she said.

He understood without explanation. Whatever she asked of him, he would do, no matter what the cost. If she left, he would wait like an obedient servant for her return.

She kissed his mouth as she rose and slid back down his cock, moving in time with the ancient rhythm of mating, drawing him to the brink of release. He held her tighter and savored her mouth under his.

Her rhythm increased and she rode him mercilessly, her hips moving forward and back. She ran her tongue up one of his fangs and down the other, and he shuddered at the pleasure.

His need to release his seed grew painful. She used him as she wanted; her cunt swelled and tightened around him.

In one swift movement, she drew his head to one side and bit his shoulder.

He cried out, but not in pain.

Her spasms of release pushed him past what reason remained, and he sank his fangs into her neck again.

This time, he drew out her orgasm, tasting it as his own, and his seed finally erupted, sending him to dizzying heights of bliss.

He clung to her and drew harder as his cock pumped.

When she pulled his mouth from her flesh the second time, they looked at each other and smiled. Blood dripped from her canines and satisfaction glowed in her eyes, surely matching his own.

His animal nature retreated, allowing back in basic thoughts and the prickling of concern over what had just passed between them.

"What are we?" he asked.

"Creatures of darkness," she said, stroking his hair back from his face, "as eternal as the stars."

She ran her index finger across his bottom lip, removing the last drops of blood, and sucked it from her fingertip.

By the time Star woke, it was well into the day and she was alone in bed. She stretched, sat up, and looked around.

The fireplace stood cold and dark, and Wendy's bag lay open next to her own backpack. Judging by the lack of clothing draped over the furniture, the others were dressed and out.

Star hopped up, ran to her backpack, and dug through it until she located the portable USB drive. Reassured, she sighed. What the hell was she going to do with the thing? Jones wouldn't look for her so far from home, not for a simple list of weekend wagers. He'd piss and moan about the fact that his flash drive was stolen, pay off his dozen customers, then start over. No big deal.

Still, she didn't want to carry the thing around. It was a part of the life she'd left behind and wanted long gone. She'd only taken it to piss him off.

Tucking it into a side pocket of her backpack, she dug out clean clothes, dressed, and checked the kitchen for coffee. Finding none, she stepped out the front door into midday sunshine.

Nothing was left of the storm except small branches in the road and yard. Birds chirped from every tree.

Once through the gate, Star turned back to study the house in the light and sucked in a breath of surprise. She thought they'd stumbled onto a mansion, but it looked more like a freakin' castle. The walls, built of dark brown and gray stone and partially covered with vines, rose at least three stories and stretched for twice the length she'd guessed. Above the third floor were towers: a large one at the back and small one at the front, both with windows all the way around. The view must be fantastic from up there.

Huge trees hid a lot of the building from the road, but standing among the trees, the place felt majestic, and a little intimidating. Like its owner.

Who the hell lived in a castle in the United States? Benjamin Bartlett must be filthy rich.

"'Bout time you got up." Wendy bounded across the empty street. "Isn't this day amazing?"

With her attention pulled from the building, Star realized the temperature was perfect and the sky above held no hint of clouds. "Not bad." She glanced to where Jack and Kyle stood half hidden under the van's hood. "What's up?"

Wendy shrugged. "They're still trying to figure out what's wrong."

"Great."

"Hey, we could be stuck in a worse place."

Star pictured Benjamin's face when he returned home to discover them still there. Something about the way he carried himself suggested he might not be much fun to be around if he were truly angry.

"Come on," Wendy said, "help me fix something to eat."

After one more appreciative look around, Star followed her friend back inside. They dug through the pantry and found three cans of chicken soup, a box of crackers, instant coffee, and several tins of sardines. Star leaned against a counter and peeled back the top of a sardine tin. She'd certainly lived on less.

Wendy stirred the soup. "Where do you think he went?"

"Who?"

"The guy who owns this place."

Star shrugged. "Who knows?"

She thought back to the night before. After Benjamin ran up the stairs and disappeared, she hadn't seen any sign of him again. He must have left; the house was too quiet. She hadn't heard a car drive off, but engine noise could have been drowned out by the storm. As nice as the weather was now, they should hear him return.

The guys came in covered with grease and grime, and made no effort to keep from leaving it behind them.

"Watch it!" Star wiped off a dark smear Kyle left on a cabinet.

"Fuck you," Kyle said. "What do you care? This isn't your place."

No, her place had been a pigsty. This place was a palace.

Why did a grease mark on someone else's cabinet bother her?

Because Benjamin's castle demanded respect, that's why.

Weird thought. Shaking her head to clear it, Star dropped the sponge in the sink on her way to the pot of soup.

She carried her bowl to the kitchen table where the others joined her. They slurped up the soup without speaking, and then lounged over the sardines and crackers.

"You find the problem?" she asked Jack.

He nodded. "Leaky fuel line."

"I thought I smelled gas," Wendy said.

Star shot her a glare. "Why didn't you say something?"

The woman loaded a cracker with a sardine, and shoved the whole thing into her mouth without further comment.

"We'll go down to the highway and look for a gas station," Jack said, motioning with his head to include Kyle.

"We could all go," Wendy said.

Jack shrugged. "What if the old man comes back and decides to lock us out? We might not get our stuff back."

"We could put everything in the van," Wendy said, her voice betraying her rising level of concern. "I'm not staying here without you guys."

"The inside of the van's all wet. And what if he decides to tow it? Then—"

"I'll stay," Star said.

They all looked at her as she ate another bite of sardine-covered cracker.

Funny, the idea of staying at Benjamin's alone didn't bother her at all, and she knew it probably should. She'd grown up on the same horror movies as everyone else. She even knew a few real horror stories her traveling companions most likely didn't. Yet, she was quite happy with the prospect of spending time looking around. And if Benjamin came home before the others got back, well, she'd stand up to him like she had the night before.

Her stomach quivered at the prospect.

With the place to herself, Star studied the painting a while longer. It really was spectacular, not that she was much of an art critic. The thing just sucked her in and she was there. She wondered what life had been like back on that ship. Somehow, she was sure it had really existed, and not been the result of an artist's imagination. No one could be that good.

After getting her fill for the moment, she checked out the rest of the room. A bookshelf covered a whole wall to the left of the fireplace. The books looked old and interesting, but pulling out one created a dust storm. She scanned those with titles she could see, and found books by authors whose names she recognized, like Edgar Allen Poe, Arthur Conan Doyle, William Shakespeare, Benjamin Franklin, and Mark Twain, and a lot more by authors she'd never heard of. She followed one row, just trying to pronounce the names. She could spend years in here reading without finishing all these books. The thought made her giddy, and she laughed.

All her life, she'd loved to read, but her chances had been limited by circumstances. At the Home, there hadn't been many choices, and she'd been pretty young. Her first foster mother had said reading anything but the Bible was a sin, so she'd discovered the public library and sinned as often as she could sneak away. After that, it was hit or miss, until she'd had to put aside reading for two full-time jobs. Then she'd started hanging with Jones. He got annoyed if she read, said she was ignoring him. Over the last three months, she'd watched a dozen movies a week. How long had it been since she'd read a whole book through? Five years?

She abandoned the bookshelf to explore, wondering what other treasures the place held. Benjamin had said he'd be back this evening, and it wasn't quite evening yet.

She stopped at the bottom of the long staircase, one hand on the rail, and listened.

Benjamin had also said they were to stay on the first floor, but she heard no hint of anyone on the floors above. What would it hurt if she just looked around? Hell, he wouldn't even know. She didn't want to take anything. Just look.

Sucking in a deep breath and blowing it out, she started up the marble stairs, tiptoeing. She couldn't hear anything over the sound of blood rushing through her ears.

The second floor was darker than the first and had several rooms with locked doors. On each end of the floor, she found a bedroom open with the bed made, fireplace filled with logs ready to be lit, bathroom clean, but dust everywhere.

The third floor at first proved just as uninteresting, until she stepped into a room that was different from all the others. It had no windows, a low ceiling, and walls of solid wood. Although the room held a fireplace at one end and a narrow staircase at the other, it had the feel of the inside of a ship. Maps covered a table in the middle, and a desk had been placed across the back corner to take advantage of light from the fire and provide a view of the room. Behind the desk was another floor to ceiling bookshelf, but this one held books that looked much older than those downstairs. The covers appeared to be homemade, some out of leather even, and must be absolutely ancient. Another difference between this bookshelf and the one downstairs was the lack of dust.

The room smelled of rich pipe tobacco and cold fireplace ashes. It must be Benjamin's hangout. It fit him, somehow.

She walked behind the desk, which held an old oil lamp, one of those quill pen gadgets you can get at a hobby store, and several stacks of yellowing paper. A large book lay open in the middle of the desk, filled with lines of ornate and flowing handwriting, nearly impossible to read. Most of it was smeared and stained, too, which didn't help.

Star leaned forward and raised the edge of the book toward the light from across the room. She could just make out something at the top of the page that looked a little like a date. March something, 1891. Damn. The book was old.

Wait. She leaned closer. Not 1891, but 1691. Holy shit. This thing was historic. It should be in a museum somewhere.

She studied the feel of the paper under her thumb and realized it wasn't paper but material of some kind. Very carefully, she turned to the first page and worked to read as much as she could. "Log book . . . something . . . Spencer." She gave up on a whole smeared paragraph and moved on. "Captain Benjamin Bartlett, Bofton. Bofton?" Scanning down the page, she realized the *s*'s looked like *f*'s. "Oh. I get it. Captain Benjamin Bartlett, Boston."

A shiver ran through her. Another Benjamin Bartlett, and a captain, too, but this one had lived centuries ago.

Reopening the book to its original place, she tried to make out the flowing words, but only got something about "returning to Boston," and "heavily laden," and "impending storm." The next page was empty.

"Wow."

Straightening, she circled the room, admiring paintings adorning the walls. Most were of sailing ships, amazingly realistic and detailed like the huge painting downstairs. Benjamin must know the painter. Star stood before each and studied it as well as she could in the dim light.

The last painting she found, in a small round frame about a foot high and two-thirds as wide, was a portrait. The subject, a man, wore a dark coat with a tall, stiff collar and a white shirt with something frilly at his throat, and he looked directly ahead, which gave the illusion of his eyes following Star as she moved closer. She read the inscription at the base of the painting: Captain Benjamin J. Bartlett. So was this the man whose log book lay open on the desk? He had wild black hair that brushed his shoulders, black eyes, and dark, heavy eyebrows. The only thing delicate about his face was his mouth. He looked so much like the current owner of the house that he had to be an ancestor. Obviously Benjamin had even been named for him. Both Benjamins looked like someone you wouldn't want to piss off. Or, if you did, you wouldn't want to turn your back on either of them.

A small flame of jealousy flared in Star's chest. What could it possibly be like to know exactly where you came from? And not just who your parents were, but your family back dozens of generations. It must be wonderfully stabilizing and comforting.

If the log book date really was 1691, the two Benjamins had been born about three hundred years apart. Was this house that old? She glanced around for some clue, but found nothing obvious.

The only light in the room came from above the narrow staircase. Star climbed it and found that it opened into one of the towers she'd seen from outside.

The tower room, about ten feet wide and round, had windows on three sides facing the inland forest. Trees displayed spectacular fall colors that danced in a breeze, and she saw no signs of another house anywhere. Far below to her left, she spotted the van, barely visible between tree branches.

The back of the room held a small, wooden door that opened to the roof of the house. A narrow walkway with a handrail on one side connected this tower to the one in front.

After testing the doorknob to be sure she could get back in, she started down the walkway. Although the roof was fairly wide at this point, the height still made her heart race and tightened her grip on the railing.

As soon as she made it to the front tower and stepped inside, she relaxed and enjoyed the unbelievable view. The smaller tower room had thick glass all the way around that reached almost from ceiling to floor, reminding her of a lighthouse without the light. She pulled one of two wooden chairs from the edge to the middle of the space, sat, and soaked it all in.

In front of her was the ocean. Waves crested in whitecaps and surfed into the shore. The sky, perfectly blue, stretched forever, drawing her imagination toward it. She pictured windswept islands and European castles defending the far shore.

Closer in, she could see a hint of the bar they'd driven past the night before, and the road appeared as dark spots among the trees. Birds flew past, some even below her, and a few chirped at the unfamiliar observer.

She'd never been in such a perfect spot, and found herself relishing the beauty and peace. All memories of Atlanta, her asshole boyfriend, Jones, and long hours at the Kitty Klub mixing drinks for horny old men slipped away. For the first time, she truly felt as if she were starting over. This was it, day one.

Smiling, she watched a large wave make its way inland, crashing against the shore somewhere out of her vision.

She should be able to see or hear Wendy and the guys coming back up the street, or any sign of Benjamin returning. Stretching her legs and crossing her feet, she leaned back and folded her arms across her chest.

As she watched, clouds grew on the horizon, broke loose, and blew by. The sky brightened to spectacular shades of orange, red, and yellow, and then darkened as the sun set behind her.

With a start, she realized she must have been sitting in the tower for hours.

Moving the chair back to the edge of the room, she turned and hurried along the walkway in the dusky light to the back tower, and eased the door shut behind her.

Wendy and the guys must have gotten past her. They had to be back by now. They could have gone halfway to Boston and still had time to return. Hopefully, they'd fixed the van and were waiting on her.

She descended the narrow staircase and started toward the door to the hallway when movement caught her eye.

Benjamin rose in front of the fireplace and spun to face her. The fire he'd just lit sparkled and spattered behind him. He looked ferocious with his hands balled into fists at his sides.

"What the hell are you doing here?"

4

Star stood frozen in place as if she'd stepped in Super Glue. She couldn't have moved if the house had been burning down around her.

Fighting a suddenly dry mouth, she managed to get out, "I, uh, didn't mean any harm."

He took a step toward her, filling more space than he should. The top of his head seemed less than an inch from the ceiling. "You were told to stay on the first floor, were you not?"

Anger swelled inside her, bursting her bubble of terror. She dropped one fist to a hip and purposely slid her gaze around the room. "Yeah, I was told."

"And do you always have difficulty following orders?"

She shrugged and cut her gaze up to his. "Most of the time."

He stared at her for several long minutes, but didn't make a move forward.

"I was just looking around," she said. "That's all."

"Get out." He pointed toward the door.

Anger flamed into rage. If he thought she was going to take

off running because he was a big bad-ass with a deep voice, he was wrong. She didn't back down from bullies.

"Hey!" She closed the distance between them and poked a finger into the middle of his chest. "You need to back off, Jack."

She might as well have poked her finger into a steel plate.

He continued to stare, his brows thickened by a frown.

"Benjamin," he said.

"Huh?"

"My name is *Benjamin.*"

She narrowed her eyes and dropped her arm to her side. Was he screwing with her? He actually sounded serious. "I know."

"You called me Jack."

He was serious.

"You don't get out much, do you?"

Unsure if he was about to bellow another order or physically toss her out, Star watched, prepared to yell back or defend herself. Instead, he took several steps backward and returned to his position before the fire.

She stared at his wide back for a few moments, dazed, then turned and ambled toward the paintings. She'd leave the room in her own sweet time. Stopping in front of the oval portrait, she asked, "Who is this?"

He glanced over his shoulder and spoke with his back to her as he moved logs around. "One of my ancestors."

"Looks just like you."

"So I've been told." He rose, picked up a pipe from the mantle, and packed it with tobacco from a leather pouch. He watched her from the corner of his eye.

"Who painted these?"

He struck a match and held it to his pipe. "Another ancestor."

God, he looked like a duke or something standing in front of the fireplace wearing a coat from another century and knee-high black boots. She'd never met anyone quite like him. Again, her belly quivered, and she wasn't sure why. She wasn't actually afraid of him. At least, not much.

"So this is like your family home, huh?"

He nodded as he drew on his pipe and puffed, filling the room with the sweet smell of pipe tobacco.

"You stay here all by yourself?" She couldn't imagine living in a place the size of a hotel and not having it stuffed with people.

"At times."

"A lot of space for one guy."

He didn't rise to the bait, and her anger faded. Maybe if you were raised in a place like this, you didn't even know there were people out there living in cardboard boxes.

"Your ancestor, the captain, was he the one who built this house?"

"Aye."

"How did he end up here?"

Benjamin studied her long enough to make her uncomfortable, then rested his pipe on the mantle, turned, and sat on the edge of his desk. "He was shipwrecked on the rocks just beyond the point, and nearly lost his life. No others survived. The captain was nursed back to health, and could never bring himself to leave. He started building the house a year later."

"Who nursed him?"

"No one knows for certain."

She searched the portrait for any sign of tenderness in the captain's cold black eyes. "So, maybe it was some Native American woman who helped him and he fell in love with her. Maybe this place is the result of a fairy tale romance."

She glanced at the modern Benjamin, who watched her intently with identical black eyes. Heat rushed through her and she swallowed hard. "Too bad fairy tales aren't real."

Dragging air into her lungs, she turned toward the door. "I guess I better see if the others are back."

"They are," he said.

She took one more look at him and nodded, then left the room.

Once she was hurrying down the dark hallway, she realized her hands were shaking and she couldn't quite catch her breath. The man had a strange effect on her. Working hard to calm her nerves, she continued to the first floor and found it, too, dark.

"Wendy? Jack?"

A hint of music drew her toward one of the guest rooms where she found the three. Wendy had hooked up her MP3 player to tiny speakers and had strip music vibrating off the walls. Star closed the door behind her.

Wendy, dancing in front of the fireplace, winked at Star before turning her back on the two men. She was already down to her T-shirt, thong, and heels, and slowly, teasingly, drew her shirt up to her shoulders.

Jack lay back on one elbow, rubbing the bulge in the front of his jeans, and Kyle groaned.

Star sat in an armchair in the corner.

Wendy had wonderful skin, smooth and lightly tanned. The tat just above her butt was actually well done, not heavy-handed like the usual tramp stamp. And the woman knew how to move. Back at the Kitty Klub, she'd been the highest grossing stripper. No doubt Bud was missing her about now. He'd probably lost half his business when Wendy took off.

Her long, fluid movements in time with the music were perfect as she pulled off her shirt and dropped it to the ground. Then she turned, her breasts squeezed between her arms, and leaned over as she ran her hands down the front of her thighs and back up the insides. Her parted lips and heavy eyelids suggested she was halfway to an orgasm already.

"Oh, shit," Kyle moaned. He reached inside his pants to straighten his swelling prick.

Wendy hooked her thumbs in the sides of her thong, stretched it out, and wriggled it down her legs a little at a time.

"Yeah, baby, take it off," Jack said.

She stepped out of the thong and shot it like a rubber band at Jack's face. He laughed.

Wendy used the post at the corner of the bed like a strip-club pole, straddling it and riding slowly up and down with the beat.

Kyle shed his pants and then his shirt and patted the bed beside him. "Come on, Wen. Let's get to the contact phase of this dance."

Wendy raised one foot and placed it on Kyle's leg, exposing her pussy to his view and marking his skin with the spike heel. Ignoring the spike, he reached out, grabbed her ass, and planted his face in her crotch. Grinning, she pushed him away.

"Damn, that smells good enough to fuck," he said.

"To you, everything smells good enough to fuck," Jack said.

Kyle shrugged and lay back to watch and stroke his cock.

Wendy danced in front of Jack as she raised his shirt off over his head. Then she turned and moved her ass inches over the top of his pants. He caressed her firm butt. She turned, pushed him to his back, and unzipped his jeans, and his thick cock sprang free.

Keeping the beat, Wendy leaned over and ran her tongue around the head of Jack's cock, leaving it wet and harder. Jack's body jerked with involuntary movements.

Something about the way Wendy controlled the situation turned Star on. She slipped her hand under her shirt, messaged her tightening tits, and pinched the sensitized nipples.

Wendy took Jack's cock into her mouth, sliding her bright red lips down the length of the shaft.

"Hey," Kyle said. "Where do I fit in?"

Wendy rose, grinning, and climbed up on the bed. On her

hands and knees, she looked back at the redhead and slapped her own ass. "Right here."

As Kyle worked his way into Wendy's pussy, she slid her mouth back down Jack's prick.

Star swallowed hard. She'd never watched like this before.

Finally buried, Kyle gripped Wendy's hips and held her up close. Wendy groaned and raised her ass higher.

The music changed tempo to something slow and steady, and the three moved in time with it. Kyle withdrew halfway as Wendy raised her mouth up to the tip of Jack's prick, and then both cocks disappeared again.

Star slid her hand down the front of her pants to her clit, easily finding juices to lubricate her fingers. As the fucking continued, punctuated with groans and grunts, her clit swelled with need and she rubbed it harder.

Kyle's arm and shoulder muscles bunched and his buttocks clenched with each stroke, and he closed his eyes. Jack fondled Wendy's puckering nipples as his prick reached full size, slick and hard.

Star closed her eyes and imagined the feel of big, strong hands around her waist, gripping her and pulling her back against a massive cock, slick with her juices and aching for her. She felt hot breath on the back of her neck.

"Oh, fuck," Kyle groaned. "This feels too good." He broke the rhythm, pounding flesh to flesh.

Star leaned her head back and rubbed her clit faster until everything tightened. She imagined a mouth crushed to hers, hands touching her flesh, urgent thrusts, a hard body. Pulling a nipple, she slid three fingers into her pussy. Spasms squeezed her drenched fingers, and she bit her bottom lip to remain quiet as release swept over her.

When she opened her eyes, she found Kyle lying on his back and Wendy riding Jack, her hands splayed on his chest.

As she watched Wendy approaching a climax, Star realized with a start whose hands she'd fantasized about, whose mouth and hard body.

Benjamin.

She drew her hand from her pants and swallowed hard. Why in the hell had she fantasized about him? He wasn't even close to Brad Pitt.

Wendy's head dropped forward and she grunted with each thrust as she came. Jack's hips rose up from the bed as he matched her movements, groaning with pleasure. Finally, Wendy collapsed to her side and lay on her back between Jack and Kyle. The music continued on with its raunchy beat.

Star rested her head against the back of the chair and recalled the way Benjamin had looked at her when he discovered her in his study. He was angry for sure and surprised, but there was more, a touch of something like fear in his eyes. What could he possibly be afraid of?

Benjamin sipped whiskey and watched flames crawl over the newest log. At least the blasted music had stopped. He'd noticed it when he first rose and realized his house guests were still in residence. It was cheap music, suggestive of sex, and he'd tried not to picture the foursome from the night before.

It wasn't that he hadn't enjoyed watching them. He had. In fact, he'd wakened with a vision of Star, her hair darkened with sweat, her head thrown back in ecstasy, riding him with abandon, her nails digging into his chest.

He'd spent twenty minutes wrestling his hunger back to its corner.

And then he'd discovered her in his study. Had she arrived a few minutes sooner, she'd have seen him emerging from his hidden room. No one but Cassandra knew of his inner sanctum.

The most insane part of the whole encounter was that through his haze of anger, he'd wanted to grab her shoulders and drag her to him. He'd wanted to part her thighs and claim her as his own.

What the hell was he thinking? She was a vagabond, nothing more, wandering through. She'd soon be gone and he'd never see her again.

Why did that thought bother him? And what was it about her he found so damned appealing?

He watched the fire burn until the newest log was consumed.

Downing the last of the shot, he deposited the glass on his desk and rose. It was time for him to determine exactly what his guests had planned.

He found the four mortals in his kitchen making use of the stove. Scents suggested some form of food he wasn't familiar with.

"Come on," one of the men said. "Put olives in it."

"Olives?" a woman answered. "In chili? That's disgusting."

"No, it's—"

They fell silent as he entered the room.

Wendy and Kyle stood at the stove where they had been arguing over ingredients. Jack spread dishes around the table and Star filled glasses with a purple liquid. She glanced up, spotted him, and spilled some of the purple drink onto the counter before righting the bottle.

He stayed just inside the doorway, trying not to show his disgust at the strange aroma. "I take it you're finding sufficient food?"

"We picked up some stuff at the Stop & Shop," Jack said. "You want to join us?"

"No, thank you." He crossed the room to lean against the counter near Star and noted the increase in her heart rate with a degree of satisfaction. "I apologize for the lack of rations. I'll have some brought in for the morning."

"Cool," Wendy said. "Thanks."

Star maneuvered around him to deliver glasses to the table,

almost but not quite touching him. His fingers itched to reach for her, and a dull ache started at the base of his canines. He tried his best to ignore it.

"And your vehicle?"

"We had to order a fuel line," Jack said. "Should be in tomorrow. Won't take long to install."

And then you leave.

Star glanced up from the table, met his gaze, and looked away.

Disappointment settled in his gut. Now he knew their plan. He should, by all rights, be happy to be getting his privacy back.

For some inexplicable reason, he wasn't.

"Well," he said, straightening. "I leave you to your meal and wish you all smooth sailing."

Without looking back, he left the kitchen, anxious to get away from emotions better left unexamined. He'd long since abandoned loneliness, and had no intention of letting it back into his life.

No, he would take to the woods and taste the freedom of the night. He enjoyed the sounds of owls rising from low branches and bats overhead. He would savor the salt water in the air and let it wash away thoughts of this strange mortal woman.

His sense of restlessness had done nothing but increase since his visit to the Tangled Net. Perhaps Cassandra was close.

Benjamin slung his cloak over his shoulders and pulled the front door shut behind him.

"You feeling okay?"

Star glanced at Wendy and nodded. "Yeah."

"You sure?"

"Yeah." Her heart still raced from being so close to Benjamin. Now when she saw him, she pictured him leaning over her to kiss her, taking her in his arms.

Insane.

"Think we'll be able to get out of here tomorrow?" she asked Jack.

He shrugged and exchanged a meaningful look with Kyle. "Maybe."

Star narrowed her eyes. "What do you have planned?"

"We have to put the fuel line in, that's all. Sometimes that isn't as easy as it looks." He tried his innocent look on her, but it didn't work. "Besides, it won't hurt my feelings to stay here a few days while we work on it."

"You're going to take stuff, aren't you?"

Jack turned his attention to his bowl of chili.

"Don't," she said.

"He won't miss it," Kyle said. "Look at this fucking place, will you?"

The thought of stealing from Benjamin had grown from distasteful to downright rotten. But how would she stop them? If she told Benjamin and he called the cops, they'd all be in trouble.

A feeling of dread skipped up her spine. Jones always said he had connections with cops all over the country. Had he just been blowing smoke, or did he really know cops in Boston? If they picked her up, would he be the one to bail her out? Chances were good he'd be pissed that she'd taken off in the middle of the night. In his mind, it didn't seem to matter that he'd been screwing around; she was still supposed to be his girlfriend. What the hell had she seen in him in the first place?

After polishing off the chili and halfheartedly cleaning up, the other three padded off to bed. They'd spent half the day walking to and from the gas station, and had then exercised, as Wendy called it. Star wasn't the least bit tired. She'd spent most of the day sitting in the tower, daydreaming.

She washed the dishes, dried them, and put them away, then wandered back to the main room where she drew a book, *Call of the Wild*, from the shelf and blew off the dust. She settled onto a sofa directly in front of the painting of the ship, opened the book, and began to read.

The story quickly drew her in. She had no idea how long she'd been reading when the front door swung open.

Star jumped, spilling the book from her lap. "Dammit." She spun around as she snatched the book from the floor, but forgot to be annoyed when she caught sight of Benjamin.

He shrugged off his cloak and hung it up as he stared at her. His hair was wind-blown and a stark contrast to the white shirt he wore. Black pants hugged muscular thighs, and his boots once again glistened with water, although it wasn't raining. He strode toward her and all the air seemed to disappear from the room.

"It appears I've interrupted your reading," he said. "Forgive me."

She held the book at her side. "No big deal."

"No?" Benjamin stopped two feet in front of her and glanced at the book, then continued on to the cold fireplace where he knelt. "Mr. London told quite exciting tales."

In a few short moments, he had a fire roaring in the fireplace and stood, turning to face her. It had taken her half an hour to figure out how to get a fire started in the guest room, and it never had roared.

"Have the others retired?"

"Yeah."

"I see. And you chose to read instead."

She shrugged. "I wasn't tired."

He frowned and looked around as if studying new surroundings. "I wish to apologize for my earlier behavior. Please forgive me."

He was apologizing? Since when did bullies apologize?

"No problem."

He turned his frown on her, and then released it and nodded as if formally bowing. "Thank you."

Star swallowed hard. The white shirt he wore showed off more of him than the black one had. In the kitchen she'd been too uncomfortable to look very closely. Now she had a chance.

He had to be well over six feet tall, his shoulders and chest were broad and muscular, and his belly showed no hint of a bulge. He must spend a lot of time working out. Jones was obsessed with working out, and he'd never looked half as good.

There was something truly different about this man, however. Star tried to find a single word for it, but couldn't. He had an air of authority about him, as if he were used to having his orders followed without question. And even in his own home, he seemed a little out of place. He was . . . what was it?

Realizing she was staring, she mentally shook herself. "Uh, these are your books?" She used *Call of the Wild* to point to the bookshelf.

"Aye, that they are." He clasped his hands behind his back and stood with his feet spread.

"How many of them have you read?"

"All of them."

Was he serious? There were more books here than she could read in fifty years. "Holy crap," she muttered.

His eyebrows arched up and one corner of his mouth rose.

Heat crawled up her throat to her cheeks. She hated being laughed at.

Clenching her jaw, she marched to the bookshelf, slid the book back into place, and then turned to leave. "Good night."

"Wait." He grabbed her arm.

Star tried to jerk her arm from his grasp, but nothing happened. Although he wasn't hurting her, his grip was like a vise she couldn't shake. "Let go."

"Don't leave."

Something in his voice stopped her. She looked up into his dark eyes and saw raw emotion that caused her chest to clench. She saw sadness, and loneliness, and a hint of desire.

Her belly did somersaults.

He drew her slowly toward him until they stood inches apart and he towered over her.

She fought to drag air into her lungs.

His gaze slid down from her eyes to her mouth, and she began to tremble.

Was he really going to kiss her?

God, she wanted him to kiss her. She wanted to know how his arms felt around her. As he leaned close, she caught a scent of wildness—the woods, wind, and dewy grass.

He caressed her jaw and drew her mouth up to his.

When his lips met hers, a jolt of excitement shot through her. His lips were cool and moist, and they demanded surrender.

Star sucked in a breath of surprise.

He drew back, then cocked his head and took her mouth completely, parting her lips.

She clung to his shirt.

His hand slid up her arm and across her shoulder, and he encircled her.

His tongue tested, explored, seduced. And she welcomed it.

God almighty, was this what a kiss was supposed to be like?

Her entire body turned to mush. She might have collapsed if he hadn't held her.

She melted against him, warm mush to a wall of cold steel, and a soft, vibrating groan rose up through that wall.

They crashed into the bookshelves and he pinned her there with his weight as he drew her legs up around him. He tore his mouth from hers to press it to the side of her neck.

His hips bruised the insides of her thighs as he pushed against her, and his chest flattened her breasts. Bookshelves dented lines in her spine.

Christ. If she could have reached his waist, she would have ripped his pants open. But all she could do was push back, thrusting her crotch against his bulging hard-on.

And what a bulge it was. The feel of it swelling against her liquefied her insides.

With a handful of his hair in her fist and clinging to his massive shoulders, Star dropped her head back to a shelf.

Benjamin kissed her bare throat, and sucked on it, probably leaving a hickey. She didn't care, she just wanted more of him.

His right hand rode up under her T-shirt to the side of her breast, and his thumb slipped across her nipple, creating lines of electricity between his touch and her crotch.

Her clit swelled with need and juices gushed from her pussy.

With one hand on her ass, he drew her up against him and eased her down, using her throbbing pussy to stroke his erection through their clothes.

No one had ever caused her body to do such crazy things. Goose bumps covered her from head to toe, and she shook with desire.

He covered her jaw and cheek with hungry kisses, took her mouth again as she struggled to breathe, and then locked his lips on the side of her neck as he rubbed harder, faster. Her neck tingled and then warmed.

Her body exploded with pleasure that quivered through her backbone and bounced off the bottom of her feet.

Gripping him tighter, she cried out. Amazing tremors of satisfaction racked her body and fogged her brain.

And the world disappeared.

Benjamin dragged the back of his hand across his mouth as he knelt beside the sofa. Star's eyes moved back and forth beneath the lids as if she fought monsters in her dreams. Had she sensed the beast she'd just held while awake?

He hoped not.

He hadn't meant to bite her, or even to kiss her. What was it about this mortal woman that drew him like a moth to a flame?

The intensity of her emotions had taken him off guard. He'd wanted all of her as a result, and that terrified him. When had he even come close to making a mistake such as this?

Never. Not since Cassandra taught him how to control the minds of his victims and leash his hunger.

But he'd sensed Star's strength, even before he tasted her blood. Perhaps he'd felt it when he first met her. Something had caught his attention.

Now he knew it, the strength. She'd faced many difficulties in her short life and learned to survive alone. She didn't need anyone. She stood with fists at the ready, protected by a wall of stone.

Damn. He wanted more of her, even now as she lay unconscious. The small holes in her skin puckered and lightened as he watched. If he drank from her again, she wouldn't heal so quickly.

Benjamin pressed his lips to her warm forehead and pushed forward peaceful thoughts. Then he staggered to his feet. Plucking *Call of the Wild* from the shelf, he opened it, placed it face down on Star's stomach, and rested her hand on top of it.

He must leave before she woke, and he wanted to be alone to enjoy the remnants of her in his system.

5

"What'd you do, fall asleep reading?"

Star forced open her eyes and stared up into Wendy's face. "Huh?"

Wendy snatched the book from where it lay. "What's it about?"

She sat up and rubbed her eyes. "A dog."

"Yeah? Like Scooby Doo?" Wendy thumbed through the pages and then tossed the book to the sofa.

"Where are the guys?" Star asked.

"They're hitching down to the garage to get the fuel line. Should be back soon. There's coffee in the kitchen."

"Really?" Star's mouth watered. She quickly stood, and then fell back onto the sofa with the room spinning. "What the hell?"

"You okay?"

In a rush, the memory of a dream swept through her, a dream in which she and Benjamin kissed.

And more. She remembered him touching her breasts and pinning her against a bookshelf. She remembered desperately needing more of him.

Christ. Now she was having truly erotic dreams about the man.

The room stopped spinning, and Star tried again. This time she remained on her feet, but she felt shaky. "I don't guess there's bacon and eggs in there, too, huh?"

Wendy shrugged. "I don't know. I didn't look."

Stretching her shoulders and back muscles, Star winced at the tender spots on her spine. The sofa cushions must have poked into her back as she slept.

All through scrambling eggs, browning sausage, and making toast, she tried not to think about the dream. The more she tried not to think about it, the more vividly she recalled details. She could smell his hair, feel his shirt in her hands, taste his mouth. And she remembered how violently blissful her orgasm had been.

Could dreams really leave such strong impressions? She'd never had any do so before.

If she hadn't known better, she would have sworn this dream had been real.

But it wasn't. It was only a dream. She'd fallen asleep on the sofa while reading.

Damn, her neck was tender, too. She rubbed the side where a crick threatened to set in. That sofa wasn't nearly as comfortable as it looked.

She dished out half the eggs and sausage, leaving the remainder in the pan for Jack and Kyle, and sat at the table with Wendy to enjoy the meal. She couldn't remember when anything had tasted so good. Probably because they'd been living off junk food for so long. With each bite, her earlier shakiness faded.

"You want to explore this place?" Wendy asked. She carried her plate to the sink.

"Nah, there's nothing else to see. Just a bunch of rooms with dusty junk." The thought of the others finding Benjamin's hangout bothered Star. The room held marvels that they'd see only as dollar signs. "Why don't we go for a walk?"

"A walk?" Wendy looked at her like she'd suggested acupuncture.

"Yeah. We could go see the ocean."

Wendy continued to frown. "I saw it yesterday."

"Yeah, but we could look for sailors."

Wendy's frown disappeared at that one. "Okay."

After washing the dishes, Star grabbed her jeans jacket, shoved the flash drive in her pocket, and led the way out the front door.

Wendy stopped in the doorway. "We won't get locked out, will we?"

"No. I unlocked a window in the back. Besides, Benjamin's gone."

"How do you know?"

"I searched the place yesterday. He left early in the morning and didn't get back until dark."

Wendy followed Star down the sidewalk. "I wonder what he does."

"Something having to do with ships, I bet."

"*Duh.*"

They walked in the hazy sunshine the few blocks to the coast, talking about people they knew back at the Klub, wondering if they'd been missed. At the corner across from the Tangled Net, they ran into Jack and Kyle hopping from the back of a pickup truck.

"You get the hose?" Star asked.

Jack held up a paper bag.

"We're walking down to the beach," Wendy said. "Wanna come?"

"You know I always wanna *come*," Jack said, wrapping an arm around her waist.

"Me, too," Kyle said.

They seemed to be turning into a threesome. Star might have felt left out, if she'd cared. Instead, she found it convenient. They wouldn't have any reason to protest when she struck out on her own. And at the moment, she really wanted to be alone so she could get rid of the flash drive.

"What about the van?" she asked.

Jack shrugged. "We'll get to it. Gonna join us?"

"No, thanks. I think I'll walk down the beach." She glanced around. "Besides, someone might see you."

"It's too damn cold out here for tourists." Jack grinned.

"Don't worry," Wendy said, flashing a pout at Jack. "I'll warm you up."

"I know you will, sweet *thang.*"

The three of them dashed across the road and then started south along the beach. Star headed north.

Something about the coast thrilled her in a primal way. Cold, salty air against her face woke her completely and made her want to run into it. Waves lashing the rocky shore washed away all other noise except for an occasional gull's screech.

A ship, made miniature by distance, seemed about to drop off the edge of the earth. It looked gray and multilevel, like some kind of military vessel. Certainly nothing like the sailing ship in the painting at Benjamin's.

After half an hour, Star stopped, looked around, and dug the flash drive out of her pocket. She drew back and threw it as far as she could, and it plopped into the water. Feeling as if she'd just gotten rid of a great weight, she continued walking, enjoying the squish of wet sand under her shoes.

As she stepped into a shadow darkening the beach, Star glanced to her left and stopped.

Twenty feet to her left was a rock ledge. It started about head high, and then rose to a wall of rock at least fifty feet tall. Gnarled limbs of trees peeked over the edge.

Her breath caught in her throat when she realized that this was the rock wall from the painting.

"Wow."

Whoever had produced the painting had seen this cliff from some distance out at sea.

She shuddered at the creepy feeling of stepping into the painting and another time.

Taking a deep breath and blowing it out, she walked, studying the cliff and the shore as she went. The tide seemed to be going out at the moment. If it were coming in, it might reach the rocks, eliminating the beach altogether. And not far off the beach, the tips of massive rocks broke the surface of the water between swells. Certainly not an inviting area, but exciting and full of raw energy.

As a strange feeling crept up her spine, Star stopped and turned a circle, looking for intruders. She had the distinct feeling of being watched. Her heart rate sped up as she thought about Jones.

It couldn't be him. Why would he chase her this far? The first time she'd started to leave, he'd said she wouldn't be able to run far enough to hide from him, but she knew that had just been the booze talking.

No, there was no one watching, no one following her. No one had seen her toss the flash drive.

Star hurried on, anxious to get back to the gentler part of the beach.

Just as the rock wall began to fall away to sand dunes, a dark spot in the face of the rock caught her eye. She stopped again.

The spot was about twenty feet up and surrounded by bushes that were losing their yellow and brown leaves. If not for that fact, and the way the sun hit the wall at that particular moment, she never would have noticed it.

It looked like an opening of some kind. A cave, maybe?

She'd loved exploring caves in north Georgia when she was young. The kids from the Home had taken two trips up there during summer vacations, once when she was seven, and again when she was nine. She'd never forgotten the excitement of stepping into cool, damp caves.

Star scrambled up the cliff, sending several small pieces of rock tumbling down from beneath her feet. The rock face wasn't as steep as it looked from below, but still wouldn't be much fun to tumble down.

When she reached her goal, she found an opening about two feet wide. Easing the bushes aside, she leaned into it and strained to see how far back it went. All she could see was darkness.

Rolling to her side, she dug a book of matches from her pocket, struck one, and held it above her head. Just inside the opening, the tiny light illuminated a room just tall enough to stand in, and she saw no sign of snakes or other undesirables on the dusty floor.

"Cool." Her voice echoed, suggesting the cavern stretched back beyond the match light.

Star shook out the match, scrambled in, and squatted just inside the opening, giving her eyes time to adjust. She could see clearly toward the opening, and could make out the walls right around her, but the room faded out a few feet past her reach. One step at a time, she moved forward, following the wall. The place looked sort of unnatural, as if carved by humans. Maybe the cave had been chiseled out by a group of early man for protection. She doubted anyone knew it was here now, because it wasn't trashed with empty beer cans and used condoms, and the walls hadn't been tagged.

Maybe she was the first human to see this place in a thousand years.

She moved deeper into the room, wondering just how far

back it went. The ceiling sloped down; she had to walk stooped over. When she reached a spot where the main path wound around to the left, losing the advantage of natural lighting, she stopped. The ground seemed to be filled with rubble, as if the walls were crumbling.

Star struck a match, and frowned at light gray rubble piled against the dark rock wall. "Weird." She reached down and picked up a rock, surprised by how light it was. As she held it close to the light, she realized it wasn't a rock.

It was a bone.

She dropped it as the match flame hit her fingertips. "Shit!"

After sucking the burn from her fingers, Star struck another match and scooted forward on her knees. Maybe early man had cooked bear or something here and left the bones. This was better than going to a museum.

She held the match close to a large round bone and found two empty eye sockets staring up at her.

The skull was human.

"Son of a bitch," she whispered.

Before the match could burn her again, she shook it out and lit another, her last.

From what she could see, these were the remains of a dozen humans, at least. Some things scattered among the bones glistened in the match light. She picked up one, rubbed it on her jeans, and realized it was a brass button. Damn, it must be really old. She dropped it and picked up another that turned out to be a silver crucifix with a chain wrapped around several neck bones.

All the skeletons leaned up against the wall as if the people had been just sitting there when they died.

A chill ran through Star's entire body, making the match flame dance around the bones. She blew it out and backed quickly to the opening of the cave, then slid down the rock wall in a shower of small rocks.

Glancing around for witnesses and seeing none, she ran north until the rock wall and cavern with its gruesome contents lay far behind her. Gasping for breath, she dropped to the sand.

It wasn't that the bones freaked her out. She'd seen a lot worse. It was just that she hadn't expected to find these, and they put her in a difficult position. She should call the cops, but she couldn't take the chance. They'd want her name, and then there might be an investigation.

She could call in anonymously, if she had access to a phone. Benjamin didn't have one; she'd found that out the first night. The bar probably had a phone, but the town was so damned small, everyone would know who had placed the call.

"Shit."

Staring out to sea, she purposely slowed her thoughts.

She'd just found a cave where a dozen people had died, and no one knew about them. Except whoever killed them, of course, assuming they were murdered. But why else would a bunch of people die sitting against the wall of a cave? Hell, the killer was probably long dead. No telling how long the corpses had been there. They definitely weren't early man, though. Not with buttons. Somewhere, families were missing members. What would it be like to have someone you love just disappear?

She had no way of knowing. First, she'd have to have someone she loved.

What if she'd never looked up and seen the cave? The skeletons would still be there, undiscovered. And no one had seen her climbing in or out of the cave. All she had to do was add this to her list of secrets no one else would ever know.

That wasn't so hard.

Standing, Star slapped sand from her jeans and hands, and started back toward the house. She couldn't help but look up at the cave opening as she passed it, and was surprised to find it now impossible to see, as if wiped off the face of the Earth.

That's it. It didn't really matter. She could convince herself of that.

"No big deal."

Star trotted down the beach, enjoying the way the sunshine warmed the top of her head, purposely forgetting the skeletons.

The sun was dipping toward the horizon by the time she reached the other three, a quarter mile past the Tangled Net. They lay on their shirts, soaking up the last of the sun's rays. Judging by the lack of wood between them, the guys had already gotten off.

Jack smiled up at her. "We missed you."

"I bet you did."

Wendy, lying on her stomach, turned her head in Star's direction. "Have fun?"

"Yeah. So, did you fix the van?"

Jack held up the small bag. "Haven't made it back yet. We'll start on it first thing tomorrow."

Star bit back a complaint. She hadn't told the guys about Jones, but Wendy knew. The last thing she wanted to do was sit around another day.

At the same time, the idea of sticking around long enough to see Benjamin again didn't really upset her. "Meet you back at the house."

"We'll be along in a few minutes," Jack said.

Star found the front door still unlocked and the mansion quiet. She climbed the stairs to the third floor and peeked into Benjamin's room. Disappointment burned in her chest when she found it empty.

What would she have said to him, anyway? "Hi, how's it going?" He just didn't seem like a small talk kind of guy.

She tiptoed through and climbed the stairs to the back tower where the sunset had splashed spectacular reds and oranges across the western sky. Entranced, she walked outside and circled around to the west side of the tower on a catwalk where she leaned on the wooden handrail and watched the sun go down. The approach of night seemed almost magical from so high up as shadows in the woods thickened and merged until they formed a blanket of darkness. When the first stars began to appear in a clear sky, she turned.

"Shit!" Her heart jumped.

Benjamin stood facing her, once again wearing a white shirt, black pants and boots, and his stern frown.

"Are you trying to scare me to death?" she asked.

"What are you doing?"

Star took a deep breath and blew it out. "Enjoying the sunset."

He glanced out toward the darkened horizon for a long moment, and then zeroed in on her again. "Your vehicle is not repaired?"

"Uh, no, not yet."

A breeze lifted his hair from his shoulders and Star suddenly remembered his kiss the night before.

It hadn't been a dream. It had definitely been real.

Why had she thought it was a dream?

Her stomach knotted.

"You kissed me," she said.

Benjamin's eyes widened.

"You did, didn't you?" There was no longer any doubt in her mind. He had definitely kissed her.

He turned and strode to the stairs, which he hurried down.

Star followed. "What the hell are you, some kind of hypnotist?"

"Something of that sort," he muttered, facing the fireplace.

She stopped in the middle of the room. "Hey!"

Benjamin spun to face her.

"What the fuck's going on here?" she said.

He growled in frustration. "You ask too many questions."

"Oh, yeah? Well, tough shit. I want an answer."

He took a step toward her that she barely resisted matching in reverse, but she managed to stand her ground. The man was more intimidating than a six-pack of bouncers.

He took another, practically closing the distance between them.

As he stood before her, glaring down at her, his hair again wild and his dark eyes shining, she knew for sure exactly what had happened between them, at least up to the point where she must have passed out.

"What did you do to me?" she asked. "Why don't I remember everything?"

He grabbed her shoulders roughly and drew her close. "I did nothing."

It was a lie. She knew. Her hands ached to feel his hair and skin, but he held her in place.

She drew in a stuttered breath as her body vibrated with excitement.

Benjamin slowly released her, sliding his hands down her arms. He spun again and returned to the fireplace, where he worked on starting a fire. In moments, flames burst forth and he rose, leaning with one hand on the mantle as he stared into the fire. "Go away, Star."

Had he yelled at her to leave, she would have yelled back. Instead, he spoke her name in a voice filled with pain, and her heart wrenched. She walked toward him, her hand outstretched to touch him, to caress away his pain.

At the last moment, he whirled around and caught her hand.

His eyes seemed to glitter a strange gold color in the dim light.

Holding her gaze, he slowly drew her arm up to his mouth and pressed his lips to the inside of her wrist. His eyes rolled shut.

Her whole body quivered. At such a simple touch, her nipples hardened to the point of pain, and her panties felt suddenly drenched.

He straightened and opened his eyes. "You shouldn't be here."

"Why not? I don't get it."

"You don't know me." He released her hand. "You should have left long ago. Do so now, before it's too late."

"What do you mean, before—?"

"Go! Now!" His voice shot through her like rifle fire at close range.

She took a step back.

For the first time since she was a kid, she felt tears burning the backs of her eyes. How could he send her away when she was offering herself to him? Damn him for making her want to cry!

Hardening herself, she sneered. "Screw you." Then she turned and left.

As she wound down the stairs, she tried to figure out what had just happened. The man was drawn to her, but insisted on sending her away. And he had kissed her the night before. Hell, she'd even had an orgasm, and then passed out. That was a new one.

And so was this. Benjamin ran hot and cold in thirty seconds. Who the hell needed that?

She might be attracted to him, but she'd get over it. She obviously had crappy taste in men. All she had to do was light a fire under Jack and Kyle to get the van fixed.

Wendy looked up from the living room floor where she'd just rested her head on one knee while in a split as part of her daily stretching routine. "Hey."

"Hey." Star plopped down on the sofa next to Jack and swiped a sip of his beer. He and Kyle drank and watched Wendy stretch. "What's the plan for dinner?"

"The bar down the road is having happy hour," Kyle said.

"Thought we might have a few more of these." He raised his bottle.

"Sounds good." The sooner she got away from Benjamin, the better. And if the guys didn't start work on the van first thing the next morning, she would.

From the widow's walk, he watched them stroll out to the street and turn toward the ocean. The four walked arm in arm, laughing and joking.

Damn her.

How was it she remembered their encounter? By all rights, she should have forgotten it.

He hadn't forgotten. The exquisite taste of her blood haunted him. Her strength and abilities were unlike any he'd encountered. Her emotions, usually well hidden, ran deep. Since she first stepped into his house, he had been unable to stop thinking about her. Now she would be in his thoughts for decades after she left.

Damn her to hell.

An irrational jealousy swelled in Benjamin's breast as he watched Jack drape his arm around Star's shoulders.

With a growl, he vaulted over the railing and dropped silently to the yard.

6

A wave of warmth met them at the door of the Tangled Net. Wendy hurried in and Star followed, leaving the guys to bring up the rear.

The place was cozy, decorated with nets, anchors, and stuffed fish, and dark enough to be considered intimate. Two tables of patrons, one of men and one of women, followed their progress.

Wendy picked out a table and Star sat across from her. The bartender was a tall man in his forties or so, and a small dark-haired woman carried drinks to one of the other tables. Everyone seemed to know each other, which wasn't surprising.

Once they were settled, a waitress with bright red hair and a few extra pounds in all the right places stopped at their table. "What can I get you?"

"We'll take a pitcher of whatever's on tap," Jack said.

"Got any nachos or peanuts?" Kyle asked.

The woman nodded toward a table against the back wall. "Happy hour snacks are over there. Help yourselves."

Kyle and Jack headed for the food.

"What's up?"

Star met Wendy's questioning gaze. "Huh?"

"What happened back at the house? You can tell me, you know."

She shrugged. "Nothing."

She considered telling Wendy about Benjamin, about the kiss the night before, and about their yelling match earlier. But it all seemed too personal to share, even with Wendy. Maybe because he'd wounded her, and she hadn't let anyone do that in years.

She also thought about the cave with the bones, and couldn't share that, either. Wendy would freak out and tell everyone, and then where would they be? Cops would get called in and they'd want Star's name. Funny, even if she didn't have to worry about Jones, she'd have felt compelled to keep the cave a secret.

Jack deposited two bowls of chips and salsa on the table, Kyle added a plate of Buffalo wings, and the redheaded waitress dropped off a pitcher and four glasses.

Star guzzled half her beer and licked foam from her lips.

An old-fashioned juke box whined out rock and roll, and one of the men who'd watched them walk in sauntered up to their table. "You want to dance?" he asked Wendy.

"Sure." She jumped up and took the man's hand, winking back at Star as she led the guy to the middle of the room. He was good-looking—tall, blond, and muscular—and a little on the scruffy side. He had no idea what he was getting into with Wendy. She'd charm the pants off of him right there in the bar, and have him paying for drinks for the rest of the evening.

Star finished her beer.

"I'll be back," Jack said. "I see a cute young thing over there who needs my company."

"Good luck." Kyle raised his glass. "Just don't start a fight," he muttered.

Wendy pulled some kind of dirty-dancing move on her partner, who grinned in response, and his buddies at the table whistled encouragement.

Star refilled her glass. What she needed was a really good buzz.

Until three days ago, she'd been happily on her way to a new life God-knows-where, not really caring what the future held. How could some crazy-ass captain who lived alone in a mansion in Massachusetts have ruined it for her? She knew from now on, she'd compare every kiss, every touch to his. Every night would be spent thinking about him. Why the hell did the van have to break down in front of his place?

"Look who's here," Kyle said.

A gust of cold air swept across the room and Star turned in time to see Benjamin step through the doorway.

"Oh, crap," she muttered.

"Captain," the bartender said. "We didn't expect you back so soon."

Benjamin scanned the room. When his gaze met Star's, she stiffened and turned to stare at her glass. What the hell was he doing there?

She felt him watching her in a very physical way, as if his gaze were a hand sliding down her arm.

"Welcome back," a woman said.

Star glanced over as the redheaded waitress kissed Benjamin soundly. When she stepped aside, he smiled at the woman.

Holy shit. He had one hell of a sexy smile. Star would never have guessed.

A ring of anger tightened around her throat. Why should she care if Benjamin kissed someone else? He'd made it clear he wanted her to get lost, and she sure as hell didn't need him.

"I've, uh, gotta find the bathroom." Star jumped up and hurried toward an alcove across the room. She considered bolting for the door, but would have to run right past Benjamin.

In the darkened alcove, she fell against the wall and worked to catch her breath as she looked around. She'd hoped the place had a back door, but didn't see anything promising.

"Dammit."

This whole thing was stupid. What the hell was she doing hiding? And if she had found a back door, where would she run except back to Benjamin's? He could certainly find her there if he wanted to. She had no desire to sleep in the cold, wet van.

He'd told her to leave and she had. It wasn't her fault he'd decided to show up at the same bar. He couldn't blame her for that.

Star straightened and squared her shoulders. He would not see her sweat, no matter what. She would go out to the bar, work on her buzz, and have a good time. This time tomorrow, she'd be miles away from Captain Benjamin Bartlett.

After a few deep breaths, she marched out, guzzled her beer while standing beside the table, then crossed the room to the group of men and smiled at the biggest guy. "Wanna dance?"

One of his buddies slapped him on the shoulder as the man's face reddened. He nodded, rose, and followed Star to the dance floor.

The guy was six-three or more and two-fifty at least, probably a guard on the football team when he was in high school. He wasn't used to women asking him to dance. When he took her hand and held her waist as if they were about to waltz, she also realized he smelled like fish.

Well, this would take her mind off Benjamin. And maybe he'd leave when he saw her having fun.

"I'm Star. What's your name?" she asked.

"Moose," he said, and his face reddened again.

She nodded as she quick-stepped in order to avoid his size-fourteen work boots.

"You live here?" she asked.

"Yep. All my life. Where are you from?"

"Georgia."

"Cool."

They danced without talking, and Star purposely resisted looking around.

"Excuse me."

She jumped at the sound of Benjamin's deep voice right behind her, and her dance partner glanced over her shoulder with wide eyes.

"May I?"

Moose swallowed hard and stepped back. "Sure."

Great. He intimidated everyone.

Benjamin grabbed her wrist, and she turned to look up into his stormy expression.

"You're going to dance with me?"

"Nay," he said, "it's not dancing I have in mind."

He turned and dragged her after him across the dance floor where Wendy humped some guy's leg as they danced, past the bar with the tall, graying bartender who simply smiled, and to a doorway she hadn't noticed before. Although she tugged against his grip, her heart pounded with excitement.

In spite of the fact that he'd yelled at her to get lost less than an hour ago, she would have followed him willingly.

"Where the hell are you taking me?" she said.

He glanced back at her but didn't answer.

Benjamin closed the door behind them and turned to Star. She stood halfway across the room glaring at him, her hands on her hips.

What, exactly, was he to do now?

He'd burned with rage watching her in another man's arms. Visions of her body writhing with passion had driven him to his feet.

He couldn't take any chances. She was stronger than any woman he'd encountered; he couldn't clear her memory.

At least she hadn't yet remembered his bite. But she would. And he would never forget it.

Even now as he stood with her in the empty upstairs room, his teeth throbbed and his cock swelled. What was it about this one that he had such difficulty resisting?

"So, now what?" she said. "You got me up here. What's the plan?"

"Be quiet," he said.

Her eyebrows shot up. "Or what? You gonna slug me? You'll never get away with it. A dozen people saw you drag me up here."

"I have no desire to hurt you." He curled his hands into fists to keep from reaching for her.

"Yeah? Then what exactly do you have a desire to do? You figure I'll take off my clothes because you're strong enough to—?"

Growling, he strode to her, grabbed her shoulders, and drew her mouth up to his. His intention was to stop her from talking, but as soon as he felt her lips under his, the intention slipped away.

He slid one hand behind her head, buried his fingers in her soft hair, and held her in place. Her lips were hard at first, but he opened her mouth with his own and she softened. He took her mouth with greed, filling his senses with her taste.

Her hands seared his chest through his shirt.

This was what he'd wanted: her surrender. He wanted all of her—her kiss, her body, her blood. He wanted her to need him.

She drew him deeper into her mouth as she clung to his shirt.

He knew the taste of her desire, and wanted to savor it again.

Benjamin straightened, reluctantly ending the kiss. He could no more resist her than the tides could resist the moon.

She looked up at him with her startlingly blue eyes as if she could see through his disguise.

"You don't understand," he whispered.

She pushed out of his grip. "No shit, Sherlock. I'm completely lost here. What the hell do you want?"

"I want you, Star."

His honesty stopped her; he saw the surprise in her eyes.

"What?"

"You heard me. I want you." He started toward her slowly. "I want to touch you, and kiss you, and please you in ways you can't imagine."

She swallowed hard and stared up at him, finally quiet. "Why?" she whispered.

He smiled. "Because I can't seem to do otherwise."

"Oh." Shaking her head as if to clear it, she looked around. "Here?"

"Aye." He stroked his fingertips down her smooth cheek. "To start with."

Her heart raced, promising delights that threatened to make him shake.

She laughed nervously. "Do I get any say in this?"

He leaned close, watching her lips respond by parting. "You may try to deny me, if you wish."

Her eyes darkened as she stared at his mouth. "No thanks."

He took her mouth gently this time, letting their lips come together in quiet hunger until he felt her tongue searching for his. Then he lifted her from the ground and walked her to the bed. Springs squeaked as he lowered her to the mattress, their mouths locked in a torrid kiss.

She clung to his shoulders and locked one leg around his.

Already hard enough to be uncomfortable, Benjamin rubbed his cock into the cleft of her hidden cunt. She responded by pushing up into him, and he groaned.

He kissed her face and neck, and she combed her fingers through his hair. Her warm skin held a hint of salt and something sweet and mysterious, something uniquely her. He craved more of it.

Moving back, he drew her up so that she sat on the edge of the bed, then pushed her jacket back off her arms and raised her shirt over her head. She unbuttoned his shirt and slid her hands inside.

Benjamin shuddered at the pleasure of her touch, and she smiled.

Drawing her hands away from his skin, he pressed kisses into her palms, and then kissed her neck. As he listened to the song of her heart, he moved down her body, sampling every inch of her marvelous flesh.

She sucked in a breath when he closed his mouth around her left breast, drawing the hard nipple carefully between his teeth. He licked and suckled as he caressed the warm flesh of her back and waist.

She kneaded his shoulders with hands stronger than he'd expected, and locked her legs around him.

When he moved to her right breast, she groaned, cradled him, and pressed her lips to the top of his head. He wanted to take her into him, to become one with her for eternity. Why did she cause this strange desire to burn inside him?

He slid his lips across her chest and rested his forehead against her breastbone.

"I smell your tempting cunt and hear your heart pounding for me, my sweet."

She whimpered in response.

He unbuttoned her pants and drew them down under her. She helped, kicking them off to one side and then spreading her legs around his chest again. He had her in his arms now, perfect and naked, to do with as he wished. That thought frightened him a little as he considered exactly what he wanted.

He couldn't hazard taking her blood here, not with the way the monster thrashed inside him, but he had to have her. If nothing else, he would bring her to a slow, calculated release, something of which her incompetent traveling companions were incapable. He would show her exactly what true pleasure was.

With his hands around her waist, he urged her over until she lay on her back watching him.

Her skin was darker than his. The hair between her legs matched the color of that on her head so that she seemed to be all subtle shades of brown, except for her eyes. Her eyes glistened like ice crystals against a midday sky, and he had to force his gaze away from them.

He pressed his cheek to her stomach and slid it across her smooth skin, then tasted her flesh. Her body twitched and jumped under him as he moved down, closing in on her eager cunt. He inhaled her intoxicating scent and closed his eyes to let it print on his memory where it would stay for the rest of eternity.

His fangs ached and hunger rose up inside him to push him to his limits. He searched for her thoughts, but found them out of reach. It would take more concentration to connect than he had available at the moment.

Locking his mouth on the inside of her tender right thigh, he raised her left leg out of his way. His fangs rested against her tempting flesh and the memory of her blood teased him.

He could not give in just yet. Not now.

Holding her firm ass, he drew her cunt up to his mouth and finally tasted her, linking her taste with her scent, savoring her thick salty cream.

She cried out and gripped her own legs, digging her fingers into to undersides of her muscular thighs.

Using an expert touch, he licked and nipped her swollen clit and felt her react to him as if they were connected by something deeper than flesh, deeper than blood even. He felt as if her very soul called to him.

He drew her to the edge of arousal, felt her release approach, and turned his head to carefully nick the tender flesh of her inner thigh. A single drop of her precious blood rose to the surface and he licked it away, letting it settle on his tongue and into his brain where it hummed as he drew her to a climax.

She cried out, her hips rose from the bed, and she flooded his mouth. He fought to stay focused, wrestling with the monster in his heart. Matching her rhythm, he drew out her pleasure until her hips fell back to the mattress and she lay panting.

Then he crawled up and, fighting the desire to urgently mount her, took her in his arms. Lying on his back, he drew her head to his shoulder. Her soft breath warmed his chest, and her fingers caressing his belly, eliciting dangerous thoughts of taking more. He covered her hand with his.

He couldn't risk releasing the monster now; he wouldn't be able to control it.

"So, uh, what now?" she asked.

The uncertainty in her voice made him smile. She had no idea how much her very presence affected him.

"I suggest a more private location."

She rose up to her elbow to look down at him. Satisfaction warmed her eyes and darkened her skin, but he saw a spark of suspicion. "How private?"

They'd walked up the street without talking, too far apart to touch. This wasn't exactly a hand-holding situation. Star felt desperation and sizzling lust in Benjamin's touch that confused and excited her, and mirrored her own feelings.

In the still night, the only real noise was his boots thudding on the sidewalk.

Star's mind worked to sort out what had just happened. The man she had the hots for had angrily dragged her upstairs into a bedroom as if he planned to rape or beat her, but had unselfishly given her pleasure instead. She'd never had a man bring her to a climax with his mouth, or any other part of his body. Benjamin was up by two.

She knew he wanted her. His erection had been as hard as

rock when he lay on top of her. Now she was on her way to his house to . . . what? Have wild, passionate sex? Be hypnotized? Get yelled at and sent away? Who the hell knew?

He opened the front door and stepped aside, letting her enter first. Then he waited in silence at the bottom of the stairs for her to decide.

She'd told Wendy they were headed back to Benjamin's, and Wendy had shaken her head in disapproval. "I knew it. Don't let this guy get to you, we're leaving tomorrow."

Too late for that. This guy had gotten to her the first time she saw him. He was different from any man she'd known, someone with great strength and dark secrets. And he knew how to please her. Granted, sex wasn't everything, but somehow it seemed like more than just sex with him. She felt a connection of some kind that ran deeper than should be possible.

Shit. She'd sworn off commitments after Jones. Sex was fine, emotional connections weren't.

She turned to study Benjamin and found him watching her, his feet spread and his hands clasped behind his back. His intense black eyes took in every detail, and his thick wavy hair rested on broad shoulders. Dear God, he was truly gorgeous.

Star swallowed hard and started up the stairs.

Benjamin followed her to his office and left the door open behind them.

She stopped in front of the fireplace. "Will you show me how to make this thing work?"

He smiled that amazingly sexy smile she'd seen just once before. "Aye, with pleasure."

She stood beside him as he crouched and constructed a fire. In mere seconds, he had it lit.

When she rested her hand on his shoulder, he noticeably stiffened, as aware of her touch as she was of touching him. They both stared at flames licking lines up crackling logs.

Her insides quivered from being close to him, and her thoughts and emotions jumbled into endless knots. Not knowing what was next both bothered and excited her. No matter what, she still had the hots for Captain Benjamin Bartlett.

He placed his hand over hers and drew it from his shoulder as he rose and turned to face her. Firelight made him look even sexier and sparkled golden in his eyes.

"I want all of you," he said, his voice deep and barely more than a whisper. "I want every inch of your body, inside and out, and more."

"More? Like . . . what?"

He smiled as he drew her closer. "I want your thoughts and emotions, your fantasies."

She pulled her hand away. "More of that hypnosis crap?" Backing away, Star stepped around the edge of his desk, putting the massive piece of furniture between them. "I don't know about that."

He nodded. "Fair enough." He stood across the desk from her. "I offer you the truth. I can take what I want from you, Star. You have no way to deny me."

Fear tickled like a bead of sweat down her spine. Coming to this empty house with him had been a mistake. She glanced at the door, judging her chance at making it past him to be some-where between slim and none. She searched the desk for a weapon.

"Hear me out," he said. "I will do you no harm."

Her gaze jumped up to his. Did he know what she was thinking? Or had she just let her guard down long enough for him to see her fear?

"Allow me to show you what I want. If you refuse, I will not force you. You have my word."

She searched his expression and his eyes, and found only honesty. If there was one thing she knew how to spot, it was a liar.

Benjamin wasn't lying.

Still, why should she trust this stranger she knew little to nothing about? Twice she'd let her guard down around him, both times without really meaning to. This time would be on purpose.

A strange memory flashed through her brain. Charlie, her first boyfriend, had taken her fishing in north Georgia once. He'd tied some kind of shiny red and purple lure with feathers to a hook and tossed it in the water. She'd watched a fish rise slowly up to the lure and wondered what the fish was thinking. Didn't it know the lure was too pretty to be real? When it sucked in the red and purple feathered lure, hook and all, she'd decided fish weren't very smart.

So here she stood considering an offer of sex from a man who was too attractive to be real. Was she as stupid as a fish?

Star took a deep breath and walked out from around the desk. "Okay. Show me."

He extended his hand, palm up. She took it, and he led her across the room. "Let us retire to my room."

"Why?"

"I cannot reveal the truth out here where we might be interrupted."

Something about the way he said *interrupted* sent a shiver through her.

He waited.

She nodded, trying her best to ignore her concerns.

7

Noting the slight tremor in Star's hand, Benjamin studied her face as he led her to the bookshelf. Her eyes showed none of the concern he knew she felt.

"As you will soon understand, I'm trusting you with my very existence." He drew out the top corner book and pushed the hidden button.

She took a half a step back as the door opened. "What the hell?"

"Please, allow me to go first. It's rather dark."

She stopped just inside the door as it closed behind them. "*Rather* dark? Shit. I can't tell if my eyes are open."

He lit the lamp by his bed and a dozen candles around the room then turned to watch her.

She scanned the room as she approached, taking in details. "Wow. You must really like antiques, huh?"

He glanced around at his possessions. "I suppose."

"Why the secrecy? Afraid you'll get ripped off?"

"No."

Now that he had her in his room, he worried that he'd made

the wrong decision. True, Abby had accepted what he was, but she'd had many months to slowly adjust to the idea. At any moment, Star could easily remember sharing her blood with him. He'd feel better if he had her in his arms when she did.

Benjamin poured two shots of scotch and handed one to Star. He settled into his favorite chair. "I like my privacy."

She sat in the chair beside his and sipped from her glass. "Good scotch. The expensive stuff."

"That it is."

"How many women have you brought in here?"

She was testing him. He heard it in her voice.

"You and one other, many years ago."

She met his gaze and he read surprise in her eyes. It transformed slowly into suspicion. "Why me?"

He downed the rest of the scotch and deposited his glass on the tea table. "You are a special woman."

"How?"

"You are strong in body and spirit, Star. And you arouse feelings in me I'd thought long dead."

She swallowed hard and stared at her glass.

"Are you going to tell me how you do the hypnosis thing?" she asked.

"In time." He rose and removed his shirt as he walked to the bed. Tossing it to the floor, he sat on the edge of the bed facing her. "At the moment, I'd prefer to continue where we left off." He removed one boot at a time.

Star sipped her scotch and watched.

"Join me," he said.

After a long moment, she finished her drink and rose, walking toward him slowly. "If you can hypnotize people, can you force them to do what you want?"

"In most cases, I can. You, however, are stronger than most people."

She peeled off her shirt. "Oh?"

Her breasts, full but not large, demanded his attention, and he focused on the small, hard nipples, a dusky rose color set against café au lait skin. Although he'd only seen her bare twice, he felt as though he were coming home as he watched her undress.

She unzipped her pants and stepped out of them, then pushed off her underwear.

Her beauty amazed him, and he clutched the bedspread to keep his hands still.

"So?" She raked her hair back from her face and then dropped her hands to her hips. "What now?"

"What do you want, Star?"

"What I want," she said, "is to know exactly what's going on. No funny shit in my head this time, okay?"

Without control of her mind, he would be unable to completely control the monster. Before long, she would know exactly what he was. But if it was honesty she wanted, honesty was what she'd get. He had no will to defy her.

He dipped his head in concession. "None."

She stood naked before the man she craved, enjoying the way his gaze ran up and down her body. Her life of growing up with large groups of relative strangers had left her with little modesty, but she'd never experienced this kind of excitement from another person's obvious admiration. Or maybe it was his amazing torso that turned her on.

Whatever it was, she'd decided to go for it. No holding back. If this was her one chance to have sex with Benjamin before she left, she planned to make the most of it. Might as well store up the fantasies for later.

She stepped between his feet, placed her hands on his amazing shoulders, and straddled him, settling onto his lap. His large hands slid up the outsides of her thighs to her ass. A wave of desire ran through her as she remembered him gripping her ass and drawing her up to his mouth.

Pressing against his swelling erection, she touched her lips to his. He didn't resist, but let her lead the kiss. She tasted first the scotch, and then his exotic flavor, already somehow familiar. She nipped his bottom lip, and sucked his tongue into her mouth. He groaned, and she warmed with a rush of power and arousal.

His arms encircled her, and he held her to him as he lay back, turning to pull her under him. She skimmed one hand up his wide back, enjoying the outlines of thick muscles.

He had control now, taking her mouth as if feasting. One hand caressed her breast as the other cradled her head. His thumb grazed her sensitized nipple, and she sucked in a breath against his lips.

He raised his head and stared down at her, his black eyes intense and glittery in the lamplight. "My desire for you is stronger than I'd realized," he said, his voice deep and rough. "But I will keep my word."

He rolled to his side and worked between them to remove his pants without taking his eyes from hers. She felt a little foggy, but decided it was her own fog this time, a fog of lust.

With his pants gone, he rolled back toward her and his cock rested against her belly. She reached down and explored. Cool velvety skin stretched over a prick already as hard as rock.

He pressed a kiss to her lips and then gazed at her again and raised one eyebrow. "Do you wish to continue?"

She nodded, not trusting her voice. Hell yes, she wished to continue. Her entire body seemed to be melting from the inside out.

He rose up over her, spread her legs with his own, and settled between her thighs, his weight on his elbows. He must be twice her size, but he didn't feel heavy. He gazed down at her, his dark eyes smoldering with desire, and her world focused down to Benjamin. He cradled her head in one hand while the other teased and caressed her neck, and shoulder, and breast.

"I hunger for you," he whispered.

She couldn't respond. No words came from her brain or her mouth. All she could do was watch, feel, and want.

She felt the head of his prick pressed against her pussy, poised to enter her, hard. And yet he waited. She raised her knees on each side of him, inviting him to continue. She needed to feel him inside her.

The corners of his mouth curved up into a grin. "You will come when I fill your lovely cunt."

God, she wanted that to be true. As turned on as she was, she needed to come.

He kissed her mouth and her face, and moved down to her neck. She squirmed against the pleasure.

He pushed, and the head of his prick shoved her swollen clit aside as it entered.

Her breath caught in her throat, and her body tightened with heightened desire.

"I've needed this," he whispered, his mouth near her ear. "I've needed you."

He pushed deeper, and her body responded instantly, drawing her up against him. He slipped his arm under her and held her tight.

Stretched against him, she felt every move his body made, felt his stomach muscles tighten as he thrust slowly into her, felt them relax as he withdrew.

He kissed her forehead and lifted his head to watch her face as he pushed again.

Star's head went back and she closed her eyes, unable to do otherwise. Her body swelled to the point of exploding.

When he stopped, she opened her eyes to find him smiling, his eyes smoky with lust. As he held her gaze, he started his rhythm again, thrusting deeper each time.

Her thoughts massed into nothing more than raw emotion as the peak approached. With her arms wrapped around him, holding tight, she gave herself over completely to the need.

Her body hardened, open and ready.

He thrust into her one last time, reaching her limit, deep and hard.

She groaned as the orgasm started. Hard pulses of release rolled through her body like ocean waves, crashing over her senses. She rose against him, taking more, needing all. He moved in time with her.

The pulses continued, unending, powerful. She clung to him.

Her cunt clamped hard with each pulse, squeezing, holding. She opened up and took all of him.

Finally, as the need eased and her senses began to clear, she remembered something strange.

The night downstairs, when he'd first kissed her, there'd been a connection between them. A moment unlike any she'd ever known. She remembered a strange tingling, and then pure bliss. His mouth had been on her neck.

Now, with his mouth pressed to her neck, the memory made her tremble.

He groaned and held her tighter, kissing her jaw and mouth. And then he withdrew from her, his prick still swollen with need, and she felt suddenly abandoned.

"What are you doing?" she asked.

He held her, his face pressed to her chest as if he were listening to her heartbeat.

"Benjamin?"

He raised himself up on his elbows and looked down at her, his expression as dark as ever. "It's time for the truth, my sweet."

She waited, her heart racing and her lungs fighting to keep up.

He kissed her lips tenderly as he rolled over to his side, facing her.

She lay on her back, her head turned to him. "Okay. What's the big secret?"

He spread his hand over her stomach. "Do you remember the night we first embraced?"

She nodded. The strange memory began to nag at her again, as if there were something she should understand but didn't. She raised her hand to the side of her neck, which suddenly tingled again. "That's the night you screwed around with my head."

"What do you remember?"

She shrugged and dropped her hand to the bed. "I don't know, exactly."

"Do you remember the way we were linked when you came?"

Heat flashed in her cheeks and she nodded. Yes, they had been linked.

"I was feeding off your emotions and your joy." He leaned closer. "I was feeding off you, Star."

"I don't . . . get it." Something about the way he'd held her, his lips on her neck, connected but not.

"I'm not a hypnotist." He leaned closer still. "I'm a vampire."

He sat in his chair again, wearing only his pants, sipping on another scotch and watching her. Star had donned her underclothes and shirt, and sat with her chin resting on one knee. She poked the fire, stirring up sparks and ashes.

The scotch wasn't doing much to take the edge off his need for her. He listened to her strong, steady heartbeat.

She turned her head to look at him, and the reflection of the fire glistened in her eyes. "How many people have you killed?"

"I'm a vampire, not a serial killer," he said.

"Aren't they the same thing?"

"No." He placed his glass on the table and gripped the arms of the chair. "I'm no worse or better than I was as a mortal." The screams of his men echoed in his head. "I sent more good lads to their deaths when I was alive than I have since."

"You're trying to tell me you've never killed anyone since you became . . . ?"

"A vampire?"

She frowned.

"No, I would not swear to such a lie. There have been times in my past when I had to choose between taking a life and risking exposure."

"And?"

"I'm still here."

"Shit." Rising to her feet, she raked her fingers through her hair. "What do you want from me?"

"I want you, Star. I want you to stay here with me."

At that moment, he realized exactly what he wanted. He wanted her with him forever. As his mate.

"For how long?"

"For as long as you wish. You will want for nothing."

She raised her hands in confusion and dropped them to her sides. "What if I don't want to stay? You tell me you're a vampire and I get to walk out of here? Or do you plan to get rid of me?"

"No matter what happens from this time forward," he said, "I will not harm you."

"Won't you be risking exposure?"

"Aye."

She stared at him, blinking hard.

He rose and crossed the room to stand near her. "Perhaps the Fates dropped you at my doorstep. Or perhaps the Fates don't exist. I have no answer. I simply know that I'm drawn to you in a way I haven't been drawn to another. I've spent many years alone, Star. I've never felt lonely until now."

"How many?"

"How many what?"

"How many years?"

"Ah." He strolled back to his chair and sat. "You want to know how old I am."

She nodded.

"Many have asked that question." He took another sip of his scotch. "Only one knows, and she's the one who made me a vampire." He met her unblinking gaze. "Until now. I was born in 1659."

"Son of a bitch," she whispered.

He smiled. "Now you're trying to decide if I'm telling the truth or not."

"I'm trying to decide if you're whacko."

Her response made him laugh.

She shook her head as if to clear her thoughts. "Look, I, um, think I need a little time alone."

"Of course." He stood and waited as she pulled on her pants and shoes, then he escorted her to the door. "The link. You felt it as I did."

She looked up at him and nodded.

"When you're ready to speak, you know where I am."

She nodded again.

He pushed the door open and she disappeared through it.

Benjamin stood listening to her footsteps. She hesitated at the door between his study and the hallway, and then ran down the stairs.

He let the door swing shut and returned to his chair to finish his scotch. After emptying the glass, he stared at it.

Perhaps he'd made a mistake letting her leave. She was frightened, and might run. He knew how much she detested fear. She might tell the others about him. Yet, he could not change his actions now. He'd promised her he would not harm her, and he'd meant it. If she chose to leave him, his existence would mean nothing anyway.

A log popped and settled in the small fireplace.

He'd watched her build the fire with trembling hands, imitating his earlier fire construction. She was a quick study, which didn't surprise him. And he knew she focused on starting the fire to sort through her thoughts.

What would she do now? He wished he knew.

The strange restlessness he'd felt before returned with a vengeance.

Star sat in a dark corner of the guest room on the floor, shaking. Her world tilted too far to one side for her to stand.

Benjamin thought he was a vampire.

Either that or he *was* a vampire.

"Shit."

She'd known people who called themselves vampires. A group hung around the Dungeon where she'd first started bartending. They were people who had dyed their hair, changed their names, and drank each others' blood occasionally. Some even had fang implants, but they didn't claim to be hundreds of years old. As different as they were, she understood them.

Benjamin had her more than just confused, he had her terrified.

She hated being terrified. If she could sort things out, she'd know what to do and could overcome the terror. The problem was thinking clearly enough to sort things out.

Star held her head in both hands and closed her eyes.

She saw his dark eyes watching her face as he pushed her over the edge, felt his cool skin against hers—

Christ. His skin had been cool every time she touched him. Why hadn't she noticed that?

Still, that didn't prove anything. Vampires weren't real, were they?

He'd asked her if she remembered the link. *I was feeding off you, Star.*

She raised her head and lowered one hand to the side of her neck. Two small spots on her neck tingled.

Oh, God, she remembered. She remembered feeling his teeth pierce her skin. He'd been kissing her, and touching her, and she'd been about to come. And then he'd bitten her and she'd exploded. Christ, she'd never come like that before.

Son of a bitch, he'd bitten her!

But, how could he have? There were no holes, partially healed or otherwise. Still, she remembered it happening.

The real question was what now? Did she run down to the bar and tell the others? If she managed to convince them that it was true, what then? They couldn't easily fix the van in the dark, and Benjamin would see them doing that anyway. They couldn't push it. They'd have to hitchhike. No way would she convince the others to leave the van and all their stuff behind.

If they did believe her, the guys might decide they should get rid of Benjamin. She pictured him lying on his bed with a wooden stake through his chest and shuddered.

Had he really meant it when he said he wouldn't harm her? She would have sworn he was telling the truth. She'd always been a pretty good judge of character, but she had no experience with vampires. How would she know if he was lying?

The stupidest part of the whole thing was that she still wanted him. The memory of him entering her aroused her all over again. The sexiest man she'd ever met wasn't a man at all, he was a vampire. Jesus, how nuts was that?

The one thing she wondered about was the question he'd never actually answered. How many people had he killed? A few? A dozen? Hundreds?

Did the number really matter? He'd admitted to killing. That should be enough.

Somehow, though, it made a difference.

Another thought sent a shiver up her spine. She'd found his hiding place. She knew where he stashed the bodies. It couldn't be a coincidence that there were at least a dozen skeletons in a cave less than a mile from his house.

Star held out her right hand and stared at it. It wasn't shaking anymore.

Good. She needed to be in control when she went back to face him.

Benjamin considered pouring another drink, but decided against it. The scotch wouldn't make him drunk, as it would have when he was mortal, and it had done all it could to lessen his hunger. He sat with the glass in his hand and stared at the fire.

He couldn't hear Star moving around. Had she left?

He wanted to hold her again. He ached for a taste of her. His skin felt too weak to contain the need that filled him like a gale-force wind in the sails.

Why had he given her a choice? He could force his way into her mind, even if only for a short time. Or he could hold her prisoner until she grew used to him.

No, she would never give in if he held her against her will. That much he knew.

"Bloody hell." He hurled the glass at the fireplace. It shattered with a satisfying crash and wet shards sizzled in the fire.

He could sit and wait no longer. He rose, snatched his shirt from the floor, and slipped it on as he started toward the door, but he stopped in his tracks when the door began to creak open.

Star had returned. She had watched him open the door and remembered the combination, as well she would. Renewed excitement blossomed in his chest. He dashed forward but stopped again halfway to the door. The shapely figure that filled the opening didn't belong to Star.

8

"Benjamin." Cassandra swept the hood from her head and shook out her golden curls. "What on earth are you doing inside on such a beautiful night? Have you missed me so dreadfully that you've taken to brooding again?"

Benjamin kissed her cheek and took the cloak from her shoulders. The tailored red silk blouse she wore complimented her figure and black slacks hugged her hips. She was as striking as ever.

"I thought you might show up." He didn't comment on her timing.

She turned and smiled at him. "As I always do. You know I would never desert you for too long, my love. It breaks my heart to think of you lonely."

"You have no heart, Cassandra."

"Ah, well, that may be so. Still, it's always wonderful to see you." She circled the room as if surveying her kingdom. "A fire in the fireplace and candles lit. How romantic." At the bed, she stopped and sat. "Aren't you going to show me how much you've missed me?"

He tried not to think about Star as he crossed the room to sit facing Cassandra.

She stroked his cheek with her slender fingers as she studied his eyes and mouth. "You look quite well," she said. Fangs dented her bottom lip.

His fangs descended in a rush as he considered the pleasure to come. After more than three centuries, Cassandra certainly knew how to please him. And he knew exactly what she expected of him.

He leaned forward and kissed her lips, trying not to compare their cool firmness with Star's moist warmth, and worked at not remembering Star's intoxicating taste.

He must remove Star from his thoughts before letting Cassandra in.

As he unbuttoned Cassandra's blouse, he recalled the first time they'd shared a mortal, several months after she'd made him.

The woman had been young, less than twenty years in age, and had long, raven hair, dark brown eyes, and smooth warm skin. She'd wandered too far into the woods in search of herbs and found Cassandra, instead, who had escorted her to the cabin.

Benjamin spoke just enough Algonquin to communicate the basics. He invited her in for a meal of smoked meat.

"Your name?" he asked.

"Kimi."

He smiled at Cassandra. "Her name is Secret."

Cassandra drew out a chair at the table. "Kimi. What a beautiful name. And so appropriate for the occasion. Please, eat."

Benjamin poured water into a cup, watching Cassandra for cues. She'd only hinted at what was to come, but her hints had excited him.

"Where are you, my love?" Cassandra's question drew him back to the present. "Memories?"

"Aye, memories."

"Share with me."

He shed the shirt he hadn't gotten around to buttoning and drew her to him, raising his chin.

Without ceremony and with great precision, she bit into his shoulder.

A heavy fog of erotic pleasure settled over him and he waited a moment to savor it before drawing back her blouse and biting her exposed shoulder.

Locked together, their thoughts melded into one clear picture, both remembering the scene exactly as it had unfolded, complete with sensory input.

Cassandra stood beside the chair and stroked Kimi's hair. "Isn't she lovely, Benjamin?"

He nodded as his fangs lengthened and his cock swelled.

Cassandra took the woman's hand and led her to the hearth. "It's warm here," she said, speaking to Kimi in a language the young woman couldn't possibly understand. "You can remove your clothes without shame, my dear."

Kimi began to remove her buckskin clothing.

"How is it she understands you?" Benjamin asked.

"Her mind is open to me," Cassandra said. "It is open to you, too. Reach and feel her thoughts."

He tried to do as his mistress wished, but had no idea how to even start.

"Don't fret, my love," she said in a calm and soothing voice. "It will be easier when you're joined with her."

Cassandra removed her own shift so that the two stood facing each other, a study in contrast. Where Cassandra was light, Kimi was dark. Cassandra's silver eyes reflected the firelight, and Kimi's brown eyes absorbed it. Cassandra's body was unadorned. Kimi wore a loose buckskin strap of shells around her neck; the shells rose and fell at the top of her breasts with her breathing.

Both women were beautiful.

Cassandra stroked Kimi's long, straight hair. "So like precious silk. Come, Benjamin, touch her hair."

He stepped up to Kimi's side and ran his fingers down the length of her hair to her waist, enjoying the curves beneath. She stood very still, unafraid, her gaze locked on Cassandra's.

"Shed your clothes and stand behind her, my love."

Benjamin did as instructed. He touched her shoulders, amazed to find them lean yet well-muscled like a sailor's. Following his touch with his gaze, he noted her small waist and tight buttocks. She did not appear to have yet borne children, but would certainly have a mate somewhere, most likely an important warrior. She was too beautiful to be alone.

His hunger surged into a growl, and Cassandra lifted her gaze to meet his. She smiled, but withheld her permission to feed.

"Listen to the strength of her heartbeat. Hear how her blood calls to you."

He heard the beat as if it were a bass drum, keeping time for a primitive dance. The sound called to his body to match the rhythm, slow and steady, and he slid his hands around her waist. His stiff cock rubbed between her solid buttocks, and he nuzzled her hair as he drew her to him.

Kimi dropped her head back to his shoulder.

"She wants you to take her as a man would, my love. Can you feel her wet heat?"

He pushed farther between her legs and found a well of hot fluids.

"Aye," he whispered. "I can."

Touching her, he found her small breasts rising and falling with her quick breathing, and her clitoris drenched and swollen. The urgent desire to fuck her drew a groan from deep in his chest.

"Not yet," Cassandra said. "We will be three as one. Kiss me."

Leaning over, he met Cassandra's hungry kiss with his own,

shuddering when her tongue ran the length of his incisors. She smiled against his lips.

Breaking the kiss, she turned her attention to Kimi, caressing her breasts and kissing her face. The young woman's heart beat faster.

The fog thickened until he no longer felt able to think at all. He touched Kimi, and tasted Cassandra, and ached for more of both.

"Now," Cassandra whispered inside his head.

He drew Kimi's hips up until he found entry into her wet cunt and thrust hard and deep, desperate to be sheathed in her velvety, tight heat. She dug her nails into his thighs to hold him close and sucked in loud breaths, and Cassandra kissed her neck.

Soaking in the bliss of Kimi's cunt, his arm tight around her waist, he withdrew and thrust, slowly filling her with his entire length. Her internal muscles tightened and wet heat ran down his scrotum. Glorious, delicious desire stoked the fire of hunger burning in his soul.

She murmured words he barely heard, and moaned.

Cassandra growled softly and buried her fingers in Benjamin's hair.

He watched her face as she moved closer, rubbing the front of Kimi's body with her own, writhing with excitement.

Kimi's breaths came out as grunts as she approached release.

Cassandra held his gaze for a long moment. She opened her mouth, then closed her eyes and fell on Kimi's neck.

Benjamin staggered to keep his balance. Kimi's cunt grabbed his shaft, drawing him impossibly deeper. His cock ached for release, and the beast demanded blood.

Gripping his hair in her fist, Cassandra guided his mouth to her own shoulder, and he instinctively bit.

His cock responded by erupting, filling Kimi's cunt.

He reached around her to hold Cassandra to them both, and savored the moment of blessed relief.

And then his world capsized.

The night shattered into bright lights that tore him apart, left him open and unprotected. He felt no boundaries, no edges to anything, even his own body. He heard soft voices and the beat of nature, steady and pure.

"I'm here," Cassandra whispered from nowhere and everywhere.

"And I," another voice said.

Kimi? It must be, but in English.

"Her thoughts," Cassandra said. "Her mind is yours. Feel her pleasure."

Intense satisfaction bubbled around him, lifting away all doubt, leaving him drunk with joy. This perfect freedom, unlike any before, was unlike any could be again. His very being swelled with strength to fill the night sky.

He drew more, drinking deeper, savoring both women until their pleasure faded. Kimi's thoughts left him first, then Cassandra's. He stood alone.

Raising his head, he opened his eyes to find Cassandra licking her lips and smiling at him.

"Lovely, isn't it?"

"Aye, it is."

And then he felt Kimi's cool skin against his, her body limp in his grasp. He lifted her, placed her on the bed, and knelt beside her.

He heard her heartbeat, but barely. "Kimi," he whispered, brushing her silken hair back from her face and drawing the blanket over her.

"Do not concern yourself, my dear. She needs rest. She will survive." Cassandra mussed his hair as she passed him. She picked up her shift from the floor and slipped it over her head.

"Are you certain?"

"Quite." She smiled. "Now, let us enjoy the rest of the night, shall we?" She held out her hand.

He glanced once more at Kimi, then rose and took Cassandra's hand.

With perfect precision, Cassandra withdrew from his shoulder as he withdrew from hers, and the past disappeared like an apparition.

"Ah, yes," she said. "What a lovely night that was. We wandered the woods for hours, chasing game and each other."

Benjamin nodded. "And when we returned, she was gone."

"Yes. I told you she would survive."

The both turned at the sound of knocking on the wall of his study.

"Benjamin?"

He jumped to his feet.

"Are you expecting company?" Cassandra asked, rising to stand beside him.

"I want to talk to you," Star said.

The secret door squeaked open.

Star stood in the doorway, waiting for the panel to complete its turn.

When it did, she stared at the couple standing on the other side, watching.

Benjamin she'd expected to find. The tall, gorgeous blonde was a complete surprise.

"I, uh—"

What the hell was she supposed to say?

As she spotted the marks on Benjamin's shoulder, anger sucked up all her confusion.

"I'm obviously interrupting something. Pardon the hell out of me."

She headed for the study door, but stopped like a dog reaching the startling end of its chain.

"Star."

She glared at Benjamin's grip on her arm, and then up into his eyes. "Get your fucking hand off me."

"Star—"

"Hey, I'm not blaming you. I was stupid enough to fall for that line." She tried to peel his fingers from her arm. "I'm the only one, just me and the one . . . who—" Realization clawed through her anger. This couldn't be the vampire who'd made him, could it?

"Aye," he said softly, "this is Cassandra."

Star stared past him to where the blonde leaned against the secret doorframe, arms crossed, smiling.

"And who is this creature, Benjamin?" Cassandra walked slowly, purposely forward, until she stood beside Benjamin. She smiled sweetly. "Are we having a dinner guest?"

A fogbank rolled forward in Star's mind, threatening to cover her thoughts and reason. She shook her head to clear it away.

"I am not dinner," she said, snarling her worst.

Cassandra turned to Benjamin, her eyes full of surprise. "She knows?"

"Aye, she does."

"Have you lost your mind?"

He slowly released Star's arm as he held her gaze. "I've asked Star to stay with me."

The fog turned into waves of invading anger, and Star flinched.

Cassandra spun and strode into Benjamin's room, but stopped at the door. "I'll give you tonight to come to your senses. Then I'll take care of this myself."

The wall panel swung shut.

Benjamin sighed and glanced back before focusing his attention on Star. "I didn't know she'd be here." He reached up and stroked her cheek. "I'm glad you came back."

She drew away from him. "I came back to talk to you."

He dropped his hands to his sides and waited.

"You said you hadn't killed many people since becoming a vampire. How many is *many*?"

"You want an exact figure?"

"Yes."

Benjamin took a deep breath and blew it out. "Seven."

She huffed. "Right."

He stiffened. "You doubt my word?"

"Damn right I doubt your word. I found your stash, and there's a hell of a lot more than seven bodies in there."

His eyes darkened and his brow furrowed. "What are you talking about?"

"Your hiding place, the cave. I found it. I know you're lying to me."

He stepped forward and towered over her. "I am not lying to you. What hiding place?"

Star ground her back teeth, fuming. She couldn't slug him; it wouldn't do any good. And he was way too fast for her to get away from. Her only choice was to call him on it.

"The cave, on the beach. The one with all the bones."

"You must be mistaken. If there were such a place, I would know of it."

"No shit."

"Show me."

"Is that an order?"

He leaned closer, and her traitorous heart raced.

"A request," he said in a murderous whisper.

"Fine." She hurried downstairs to the guest room, where she grabbed her flashlight from her backpack, then headed outside. She didn't look back to see if he followed her.

She didn't need to. His presence was like a cool breath against her skin, even though he walked a dozen feet away.

The night seemed to have gotten quieter so that they heard the jukebox music several blocks from the bar. Obviously, Wendy, Jack, and Kyle were still mixing with the locals.

It seemed like a lifetime had passed since she'd left the Tangled Net.

After dashing across the street and scrambling down to the beach, she switched on her flashlight. A partial moon slid in and out of wispy clouds, illuminating the shore, but she needed the small beam of light to keep from tripping over things.

Benjamin's step behind her didn't falter, although he was well out of flashlight range.

Could he see in the dark? He must be able to. Damn, she had a million questions, but she was too pissed off to ask any of them.

One big question drowned out all the others as they walked. What would happen once they reached the cave? Then he'd know for sure that she knew about it. Would he add her body to his stash? Was she walking willingly to her death?

Star took a deep breath. If this was her last hour on earth, she sure as hell wasn't going to whine. No cowering, no tears. If he was going to take her life, he'd have to look her in the eye while he did it.

Pumped with determination, she charged up the trail toward the cave opening, but took a false step halfway up, fell to her hands and knees, and skidded down several feet.

Benjamin's hand appeared around her arm and he drew her up.

She tried to jerk her arm free. "Let go. I can make it by myself."

He released her, and she scrambled up in front of him.

Star paused at the opening long enough to look for unwanted critters, then crawled inside.

She watched Benjamin squeeze through the opening behind her. As soon as he was inside, he looked around, frowning.

Damn, he was good. If she didn't know better, she'd think he'd never seen this place before.

Swinging the flashlight around, she placed the beam on the closest skeleton, even more gruesome than it had been in match light. Patches of material clung to a few bones, and one hand was missing.

Benjamin crouched in the middle of the cavern, staring.

"There's a lot more than seven of them," she said, sliding the light beam to the next. "Want to tell me how they got here?"

He snatched the flashlight from her hand and scanned the room.

Cold air in the small space vibrated with some weird noise. A growl?

Benjamin rushed forward to the skeletons Star had examined before and picked up the button she'd found. He held it to the light for several long seconds, and then turned, flashing the light across all the remains. The beam fell on the silver crucifix.

"Jeffery," he whispered.

"So, you do know who they are." Star sat back and glared.

"My crew," he said, his voice so soft she barely heard it.

He moved the light more slowly now, illuminating each individually. "Collingswood, Ashby, Roland." The beam stopped on another, a different skeleton. This one had large brown patches of something like paper next to it, or maybe ancient leather. Small seashells hung from a string around its next.

"Kimi," he whispered.

The soft growl turned to a roar, and Star jumped.

The flashlight fell to the ground and rolled toward her. She picked it up and shone it around the cave.

She was alone in the cave with the skeletons and a swirl of dust.

"Son of a bitch."

Where had Benjamin disappeared to and how had he moved so damn fast?

Not wanting to spend an extra second alone with the dead,

Star scrambled out and down the slope until she reached the beach. She looked in both directions and saw nothing but sand and rocks, and small waves rolling up the beach. The tide appeared to be coming in.

Sifting through what she'd just witnessed, she walked, following her beam. Benjamin had truly looked surprised to see the skeletons. Could he really have not known about the cave? He said they were his crew. He'd told her the original Captain Benjamin Bartlett had shipwrecked here and was the only survivor.

Was that his story? Had he shipwrecked on this coast and been nursed to health by . . . ?

By a vampire. Cassandra.

Her head began to ache. This whole thing was too much.

Maybe she should stop at the bar and talk to Wendy. She sure as hell wasn't going back to the house, not to be alone with two vampires. Even if one was the most amazing man she'd ever met.

Star trotted up the small slope and started across the street to the bar.

A car skidded to a stop in front of her, and a dark window slid down.

"Well, boys, look who just showed up," Jones sneered.

Benjamin barely managed not to rip the wall panel away. He waited until it had opened and then charged into his room, his hands clenched as fists at his side.

For a moment, he thought she'd left, but then he heard her voice. "Benjamin?" She pulled open the door to the bath and stepped out in a rolling cloud of moisture, rubbing her wet hair with a towel. "Have you come to your senses yet? I must say, the shower is wonderful."

When she met his gaze, she straightened. "What is it?"

"You killed them."

She cocked her head to one side. "Who?"

He charged forward, wanting nothing more that to choke the existence from her body, grabbed her by the neck, and slammed her to the wall. "My crew!"

She wrapped one hand around his wrist and twisted.

Try as he might, he couldn't hold her in place.

When she'd freed herself from his grasp, she continued to twist until he was on his knees staring up into blood-red eyes.

"Don't ever do that again."

"You killed my crew," he said through gritted teeth.

She shoved him backward, then snatched her towel from the ground and continued drying her hair. "I did them a favor."

He watched her through reddened vision, trying to rein in his overwhelming anger.

"Do you remember that first week? I sat by your side nursing you, giving you a little of my blood each night." She sat on the edge of the bed and smiled as if telling a bedtime story. "You left me no time to hunt. If not for the sacrifice of your crew, I would have been unable to save you. Once you knew the truth of what I was, did you ever ask how I'd survived so long at your side?"

His anger began to melt into horror as he realized what she was saying.

"After you turned, do you remember when I would come home and feed you from my breast?" She drew her blouse aside to expose the rounded top of her breast where he'd drawn erotic sustenance from her flesh more than once. "Did you ever ask where I'd been? How it was that I could feed you?"

Horror jelled in his gut.

He'd drunk the blood of his own men.

He'd been the reason they'd died.

"Kimi," he whispered.

"Yes, poor thing. She didn't make it. I circled back to check on her while you were exploring the woods, and found her dying. I suppose I could have tried to turn her, but I didn't really want to share you." She glanced at the closed door leading to his study and narrowed her eyes. "I'm not sure I want to now, either."

The look in her eye shook him.

Benjamin rose to his feet and dusted off the back of his pants. "Leave Star out of this."

"My dear, I don't believe you're in any position to give me orders."

He took a step toward her, shaking with rage.

"You might try asking nicely," she said, one eyebrow raised. "After you apologize."

Glaring, he worked to control his anger. "I . . . apologize. I *ask* that you leave Star alone."

She raised her chin, her victory complete. "I'll consider your request." She combed her fingers through her blond curls. "In the meantime, I suggest you find something else to do. I don't wish to enjoy your company at the moment. Perhaps you should find your little mortal playmate."

She was throwing him out of his own room, and he could do nothing about it. If for no other reason than to keep her from hurting Star, he would comply.

He bowed formally and hurried to the door. Once in his study, he steadied himself on his desk and considered what he'd just learned.

Cassandra was right. He hadn't asked any questions as he'd taken his fill of blood and pleasure. But how could he have known she'd butchered his crew? Had she kept them captive and fed off them slowly? Poor Jeffery. The boy had done everything asked of him without complaint, only to meet his fate at the hands of a killer he couldn't fight, no matter how brave he was.

And now Benjamin must live with the knowledge that it was all his fault. He glanced at the embers left in the fireplace, thought of Star, and groaned.

Damn it all, he'd abandoned her in the cave thinking him a liar, and worse.

9

"One last time, where's my flash drive?" Jones leaned close to her, a silhouette against the bar's lights through the darkened car window.

"I told you," Star said, "I don't have it."

He backhanded her, slicing open her lip. Blood pooled in her mouth.

"You better hope you have it," he said. "I want it back, and Hammer, here, is going to help you remember where you put it."

Hammer flexed his muscles and his oversized arm tightened around her neck.

Anger numbed even the split lip as Star considered what she'd like to do to Jones. How could she have ever thought he was a decent guy?

A huge man Star didn't recognize trotted across the street and slid into the front seat. "The stripper's inside, and there's a couple guys from the club, too."

Jones nodded. "So, maybe your traveling companions will be more cooperative." He glanced at the man. "Get the stripper, Frank."

"Leave her out of—"

Hammer clamped a hand over Star's mouth, and she fought to get free until he tightened his grip around her throat. With lights sparkling in her vision, she stopped fighting and focused on getting air into her lungs.

Wendy hopped down the front stairs and hurried across the street with Frank following.

"Hey, Star, I got something cookin' here." Wendy ducked to look into the back seat. "What's . . . up?"

Before she could scream, Frank grabbed her, stuffed her into the front seat, and climbed in beside her.

"Okay, Bubba," Jones said, slapping the back of the driver's seat, "let's go to the house. It's gotta be with her stuff."

As they turned the corner, Star realized Jones and his goons must have been the ones she felt watching her. How had they located her so easily?

But why the hell had he come all this way after a simple flash drive? It must have held more than just the names and numbers of small-time gamblers.

Benjamin knew the cave was empty of life before he crawled into it. He hadn't passed Star walking back. Perhaps she'd stopped at the Tangled Net again. He'd heard music, in spite of the hour.

Yes, the cave held only the dead—the long dead. He sat in the middle of the skeletal corpses and remembered the face of each man who had served under him so many years ago. He could still hear their screams as they fell into the sea.

How could he have not known they were here?

He scrambled back out and walked down to the water's edge. Before him, the last of the rocks disappeared under the surface to lie hidden as they'd been that fateful night when they'd gutted the *Spencer*. So many decades he'd sat on this very beach, staring out to sea, not realizing much of his crew lay hidden just over his shoulder.

He'd always felt responsible for the death of his men. If he hadn't insisted they chase the villains farther out to sea when he'd been advised by almost every one of his officers to turn back, they certainly wouldn't have caught the pirate ship, but they might have made port before the storm.

Now he knew exactly how responsible he'd truly been, and the guilt was a crushing weight on his chest.

"You were the finest lads," he whispered into the night. "May your souls be at peace."

He stared out at the ocean until he stood in ankle-deep water, then turned and sloshed back to the beach.

No doubt Star had lost any regard for him she'd had, and perhaps that was best for her. Considering how truly despicably he'd survived, he had no right to happiness.

But he couldn't let go. His need for her was a fiery monster, lighting the night sky and yowling for more. He wanted to feel her body against his, to know her moment of true surrender, to taste her joy.

He did not deserve her, or the delight of her embrace. He should let her leave without trying to stop her, but such lack of action was unthinkable.

Figuratively speaking, he would put the stake in her hand and point it at his heart. It would be up to her to drive it in or toss it aside.

"Get it. Now!" Jones grabbed a handful of her hair and jerked her around.

"I can't, you asshole." Star tried to face him, but he held her too tight. "I threw it away."

"Yeah, right." He leaned close. "I'm not playing this game much longer. In thirty seconds, I'm shooting your friend. Thirty seconds later, your kneecaps are going. Got it?"

"Are you deaf? I don't have it!"

She heard the revolver click as he cocked it.

"Wait! Okay, you win. I'll show you where it is."

"Good." His voice held an evil grin she was sure he wore. The bastard.

She pointed toward the guest room. "It's down there."

What would she do now? If she got Jones to the bedroom, she could try to wrestle the revolver from him. He'd need to let go of her so she could search her bag. Or maybe he'd be worried she had a gun in her bag and insist on searching it himself. Even if he killed her, it would be better than suffering shattered kneecaps first. He wasn't going to just drive away and leave her here in one piece. Especially since she didn't have the flash drive.

"Well, what's this? A party?"

They stopped and Star looked up to where Cassandra stood at the top of the stairs, wearing a silk blouse unbuttoned nearly to her navel, black pants that did amazing things for her figure, and gold high heels. She started down the stairs with a slow strut that could have put Wendy to shame, trailing inch-long fingernails down the banister as she went.

The room fell silent. No doubt, Jones and his two homeys gawked.

In spite of her situation, Star felt a rush of hot jealousy as she remembered finding Cassandra with Benjamin. The woman was way past gorgeous. How was she supposed to compete?

Jones's grip on Star's hair eased enough that she could turn to watch.

"Isn't anyone going to introduce me?" Cassandra strolled among them, eyeing the men.

Hammer stepped forward, handing Wendy off to Frank. "I'll *introduce* you, lady."

The other two men chuckled.

"Ooo," Cassandra cooed, "that sounds like fun." She circled Hammer, touching his colossal shoulders. "Nice muscles."

The man flexed and rubbed the front of his pants. "I got one more muscle waitin' just for you."

"Yes? I'd like to see that."

"I bet you would, bitch."

"The name's Cassandra." She stopped in front of Hammer, flattening one hand to his chest. "And what should I call you? Bonehead, perhaps?"

"Huh?"

"Yes, I like that. Kneel for me, Bonehead."

Hammer's cocky grin faded to a frown as he fell to his knees.

"Hey, man, what the hell are you doing?" Jones released Star and stepped forward.

"I . . . I—" Hammer couldn't seem to get to the second word.

Cassandra stepped closer, rubbing her crotch in Hammer's face. The man whimpered.

Star glanced around the room for a weapon. If she could get her hands on the fireplace poker, she might be able to smack Jones with it. It was heavy enough to do some damage. Frank had a gun, too, but it was tucked into a shoulder holster. He'd have to release Wendy, open his coat, and draw. She just might have time to shoot him with Jones's gun first.

Anything was worth a try.

She took one step toward the fireplace, and another.

"Hey, what are you doing to him?" Brandishing the revolver, Jones approached Cassandra.

"Playing," she said. Using one finger, she pushed Hammer over and he fell to his back. "Would you like to join us?"

Frank shoved Wendy aside and drew his pistol.

Shit. If Star hit Jones over the head, his freakin' goon would shoot her. And Wendy could easily be caught in the crossfire. She froze.

"Back off," Jones said.

"I don't think so." Cassandra narrowed her eyes.

Jones's hand started shaking so violently, he had to support it with his other hand. It only quit shaking when he lowered the weapon. "How the fuck did you do that?"

Cassandra smiled.

"Yeah?" Jones dashed over to Star and caught her by the arm. "Well I can still shoot her."

The vampire shrugged. "I don't care if you shoot her."

Everyone in the room except for Cassandra jumped as the front door flew open and slammed against the wall.

"But I do." Benjamin filled the doorway and his voice shook the air. He started toward them, taking huge, angry strides.

Frank shot, hitting Benjamin in the chest, and Benjamin staggered a step.

Star gasped and her heart skipped a beat. She tried to run to him, but Jones held her close.

Benjamin lowered his head for a long moment as a red spot blossomed in the middle of his shirt. Then he raised his gaze and glared at Frank with blood-red eyes, flashing nasty fangs.

No doubt Frank tried to shoot again, but as he did, Benjamin charged forward in a blur of movement. He ripped the gun from Frank's hand, crushed it, and tossed it aside.

Frank swallowed hard.

Benjamin grabbed him by the front of his shirt and lifted him off the ground as if he were a doll.

"Hey," Jones said. "Put him down." He pressed the barrel of his pistol to Star's temple.

Time slowed to a crawl.

Benjamin stared at them as he eased Frank down to his feet. "If you hurt her, you will die a slow and painful death."

Jones huffed. "Yeah, well, everyone's got to go sometime. Now, how about you back off."

Benjamin raised both palms in a gesture of surrender as he met Star's gaze. If he moved toward them, no matter how fast, Jones would probably pull the trigger. Jones had the upper hand and he knew it.

Star couldn't just stand there and get shot. She had to do something. She mouthed, "Ready?"

Benjamin's eyes widened a bit, either in acknowledgment or warning, but she knew she wouldn't get a second chance.

She mouthed, "Now," and raised her fist against Jones's gun arm as she ducked.

The gun fired, taking out her hearing.

She fell to the floor on her side.

Benjamin flew forward, grabbed Jones around the chest, and ripped into his neck.

Star glanced across the room to see Cassandra tossing Frank aside, licking blood from her lips, one high heel in the middle of Hammer's chest to keep him on his back.

Benjamin rolled Star into his arms and examined her head. She saw his mouth move but couldn't hear him at first.

Then the ringing in her ears let up a little.

"I don't see a wound," he said.

"He missed," she said.

Benjamin drew her up to his chest and held her.

Star wrapped her arms around his neck and felt him sigh against her. Suddenly, she knew where she belonged.

"What the hell's going on here?"

Benjamin released her, and Star turned to find Wendy looking around the room, pale with fright.

"I'll take care of it," Benjamin said, rising to his feet and offering Star a hand.

Star touched the circle of wet blood on the front of his shirt, some of which was now on hers. "He shot you."

Benjamin shrugged. "Don't worry, my dear. I'm already healing."

Then she nodded toward Wendy. "She knows what you are."

"Aye," he said softly, "but she won't remember."

"Really?"

"Let's retire to my study."

"Oh, don't worry about me," Cassandra said, waving dramatically. "I'll clean up this mess when I'm done." She drew Hammer up by the hand and he just stood there looking dumber than usual. "I think I'll take my time with this one. I know he's only a pretty face, but every girl needs a pretty face now and then." She glanced back. "And big muscles."

Star watched the vampire lead her next victim away, feeling no sympathy for the man at all. If anything, he was getting better than he deserved. Her throat still ached where he'd nearly choked her.

She stopped beside Jones, who lay face down. "Bastard." She kicked him in the side and nodded with satisfaction when he didn't react. Judging by the size of the gash in his neck, he must be dead. She had to admit, this killing didn't bother her. Had all Benjamin's victims been as despicable as Jones?

She crossed the room to where Wendy stood against a wall, shaking, and hugged her. Wendy sucked in stuttered breath. "What's going on?" she whispered.

Star stepped back and took Wendy's hand. "Come on, we'll explain it to you."

Benjamin watched Star sit beside Wendy on the small sofa in his study. He turned to the fireplace, crouched, and placed fuel on the last of the embers.

"You're okay now, Wen. Really, I promise."

"But, I saw . . . what are they?"

"They're vampires," Star said.

"Oh, shit. Are they going to kill us, too?"

Benjamin flinched and rose to stand before the smoldering logs. Fire crackled across dried bark.

"Wen, they were protecting us."

"From what? Jones wasn't going to hurt us. He promised."

Benjamin glanced over his shoulder and found Star staring at her friend, her eyes widening. "What do you mean, 'he promised'?"

"When I called him the other day."

Star rose. "Why the hell did you call him?"

"I had to. Before we left, he said you were taking some kind of computer disk and he wanted it back. He said if I couldn't find it, I should call him."

"So you called him and told him where we were?"

Wendy huffed. "I didn't have to tell him. He knew. His connections told him."

"What connections?"

"You know, the mob. Organized crime."

"*Jones*?"

Wendy looked up at her with disbelief. "Of course."

"Why didn't you tell me what was going on?" Star took a step away from the sofa. "I thought we were friends."

"Hey, when a mob guy says don't tell, I don't tell."

Star stared for several long seconds, then turned and fled up the stairs to the tower.

"Wait," Wendy said, rising to her feet. "Don't leave me in here with—"

Benjamin hurried to the woman's side and grabbed her wrist, pushing forward thoughts of calm and trust. He met her gaze. "Have a seat, Wendy."

She sat, and he settled beside her.

Interestingly enough, he had no trouble penetrating her thoughts. Where Star was exceptionally strong, Wendy was amazingly weak.

"What has happened here today was nothing out of the ordinary. You witnessed an attempted burglary. The burglars were escorted away by the police, and all is well."

"All is well," she repeated softly, her brown eyes open wide.

He glanced past her to the stairs where Star had disappeared. He understood the sting of betrayal by one you trust.

"You don't remember anyone named Jones. You made no promise to him."

"No . . . promise," she said.

"Very good. When you wake, you'll be anxious to be on your way."

She nodded.

"Sleep."

Her eyes closed and her head fell back.

Benjamin gathered the woman into his arms, carried her downstairs to the guest room, and placed her on the bed. He hurried back upstairs.

Star stood on the deck of the back tower, looking out toward the woods. Clouds from earlier had disappeared, leaving a cool, clear night sky full of stars.

"You were right about the bodies, in a manner," he said.

She stiffened, but didn't look at him.

"I was responsible for their deaths, but I didn't know it. They were people I cared about."

She nodded. "I know. I saw it in your face."

He studied her profile, beautiful in spite of her anger. "You were betrayed."

She shrugged. "Nothing new there. I should have known better."

"Better than what?"

Her blue eyes hit him like a cannonball squarely in the chest. "Better than to trust her. I learned that lesson a long time ago. There's only one person in this world I can trust, and that's me."

Knowing it was time to risk all, he leaned closer. "You can trust me, Star."

Her heartbeat raced as she studied his eyes. "How the hell can I trust you? I don't even know for sure what you are."

"I told you what I am. Perhaps you don't understand what happened tonight." He moved away from her and stood near the door, finding it easier to talk to her back. "I told you I've killed before, and I have. When I was mortal, I ran one man through during a duel of sorts. He claimed I'd sullied the reputation of his sister and was intent on killing me. Another man, I hanged for mutiny. But the deaths that weigh most heavily on me are those of my crew. I sent them to untimely deaths because of pride. I knew I'd be seen as a hero if I sailed back into Boston with the pirates and the gold stolen from the Crown. I had visions of glory, of being held in high esteem by the townsfolk, of leading the raiding party on the French." He sighed. "I was a fool."

Star turned to face him.

"After I became a vampire, I killed for a different reason. I took life only when it was necessary to maintain my secret. Each death was cold and calculated, and several I truly regretted. Every one I remember with clarity.

"I'd never killed out of anger until tonight."

She stared at him, her wide eyes reflecting light from the tower behind him, and swallowed hard. She was listening, and sifting through his words.

"I've not lied to you, Star. Not since I told you what I am.

"Tonight, when I saw that bastard's hand on you and his weapon pointed at your head, I felt rage unlike anything I've ever experienced. I'd planned to rip his head from his body, and probably would have if his comrade hadn't shot me first. Once the bullet did its damage, I needed his blood to heal.

"I won't apologize for killing him."

Star took a deep breath and blew it out. She had no tears in her eyes, and he saw no accusation.

"You can trust me," he said, stepping closer. "I will never betray you."

"I can't," she said, her voice small in the night.

"You must." He stopped directly in front of her, gazing down into her sapphire eyes. "I've trusted you with everything." He reached up to touch her cheek and she flinched. He waited a moment then stroked her soft skin with his fingertips.

Star closed her eyes to his touch, and her body trembled.

Benjamin bit back a growl. He wanted to hold her and kiss her, and so much more. He wanted her to surrender to him completely, but wasn't sure she truly could, now that she knew. She'd seen the beast.

When his lips met hers, she sucked in a breath of surprise and her eyes popped open.

He waited, poised, for her answer, their lips a gnat's wing apart.

She leaned into his kiss and raised her arms to his shoulders, and he embraced her body with his own as he greedily took her mouth. Every inch of him craved every inch of her.

Need swelled with hunger, but more than just hunger. His fangs dropped in a rush, and he tore his mouth from hers and held it near her ear. "I want you like no other, Star." Holding her with one arm around her waist, he used the other hand to push her shirt up until he could tenderly touch her breast. "No, it's more than want, more than crave." He nuzzled her neck. "I exist for you."

Still trembling, she groaned softly and wrapped her legs around his hips.

"I wish to spend my nights pleasing you." He pushed her back until she leaned over the handrail.

He felt her body harden and raised his face to gaze into her eyes. No doubt his had changed color by now; his arousal was complete. He heard her heart pounding in his head, calling to him, and smelled her wonderful scent.

She gripped his shoulders and turned her head to glance down. "Shit. What are you doing?"

"Trust me, Star. I won't let you fall. You must trust me."

"I . . . don't know." She glanced down again and then frowned into his eyes. "I don't know how."

"Turn away your fear. Release it. I will not hurt you." He pressed his lips to her neck.

When she raised her head a little, he moaned at the promise of joy just below the surface of her sweet flesh. Still, she gripped his sleeves in her fists.

Pushing her shirt up higher, he exposed her left breast to his view, and ran his thumb across the puckering nipple.

She gasped softly, and tightened her legs around him.

His cock ached to be inside her, but this wasn't the time. They needed a deeper connection than sex could provide. They needed to be tied at the heart.

A cool breeze blew across them, carrying an owl's lonely call.

Benjamin moved his mouth down to her perfect breast and licked slow circles around the nipple, and then he flicked it slowly, cruelly.

Star reacted to his touch with her entire body, and her scent grew stronger.

He moved his mouth up and pressed it to the flesh just above her heart, right where her breast started to swell from her chest. The perfect spot, fully Star, smooth skin and a strong, racing heartbeat. "Let go, my sweet," he whispered.

He felt her grip on his hips ease. She unlocked her feet and slid them slowly down his legs until they hung loose against the rail.

One hand at a time, she released his shirt and dropped her arms to hang down toward the ground.

Finally, with the last of it, she rested her head back.

He had her now, holding her four stories above the ground, her body his completely.

Carefully, purposely, he pushed his fangs into the flesh above her breast, and she cried out as her essence reached his tongue and exploded in his head. Her body rose up against his mouth, but she did not try to grab him. She lay back, free, letting him take what he would.

He tasted first her arousal, on the verge of completion, and her wonder at the moment. Her strength shot through him like a wooden bolt, ripping a hole in his heart.

And then he found it, the depth of her trust, and her fear of giving it. Her trust filled the hole her strength had created, fusing them together as one. No matter what the future held for them, he'd never know another woman like this.

He withdrew his fangs and held his mouth to her warm skin, savoring the last drop of her blood as the holes closed. She was perfect, made for him.

Could he convince her to stay?

He pulled her up and into his arms, and she held him with her head on his shoulder. In silence, he carried her to his bed.

10

Star lay on her back, watching Benjamin strip. Had it been only hours since he'd told her he was a vampire? It seemed like days, years even.

Her body felt heavy, like it was filled with lead. It took all the effort she had to raise her hand to her face to brush hair from her eyes.

His bite just above her tit still tingled, even though it seemed to have healed to tiny bumps. God, no single thing in her life had ever felt so erotic!

Letting go had both terrified and thrilled her. She'd been truly exposed for the first time in her life, with no control over anything. When his teeth had pierced her skin, something else had pierced her heart. Something horrifyingly wonderful, something she couldn't begin to put a name to. And she'd felt him inside her head, as if he were suddenly a part of her.

Now what?

She was so turned on, he could probably just blow in her ear and she'd come. His body was magnificent, big, masculine, charged with strength. Muscles rippled all over when he moved, and what had once been a bullet hole was now just a small pink circle.

Completely naked, he knelt on the bed and began undressing her.

"I can't help," she said.

He smiled that amazingly sexy smile. "You don't have to."

"My arms are so heavy."

He drew her right palm up to his mouth and kissed it. She closed her eyes to enjoy the sensations crawling up her arm.

"You relinquished your shield of distrust tonight. You now stand exposed. It will take some time for you to adjust."

"That's why I'm so tired?"

"Aye." He drew her pants off and tossed them to the floor beside her shirt. "Come, I think I know what will help."

He gathered her up as if she were a child and carried her into the bathroom, where he placed her on her feet.

"Tile's cold," she said.

Holding her arm, he reached into the huge glass-fronted shower and turned on the water. Waves of warm, moist air rolled from the shower to fog the room.

"In you go," he said, his voice as gentle as his touch.

In spite of all the old-fashioned appliances and decorations throughout the rest of the house, this bathroom was thoroughly modern. Star stepped under a huge showerhead that blasted her with hot water.

Benjamin stepped in behind her and slid the door shut.

In no time, her blood was pumping, and her skin felt alive and vigorous. Her strength returned.

She turned to face him, trying to wipe water from her face. He took up so much space, she felt even smaller than usual. "Can't you turn this thing down?"

He reached up and flipped a switch, and suddenly the shower felt like a summer afternoon rain shower. Drops fell on her hair and her shoulders, and ran softly down her body.

"Better." She wiped water from her face again. "Now that you've got me awake, what do you plan—"

He kissed her in a move so sudden, she nearly jumped.

His mouth covered hers, nipping to be let in.

She drew hard on his tongue, as she wrapped her arms around his neck.

He'd only been partially aroused when she turned to face him, but as soon as he straightened and drew her up with him, she realized he was way past interested.

His body was hard and big against hers, and his prick rose against her crotch. He grabbed her thigh and turned to press her to the tile wall.

She fisted her hand in his damp hair and held him close as his tongue dueled with hers, caressed hers, reached deeper.

And then he tore his mouth from hers and pressed his lips to the side of her head.

"I can't get enough of you," he whispered.

His cock pressed against her pussy, hinting at the pleasure to come. She had no way to stop him from taking her, and she didn't care. He wouldn't hurt her, she knew that.

"Make me come again," she said.

He smiled against the top of her shoulder. "As you wish, my dear."

He started into her slowly, gently, kissing her shoulder and face as he did.

She felt the strain in his muscles, the hunger in his kiss, and knew every movement was for her.

His hard prick rubbed her clit with exquisite cruelty.

Halfway in, he withdrew and started again.

Warm water flowed across his shoulders and seeped between them, crossing the buds of her tits like a whispered breath.

"Damn, that feels good," she said.

"Aye, that it does."

Her body swelled, muscles tightened, and nerves fired like crazy. In less than two minutes, he had her near the edge.

He pushed deeper, and muscles in his shoulders and back bunched under her fingers. She held him tighter, clamping her legs around him.

"More," she breathed.

He complied, pushing deeper still, until he'd reached her limit. Then he eased out and back in, creating an amazingly torturous rhythm. So close to release, she could do nothing but cling to him and wait.

He gripped her ass, and leaned over to kiss her mouth, matching the movement of his cock with his tongue as he pressed her to the wall, and she felt as though she were being fucked all over at once.

Wet heat surrounded her, touching, caressing.

She cried out against his lips.

Her body exploded, muscles contracting hard, satisfaction rolling up and down her spine.

He matched her needs, stroking against her movements, filling her completely.

The climax went on and on so long, it bordered on pain. Waves of glorious release crashed over her.

And then the need left her body in a rush.

He held her against the wall, and she panted into his mouth.

"That's un-fucking-believable," she said.

He laughed as he withdrew from her and eased her back to her feet. "Your language reminds me of my life at sea."

She pushed out of his grip, stopped under the warm water for a moment, then stepped from the shower. "Good. Then you're used to it."

Pulling two towels from a shelf, she tossed one to him and used the other to dry off. She watched him in the bathroom mirror watching her and found her body reacting to his all over again.

Christ. Just the sight of him turned her on. And the fact that he was still hard interested her.

Why hadn't he reached a climax yet? Did vampires do that?

"You have questions," he said, grinning.

She shrugged. She didn't like the possibility that he could read her thoughts. No matter how much she trusted him, her thoughts were her own.

Draping the towel over the shower door, she returned to the bedroom and flopped onto his bed. The satin cover felt amazing against her skin.

Benjamin didn't hesitate to stretch out beside her. He touched her arm and her shoulder, and then moved his hand down to her breast. He rubbed his index finger over the nipple and shoved it around in a circle.

God, his touch felt good.

Holding his gaze, she reached down and wrapped her fingers around his rock-hard prick and he rewarded her with a soft exhale. A hint of gold flickered in his eyes. When she pushed, sliding her hand down the length of him, he growled low and long.

As she started the maneuver again, he grabbed her wrist. "No," he whispered. "As much as I want to, we must not."

"Why not?"

Silence grew between them like a mushroom cloud, and her heart began to race.

He studied her eyes and frowned. "We cannot continue until you're ready to join me."

She also frowned. "What do you mean?"

He drew the back of her hand up to his mouth and kissed it, then held it to his chest. "I want you to be my mate, Star, my wife."

Her heart pounded as she understood the meaning of his statement, and she sat up. "You want to make me a vampire?"

He looked up at her from where he lay and nodded.

"You're telling me we can't have sex again until I'm ready to become a vampire. Is this a threat, or some kind of a weird bribe?"

He raised up to one elbow. "It is neither a threat nor a bribe, my dear. I have simply reached my limit." His voice lowered a notch and the corners of his mouth drew up into a wicked grin. "You spread those luscious thighs for me again, and the beast will take over. You will not survive."

Holy crap. She sat naked in bed with a man who had just admitted he was ready to kill her. When the hell had she lost all common sense?

Star scooted off the bed. "Look, this is nuts. I, uh, need to think about it." She grabbed her clothes from the floor and yanked them on.

"Before you leave—"

She screeched and spun around to find him suddenly standing between her and the door, wearing pants. "Son of a bitch! Quit doing that."

"My apologies," he said. Then he stepped closer, towering over her. "Before you leave, I want you to understand exactly what I'm offering."

She couldn't resist sliding her gaze over his bare chest, spread wide before her, and shuddered at the memory of muscles rippling under her touch in the shower only moments before.

"I want you to stay with me, Star, to enjoy whatever piece of eternity we have. As vampires, we'll share emotions and experiences you can't begin to imagine. But, you must also understand the limitations."

Her gaze rose back to his.

"You must give up all contact with those you care about. To them, you will be dead. And you'll never see the light of day again. You have no idea how difficult that can be."

He cradled her face and stared into her eyes with an intensity she felt to her toes.

"Make no mistake," he said. "I will gladly forfeit everything to keep you safe and make you happy. If it is possible for one of my kind to love, it is love I feel for you."

He pressed his cool lips to her forehead, and then stepped back and aside. "But you must come to me of your own free will, and with no reservations."

His words stunned her. In one breath, he told her he was ready to take her life, and in the next, that he loved her.

No one had ever told her they loved her.

Her heart clenched at the thought that he must be telling the truth. He'd taken a bullet for her. Granted, it hadn't done any permanent damage, but it couldn't have been much fun to get shot. And she'd seen the level of his anger when he'd grabbed Jones.

To them, you will be dead.

Did she have anyone who would miss her? There had been a few kind people in her life, but had any really cared about her? She couldn't come up with a single name.

Her head swam with questions and thickening emotions.

"I've got to go."

He bowed.

With a trembling hand, she pushed open the hidden door.

Benjamin closed his eyes for a moment as he listened to the door close behind her.

Once again, she'd left him alone, and, once again, he feared she might not return.

Star had no idea how close she'd come to losing her life in his arms. The thirst for her blood was like nothing he'd fought before. It rattled his forfeited soul.

Perhaps he should have tried harder to persuade her to stay. He could have told her of the joys of roaming the forest, seeing in the darkest night, having the strength to leap to the treetops, connecting with the wolf on a hunt. He could have told her of the nights they would spend sharing every thought, memory, and emotion as they rose to dizzying heights of erotic pleasure.

Would any of it have made a difference?

He must keep his hope alive. She was made for him, so perfect he could want no other. She must choose to stay. He could entertain no other possibility.

While he waited, he should clean up the mess downstairs before others found evidence of the killings. It would be difficult to wipe clean the memories of Kyle and Jack at the same time. No doubt Cassandra could do it, but he might have to resort to physical restraint while he worked on them. He didn't have the patience at the moment.

After dressing, Benjamin descended the stairs to find the bodies gone, but the floor still stained with drying blood, and he glowered at the waste. He prepared a mop and bucket, and wondered if Cassandra had used the cave to hide her latest victims—and his own—as he mopped the tile.

"I see you still remember how to swab the deck."

He glanced up at Cassandra. "It's not something one forgets."

She laughed. "And where is your little *friend*?"

He bit back his anger. "I don't know."

"You mean you're letting her run around loose with the knowledge of what we are?"

"Aye." He planted the mop in the bucket and carried both to the laundry where he rinsed them out and left them to dry.

Returning to the living room, he found Cassandra lounging in an armchair.

"The night is nearly over," she said. "I assume you've realized what you must do."

He tried to ignore the ache of dawn in his bones as he stood beside her and stared at his painting of the *Spencer*. He'd carry the guilt of the loss of his men for as long as he existed, but he could no longer blame Cassandra for their deaths. If she had not made him a vampire, he would never have known the exquisite, wondrous, pain-filled joy he felt now thinking about Star.

"I've asked her to stay as one of us."

Cassandra laughed again, but this time dryly. "You plan to make that little wretch a vampire?"

"She has great inner strength and true heart." He glanced down at Cassandra. "I don't wish to carry on without her."

Anger flashed in her eyes as she rose slowly from her chair. "I gave you eternity. You think you can just throw it away?"

"I'm not throwing it away. I've found the woman I want to share it with. Can you truly not understand that?"

She stood in front of Benjamin, glaring at him. "And how, exactly, do you plan to do this? You don't know the first thing about making our kind."

He raised one eyebrow. "You do."

Star sat under a tree, shivering, staring at the dark walls of Benjamin's mansion as the night sky lightened with dawn.

The whole thing should be a fairy tale. A tall, dark, handsome stranger with more money than God and a magnificent castle told her he loved her and asked her to stay with him.

But in her life, fairy tales always got twisted into horror stories somehow. In this case, the tall, dark, handsome stranger was a vampire. In order to stay, she had to die.

Jesus Christ.

She'd waited all this time to have someone say to her exactly what Benjamin had said. Wasn't that enough? And who wouldn't want to live five hundred years?

"Me," she muttered.

Benjamin had told her he remembered every life he'd taken with perfect clarity. And he obviously remembered the crew he'd lost. What if every bad memory from her life stayed with her? Would she really want to carry all this shit around forever?

Still, he was the only man, living or otherwise, she'd ever completely trusted. Didn't that mean something?

No matter what, she couldn't go to Maine with Wendy, Jack, and Kyle, not after finding out Wendy had ratted her out. That one had caught her completely off guard. How could someone she'd considered a friend do something so vile without her catching on?

Wendy had a better mask than Star would have guessed.

What the hell was she going to do now?

She could hitchhike into Boston and get a job, as she'd considered earlier. That option was looking better and better. At least she didn't have to worry about Jones anymore.

But for some reason, the thought of leaving the place produced a knot in her gut.

A car crept up the street and stopped in front of the house. Laughing, Jack and Kyle stumbled out. Jack leaned back in to kiss someone, and then both men watched as the car pulled away.

"Damn, I'm tired," Jack said.

Kyle slapped him on the back. "No fucking surprise there. You've been screwing for the past two hours. What are you going to do when the dingy girl's boyfriend comes looking for you tomorrow night?"

Jack shrugged. "We'll be gone by then. Shouldn't take more than a half hour to change the hose."

"I don't know about you, but I need some sleep first."

"Good plan. Then we can load up a few things and be on our way."

The two disappeared through the front door, their voices replaced by quiet.

11

"I don't know when I've, slept so well." Wendy stretched and then rose from the bed. "Wasn't that weird with those guys breaking in?"

Star watched her as she drew clean clothes from her backpack. "What do you remember?"

Wendy met her gaze. "What do you mean? I remember what you do, the three guys breaking in, the cops showing up, and the three guys going to jail. Why?"

"Just wondering."

"Where are Kyle and Jack?"

Star motioned with her head. "Outside, fixing the van."

"Cool. We should be able to get out of here by noon."

"Yep."

Wendy knitted her brow. "What's up?"

"Nothing."

"Yeah? Then let's go make some coffee."

"Good idea."

Star struggled to keep her anger and hurt hidden. As far as Wendy knew, nothing involving Jones, the flash drive, betrayal, or vampires had happened. If she and the guys were to be allowed to leave, it must stay that way.

She followed Wendy to the kitchen where they filled the coffee pot and waited for it to drip.

"What happened last night between you and the captain?"

Star shrugged. "Not much."

"Oh, girl, I think you're full of shit. What aren't you telling me?"

"Nothing. We kissed, that's all."

Wendy's mouth fell open. "He *kissed* you? And you let him? And nothing else happened?"

"Yep." It was none of Wendy's business what had transpired between Star and Benjamin. Even if she'd still considered Wendy a good friend, she wouldn't have told her about any of it. The whole thing was beyond personal.

Suddenly, the weight of Benjamin's secret became clear. He could only share what he was with a few, trusted people, and then had to wonder what would happen. Did he wonder now what she was thinking? If she'd told her friends?

He must know her better than that.

"Is he any good at kissing?" Wendy's eyes twinkled.

Star shrugged.

Wendy filled a mug with coffee. "Yeah, that's what I figured. Lonely old guy, probably forgot everything he ever knew."

Star had to turn her back on the woman so she wouldn't see her smile. For one thing, he was a hell of a lot older than Wendy knew, and he certainly hadn't forgotten anything about kissing, or anything else. Her knees felt weak just thinking back to his touch. And when he bit her—

Her spoon slipped from her hand and clanged to the floor. "Damn." She picked it up and tossed it into the sink.

"Come on, klutz. Let's go see what we can do to get the van rolling."

* * *

Benjamin couldn't remember when he'd ever felt so trapped by daylight. He sat in his room, sipping whiskey, listening to noises from outside.

He heard the young men working on the vehicle, and he heard Wendy jabbering about nothing in particular. He only knew Star was with them because of her occasional one-word answers.

What was she doing? Was she getting ready to drive away and leave him? Was she considering staying?

"Bloody hell." He rose, paced across the room, and stood before the cold fireplace.

He'd never felt such anxiety, even when he'd been walking the coast looking for his crew. As horrible as that had been, it had only been a matter of life or death. After all these years—centuries—this was much more. He would either have the one being who could make him whole, or he'd have nothing. Knowing she existed meant he'd now know what he was missing if she left.

The thought terrified him.

He turned to study Cassandra who lay in his bed enjoying death's sleep. Her beautiful, pale face showed no hint of vitality.

What role would she play in all this? She could help him, or doom him to despair. And if she decided to hurt Star . . .

He shuddered to think of what the future might hold.

There was little point in staying awake to fret. Nothing would likely happen before dark.

Stretching out on the bed, he lay on his back, crossed his hands over his stomach, and closed his eyes. He would not allow himself to drop off completely, just in case Star came calling.

He wished he'd established a link with her already so he could send her his wishes. She couldn't possibly know how much she meant to him.

* * *

"Coming?"

Star stood at the gate, backpack slung over her shoulder, looking first at Wendy, then at the van, and then back at the house.

She'd told Wendy and the guys that she'd decided not to go to Maine with them, and they'd offered her a ride to the closest highway where she could hitch back to Boston. But now that the time had come, she was having second and third thoughts.

"Come on," Kyle said, pushing past her with a bag that clanged. "Time to go, before the old man shows up."

Star lowered her backpack to the ground. "I guess I'll stick around a little longer. You guys go ahead." She followed Kyle out to the van. After he shoved the bag into the back and closed the door, she opened it again and drew the bag out.

"Hey!" Kyle reached for her, but she stepped aside. "What the fuck do you think you're doing?"

"I'm taking Benjamin's stuff back to him."

"Are you nuts? The old man has more crap than he can ever use. We're just taking a few insignificant things, trinkets." He stepped toward her.

Star matched his step backward. "No."

"What are you, suddenly righteous or something?"

"You don't need this."

"You think I can't take it from you?"

"I think you can try." She curled her free hand into a fist at her side. If he got the bag back, he'd also have a bloody nose and swollen balls, at the least.

Wendy grabbed Kyle's arm. "Come on, forget it. She's flipped. Let's just go."

"Stupid bitch," Kyle said.

Star grinned and shot him the finger.

With a look of confusion, Wendy glanced back at her, shook her head, and climbed into the front seat of the van. The engine roared, sputtered, and evened out as they pulled away.

And they were gone.

Star stood at the gate for a while longer, making sure they didn't circle back, then carried the bag and her backpack inside and left them in the living room.

She still hadn't made up her mind about what to do.

Surrendering herself to Benjamin on the catwalk had been tough, but not impossible. After all, it was only for a short time, and there was something about him she truly trusted, as strange as that was. Surrendering herself forever was something entirely different.

She'd never known any couple to last more than a few months. It was understandable. She'd never been able to stand being around anyone longer than that.

Her last foster mother had told her she had trouble with relationships because she was afraid to open up, afraid of getting hurt. The woman had been wrong; it wasn't fear. It was avoiding the inevitable. Every person Star had ever trusted had turned on her. Every foster parent had sent her away. Most had slapped her around. One had raped her. Hell, Jones had been ready to kill her. And even Wendy, the one person she'd considered a true friend, had betrayed her.

So, now what? Why did she think Benjamin would be any different?

Maybe because he *was* different.

Star climbed the stairs and slipped into Benjamin's study. She stood in front of the secret door, pressed her palms and forehead to the wallpaper, and sighed.

It was crazy the way she knew he was on the other side of the wall. It wasn't just a hunch, or even a logical thought, it was a feeling deep in her gut, like a tugging from the inside. She *felt* him on the other side of that wall.

Okay, so maybe she loved him, or something close to it. But was she ready to die for him?

Tiptoeing away, she climbed the narrow stairs to the tower and walked out to the catwalk. She stood at the spot where he'd held her over the handrail and demanded her trust. The memory of that moment left her both queasy and excited.

But dying was not something she could take back. And what if he screwed it up and she just died? She was too young to die.

Why the hell was she even considering any of this?

The smart thing to do was leave before the sun set.

After one last look around, Star turned and headed down the stairs.

Benjamin waited as long as he could. With the sky still darkening, he shoved open the secret door and dashed out, ducking around shafts of light falling down the stairs from the tower.

"Star?"

The house felt empty.

"Star!"

He trotted down the stairs to the guest room, where he found nothing but rumpled bedclothes and a bag full of candlesticks, silverware, and other odds and ends. He checked the bathroom and poked his head through every doorway as he made his way toward the front of the house. His boot heels echoed across the tile floor and the sounds bounced off walls as he traversed the hall. Darkness swelled in his chest. Had she really left him?

"Bloody hell, Star. Where are—"

He skidded to a halt at the entrance to the living room where she sat on the sofa, staring at the painting of the *Spencer*.

She looked different than she had when she left his room. Her stone wall seemed to have cracked, maybe even crumbled a bit. She turned and trained her blue-eyed gaze on his.

Damn, she was beautiful, like a storm blossoming on the horizon. Her power whispered to him in a language he felt more than heard. Her heartbeat pounded like distant thunder.

As her gaze slid back to the painting, he approached slowly, afraid of spooking her.

"Was this your ship?"

"Aye."

"Who painted it?"

"I did."

Her gaze snapped back to his. "Really?"

He nodded. "Given enough time, anyone can learn such a skill."

She huffed a laugh and retuned her attention to the painting.

"Have you made up your mind, Star?"

She sighed. "I thought I had. I'd planned to leave before sunset."

Darkness faded from his soul as he considered her words. "But you haven't left."

"No."

"You'll stay, then?"

She shrugged. "I don't know."

In a flash, he stood beside her, grabbed her by the wrist, and drew her up into his arms.

"Hey!" She pushed against his chest. "Back off."

Her scent teased his senses and he smiled. "I will not."

She snarled up at him. "You said I had to come to you of my own free will."

He wrapped his arms around her and held her tightly to him, thrilling to the feel of her lean, hard body. "That's when I was certain you would. Now I'm not so sure, and unwilling to risk you leaving."

"That's not fair."

He watched her struggle and realized she was only half-heartedly working at escaping.

"Put me—"

He covered her mouth with his own and first met hard lips, but as he waited, she gave in. Her taste weakened his spine and he felt a groan rise in his throat. When she opened her mouth under his, the groan deepened into a growl.

So perfect, so delicious. How could he ever want anyone else? And how would he ever get enough of her?

Her hands slid up over his shoulders and he lifted her against him. Forcing himself to abandon her mouth, he kissed her face and neck, and then he held his mouth near her ear. "Stay," he whispered.

Her heart pounded. He felt it against his chest and arms.

"I don't know," she finally whispered back.

He drew back to meet her gaze. "What don't you know?"

"What if . . . I don't know, what if we end up hating each other? Three hundred years is a long time."

He eased her to her feet, then drew her down to the sofa and sat beside her. With his arm around her shoulders, he brushed her silky hair back from her face. "It will be but a moment with you beside me."

"Easy for you to say." She looked away, frowning.

"You're afraid you may grow weary of me."

She shrugged. "Something like that."

He drew her face back around to his. "Listen to me, Star. You have my commitment. I know you, and I want you. But I make no such demand on you. If you tire of me, you are always free to go."

"Oh, yeah? So you'd just stand there and let me leave?"

He sighed at her apparent anger. "Not willingly, but I would not force you to stay if you truly wished to leave."

Her eyes suddenly glistened as they studied his.

"What is it, my dear?" He stroked her cheek with his fingertips.

"I'm trying to figure out why this isn't going to work."

He smiled and kissed her forehead. "It will work."

She reached up and touched the side of his neck, and he shuddered.

* * *

Star studied Benjamin's wide shoulders and tight butt as she followed him up the stairs. Something about their pace reminded her of a funeral. But she knew he was trying to give her time to be sure about her decision.

How the hell could anyone be sure about becoming a vampire?

The closer they got to his study, the shakier she felt. By the time they stood in front of the secret door, she trembled all over, and hated the fact that she couldn't hide it.

"Must be cold in here," she said, by way of an excuse.

"It is?"

"Yeah. Or something."

He pulled out the top corner book, pushed the button under the chair rail, and stepped back to allow her to go first.

She took a deep breath, and then stepped into the candlelit room. A fire burned in the fireplace, and pillows stacked at the head of the bed looked inviting.

She turned to face Benjamin, who stood watching her. "How does this work?"

"Quite naturally, my dear." He flashed his killer smile.

Star gulped, crossed the room, and sat on the edge of the bed. "Think we can have another shot of scotch?"

"Of course." He filled two shot glasses from a glass decanter and handed one to her. Then he raised his glass. "To the future."

She clinked her glass to his, and downed the contents. The burning scotch felt good going down. She pounded her chest with her fist. "Good shit," she managed to croak.

He took her glass and placed it on a table with his own, then sat beside her on the bed.

"I feared you might leave," he said.

She met his steady gaze, and saw how hard his fear had been for him to admit. Perhaps they were more alike than she'd realized.

She shrugged. "I couldn't."

"Why not?"

She shrugged again.

He leaned closer, and his voice dropped several notches. "Tell me why you couldn't leave."

Yes, it was time for honesty. If she planned to give her life to this man . . . er, vampire, she damn well better be able to trust him with the truth.

"I couldn't leave you."

He smiled, and gold flecks appeared in his eyes. "I'm glad."

He drew her face up to his and took her mouth, commanding her attention. As usual, his kiss swept her senses away, and she didn't fight it. His tongue stroked hers and led it in wildly seductive circles. All she could do was hold on and follow.

When he let her up for air, she found her fists clenched around handfuls of his shirt.

The fire crackled behind him.

"Last chance," he whispered. "If you wish to go—"

She shook her head.

"Good," he growled.

He drew her with him up the bed until she lay in the middle and he leaned over her. His eyes were completely gold now, ringed in red, and when he opened his mouth, she saw his fangs.

"I've hungered for you like this since I first saw you, Star. I will try my best to go slow, but I make no promises."

Her insides quivered at the thought of him losing control.

Movement suddenly drew her attention to a figure standing near the fireplace.

"What's she doing here?"

Benjamin didn't take his eyes off of hers as he slid his hand under her shirt. "I've asked Cassandra to assist me."

"Assist you?"

"Aye. I've never made a vampire, and she has."

Star's gaze snapped up to Cassandra's, and the woman bowed her head in greeting.

Star frowned at Benjamin. "I don't know . . . I, uh—"

"Don't worry, my sweet." He fondled her breast as he spoke. "Cassandra is only here to keep me from making a mistake."

Her body responded to his touch, even as she worked on the meaning of his words. The woman who had threatened her the night before, then saved her from Jones and his thugs, now stood by to make sure Benjamin didn't screw up when he made her a vampire.

The whole situation was bizarre. What difference did it make if someone else watched?

Star raised her arms and let Benjamin draw her shirt off, and then she unbuttoned his as he tenderly kissed her face. He touched her body with firm, cool hands, caressing and stroking her skin as if worshipping her. The effect was intoxicating, and Star's head swam with giddiness.

When she finally pushed his shirt back, he shrugged it off and stretched out on top of her. The bulge in the front of his pants reminded her of just how wonderful he felt entering her. She whimpered.

"We'll get there soon," he said. "But this time, when we become one, more than just our bodies will be entangled."

She gulped at his words, wrapped her arms around him, and pressed her mouth to his bare chest. His skin tasted as exotic as ever, and he groaned as she sucked hard.

Gripping her right leg and drawing it up beside him, he captured her mouth again and pressed the bulge of his erection into her crotch as he kissed her. She raised her hips in response.

Her insides filled with the joy of it all as she tasted his desperation. He wanted *her*. He craved more, just as she did, and when she raised her hips again, he grunted softly.

Star tore her mouth from his. "Too many clothes," she said.

He nodded. "Aye."

Fabric tore in their rush to remove clothing, and pieces flew to the floor without care. Somewhere in the corner of her mind, she thought about Cassandra watching from the far side of the room, but that thought drifted away as soon as Benjamin drew her into his arms again and kissed her. She ran her hands over his smooth skin, and thrilled to his touch.

He rolled over to his back, drawing her up on top of him. His body was big under hers, heavy and hard, like the anchor she hadn't realized she needed.

When she straddled him and sat up, he slid his hands down to her thighs and smiled up at her. She understood that he was letting her set the pace.

With one hand in the middle of his chest, she reached between them to touch the velvety skin of his prick, and saw the immediate effect in his eyes as they glittered gold and silver. The tip of his tongue ran across his bottom lip and up one fang, and his gaze slid down to her neck.

Excitement and power surged through her as she considered the beast she controlled with a simple touch. How far could she push him?

Her tits tightened and desire crawled up her spine.

Straightening, she pressed his prick against her cunt, drenching it with her juices as she moved forward and back.

His grip on her thighs tightened.

At the head, she arched her back and stopped with his swollen prick pointed into her cunt. As much as she wanted to impale herself on him, to feel him filling her completely, she wanted more to watch his need build.

He waited, completely still except for his lustful gaze.

She slid back an inch, and his cool, hard cock parted her lips.

He could have shoved her onto his prick, but he didn't. He waited. His eyes rolled shut and his head went back.

She leaned forward then and pressed her lips to his chest. She licked a trail up to the side of his neck, and he turned his head and groaned. Trying to imagine what it would be like, she opened her mouth against his skin and nipped.

He ran his hands up her back, and his groan deepened into an animal-like growl that vibrated through her entire body, leaving trails of excitement.

"Careful," he whispered, his voice hoarse.

She sat back up and met his blood-red gaze, and felt no fear, not even a little hidden somewhere. This was the form she would take with no regrets. She would lie in Benjamin's arms during the day, and enjoy fucking him at night, and she'd never wanted anything more desperately.

Grinning, she started slowly down the length of his cock, feeding her hungry cunt, stretching to take in all of him. Before she made it, her body started a rhythm she couldn't deny.

Suddenly, he sat up and wrapped his arms around her. "Not yet."

"I'm ready now," she said, riding his cock.

He held her to him, stopping her movement, and she frowned.

"Wrap those lovely legs around me."

If she did that, she'd have no control. "I don't—"

"Do it," he said, his voice deep and commanding.

Star straightened her legs and then wrapped them around his hips, and felt as if he dangled her over the handrail again. Her skin tingled.

He held her poised, halfway down his cock, one hand gripping her butt and the other arm around her waist. "You must learn control," he said, nuzzling the side of her head. "The hunger is much stronger than the desire you feel now."

A shiver ran through her. At the moment, every ounce of her was focused on their union, on the ache building between her legs, on the need to flood him with her cum. How much stronger could the need to drink blood be?

She frowned as she closed her eyes and concentrated on the

feel of him in and around her. He pressed his lips to her jaw, and she raised her chin.

"Much stronger," he breathed.

She clung to him as he lowered her fractions of an inch at a time. Heat built in her body as if from flames eating up fresh logs in the fireplace. More. She needed more. She gripped a handful of his hair and pressed her mouth to his shoulder.

His body moved against hers in subtle flexes, and he pressed his teeth against her neck.

Her breathing closed to small gasps as need radiated out from her to fill the air in the room.

He slid his cool, wet lips down to the top of her shoulder.

Her clit throbbed.

"Oh, god," she whispered, "make me come."

As he eased her the rest of the way down his cock, he sank his fangs into her shoulder.

Her body exploded.

Holding him as tightly as she could, she rode out the convulsions of pleasure. Spasms shot through her body from her cunt like bolts of electricity. She yelled through gritted teeth at the intensity.

He sucked hard on her shoulder and she felt waves of release flowing from her to him. Could he feel her pleasure? Or taste it?

Then he withdrew his fangs and she collapsed against him.

His cock still filled her, fully erect and hard, and he rocked her against him with subtle movements.

God, she was still turned on.

Pushing against his chest, she leaned back, exposing her tits to him, and he matched her movement. His tongue, now warmer, circled her tits, and then slid back and forth over budded nipples, and she writhed with delight. How could anything feel so damn good?

Her cunt tightened again, and she felt the second round approaching like a rumbling freight train. "Oh, fuck."

His teeth pierced the flesh above her tit, and she came.

Her cunt contracted and his cock pushed deeper, reaching for her center.

The erotic pull from his mouth drew her up to him, arched her back more.

He held her tighter, and she dug her fingers into bulging muscles in his arms.

He raised his head and the orgasm eased away.

Star panted as she opened her eyes to meet his gaze.

He licked his lips and then grinned.

His canines had grown into huge fangs, and his eyes had a distinctly animal appearance. "You are mine," he said.

It was true. She was completely his. She knew at that moment she'd never be able to hold anything back from him. Anything he wanted, she'd give willingly. Even her darkest secrets.

She nodded slowly, and his grin broadened.

Holding her, he turned and laid her on the bed beneath him. He tenderly kissed her lips, and her face.

"It's time," he whispered near her ear.

She shuddered in response, shaking off the last remnant of doubt.

He froze. Did he think she'd changed her mind?

She bit his shoulder, and he jerked and grunted as he thrust deeper into her cunt. Her body felt as though it were being tortured with pleasure. She couldn't take much more.

Benjamin moved his mouth to her neck, and pressed the sharp tips of his fangs to her skin.

She clenched her teeth against the impending flash of pain, but it didn't come. Instead, he began to fuck her in a slow, wet, relaxed rhythm. Her clit swelled again under the sweet torture, and she spread her legs wider.

She knew when she came this time, he would take her as a

vampire and drain away her life. Her heart pounded against her ribs.

A strange peace seemed to seep into her mind, even as the muscles in the back of her legs strained with need. He moved faster, matching her rising level of desire, and she felt the subtle sting of his fangs piercing her flesh.

Her hands closed into fists against his back as the first pounding wave of release raised her up against him, and something inside her snapped.

Every cell in her body seemed to fly off in a different direction.

His fangs sank deeper, tapping into her heartbeat.

Her very being screamed with joy as her soul stretched out past her skin.

His cock erupted, reaching for her core.

And then the space between them disappeared.

He held her with more than his arms. He shared his joy with her as if sharing a taste or a scent. He caressed her without touch, whispered to her without words. She marveled at the expanse of his feelings opening beneath her like an ocean.

Clinging to him, she fell.

Together they sank in the dark water, and cold inched up her limbs. She tried to hold on to him, but lost the feeling in her fingers and hands, and he slipped away.

As the cold moved deeper, creeping toward her heart, she opened her eyes but found only darkness. Total, complete darkness.

And then even the darkness disappeared.

Benjamin felt her life ebb away, and followed the receding wave.

"Release her."

The words echoed in his head without meaning.

"Release her, now!"

He responded to the hand pulling on his shoulder by withdrawing his fangs from Star's neck. He turned his head and snarled at the intruder.

"Benjamin, listen to me."

The soft voice soothed the beast until it quieted and stepped back.

He looked down at Star's face. Her lips were pale and parted, and her eyelids drooped over lifeless eyes.

Fear clenched as a fist around his heart and soul as he backed away from her. "I've taken too much." He grabbed her hand and pressed it to his mouth. How could he have destroyed the one he loved?

"No, my dear, you've done all as you should. Now you must bring her back."

His gaze snapped up to Cassandra's.

She nodded her reassurance.

As his senses began to return, he recalled her instructions and moved around to crouch beside the bed. Tearing a gash in his own wrist, he held the wound above Star's lips and gave her back what he had taken from her.

He watched as blood filled her mouth. Had he been able to pray, he would have. But all he could do was wait and hope.

"Come back to me, my love," he whispered.

Could she hear him? Had he let her stray too far?

He saw her swallow and nearly yelled his joy.

Her eyes popped open and she stared at him. The amazing blue of her irises mixed with gold, producing the most beautiful eyes he'd ever seen.

With one shaky hand, she clasped his arm, drew his wrist to her mouth, and sucked hard.

He closed his eyes, nearly swooning with delight.

He felt the wound in his wrist close, and she pushed his arm away.

Licking the last drop from her lips, she reached for him, wrapping one arm around his neck. As he drew her from the bed and into his arms, she sank her fangs brutally into his shoulder, growling.

He gasped and held her close.

His mind reached out for hers, but found only darkness.

He held her tighter, stroking her hair. "Take what you need," he whispered. "I am yours."

And then he felt her open to him, a little at first, and then more. He pressed forward, offering her his happiness.

The growling stopped, but she continued to drink.

His arms weakened, and he fought to hold her. He could not deny her, even if it meant he wouldn't survive.

Her hand slid slowly up to the back of his head, and she drew his mouth to her flesh. Enraptured, he accepted her offer.

Finally truly connected, he opened himself to her, laying his dreams, and hopes, and joys, and fears on her altar. As she touched each, tasting, rejoicing, he finally saw the true depth of her strength and knew he'd made the right choice.

They merged into one, forever bonded, the link forever open.

He withdrew his fangs from her shoulder, and she did the same.

She trembled against him, and he scooped her up so he could return to the bed and lay with her in his arms, touching the edges of her mind as he caressed her body.

"Well done."

He opened his eyes and looked up to where Cassandra leaned over him.

"But a little too sentimental for me," she said. She stroked his hair. "I'll check in on you, my dear. I hope you don't regret this decision."

"I won't."

She shrugged, straightened, and headed toward the door. "I think I'll head west. I have a friend in New Mexico I haven't seen in a while."

"Cassandra."

She stopped and glanced back at him.

"Thank you."

She shrugged again, but a twinkle in her eyes gave her away.

He watched her wrap her cloak around her shoulders and disappear through the concealed doorway. The panel screeched shut behind her.

Overcome with exhaustion, Benjamin turned to his side and drew Star's body into his. She snuggled back against him and sighed.

He studied the outline of the star on her shoulder and realized how truly appropriate choosing her had been. Every sailor knew the importance of a guiding star. He would set his course through eternity by her.

Inhaling her wonderful scent, he drew her closer and closed his eyes. As soon as he was able, he'd make love to her again, but as his vampire mate. The thought made him smile.

12

Star turned the pages of the book, soaking up words faster than she would have thought possible, and laughed with glee.

Benjamin kissed the top of her head and she smiled up at him. "I'm off to take a shower, but I'll be back shortly, and you will be required to pay attention to me, do you understand?"

"Aye," she said.

He grinned and winked.

She watched him climb the stairs before returning her attention to the book.

In less than twenty hours, she'd decided she liked being a vampire. True, the hunger was startling, but Benjamin kept a stash of nourishment in a hidden refrigerator in his room. He gave her enough to take the edge off.

So far, they'd had sex twice since waking at sunset, and it wasn't even nine o'clock yet. She decided it would take awhile before she got tired of fucking him almost constantly, but made him promise to give her at least an hour each night to read. He'd agreed, and offered to read books of poetry to her. She'd never paid much attention to poetry, but imagined she'd enjoy it. She loved listening to his deep, sexy voice.

The knock at the door made her jump. It was followed by the doorbell.

Star stood and listened.

She heard two men outside.

"You sure this was where they were?"

"Hell, yeah, I'm sure. I was waiting right there."

She recognized the second voice with a start. Bubba, Jones's asshole driver.

"Oh, shit," she whispered.

One of them knocked on the door again.

Straightening her clothes and combing her fingers through her hair, she walked to the door and opened it.

The man she hadn't recognized turned out to be a cop. Christ, only Bubba could be stupid enough to call the cops after kidnapping her.

The cop tipped his hat to her. "Good evening. I'm looking for—"

"That's her. She's Jones's girlfriend."

Star clamped her mouth shut as she felt her fangs growing. She hadn't been around anyone except Benjamin since she turned, and suddenly couldn't hear anything but their thundering heartbeats. She watched the pulse rise and fall in Bubba's neck and imagined what it would be like to sink her fangs into that pulse. Hunger clawed at her gut.

Bubba's eyes widened and his gaze rose over her shoulder.

Benjamin's hand came to rest on the small of her back, and suddenly the heartbeats faded.

"Officer," he said. "What can I do for you?"

"Good evening, Captain. This man, Mr. Smith, says three of his friends disappeared inside your house last night."

"They was with her, Jones's girlfriend." Bubba pointed at Star.

"There must be some mistake," Benjamin said. "This woman is my wife."

Star felt waves of soothing emotion coursing through the air, and glanced up to find Benjamin staring at Bubba.

Bubba's eyes widened.

"I didn't know you'd gotten married," the officer said. "Congratulations."

"Thank you." Benjamin nodded at the young man, and then smiled down at Star.

"Still, I have to follow up on—"

"I made a mistake," Bubba said, his excited, nasal voice suddenly monotone. "They wasn't here."

The cop looked at the man and frowned. "Are you sure?"

Bubba nodded, then turned and walked away.

The cop shrugged and shook his head. "He's a strange one. I'm really sorry to bother you." He tipped his hat to Star again. "Nice to meet you, Mrs. Bartlett."

Star smiled. Mrs. Bartlett? She hadn't considered that. A little old-fashioned, but not so bad. She could get used to it.

The cop followed his confused witness back to the sidewalk and Star closed the door. She turned to gaze up at Benjamin. "You have got to show me how to do that."

"With pleasure," he said. He leaned forward, trapping her against the door between his arms, and kissed her mouth. "But not now."

"Oh?" She looked up, her eyes wide with feigned innocence. "Why not now?"

He grabbed her and lifted her from the ground, holding her at eye level as he walked toward the living room. "Because now I plan to fuck you again."

Her fangs descended and she wrapped her arms around his neck. "But you promised me an hour to read."

"Aye," he said, "I did. But I didn't say it would be all at once." He kissed her neck.

She laughed as he lowered her to her feet before the fire and began drawing off her clothes.

"I don't know why I bother getting dressed," she said, shoving his shirt over his gorgeous shoulders.

"Perhaps you shouldn't." He drew her down to the floor with him where he sat and settled her onto his lap.

She pressed her mouth to his, ecstatic to be back in his arms, and enjoyed the feel of his hands running up and down her bare skin.

"My cock aches to be inside you," he whispered against her lips.

She didn't have to tell him how much his words turned her on. He knew. He knew everything about her, just as she knew everything about him. He even knew her darkest secrets, and accepted them without judgment.

Raising herself against him, she found his stiff cock easily and slid slowly down the length of it as she kissed him, amazed at how perfectly they fit together. Her fingers tangled in his thick hair, and she felt a low growl rumble in his chest.

Hunger for him filled her completely, and she leaned back to meet his golden gaze.

She didn't have to tell him she loved him. He knew.

She stroked his face and opened her mouth to reveal her fangs. As she ran her tongue teasingly over one, he groaned.

"Will you make me come?" she asked.

"Aye, with pleasure, my love. For all eternity." Closing his eyes, he raised his chin and surrendered to her.

Blood Lust

1

"You look delicious in moonlight. More wine?"

Rachel gazed up into the dark eyes of her unusual host and smiled. "Sure."

At something like six-four and amazingly handsome, Max's high cheekbones, firm jaw, and thick, dark, shoulder-length hair gave him an exotic air. She'd never seen anyone quite so attractive.

She'd certainly never spent the evening with anyone so attractive.

He filled her glass with cabernet.

She turned to watch the full moon shatter on the Gulf's surface, trying her best to appear mysterious, and enjoyed the tropical breeze as she sipped. Warm, salty air sighed across her skin.

The wine was good. Probably expensive, like everything else—the hotel room on the beach, the food, his clothes. Max was wealthy, good-looking, and sexy as hell.

Yes, this was a date no one back at camp or at school would believe.

"You, my dear, have wonderful lines."

He spoke from right behind her, and a shiver tripped up Rachel's spine.

"Lines?"

"Yes." The tips of his fingers slid across her shoulder and up the side of her neck. "Quite classic, like Aphrodite."

His touch did strange things to her skin, leaving behind tingles that sizzled deeper into her body. She closed her eyes to enjoy the erotic sensations.

"Tell me, dear Rachel, what are you doing so far from home?"

She swallowed hard. "I was, uh, working a dig. For school."

"A *dig*?" His fingers blazed trails down the outsides of her arms.

"Yeah. Archaeology. You know, Maya ruins and all."

"Ah, I see." He spoke directly into her ear in a quiet voice full of lust and danger. "Looking for secrets perhaps?"

Rachel grabbed the railing with her free hand to stabilize her spinning world. "Yeah, secrets." She hadn't had enough alcohol to be drunk, but she felt intoxicated nonetheless. "Legends."

"Hmm, legends." His palms grazed her hips, and then slid up to the tender sides of her breasts. "I know several legends from this place. Which is it you seek?"

Even through her cotton blouse, his touch felt incredibly intimate, as if she were standing before him naked, unable to move. When his lips brushed the top of her shoulder, her breasts swelled with desire and her nipples puckered.

She tried to focus. Although she'd accepted Max's invitation to his room knowing she'd likely end up in his bed, she didn't want to appear too eager. Stanley, her ex, had told her that men enjoyed a challenge, just before he left her for her prudish former roommate.

Focus.

Work. What was it he'd asked about work?

"Legend," he whispered, as if answering her silent question.

"In Mutankah, near Chichen Itza, a priest created a talisman that was supposed to be magical or something. Probably . . . worth a lot."

His fingers traced a line around the top of her jeans, grazing bare flesh, and his mouth moved to a tender spot at the side of her neck. He kissed and gently sucked, and her knees began to tremble. His hands moved around her waist and he eased her back against him as he unsnapped her pants.

She drew in a breath of surprise at the size of the erection pressing into her lower back.

"Ah, yes, the Mutankah talisman," he said. "And have you found it?"

"No." She rested her head against his solid chest, marveling at the scent of cloves and strange herbs. Wild aftershave, unlike anything she'd encountered before. Ancient and enticing. "We, uh, don't even know . . . if it exists. No proof."

"But you will continue to search?"

"Not me. I'm going . . . home. Others will."

He caressed her breasts with an expert touch, teasing the sensitive nipples through the cotton, and desire tightened her crotch. She wondered how long it would be before he removed her clothing. Would he take her gently, as he now seduced her, or would he throw her onto his bed and fuck her brains out? Just the thought brought juices that soaked her panties.

"Max," she whispered, "you're good."

"Hmm," he said, his chest vibrating against her. "And you are quite lovely."

One hand slid down her belly and into the front of her pants.

A strange fog invaded her thoughts, making it hard to decide what to do, as if he had total control over her. She couldn't move away from him, and wasn't even sure if she wanted to.

She wondered if anyone stood on the beach, watching them, and surprised herself when she realized she didn't care. Let them watch. At the moment, she just wanted to come in this man's arms. As his cool fingers slid between the folds of her wet pussy and across her swelling clit, she nearly did.

She pushed back against him, and then rocked her hips forward, and his fingers hinted at entering her. Muscles tightened and she groaned at the promise of ecstasy.

"Oh, yes," he said. "Delicious." He kissed the side of her neck.

She moved her head to one side to give him access to more, as she pushed back and forward again, drawing his fingers inside.

He sucked on her neck, and her pussy tightened.

He slid out and back in, deeper, and again.

Her back arched at the impending release, and her world narrowed to just his touch.

"Yes," she breathed, "yes."

He slid deeper still as her climax started with hard, urgent pulses. She cried out and her entire body convulsed from the inside out. His arm tightened around her waist, holding her close.

A scream froze in her throat when he pierced the flesh of her neck, and the wineglass tumbled from her hand.

"I need more light over here."

Chris looked up from his notebook as Nicole sat back on her heels and drew her forearm across her face, pushing chestnut hair from in front of her dazzling green eyes. The sleeveless cotton blouse she wore exposed more of her flesh to his gaze than he found himself able to ignore, and he had to purposely look away.

"I'll get it," he said. Closing the notebook, he rose, picked his way over electric cords and string grids to one of the portable spotlights. He moved it closer to the lovely professor. "Here?"

She nodded. "Yeah, that'll do." Then she fell back to all fours to remove dirt from a rock with a camelhair brush.

The swell of her hips and length of her muscular, brown legs made Chris want to growl. Why did Dr. Nicole Stephenson have to be so damned alluring?

Under normal circumstances, he would simply unleash his preternatural charms and seduce her, taking what he wanted and needed. But this wasn't normal circumstances. He could run no risks with her physical well-being. If the good doctor found the object he sought, his very existence could instantly change.

Chris raised his gaze from Nicole to study the surrounding jungle and ruins, searching the darkness outside the ring of buzzing lights for any sign of movement. There were others who wanted the talisman, and who would probably stop at nothing to get it. His only hope was that Nicole and her students would uncover the truth, whatever it was, before any of the others appeared. Otherwise, the entire world could be transformed, and most likely not for the better.

Reassured by the stillness of the night, he returned to his canvas chair, hunched over the folding table, and continued working on his notes. A Coleman lantern hissed at his right ear and cast a great deal more light than he needed on the half-filled page.

After recording the evening's progress, he discreetly surveyed the other workers. Nicole's doctoral students, Eric, a broad-shouldered Nordic blond, Megan, a lusty redhead, and Brandon, a brainy, dark-haired, wiry man, were the only ones allowed to actually uncover new ground. Half a dozen other students, whose names he didn't know, hauled buckets of earth to screens where treasures were sorted from debris. The faces of those others had changed over the first half of the summer as students had flown in and out of Merida to serve their time. Most seemed anxious to return to their beer-soaked summer activities back home. None appeared to pose a threat to the project. The doctoral students, moreover, exhibited true enthusiasm for the work, exceeded only by their charming professor's.

Closing his journal and sliding it into the leather sleeve, Chris stood. He considered where his efforts would best serve the project. He could help Brandon's group excavate the waste pit, joining the line of students carrying buckets. Or, perhaps he should—

"Oh, my God! Look at this."

Nicole's exclamation spun him around, and anticipation rose in his chest. He trotted across the site and dropped to his knees beside her.

The stone ledge she'd just uncovered held a column of Maya glyphs.

"Does this say what I think it says?" Nicole asked.

Chris sounded out each glyph, letting ancient words form in his mouth as the meaning became clear. He interpreted for himself and the group forming behind them. "The high priest, Ahcaanan Uxmaal, is the creator of great power."

"The talisman?" Nicole whispered.

Chris nodded slowly. "It's possible."

"Yes! This must be his tomb!" Still on her knees, Nicole threw her arms around Chris's neck.

Instinctively, he drew her to him.

All noise disappeared except the thunder of her heartbeat in his ears. The sweet sound wound through his brain, and then his chest, whispering to the beast within, "Feed."

She smelled of sweat, damp earth, and crushed vegetation, but above all, woman. Pure, lovely, tempting female.

His fangs dropped into place as the beast rose to the call.

He held his mouth an inch from her neck, listening to the steady *whoosh*, so close he could taste it. He spread his hands on her back, savoring her warm flesh.

She made no effort to escape. She offered herself to him.

The beast surged forward.

Time stopped, and the earth stilled.

"We found it!"

Her words shattered the moment and Chris drew back.

Closing his eyes, he shoved the unquenched beast into a corner, struggling to reattach the chains.

As soon as he was able, he released Nicole, staggered to his feet, and glanced around.

Workers whooped and hugged each other, and Brandon helped Nicole stand. None of them noticed the monster in their midst. Nicole hadn't spotted the shadow that had swooped down upon her, nearly claiming her life.

With his mouth clamped shut, Chris backed away from the celebration until he'd melted into the shadows. Then he turned and dashed to his waiting Land Rover.

He drew two pints of O-positive from the ice chest he kept hidden in the back, punctured the plastic with elongated fangs, and drained the bags quickly. As the liquid spread through his body, its effects saturated his brain, soothing the beast for now. Hints of human emotion nearly gone from the donated platelets skipped across nerve endings, reminding him of the life that wasn't his to celebrate. The fluid did little more than squelch his need, but that was all he'd expected.

Leaning back against the vehicle, shielded from the camp, he gazed up at the moon as he waited for his appearance to normalize and recalled the first time he'd encountered the beast, three centuries earlier. The first thirst, unbelievable in strength, had nearly driven him to recant his decision . . .

Clouds passed overhead too quickly, as if the world were ending. Chris watched, unable to move so much as an eyelash. He'd never experienced such silence; his heart had stilled and he felt no need for breath.

He'd been a fool to believe the handsome stranger. Now he'd forfeited his life, and would only be able to watch as the stranger took possession of his purse, too. How could he have been so gullible?

" 'Good night sweet prince, and flights of angels sing thee to thy rest.' " A low, rumbling laugh accompanied the quote. "That's what you're thinking at this moment, isn't it? 'I'm dead.' Ah, well, right you are."

In a sudden rush, Chris drew air into his lungs and sat up. He whirled around on his hands and knees to glare at Max. "What is this? What have you done?"

"I've killed you, dear Christopher, in order to keep you young and strong forever. Isn't it lovely?"

Chris staggered to his feet, and fell against the brick wall as a wave of hunger swept over him like a tidal bore. His mouth ached, and his vision grew strange; the night took on a deadly glow. He shook from head to toe, weakness facing off against strength of desperation.

"I'm hungry," he said, his voice a croak.

"I'm sure you are. What you need is a meal unlike any you've had before." Max stepped close and stroked the side of Chris's face with cold fingers. "Try this." He held out a bottle.

A coppery scent wafted up to Chris's nostrils, and desperation won out. He snatched the proffered bottle and gulped down its contents.

Halfway through, Max grabbed it back and pushed him away with one hand as if he were no more than an annoying child. "Slow down, or you'll retch. You don't want to waste such precious drink."

Leaning against the wall again, Chris dragged his arm across his mouth as he watched the bottle, considering the possibility of wresting it from the stranger's grip. Max sipped slowly, delicately, teasingly, and, after a long moment, handed it back.

Chris raised it to his mouth again. The cool, thick liquid did amazing things to his senses as he drank. It didn't fill his stomach, but his mind and emotions. And he felt things that were not his to feel: the chill of a knife against his arm, the burning slice of metal into skin, the weakness from blood letting. And then more, deeper sensations: joy of fatherhood, love of a gray-haired woman, and the deep sorrow of love lost. None of these memories were his, and yet they became so. They were old memories, shadowed with time.

"Wonderful, isn't it?" Max whispered. "And it gets so much better."

A shiver ran up Chris's spine as he stared at the empty bottle.

The cathedral bell tolled once; sound crashed through the Boston streets like thunder from a lightning strike mere feet away. Chris fell to his knees covering his ears and yelling against excruciating pain. The broken bottle glistened in moonlight from paving stones before him like ice crystals in morning sun.

Grabbing his arm, Max raised him gently to his feet and urged his hands away from his ears. "You'll soon be used to your abilities and senses. It's but a matter of time."

Suddenly tired, Chris thought of his sweet mother and dear sister, asleep in their beds, believing him safely tucked into his own. "I must go."

"To where?"

"To my home, my family."

"Oh, no, my boy. To them, you are dead. I am your family now."

The horror of Max's words chilled Chris's soul, and he turned to stare at the man. "Dead?"

"Yes. Feel your chest."

Chris pressed his palm to his chest and felt nothing. How could this be? He was alive, and yet he wasn't.

"You asked for eternity. No such gift comes without a price."

"But—"

"Ah, now, don't fret so." Max wrapped an arm around his shoulders. "I have a lovely treat for you, a special celebration for this night. Come."

Terror settled over Chris as he let himself be led down a

dark alley by this stranger, his *family*. How could he have made such a mistake? Would he truly be lost to those he loved? After all the times his mother had wept into his coat when he'd returned to her from the sea, would she now weep into her hands?

"This hunger," he said, wanting to ask but not knowing how.

"It is the call of blood," Max said. "Never fear. You will learn to control it in time." He spread his free arm wide, motioning toward the sky and earth around them. "All of this is now yours to do with as you wish. Isn't it as I promised? No man can harm you, and no woman will break your heart. You have but few things to fear."

"Fear?"

"Well," Max said, "you must avoid sunlight. You walk in the night. And a wooden stake through the heart will turn you to dust. But we won't discuss those things now." They stopped before a small stone building, and Max smiled at him. "Time to enjoy." He pushed open the thick door with one finger.

Inside, warmth glowed from an open hearth, softening a small room to orange. A heavy wooden table held bowls of food, none of which looked appealing. This was all he saw as he peered in, but he knew there were people in this room. He heard them. And smelled them.

He *heard* their heartbeats.

"Go on, sweet prince," Max said, urging him forward with a gentle shove to his shoulder. "Our treats await."

Ducking through the doorway, Chris realized the occupants were women before he saw them, and he wasn't disappointed. Two women, neither more than twenty years of age, sat on a large bed, each wearing only a chemise. Their similarities— both had reddish brown hair, blue eyes, large breasts, and enticing figures—suggested a family tie. Not quite twins, but doubtless sisters.

"Allow me to introduce the young ladies," Max said, "Susanna and Margaret Clarke. Their father is the good Reverend Clarke. Aren't they lovely?"

Chris felt as if he were rooted to the floor. Scents swirled around him and into his head, and again his vision changed. Orange faded to shimmering red. The women sat like amazing creatures, sirens, threatening to capture his soul with their smiles.

He'd always had a way with the ladies, but had never lost his heart. As he stood before these two, he felt as if he were about to lose much more.

Max's hand on his shoulder stopped the forward progress he hadn't noticed he was making.

"The young ladies are anxious to experience pleasures of the flesh, as I'm sure you are." Max leaned close to whisper to him. "They will be your first lesson in restraint. Remember, creatures such as these require delicate handling."

Chris's vision cleared a little and he licked his dry lips.

Margaret stretched a hand toward him, and he enveloped her fingers in his and bowed. He didn't trust his voice enough to speak.

Susanna covered her mouth to muffle a giggle. Her blue eyes glistened with mischief in the lamplight.

Suddenly, Chris felt a festive excitement in the air, and smiled as he settled into a chair beside the bed.

Max made a production of pouring wine and distributing goblets to each of them, then raised his in toast.

"To love," he said. "May it be as eternal as I am."

Susanna giggled again and drank.

Chris sipped from the goblet, expecting the rich taste of a hearty wine, but found nothing more than watery, tasteless liquid.

He frowned at Max, who shrugged. "You'll soon understand."

Holding the goblet helped Chris cling to restraint. The strange hunger from earlier had returned, this time tugging at his entire being. He listened to the steady beats of hearts, at first drowning out all noise, but then softening to the background as he grew used to the sound. Max chatted with the women about Boston and their family's history, but none of the words interested Chris. Instead, he was drawn to the beauty of Margaret's warm, pale flesh in candlelight, the way it glistened and changed hue as she moved.

He followed the progress of her fingertips as they traced the neckline of her delicate chemise, rising and falling over the swell of each barely hidden breast. She watched him watching her, her eyes darkening with desire, and Chris's body reacted to her invitation. He glanced at Max, who had settled onto the foot of the bed, wine in hand, talking as if with old friends, and he caught the warning look. Whatever the plan, it was not yet time to act.

Max's look was not the only thing stopping him, however. Chris pretended to sip from the goblet as he tried to sort out his new urges. He'd bedded women before, and understood the desire to part Margaret's sumptuous thighs and bury his cock in her waiting heat. What he didn't understand was this new need to take more than just her body. He wanted her soul, and her dreams.

At Max's urging, Susanna rose from the bed, turned her back to her audience, and slowly, mischievously, lowered her chemise to expose her back and then her pretty, rounded buttocks, and the backs of her pale legs. She stepped out of the garment and drew it up to cover the front of her body as she spun around, laughing.

Max deposited his goblet on the floor and applauded the young woman's performance as if at the opera house, and she laughed even more. Then he patted the bed and she sat beside him, facing him with her legs drawn up under her garment.

Max traced the tops of her shoulders. "You, my dear, are

more beautiful than French dancers whose performances are attended by kings and queens."

"You're teasing me, sir," Susanna said, her cheeks reddening.

"Not at all." He leaned forward and replaced his touch with tender kisses, moving from her shoulder to the side of her slender neck.

A strange, aching pulse beat in Chris's gums, and he traced the pain with his tongue. When he found his incisors growing, he gulped.

As if he'd heard the noise, Max turned his head, glanced at Chris, and smiled. His lips parted to reveal animal-like fangs. Oddly enough, the women seemed not to notice, or not to care.

"Quite lovely," Max said softly, lowering his lips to Susanna's shoulder again. Slowly, he drew her cloth covering from her grip and discarded it, leaving the young woman sitting before him completely bare.

He was right in his assessment; she was lovely. Her young, pale flesh tightened over supple curves. Her full breasts ended in bright pink nipples that crinkled and stiffened as Max continued his attention to her shoulder.

Chris had never watched another man seduce a woman, and found himself riveted to the sight.

Max touched her slender waist and then the sides of her breasts, and Susanna's eyes closed. Her breathing grew louder as Max explored more of her, caressing her breasts and pinching the little pink buds. Chris could almost feel the heat of her skin in his own fingertips.

The young woman's hands encircled Max's shoulders and she groaned softly. The noise invaded Chris's body with braided sensations of power, longing and hunger. In his mind, he saw a wolf cornering its weary prey.

Without effort, Max drew the young woman up to his lap and she straddled him, her back to Chris, and Max's hands slid up and down her sides and across her quivering buttocks.

Chris glanced at Margaret and found her also watching the scene before them, one hand inside her chemise, caressing her own breast. His breeches tightened to discomfort.

Susanna drew Max's face to hers and kissed him, and Max's hands settled on her buttocks, massaging and squeezing. The young woman began to ride what had to be the man's cock swelling in his breeches under her, if he were a man at all.

Chris discovered his body matching the rhythm with unconscious movement, and, relinquishing his goblet, he rested his hand in his lap for discreet friction. His hearing noticeably sharpened and the strange red hue invaded the room once again.

Max glanced at him over Susanna's shoulder with eyes that had changed to a golden beastlike color, and he opened his mouth to reveal glistening fangs poised at the woman's neck.

A strange growl rose to fill the air. Chris started when he realized the noise came from his own throat, as well as that of his tutor. As Max's mouth closed over Susanna's flesh, the woman cried out in ecstasy. She gripped Max and rode out the waves of pleasure against his clothed body.

Chris knew instinctively that Max fed from his prey at that moment, showing the way.

Fighting a wave of overwhelming hunger, Chris rose and turned his attention to Margaret. The woman looked up at him with wide eyes, but she didn't recoil.

He focused on the thundering beat of her heart as he extended his hand, and she took it, rising to her bare feet before him.

She was taller than he'd realized, only inches shorter than his own six feet. Her breasts rose and fell quickly with shallow breaths, and again he thought of the cornered prey.

Any sympathy he might have felt in the past had vanished.

Remembering Max's instruction of delicate handling, he eased the fine linen chemise off of Margaret's shoulder and kissed her exposed flesh. She tasted vaguely of salt and something more, something strikingly feminine. The flavor weakened his knees and he fought to remain standing.

Her scent delighted his senses, drawing forth the same growl that had risen from his throat before. Her hand scorched his chest through his shirt.

He held her waist, savoring the heat rising from under the cloth, needing more. Urging her before him, he moved to the bed and lowered her onto it, holding her in one arm as he carefully stretched out at her side.

Her lovely mouth opened under his and he tasted her, stroking her velvety tongue with his own, as he let his hand slide down the length of her. She trembled under his touch, stoking his blazing need for her.

Drawing her chemise up to her waist, he touched bare thigh and buttock, and then reached between her legs as she sucked hard on his tongue and rose up to his touch. Soft hair gave way to the cleft of her cunt and she raised one knee to allow him access.

The specter of a beast rose in his mind, a snarling creature with knifelike claws, hideous fangs, and cold, lifeless eyes. He drew Margaret under him and freed his cock from his breeches. The beast pushed him on, whispering of delights yet to come. "Feed," it said, "drink."

He pressed his cock to her waiting wetness, ready to force his way in, when he heard another voice. "Restraint, my boy."

Trembling, he closed his eyes, focused on Max's command, and mentally wrestled with the strange beast.

Margaret's heartbeat pounded in his head, and her warm breath slid across his cheek.

As a measure of control returned, he kissed her mouth, and her beautiful face. Still poised to mount her, he waited now, relishing the anticipation.

Margaret's body heated beneath him, moving with a hint of

rhythm, and her hands caressed his back and his buttocks. Delicious shivers coursed through him.

"Don't stop," she whispered, scraping her fingernails up the back of his shirt.

His earlier struggles dissolved as the beast broke free.

Pushing up onto stiff arms, he gazed down at her as he entered her in one brutal stroke, savored the pained pleasure on her face. She whimpered her submission as she gripped his shirt in her fists. With her bottom lip between her teeth, she turned her head.

He stared at the steady rise and fall of the pulse in her neck, and listened to the melodic *whoosh, whoosh, whoosh*. The beast no longer whispered demands, but controlled him completely as he opened his mouth.

He sank his fangs into her soft, sweet flesh, and his world exploded.

In a rush, her heartbeat became his, pounding in his chest, and every nerve in his body jumped to life. He felt her, tasted her, knew her. Her dreams filled his thoughts, tainted by her life, and he felt each of her joys and pains as if they were his own. He wanted to cry, and to sing, and to mourn as she had.

Then the ecstasy slammed into him with the force of a killer ocean wave, washing his world from its foundation.

He pumped his seed into her and she tightened around his cock, demanding more, screaming her release. His joy soared even higher as he felt her thrilling to the fullness of his phallus.

Too much, too intense, he drank. He needed more. She became his, melting into his soul.

Suddenly, his arms were empty and he was flying across the room.

Still shaking with pleasure, dreaming her dreams, he opened his eyes to find Max pressing him to the wall, one hand clamped around his throat.

"Enough."

Savoring the last remnant of blood on his lips, he glanced to where Margaret lay sprawled on the bed, her face pale, and her eyes closed. Blood oozed from holes in her throat.

"Is she . . . have I killed her?"

Max turned his head, perhaps listening to the room behind him. "No, but you would have." He released his hold on Chris's throat, and remained standing close. "Now that you know the intensity of the pleasure, you must learn to control it. There is a time for killing, and a time for entertainment. Do you understand?"

Chris considered the amazing sensations he'd just experienced, recalled the desire to drain Margaret of every moment of her life, and shuddered at his newfound power.

"Yes."

Max smiled and straightened Chris's shirt. "Good. Now we have time to enjoy our treats. Are you prepared for lesson number two?"

Chris nodded. A brief thought of his mother and sister skittered through his mind and disappeared. An eternity of pleasure stretched before him. Perhaps Max was right about this gift.

He turned his attention to the lovely Susanna. The younger of the two, she was even more scrumptious than her sister, whom she now caressed but without much concern.

Susanna looked up at him, demurely batting her eyelashes.

Chris knelt beside the bed, touching her silky feet and ankles, and she pushed a strand of his hair back from his face as she ran the tip of her pink tongue back and forth across her bottom lip.

"Remember, I've already had a taste of this one," Max said. "You must be extra careful."

The beast woke again.

Chris drew her hand down to his mouth and kissed it, and she laughed and pulled it away. Then she crooked a finger at him.

He crawled up onto the bed, ready to take his place between her legs, but she pushed him over playfully.

His prick rose stiffly from his open breeches, and she studied it with wide eyes, then with warm fingers.

Growling softly, he closed his eyes to the sweet pleasure. Never before had a woman's touch felt so exciting, as if his skin had taken on new abilities. His fangs extended as they had before, and he heard every breath she took.

The old feather mattress depressed, rocking him to the side as she moved around to straddle him. She rubbed his cock with both hands and pressed it to her soft mound.

Max stood beside them, stroking Susanna's hair and shoulders, but she ignored him as she rose and pointed Chris's swollen rod into her cunt. Her tightness proved a difficulty to be overcome by wiggling and writhing, and he clenched his fists to keep from grabbing her and forcing her down.

One delicious inch at a time, she enveloped him with her searing heat, until she'd taken all she could and whimpered. She leaned forward, ripped open his shirt, and used his chest for leverage to raise and lower herself onto him, stroking him with her wet heat until he was nearly lost again.

He considered drawing her down to his chest so he could pierce her neck, but managed to remember Max's warning. As she tightened and increased her pace, he lifted one of her hands to his face and sucked on her wrist, tasting her salty flesh, feeling the pounding pulse beneath his lips.

Carefully, he nicked her skin and locked his mouth onto her arm, and her lovely voice filled the room with sounds of pleasure. As her blood seeped down his throat, he groaned. Her pulsing delight drew him slowly over the edge of a capping ocean swell, and he filled her with all his body had left.

"Stop now," Max whispered.

Chris released her thin arm and her wrist rolled from his mouth, and she fell forward panting, pressing her forehead to his chest. The last few blessed pulses bit at his softening prick, drawing his lips up into a smile.

"Wonderfully done," Max said. "I knew I'd chosen well."

Ancient memories faded and Chris straightened. He'd been naïve then, that first night. Darkness had meant nothing more than the promise of illicit pleasure.

He'd paid in loneliness and regret many times over for those early years.

Now he had a mission to complete, and he couldn't allow anything to get in his way. Especially not the enticing Dr. Nicole Stephenson.

The memory of her scent nearly made him swoon. What was it about her?

Perhaps it was simply the amount of time he'd spent around her, denying his desires. That must be it.

True, she was unusually intelligent, and they'd spent many nights discussing theories about various aspects of Maya culture. Her reasoning powers were quite remarkable for a mortal.

But he'd encountered intelligent women before.

And attractive ones.

Why was this one testing his limits?

Shaking his head at his own foolishness, Chris picked up the empty bags, tucked them into the rear of the Land Rover, and started back for the lights of the camp. He ran his tongue along his incisors to be certain they'd returned to their normal size, then watched the mortals illuminated in artificial light as they clustered around the stone ledge, arguing its meaning.

Nicole glanced over at him as he stepped into the ring of light, and a blush rose in her cheek.

Chris looked away, wondering at the renewed nagging thirst.

How much longer would he be able to maintain his position as an active member of the dig without giving himself away?

"All right, everyone, back to work."

Her voice broke up the celebration and sent a shiver down his spine.

2

"I need this area uncovered before the night's over." Nicole signaled a circle five meters in diameter with the glyphs she'd unearthed the night before in the center. "Somewhere here must be an opening to a tomb."

Students went to work like a nest of disturbed ants, hammering in metal stakes, laying out grids, preparing for work. Brandon, who had abandoned his trash pit somewhat reluctantly, directed with his clipboard in hand.

Wiping sweat from her forehead, Nicole glanced out at the sound of an approaching vehicle. The sun had disappeared below the horizon twenty minutes ago. Like clockwork, Chris Marsh arrived in his Land Rover and parked on the far side of the lot. She saw his outline against the darkening jungle as he walked around the back of the vehicle.

The man confused her, and she hated confusion.

Her world was full of mystery—mysteries of the past—but orderly. As she uncovered one piece, she examined it from all sides, interpreted it based on what had been discovered before, and catalogued it for future reference. There were moments of excitement, like the one the night before when she'd found the glyphs, but they were understandable and not completely unexpected.

She had no reference point for Chris Marsh and no idea what to expect. Hell, she didn't even know where he went when he left the site.

The man was gorgeous, tall and slender with sandy blond hair a bit on the long side, piercing blue eyes, and a face that could have been carved by Michelangelo. What she'd seen of his arms when he rolled up the sleeves of his white cotton shirts suggested a tightly muscled torso, brown from hard work in the sun, yet she'd never seen him in sunlight. When he'd first approached her with financing for the project and the stipulation that they only dig at night, she'd agreed that summer heat in the Yucatan could be brutal and that night work was a good idea. She'd assumed he'd stick around after daybreak when things got interesting. Fifteen hours ago, she'd suggested they continue excavating to look for the tomb. Marsh had insisted they shut down operations, reminding her of their agreement, and then he'd fled the site as if his life had depended on it.

Strange man.

Still, his insistence on working at night wasn't what confused her. Archaeology had its share of eccentric scientists. It was the way her body reacted to being near him that had her puzzled.

At thirty-two, Nicole was no stranger to sex. Three of the men she'd slept with had been fellow archaeologists with whom she'd shared a sleeping bag or hotel room. One had been a reporter who had written an article about her winning the Letty Award. A few years ago, she'd nearly fallen for a musician, Zack, but had come to her senses when she'd found him in bed with a stoned coed.

Never had she lost control around a man. Never had she lost her head.

Chris Marsh made her blood boil. Whenever he stood within ten feet of her, she wanted to throw herself into his arms. She always felt on the verge of losing her balance around him, and found her clothing as confining as chain mail. And when she crawled into her hammock each morning, she dreamed of him. Usually, in her dreams, the two of them had sex in strange places, like on a table in a crowded room, or on the floor in one of her classrooms. Once she'd dreamt of them screwing on the wooden deck of a pirate ship, of all things, surrounded by leering pirates.

She'd never really been all that crazy about sex. No man had ever brought her to a climax, and she'd gotten fairly good at faking it. She knew, from all the stories she'd heard and books she'd read, that she should enjoy intercourse, but she just never had. She'd decided long ago that she was probably missing some necessary hormones.

Christ. Had her biological clock kicked into overdrive? She didn't want a family. She didn't even want a husband. But maybe nature had taken control of her sex drive.

Whatever the reason, Chris Marsh was making her crazy.

Ancient leather satchel in hand, he strode onto the site wearing his typical white cotton shirt open at the throat, black pants that so nicely hugged his tight butt, and black leather boots. He nodded in her direction, and then squinted against the sudden glare of the lights as he unpacked his case, laying out notes, reference books, and notebooks on the folding table, same as every night. He showed no sign of regret at closing the dig at dawn. In fact, he showed no emotion at all.

Nicole took a deep breath and turned her attention to the activity around her. She knew they were close to a major discovery—she felt it in her bones. She didn't have time for confusion.

Eric and Megan began to excavate, and two of the kids, as she thought of the groups of students, hauled off buckets of material for screening. Brandon took notes.

Nicole eased down to her knees at the side of the main excavation. She could feel a doorway calling to her, whispering like a pyramid sighing its first breath in a thousand years.

"Here's what I have so far," Brandon said, handing her his notebook.

She took it and tilted it toward the overhead lights to review the drawings and notes, all done in a perfect hand full of artistic flare that was professionally controlled. "Make sure you get this measurement."

He leaned close to see where she pointed. "Between seven and eight?"

"Yep."

"Will do."

She smiled up at the young man, who could easily rise to be one of the best in the field someday. "This is great stuff."

His olive complexion reddened a shade as he accepted the notebook, brandishing a crooked grin. "Thanks, boss."

She patted his shoulder and returned her attention to the excavation.

Brandon moved around to the far side of the pit.

"Any signs yet?"

Nicole jumped at the voice from directly behind her and glanced back at Chris. His blue-eyed gaze sent a chill up her back in spite of the lingering heat radiating from surrounding rock and sand.

"Not yet, but I'm sure it's right here."

He nodded and crouched beside her, watching intently.

She found his scrutiny unnerving, and finally sat back on her heels. "Would you mind—?"

"Look!"

They both turned toward Eric, who was pointing with his hand shovel. "Look at the way these two stones come together. No way this is freakin' natural."

Moving carefully, Nicole skirted the excavation until she

stood at Eric's shoulder. Chris followed precisely in her foot-steps, just as she'd instructed him the first night. He now stood right behind her, almost too close. She held her breath antici-pating his touch.

In front of Eric, two rectangular stones came together at a ninety-degree angle, both obviously hand-carved in spite of smoothing from ages of wind and rain.

She pointed. "Try right in front of that one."

Eric grabbed a large paintbrush from his back pocket and began to brush away sand with enthusiasm.

"Carefully!"

He grunted at her warning and continued to work until he was well below the level of the top stone. Then he sat back and grinned. "This is it."

"Yes!" Nicole hissed. She motioned for Brandon and Megan. "Over here. We need to get this open."

The four of them worked in earnest, filling buckets with loose soil and sand. In what seemed like minutes, they were down two courses of stone and a well-defined opening had appeared as if it were a gateway into the underworld. She hoped that was exactly what it was—an entrance to an underground tomb.

As she stood to stretch, she realized they'd actually been working for hours. "Take a break," she said. "I want pictures of everything before we go any farther."

Brandon picked up the camera and went to work as the oth-ers stumbled off to water bottles and collapsed.

Chris stood in the shadow of the nightlights with his hands in his pockets, a soft night breeze lifting his blond hair from his collar, watching her approach.

"Aren't you thirsty?" she asked, trying to ignore the jittery feeling in her stomach the sight of him produced.

His eyes widened a bit at her question and he shook his head.

It suddenly occurred to her that she couldn't remember seeing him drink. In fact, he didn't carry a water bottle with him, did he?

She tossed the thought away. He must carry water. No one could survive in this place without water, not even working at night.

His gaze swept over her, and then he quickly looked away, as if he were a schoolboy caught staring at a nude in a museum. Nicole bit her cheek in order not to laugh.

She drank her fill as she watched Brandon snap off a few pictures, then make notes and take measurements.

"You think this is"—she turned to look at Chris and found the spot where he'd stood now vacant—"it?" She searched the site, and then squinted into the shadows. Where the hell had he gone?

Abandoning her water bottle on a rock, she tiptoed into the darkness. Once out of the ring of halogen lights, she realized a half moon lit the surrounding clearing, leaving the jungle looming in the background as true blackness.

She thought she saw something move across the trail ahead. "Chris? Is that—?"

He grabbed her arm and she gasped as she swung around to face him. He stood as a shadow among shadows with only his white shirt and blond hair truly visible in the night.

"You shouldn't have followed me out here," he said, his voice low and dangerous.

"I wasn't following you." She swallowed hard against the lie.

He drew her closer until she stood inches from him, staring up into his glowing eyes. How could they possibly reflect so much moonlight?

"I can't seem to resist you, Nicole."

The way he said her name made her insides quake.

Wrapping his arm around her waist, he drew her up hard against him. She knew, as a professional working on a project he financed, she should protest and struggle against his embrace, but she couldn't find the will. He loomed over her as if he'd gained several inches in height, and her belly quivered.

Her hands found soft cotton over steel muscles as she opened them on his chest and ran them up to his broad shoulders.

His face, a shadowy blur, moved closer, and her breath came out in a ragged stutter. And then his cool lips pressed to hers, urging her mouth open as his hand slid behind her neck, cradling her head and holding her close.

She melted against him, fisting her hands in his shirt. She'd longed to be in just this spot, standing in his arms, since the first moment she saw him, and began to tremble as she wondered what would happen next.

He tasted her as if sampling a precious wine, and she whimpered.

He drew her closer, one hand in the middle of her back, as his tongue found hers and circled it tentatively first, and then with more certainty.

His hand rode slowly down her spine, raising goose bumps in her flesh, pulling her focus away from his mouth. His fingers slid over her butt and she shuddered.

He groaned softly and gripped her bottom, lifting until her feet left the ground. She clung to him, her legs locked around his hips, her arms wrapped around his neck, her mouth welded to his.

He gripped her with ferocious strength, holding her as if against escape, taking her mouth with feverish need that echoed back from her very core.

She rolled her hips forward until she felt the length of his erection pressed firmly into her crotch, certain she must be drenching him through their clothes.

With one hand on her ass and the other holding the back of her head, he drew her up and eased her back down fractions of an inch, just enough to torture her swollen clit inside her saturated panties. Her whimper grew to a groan as she sucked hard on his mouth, stroking his tongue with her own. Excitement quivered through her body.

Ripping his mouth from hers, he moved it to the side of her neck and locked his lips onto her flesh.

God, she'd never been so turned on in her life.

Gasping for breath, she let her head fall back and released all semblance of rational thought as he gripped her more firmly and moved her faster, growing and hardening under her pussy. A line of erotic pleasure formed between the spot on her neck where he sucked and her clit, and every muscle in her body tightened against a promised onslaught.

She imagined the excitement of his erection freed and entering her in long, passionate thrusts, searching for her depth, uncontrolled, filling her with hot cum.

And then she felt the explosion, the amazing release of energy, and she clung to him as her body writhed in its own rhythm. Spasms of pleasure shot through her, starting in her crotch and erupting out to fill the night sky.

His mouth covered hers again, muffling her cries, as the bliss continued. Her consciousness narrowed down to the two of them, entwined under the stars, civilization shed in favor of animal lust. She prayed to ancient gods that the ecstasy continue forever.

The climax slowed to long, rolling waves, and finally faded away. Vaginal muscles twitched and pulsed.

Nicole gasped against his mouth, suddenly aware of what she'd just done. Her face burned. She was glad now that Chris had insisted on night work. At least he wouldn't be able to see her blushing fiercely. Was he amused or horrified at her unprofessional behavior?

She unlocked her ankles and he eased her slowly down the front of his hard, lean body. How had he managed to hold her like that without any hint of strain? She wasn't exactly willowy.

But he didn't release her right away. She stood in his arms, her face pressed to the front of his shirt, her heart thundering in her chest. A breeze circled them and died.

Thank God he didn't laugh.

"Too tempting," he whispered.

She leaned back and looked up. "What?"

He gazed down at her with an expression she'd never seen on a man's face before, almost like that of a starving beast cornered by hunters.

He swallowed hard and the expression faded.

Then he backed away from her, leaving her to manage on shaky legs. As she watched, he turned and disappeared into the night.

Not only had she just lost her head, she'd lost every shred of self-control and dignity. Nicole staggered to a nearby rock and sat, leaning forward to hold her face in her hands.

How the hell could she have let this happen?

Two pints did almost nothing to satisfy him this time. He huddled behind a boulder a quarter mile from the site, terrified someone might find him in this state, waiting for the hunger to diminish to a manageable level.

She'd caught him off guard. Her scent had filled the air, stronger than any night-blooming cereus, whispering to him of earth's mysteries. Jealousy had sunk its teeth into him when he'd watched her with Brandon. The two shared a love of archaeology, but there was something more. Had they shared a bed? He snarled at the thought.

He'd tried to walk away from her, but he'd needed to hold her, wanted to take her as a man would, and hungered for her as only a beast could. She had no idea how close she'd come to being drained of her life, right there in the Mexican night, not thirty yards from her coworkers.

He wouldn't have stopped; he knew it. He wanted every dream, every desire, every moment of pleasure. He wanted to steal them from her and make them his own.

He'd tasted her skin, the salty, dusty, sweet flesh at the side of her neck where her pulse rose and fell just below the surface. His fangs had ached fiercely to tap into that well of delight.

And then he'd tasted something else, something exquisite. He'd tasted the rays of the sun woven into her skin.

Would he ever feel the warmth of the sun again? Could the legend possibly be true?

How many times had he believed he'd found the cure? Max had started him on the quest long ago.

Chris wrapped one arm around his knees and shivered against the need as he raised his gaze to the heavens. There had been a night not so different than this one in the swamps outside New Orleans, where Max had dragged him off in search of a promised elixir. When had that been? 1820? Perhaps closer to 1830. The air, heavy with summer's moisture, had been laden with the scents of rotting fish and decaying plants . . .

"Must we really take this . . . this vessel?" Max stood on the shore, eyeing the hollowed-out log.

"*Oui*, monsieur." Their burly guide stiffened at the insult. "This pirogue, she is the best in the swamp. Don't you worry, you. Madame LaCour, she put a curse on me if I let you drown, *n'est-ce pas?*"

Without protest, Chris had settled into the front of the flat-bottomed boat and watched his own shadow, cast by the lantern placed in the middle, glide across black water. Yellow eyes reflected light back as they passed alligators, bullfrogs, and other unidentifiable creatures.

Pierre, their guide, stood in the back of the pirogue and pushed them through the labyrinth of cypress knees and trunks with a long pole that slurped each time he pulled it from the sucking muddy bottom.

Instinctively, Chris searched the area for shelter. Even in such a shadowed world, daybreak would bring enough sunlight to turn them both to dust. Nothing held the promise of refuge.

He cocked his head at the sounds as they approached a piece of high ground illuminated by crackling firelight. Foreign instruments accompanied voices in a strange chant.

Pierre eased the pirogue to the muddy shore, and a large, dark man offered a hand to help them out. Chris accepted the offer, as unnecessary as it was, in order not to draw attention to himself. He could easily have hopped to shore, or into the treetops, for that matter.

A massive woman wearing a brightly colored garment and adorned with all kinds of feathers, claws, and glass beads, sat on a tree stump facing the fire, holding a bottle of rum in one hand and a painted gourd in the other. She shook the rattling gourd as she sang. At least a dozen young men and women, most scantily clad, circled the fire swaying and chanting with her.

"Madame LaCour, I presume," Max said, stepping toward the hefty woman with outstretched hand.

Madame LaCour glared at Max for a long moment, ignoring his hand, and then at Chris.

Two attendants carried a log forward and placed it on the ground near the woman. She motioned for Chris and Max to sit as she drank from her bottle.

The group fell silent. Around them, the swamp buzzed and croaked with nightlife.

Madame LaCour reached into a pouch hanging around her neck and withdrew a pinch of powder which she tossed at the fire. A blue flame rose up the arc of powder, reaching for her hand, and then the fire crackled and spit, causing shadows to leap in the trees.

"You have the curse of darkness," she said. Her voice sounded dry and crackly like winter leaves underfoot. "You lookin' for gris-gris to give you light, take away the curse." She took another swig from her bottle, and then turned a toothless grin on Max and Chris. "Madame LaCour has many powers."

She shook the rattle above her head and her entourage began to dance and clap, chanting in a language Chris had never heard. Two of the dancers coaxed strange sounds from oddly shaped flutes of some kind.

One of the young women passed close in front of him, twirling and smiling. She had steel-grey eyes, skin the color of maple syrup, and full, firm breasts exposed to the night air. She wore only a cloth around her hips with nothing covering her long legs or delicate feet, and she appeared to enjoy his admiring gaze.

The group suddenly quieted as Madame LaCour lowered the gourd to her lap, but they continued to circle in subdued dance steps.

"You must first offer great sacrifice," she said, "in both blood and money before I make gris-gris."

"Of course," Max said, withdrawing a leather pouch from inside his jacket and holding it out to her. "I brought the amount we agreed to."

Madame LaCour's eyes widened and she wagged her rattle at Max. "Madame LaCour will not be soiled by greed of man. You give them foul riches to Henry."

A young man, well muscled and wearing very little, approached with a red cloth draped across his hands, and knelt in front of Max, who placed the leather pouch in the center of the cloth. Henry folded the cloth three times and laid it at Madame LaCour's feet.

With her hand on Henry's head, the woman waved her rattle and murmured something, then threw another pinch of powder at the fire.

Chris watched the grey-eyed beauty dance by again, firelight glistening off her skin. She smiled openly at him and raised her eyebrows suggestively.

Once the bonfire had settled back down, Madame LaCour nodded to Henry, who picked up the folded cloth and tossed it into the blaze. The group cheered.

"Damned waste of bills," Max muttered.

"And now you prepare for blood sacrifice." She stood, motioning for Chris and Max to do the same.

As soon as Chris rose, a man and woman ran to him and drew off his clothing to bare his upper body. The man held his arms from behind while the woman pulled off his boots and tossed them aside. As he stood in nothing but his britches, the grey-eyed woman approached, offering a bottle.

Chris glanced over to find Max accepting a similar offer from Henry with a nod and raising the bottle to his lips.

Chris sniffed the bottle first, noting several smells he could identify: saffron, rum, and opium. Had he been human, the mixture would probably have knocked him out. As a vampire, it most likely would have little effect.

Resigning himself to do whatever he must for a chance to escape eternal night, he sipped the liquid. It was unpleasant but bearable, so he swallowed a mouthful.

He glanced down to where the grey-eyed woman ran her hands over his stomach and along his sides.

"What's your name?" he asked.

"Angel," she whispered.

"Angel. How appropriately unusual."

She smiled up at him as her heated palms circled his chest.

He drank some more from the bottle.

"You are handsome man," Angel said, her voice heavily accented. "We dance together, no?"

"Yes."

Letting her lead him by the hand, he circled the fire, sipping from the bottle and enjoying the sight of Angel, her hips swaying and thrusting provocatively with every step.

Glancing back, he saw Max following Henry in much the same way, eyeing the young man with interest.

Long before he'd emptied the bottle, Chris began to feel giddy. Laughing, he pulled Angel into his arms. She didn't resist as he took her mouth, enjoying her unusual taste. Her tongue circled his own, teasing his desire forward. His head filled with thoughts of trade winds blowing across open oceans and swaying palm trees, heavy with coconuts.

She pushed him away playfully, raking her nails across his chest and leaving red welts swelling with blood. The scent excited him, and he drew her back more roughly. Her laughter bounced through his muddled brain as he pressed his mouth to the side of her slender neck, fighting the urge to sink his fangs into her flesh.

She drew him down with her as she dropped to her knees, and then to her back, cushioning his hips in her open thighs.

The music and dancers faded into a blur of sound and scent as Chris focused on the steady beat of Angel's heart. Her body whispered to him of pleasures he had not enjoyed in many years, and never in a situation such as this, surrounded by human witnesses. He knew they watched, but he didn't care. What difference would it make if they discovered his secret?

On straightened arms, he gazed down at Angel whose form seemed to shimmer and swirl under him. The thin cloth around her hips had fallen away, leaving her uncovered, a tempting shadow in the firelight.

She gripped him between her knees and clawed at his torso as she writhed and raised her hips. Her grey eyes widened in invitation, and her tongue flicked across her upper lip.

Madness overtook him, a beast shredding his insides to get out. Desire darkened to hunger and greed. He withdrew his swollen phallus from his britches as he licked elongated fangs. With a growl, he drove his cock into tight, wet heat and fell onto her, piercing hot flesh, releasing sweet nectar, drawing out her screaming soul as he filled her throbbing cunt.

Time stopped, the earth tilted, and he slipped below the surface of a dark pool. Seaweed rose around him, entangled his ankles, and drew him down to impossible depths where water threatened to crush his bones.

White light suddenly exploded in his brain.

Howling in pain, he withdrew.

Cradling his head, curled on his side in wet grass, he watched a group of dancers lift Angel's limp body from the ground and raise her to the heavens. Past them, he saw Max gripping Henry's waist, thrusting against meaty buttocks, his head thrown back in bliss and his fangs protruding from his open mouth. With a roar, Max sank his fangs into Henry's muscular shoulder. The young man rose up against the attack, reaching back for Max as his own seed spilled onto the ground.

The two male bodies joined in ecstasy swam in his vision and he closed his eyes, no longer caring what happened to him. He heard Madame LaCour's rattle accompanied by cackling laughter, and then he fell into silence and utter blackness.

When he woke, he saw the murky sky above as a blur and knew the sun approached the eastern horizon. Holding his pounding head, he staggered to his feet and glanced around the site, deserted but for an empty rum bottle, smoldering embers, and an abandoned pirogue.

The scent of blood sharpened his vision and he looked down at the line across his chest, a clean knife slice closing as he stared. When had he been cut? And why? Was this the blood sacrifice Madame LaCour required?

A groan drew his attention to Max, who lay on his back several yards away, naked and also marked across the chest, rousing in the same state of confusion as Chris.

"My clothes," Max mumbled, turning over and rising to his hands and knees. He looked up at the lightening sky. "Bloody hell."

Chris stumbled in a circle around the remains of the fire, snatching clothing from the ground. He threw Max's garments at him as he pulled on his own shirt and coat, and drew on his boots.

His legs grew heavy and his skin began to heat at the approach of dawn. Whatever they'd gone through had done nothing to lessen the threat of sunlight. Grasping at what he could of panic, he grabbed Max's arm and dragged the older vampire with him to the shore. He threw Max to the ground, dropped beside him, and drew the flat-bottomed pirogue over the top of them both. Pressed to his master's body, he gripped the inside of the boat, hoping no one would come along and right it during the day.

"What the hell happened?" he asked, his voice echoing in the small space.

Max sighed. "Ah, dear boy, I believe we were used. I doubt my bills were truly thrown into the fire, and I think Madame LaCour may now have two fledgling vampires to control. Dangerous woman." He sighed again. "Did you know I was once a general in Caesar's army? I led legions into battle. I cowered before no threat on earth. Now, here I lie like a bloody spineless slug under a rock."

Starlight twinkled above in spite of the moon, the last throes of heavenly light before false dawn. How well he knew each minute of these hours when the sun's rays warmed other parts of the planet.

Madame LaCour had been right about one thing: the curse he carried, the curse of darkness. How could he even think of risking this chance to lift that curse?

After more than three centuries of existence, how could he want one woman so badly when there was so much at stake?

He couldn't. He wouldn't. No matter what, he must stay focused on his mission.

With the hunger abated and control returned, Chris rose to his feet and dusted off his pants. He carried the empty bags to his Land Rover and stashed them under the front seat, then started back for the dig.

In less than an hour, he'd pack up and head for shelter. He could easily keep his thoughts off the tempting professor that long.

"Hey, this rock's hard."

Chris froze, turning his face toward the woman's voice to his right.

"Not as hard as I am," a man answered.

For one blinding moment, he thought the voices belonged to Brandon and Nicole, and he shook with rage.

Two shadows appeared against the lighter ground, at least fifty yards away. Chris loosed his preternatural vision to identify Eric and Megan, embracing and kissing, and nearly collapsed with relief.

"Don't be crude," she said.

"Crude's my middle name." Eric laughed and pushed her against a large block, left over from construction possibly completed more than a thousand years earlier. They kissed.

Their groans of pleasure weakened Chris's knees. He stepped off the trail and crouched in the shadows, his incisors suddenly dropping into place. In spite of feeling like an intruder, he couldn't stop watching.

"Haven't you ever wanted to screw in the ruins?" Eric asked. "Just think, a millennium ago, some poor soul may have had his head chopped off right here."

Megan slapped his chest. "Oh, that's great. Now I'm really in the mood."

"Aw, come on."

They kissed again, their bodies pressing closer together.

"Wait." Megan turned her head. She spoke in a hoarse whisper. "What if someone sees us?"

"It's too dark."

"What if they hear us?"

Eric laughed quietly. "You'll just have to make sure you don't scream this time."

Their bodies leaned as one until she lay on top of the block, her bare legs wrapped around his hips, and their kissing grew more passionate.

Chris closed his eyes and listened, identifying each movement, feeling a part of the encounter as if he stood in Eric's place.

Hands brushed clothing aside, searching for flesh, hungry for more. Lips met, moved, opened to soft cries of surrender.

He heard quick tearing of a wrapper. "Wait," Eric breathed. "I don't want to drop it." Movement. "Okay, I got it."

More movement.

"Oh, yeah." Soft grunts as flesh met flesh.

Chris felt the surge of pleasure. Hardness penetrated soft wetness, pushing deeper with each enveloping thrust, releasing the scent of female arousal to the night air. He caught a hint of it on the breeze.

"Oh, fuck, that's good," Eric whispered. "Come for me, baby."

Megan's groans grew quicker, more urgent. She neared release.

Chris knew the tightness, the intensified longing, the white-hot need. His erection hardened to discomfort. He pictured Nicole under him, her head back, her mouth open, her breasts glistening with sweat, dark nipples tightening in the night air. He heard her whimper as her control slipped away, and smelled her scent as her juices flooded his cock.

Megan drew a stuttered breath, and cried out in release, her voice muffled against Eric's chest. Their bodies met faster, harder.

His muted cries of pleasure joined hers, and their rhythm slowed.

Both breathing hard, they lay together on the block.

Chris raised his gaze to them, a silhouette of satisfied lovers, and listened to the sweet song of their racing heartbeats.

"Shit," Eric whispered, "that was great."

"Yeah," Megan said. "But next time, I'm on top. You may not be hard anymore, but this fucking rock is."

They laughed together, enjoying their private joke.

Chris's chest tightened. He'd never share such a moment with Nicole, even if he allowed her close. He'd forfeited his chance at human tenderness—human love—long ago. Hunger would forever lurk just below the surface of his desire for her. The thought softened his erection, and his fangs receded, taking with them his unnatural hunger.

Silently, he got to his feet and traveled the trail to the site. Most of the remaining group lounged at the edge of imported light as Brandon completed his photographic and recording duties.

Nicole's gaze rose to meet Chris's, but her expression gave nothing away. She watched as if waiting for him to speak, then purposely turned her head.

3

Chris rode a wave of disappointment home just before dawn, and cursed himself for it. If he were lucky, Nicole would hate him for deserting her in the inky night.

The metal door clicked into place behind him.

Fighting heavy limbs and eyelids, he shed his dusty clothes and stepped into a hot shower. Steaming water washed away the dirt, but did little to ease his mind.

He needed to refocus his attention on the prize. After three hundred years of darkness, what wouldn't he give to step back into the world of light? Certainly his infatuation with a woman— even one as singular as Nicole Stephenson—couldn't hold him back.

Not even her. Not after all this time.

With renewed determination, he turned off the water, tow- eled off, and slipped into a silk robe. The fabric caressed his skin as he walked to the kitchen, poured a glass of nourishment, and carried it to the study.

In spite of the weariness of daybreak, he knew he wouldn't sleep. Not that he wasn't comfortable in the new house. In the month and a half that he'd had the place, no one had bothered him. He felt safe enough in the steel-reinforced basement apartment, and he enjoyed sitting outside listening to the ocean on his nights off.

No, it wasn't his surroundings. It was Nicole. Something about the way he was drawn to her spotlighted the fact that he was completely alone in the world. Restlessness tugged at his thoughts, leading them down paths they hadn't walked in many years. He sat at his desk and opened the top right drawer. Staring up from inside a dark frame were two blue eyes, much like his own, but surrounded by a face of sweetness and innocence.

He knew the small painting better than he knew his own hands, for he'd spent long hours accumulating into years, or perhaps decades, studying it. The woman, nineteen when she sat for the portrait, had lips the color of ripe cherries, and her hair shimmered like spun gold. Her brown dress and white lace set off her petite features perfectly, verifying her purity more surely than any words could have. In the background, a ray of sunshine fell through a window, setting ablaze a vase of cut roses.

"Abigail," he whispered, sliding one finger down the side of the beech wood frame, worn smooth by years of similar strokes.

Closing his eyes did nothing to diminish the lines of her face, a face he thought he'd never see again after Max took his life. And yet, he'd had that one brief moment years later to enjoy the perfection of her blue eyes in another's face . . .

"May I have this dance?" Chris extended his hand, palm up, and, as she bowed, he studied the top of the young lady's head where stray curls of her golden hair had escaped the bun to form a halo.

She was quite easily the prettiest woman at the ball.

"I'd be honored, sir."

She rose, placed her hand in his, and smiled.

Something about her smile felt familiar, although he knew he'd never seen her before. He hadn't been in Boston for years, certainly not since this lovely child had taken her first breath. She couldn't be more than nineteen, at most.

As they walked toward the dance floor, he sampled her scent and found it as inviting as the pale flesh left bare by the square front of her pretty pink gown.

"May I ask your name, sir?" Her voice was clear and polished, yet sweet in its cadence.

"Christopher Becker, at your service." He nodded, hoping the assumed surname sounded authentic enough. He'd practiced on the buggy ride across town.

"Mr. Becker, you're not from Boston."

"Connecticut. I'm here visiting a business acquaintance."

He listened to the steady beat of her heart, fast but not racing with fear. She was excited by his interest and the surroundings, no doubt. Music from violins and a harpsichord serenaded the elite of the city as they danced.

"And may I know the name of the most beautiful lady at the ball?"

Her cheeks flushed as she smiled. "I do not believe you mean me, sir."

"Indeed I do."

"My name is Abigail."

"Abigail." A small knot of regret tightened in his gut. "Beautiful name."

"Thank you, sir. I was named for my grandmother. In fact, I was even given her maiden name, as I was born on her birthday. Strickland. My full name is Abigail Strickland Percy."

Chris faltered a step.

The young woman turned to look at him. "Are you all right, sir? You look quite pale."

"Abigail Strickland?"

Her strawberry lips curved with a smile. "Do you know my grandmother?"

"I knew her once. She still lives, then?"

"Yes, sir, she does."

Abigail, his beautiful sister, was still alive? He had assumed her long gone from the world, as he knew his mother was since finding her grave years ago. He'd spent many nights recalling the sweetness of his sister's voice as she told him stories from her place at the stove while he warmed his frozen feet and filled his empty belly. He remembered the tenderness with which she'd tucked him into bed at night and kissed his forehead. Although only three years his elder, she'd often been like a mother to him, as their own mother had worked away her life to keep them fed.

He dropped his eyes to the small hand he held in his own and realized this young woman was his family, the grandchild of his sister. Had she been told of Abigail's brother, the one who disappeared mysteriously one dark night? Or had memory of him been erased from the pages of the family history?

If only he could see Abigail once more, know that her life had been a good one, before—

"If you know my grandmother, I must take news of you to her. I will visit her in three days. Shall I tell her I found you well?"

His gaze leapt to hers. Could he risk one brief visit?

"Ah, dear Christopher, there you are." Max appeared beside him and dropped his hand firmly to Chris's shoulder. "I should have looked for you first among the pretty ladies here tonight." He bowed to Abigail. "I hope you'll forgive me, my dear, for spiriting away your dance partner. Urgent business has arisen that demands our immediate attention."

Chris bowed and pressed Abigail's hand to his lips. Holding her gaze as long as he could, he let Max lead him away by the arm.

"What is this urgent business?" he demanded in a whisper once they'd reached the hall.

"The urgent business is keeping you from making a dreadful mistake. Can you imagine what would happen if your sister saw you now, unchanged in more than forty years? She would either know you for what you are, or assume you an apparition and die of fright. Neither outcome would be a good one, I assume."

"You were eavesdropping on my conversation."

"Fortunately."

"If I wish to visit my family—"

"I told you once before. I am your family now. You must not forget that, Christopher. If you expose yourself, you expose us all. I'm not the only one who would be upset by that prospect. And you would place your sister in grave danger. Is that what you want?"

Chris shook his head. "Of course not."

"I didn't think so."

Still gripping Chris's arm, Max led him up a large staircase, away from the music and sounds of dancing.

Just as well; he no longer felt festive. Disgust filled his mouth like bile as he realized he'd nearly fed from his own kin. He wanted to return to his room and sulk.

"Besides, I wouldn't want you to miss the little diversion I have planned."

Chris glanced at his master and found him grinning like a barn cat eyeing a limping mouse. "What diversion?"

"You'll see." He guided Chris down a long hallway of closed doors and slowed as they approached the last room. "I adore this new age, where the young people all work so hard to prove they aren't Puritans like their ancestors, don't you?" He released Chris in order to push open double doors, and ushered him in.

The oversized room sported a row of covered French windows, lavish Oriental rugs, a four-poster bed in the center, and a number of sofas and chairs. It also held two dozen guests or more, both men and women, in dress quite different from that seen downstairs. The men sported little more than breeches, and the women wore mostly chemises. They lounged around the room, playing games and eating from bowls of fruits and sweets. One couple embraced on one of the sofas, and another kissed as they stood in a corner. Hands fluttered over bare skin, and laughter filled the air.

What now?

Max leaned close to Chris. "Much better than a stuffy ball, don't you agree?"

"What have you talked these misguided mortals into?" Chris glanced at him. "They are mortals, aren't they?"

"Quite so, and I didn't talk them into anything. They played along rather willingly. Come." He led Chris by the arm again. "I've saved a few especially for you."

"A few?"

"Yes," Max hissed. "They look ever so delicious." Holding Chris's shoulders, he turned him to face three women on a sofa. A dark-haired beauty on one end stroked the waist-length blond hair of the young lady in the middle. On the other end, a redhead swung one shapely bare leg over the arm of the sofa and twirled an auburn ringlet around her fingers as she eyed Chris and Max.

"My friend here," said Max, "is not yet into the spirit of our little soiree. I do believe you ladies can help."

The blonde giggled as she and the dark-haired woman rose. Each took one side of Chris and began removing his clothing.

Normally, he would have been delighted by the prospect of enjoying three such attractive women at once, but he still felt the impact of seeing Abigail and realizing how far he must remain from one of the people he'd once loved so dearly. He wanted to shake the women off and run from the room, but he knew Max wouldn't be happy.

One thing he'd learned in forty years was that it was best to keep Max happy.

He glanced down at the redhead who remained seated, watching the other two work.

"Margaret says the men should not be allowed to wear anything," the blonde said, motioning to the redhead with her chin.

Margaret bit her bottom lip as they drew Chris's shirt off over his head. He had to admit, Max had picked three very attractive women for him.

"This is Mary," the blonde said, grazing his chest with her palm, "and I'm Anne." She smiled demurely as she let her hand slide down to his stomach. Her small, warm hand felt good on his skin.

Striding into the center of the room, Max clapped his hands for attention, and the mortals quieted. "Our first two contestants," he said, drawing two men to stand with him. "They will be the first to ascend Mount Olympus, where they will perform for the gods as all great athletes do."

The group cheered and whistled, and the two men flexed arm and chest muscles and posed. Both were well formed, and although Chris didn't completely share his master's taste for men, he admired their muscular physiques.

"Yum," Margaret said, apparently admiring them more than Chris did.

Max looked the contestants over. "Ah, but you must be as naked as the Greeks were who performed those great feats."

The two men eyed each other, and color rose in the face of the younger one, then they simultaneously unbuttoned their breeches and stepped out of them. As they glanced at each other again, it was the older one's turn to blush when he saw the size of the young man's prick.

The group laughed and applauded.

"Now, I need two volunteers."

Two women stepped forward, chided by their friends. Max handed them each a set of velvet ropes. With a bit of giggling and much showmanship, they soon had the two men's hands tied to posts on the bed so that they stood on opposite sides, facing outward, with their arms spread and their backs to each other.

Anne and Mary drew Chris down to the sofa they'd occupied, facing the bed from the foot, and caressed his shoulders and chest with their heated hands. They could see both contestants clearly. Neither man now offered much in the way of an erection. Margaret remained on the end of the sofa, ignoring her two compatriots and Chris, transfixed on the sport before them.

Max had staged some strange encounters in the past, but this one had to be the strangest.

Circling the room, Max drew four young ladies to their feet, whispered instructions to them, and led them to the bed, placing two on each side.

"And now," he said, standing before the gathering group with arms wide, as theatrical as ever, "let the contest begin. The first team to *drain* their contestant takes the prize, and the last man *standing*, as it were, is declared the champion. The spoils will be his."

The four women drew their chemises over their heads, tossed them to the floor, and quickly went to work on their captives.

Max had wisely split the two most shapely women, and paired them each with a younger, thinner mate. The two working on the younger man were both fair-haired, and the other two were darker and looked enough alike to be cousins.

The fair pair covered the young man's body with teasing touches and kisses, and soon had his cock on the rise. He wriggled and twitched under their hands, pulling against the ropes, and gooseflesh rose on his skin.

The darker pair went straight to the heart of the matter. The rounder one stood before the man and attended to her own breasts, squeezing and plucking at rose-colored nipples, quite obviously enjoying her own attention, while her cousin grabbed the man's penis in both hands and began to pull and push. The man groaned with pleasure, and quickly shut his eyes, perhaps to remove one source of stimulation.

With coaching from the audience, one of the fairer women dropped to her knees and drew the younger man's cock into her mouth. His phallus was impressive enough to reach halfway down her throat, but she managed to take in more than would have been expected. Her head moved back and forth as she fucked him with her cherry-red lips. His veined rod swelled and hardened until the glistening skin looked stretched to its limit. Her partner pinched and twisted the man's nipples, and the contestant groaned as his buttocks quivered and his knees shook.

Chris felt his own erection building inside his breeches. Anne pressed her palm to the bulge. He grunted in response to the pleasure and raised his arm to encircle her slender shoulders, inhaling a whiff of her perfumed hair.

The younger contestant had no chance. After only a few short moments of oral attention, he jerked and cried out, and the young woman backed off as his seed spewed out to the floor, splattering into her lap. She laughed and wiped her mouth with the back of her hand.

"We have a champion!" Max stepped forward, applauding, and everyone joined in. He released the older man from his bonds and raised his hand. "And now, sir," he told the man, "it is up to you to do with the losing team as you wish."

The winning contestant, sporting a raging erection, grinned as he moved the smaller dark-haired woman to the bed where she lay face down with her feet on the floor. Then he positioned the larger woman on the bed beside her.

With encouragement from the audience, he mounted the smaller woman from behind, raising her hips and entering her with forceful thrusts, and leaned forward to suckle her cousin's full breasts as he fucked her. Both women's groans could be heard over the crowd's cheering, along with the champion's grunts as his thrusts quickened. Rising to his feet, he withdrew and released his seed as an arc across the smaller woman's back.

Chris's fangs dropped into place as he watched, and the room filled with the beats of many hearts. He glanced over to find Max grinning at him.

"Lovely," Max said, stepping forward as he applauded. "Now for a more difficult challenge. This time, we will see which contestant can produce an orgasm in his female companion. Any takers?"

The game fell apart before the next contest got very far as more and more people piled onto the bed and stretched out on sofas. Groans and sighs accompanied the heartbeats as couples copulated and laughed, and sex charged the air. The earlier victor made a show of shoving a strawberry into one woman's cunt and sucking it slowly back out, to her squealing delight. He was repeating the performance for the third time when her head went back and her hips lifted into the air as she gasped. He inserted a finger into her pulsing cunt and rode out the climax as he stroked himself. She collapsed, spent, and her partner crawled up to spread her pale thighs.

Chris could no longer resist the scents assaulting him, and the sounds of pleasure rising and falling. He reached over and drew Anne to him so he could nuzzle her hair. She unbuttoned his pants.

He expected her warm hand to surround his phallus and jumped when he felt something hot and wet sliding over him instead. He looked down to find Margaret, the seemingly disinterested redhead, kneeling on the floor in front of him, taking his cock into her wide, sensuous mouth, swirling her velvety tongue around the head as she went. He groaned with pleasure.

One of the young men who had been sitting near them knelt behind Margaret. Raising her chemise over her plump hips and caressing her round ass, he mounted her, thrusting into her in rhythm with her attention to Chris's cock, causing an extra jolt each time her mouth covered him.

Had he been human, Chris would have come. Instead, the stimulation awakened the beast and it snarled and growled from its corner.

Chris pulled Anne across his chest where he could kiss her tempting mouth as he slid his hand between her legs. Over her shoulder, he watched as the young man behind Margaret approached release. Muscles and veins bulged in his chest and arms, and he arched his back. Clinging to Margaret's waist, he grunted as he pounded out his own urgent rhythm. Margaret raised her head, but continued her attention to Chris's cock with a wet, tight fist.

Anne clung to Chris, writhing against his body. He entered her with one finger, and then two, easing her tightness, dipping into her juices and spreading them over her swelling clit. As new as she was to this activity, it didn't take long for her cunt to clench deliciously around his fingers. Her hands curled into fists against his back, and he lowered his mouth to the quickening pulse in her neck.

As carefully as he could, he breached her flesh and fed, taking in her naive pleasure, thrilling to the surge of emotions. She cried out as she bucked against his hand, and he held her tighter, taking more, delighting in her simple joy.

Her climax hit his brain like thunder, and his own seed flowed in sweet release, aided by Margaret's hand.

Before he could be caught feeding, he withdrew his fangs

and held his mouth to Anne's neck. His body tingled and stolen emotions sizzled through him.

With the beast quieted for the moment, he lay back and watched, and Anne curled up across his lap. He stroked her soft hair as he enjoyed her warmth.

Margaret and Mary, the brunette who had helped disrobe him, discovered an attraction to each other that drew attention from several men. The two women laughed as they kissed. Then they took turns mounting admirers and riding them until their bodies glistened with sweat and both were panting. At one point, a well-endowed man pumped Mary's cunt while another entered Margaret's tight ass. The two women caressed each other's tits as their partners worked behind them. Finally, with men lying wasted on the floor around them like fallen soldiers in battle, the two women fell onto the rug with their arms around each other's shoulders, laughing.

"Isn't this wonderful?" Max whispered, crouched where he could speak in Chris's ear. "I told you we can have whatever we wish, do whatever we want. The world is ours."

Chris decided it best not to contradict Max but found himself thinking, I want to see my sister, and will never look upon her face again in this world.

He purposely put consideration of the next world out of his mind. If such a place existed, he doubted he'd see his sister there, either.

Max patted his shoulder and rose. "I do believe I can be of help," he said to a young man struggling to please two women at once.

Chris watched his master cross the room shedding his clothing.

In the midst of all the revelry and excitement, he felt very much alone.

* * *

Chris slid the drawer slowly shut and Abigail's innocent blue eyes disappeared. He reached down and opened the drawer below it.

Lifting out an ancient piece of cherry, he leaned back in his chair and studied it.

More than a century ago, he'd sharpened the end to a fine point, and flattened the handle. He knew exactly where he must push it in to pierce the heart, which ribs to slip between. Smooth wood slid easily against his palm, leaving no hint of a splinter.

If he didn't find the answer this time, would he have the courage to use it?

He pictured Nicole's face in the moonlight, her eyes filled with desire, her lips barely parted. She had no idea what kind of threat he posed. If she found out about him, her life would be in danger.

He heard Max's question from so long ago. Is that what you want?

"No."

The last thing in the world he wanted was to hurt Nicole.

He balanced the stake between his index fingers and spun it with his thumbs.

He couldn't face another century alone in the darkness. But could he really leave humanity's fate in the hands of monsters like Max?

"So, do you think it really exists?"

Nicole glanced out at the parking area, verifying that Chris's vehicle was gone. She told herself she'd felt relief at his departure, but that was only half true. She'd also felt a surge of sickening disappointment. After disappearing into the darkness, he'd returned to the dig to act as if nothing had happened. Maybe he was even disgusted by the way she'd thrown herself at him, humping him like some dog in heat.

Trying to ignore the memory of their brief encounter, she sighed and returned her attention to Brandon, who frowned at her.

"What?" she asked.

"The talisman. Do you think it's real?"

She shrugged. "I don't know. I hope so." She dried freshly washed tools and tucked them into the bag.

He nodded. "Even if it is, what kind of power can it possibly hold?"

Latching the canvas tool bag, she carried it to the wagon, and then returned to the table where Brandon sorted and filed notes.

"Most legends say the one who carries the talisman walks in light," she said. "If we assume the Maya culture in this area was similar to most other cultures, 'walking in light' would refer to being pure enough to stand before the deity."

He closed the folder over the night's notes and snapped the elastic band into place. "So, we're looking for something that puts the owner in the presence of God?"

"That could be what the people of this village believed."

"What do you believe?"

She smiled. "You're asking me if I believe there's a supreme being waiting for me to dig up a buried treasure so I can stand before him? Or her?"

He returned her smile with a self-conscious grin.

"I believe what I see." She gathered the lantern, water bottles, and other paraphernalia from the table, dumped everything into the wagon, and pulled it behind her toward the car.

Brandon fell into step beside her. "Doesn't it seem a little strange to you that Marsh doesn't stick around, even at a time like this?"

Nicole cast a wistful glance over her shoulder at the opening to the tomb, yet to be fully excavated. If she'd had her way, the crew would have worked until they'd exposed whatever doorway lay below, at least. Archaeologists were used to working through the fury of discovery. "I'm sure he has his reasons."

"Like?"

She studied the lanky student, who had once gone so far as to ask her out. She'd politely explained her conviction not to get involved with students, and he'd joked about changing majors. In spite of the uncomfortable moment, she hadn't regretted hiring him as a research assistant. He was excellent at documentation. And quite honestly, she might have been attracted to him after a summer of working together if she hadn't met Chris.

"I don't know," she said. "But he's financing this dig, which makes him the gift horse whose mouth we're not planning to scrutinize."

Brandon saluted playfully. "Message received and processed, boss."

Nicole loaded equipment into the Subaru and was closing the hatchback when an approaching vehicle drew her attention. For a brief moment when she turned, she expected to see a Land Rover drop over the rise and her heart raced with anticipation. Instead, a rusted brown van lumbered over water bars and through potholes, and skidded to a stop in front of her, sending a cloud of dust rolling into the air. A young man dressed in a brown uniform jumped out, carrying a cardboard tube.

"Doctor Stephenson?" he asked, approaching Brandon.

The student pointed to Nicole.

"Ah. *Lo siento*, Doctor. This package is for you."

"*Gracias.*" She took the tube, surprised by its weight.

The young man produced a clipboard. "You sign, *por favor*?"

Nicole signed, and then dug a ten peso bill from her pocket.

"*Gracias!*" He gave a small bow, stashed the money in his shirt pocket, and hurried away. Dust rose behind him as he sped out of the parking area.

Nicole ripped the top from the tube, extracted the rolled

contents, and tossed the tube through the car window into the backseat as she carried the maps to the hood.

Brandon followed, reading over her shoulder. "The GPR results?"

"Looks that way." She spread out the pages, studying the site plan on top. Dashed lines had been added to indicate possible cavernous areas in the limestone located by ground-penetrating radar. She'd never used such an expensive tool on a university project, but was instantly glad Chris had agreed to it. Just too bad she hadn't asked him earlier.

Adrenalin flooded her body as she traced the rectangular space directly south of the opening they now excavated. The tomb had to be at least five meters in each direction, and must be untouched. If anyone had broken the seal in the past, it would have filled with debris after all this time.

"Yes!"

"Hot damn!" Brandon slapped the Subaru's hood.

Nicole shook his arm in her excitement, barely keeping herself from jumping around like a kid.

Taking a deep breath and huffing it out, she returned her attention to the map.

"What's this?" Brandon asked, tracing a much larger dashed line to the north, outlining something at least thirty meters wide. The space opened into the jungle, where the radar survey had stopped.

"A cavern, maybe?" she answered.

"Yeah. If you want, a few of us could scout for an opening this afternoon, before dark."

Nicole nodded. "Not a bad idea. Maybe we'll find next year's project. See if you can get Eric and a few of the kids to go with you."

"Will do."

"But don't be late for work."

"Don't worry. I wouldn't miss this for the World Cup."

She nodded. "You sure you don't want a ride?"

"No, thanks. I'm fine."

Nicole slid into the Subaru, wedged the maps against the front passenger's seat, and cranked the engine. She waved as she passed Brandon on his bike.

On the two-mile drive to the huts, weariness set in, and she realized just how hard they'd worked once they'd discovered the stones. That and the constant level of excitement had taken its toll. Now, all she wanted to do was sleep.

Long before she heard Brandon's bike roll through the courtyard area, she'd discarded all but her T-shirt and panties, washed up, and climbed into the hammock, pulling the netting around her. A cool morning breeze blew in through the main window, aided by the overhead fan, and rattled the thatched roof.

She'd found it, the priest's tomb. She'd known it was there, in spite of all the "reputable sources" laughing at her.

If Chris Marsh hadn't believed in her, she'd never have discovered it. Funding for the site had dried up shortly after the first year of excavation. No one cared about such a small, insignificant dig.

"Ha."

The dig wouldn't be insignificant for long. She'd milk this find for years. A cover story for *Archaeology*, undoubtedly, and the center of professional chatter around the world. People would be fighting to fund next year's work. She wouldn't need the eccentric Chris Marsh with his insistence on night work.

Chris Marsh.

Her belly flipped at the memory of his kiss, and the feel of his hard body against hers. In all her fantasies, he'd never felt so perfect.

She could see the hunger in his blue eyes now, feel his hands on her butt, smell his exotic scent. His mouth moved to the side of her neck and she shuddered at the pleasure as she combed her fingers through his soft hair.

"I want you, Nicole."

His low, sexy voice slid across her skin like his touch, raising goose bumps and making her tremble.

As halogen lights faded to points of starlight, he laid her down on warm grass, cradling her head in his arm. "Now," he whispered.

His hand traveled up her side, cupping her breast, suddenly bare. "Too tempting."

She tried to ask him to stop, to point out that they were out in the open, but she couldn't get words past her throat.

He rose up above her, gazing down with glowing eyes, easing her knees apart. She wantonly spread her legs, ready to feel him enter her with urgent thrusts. Cream oozed from her achingly empty pussy.

And then he filled her, suddenly inside her, and her back arched with pleasure. He withdrew and thrust forward, again and again, abrading her swollen clit until she was about to come.

She opened her eyes and looked up at the faces of her students, drinking from water bottles and studying her as if she were an unexpected artifact.

But she couldn't stop. Her hips rolled up to take more of him, and she clung to his shoulders.

"Come on, Nicki. It's your turn. You suck me off and then we'll do it tomorrow night. I swear."

Her gut clenched and her excitement melted away as she realized Chris Marsh wasn't fucking her, she'd only imagined him kissing her and parting her thighs. Zack lay on top of her, reeking of reefer and stale beer, and annoyingly sucking her ear. Had he been out all night with the band again?

She wanted to scream at him, tell him to go find his coed girlfriend, to leave her alone. How could he expect her to have oral sex with him after he'd betrayed her with a laugh?

Were her students still watching? She couldn't see them now.

"Come on, Nicki."

Kicking and flailing, she managed to push him away. "No. Leave me alone!" But he fell back onto her. She fought him off again. "No!"

"Dr. Stephenson?"

She sat up.

The hammock swayed in the darkened hut, bolts creaking against wood.

"Nicole? Are you okay?" It was Megan's voice at the window.

She stared at the woman's shadow on the thin cotton curtain. "Yes, yes. I'm fine."

"Sounded like you were having a nightmare, maybe an argument with Dr. Wilson?"

Nicole smiled at the reference to her departmental rival. The man was a jerk but smart, and they'd had a strange kind of antagonistic friendship since she first arrived.

"Yeah. Thanks, Megan. I'm okay now."

"All right."

She lay back and listened to the woman's soft footsteps return to the neighboring hut as she stared up at a piece of thatch hanging from the roof, dancing in the fan-cooled air. Sweat ran down the side of her face.

Why couldn't men just stay out of her life and leave her in peace?

Purposely trying to relax, she considered the possibility that the dream had been a warning. As different as Chris seemed, was he just as much of a jerk as Zack and the other men she'd cared about? Would he simply disappoint her in the end?

Probably.

She didn't have time for this crap.

Taking a deep breath and blowing it out, she focused on the tomb, wondering what they'd find inside. Would it be filled with jade carvings? Or gold jewelry adorning an undisturbed sarcophagus?

In spite of her best efforts not to remember, Chris's whisper echoed through her thoughts. "Too tempting."

4

They'd managed to get through a whole night's work without exchanging more than a dozen words and a few quick glances. Would they make it through two? Nicole seemed intent on pretending he wasn't there, and Chris tried to act like he didn't constantly crave every inch of her body.

And every drop of her blood.

He couldn't let her see that when she approached, his hands shook with wanting to touch her again. She couldn't know how much he ached to bury his fingers in her silken hair, gaze down into her emerald eyes, and kiss her warm, welcoming mouth.

Focusing on his notes, he wrote a paragraph describing the entrance they'd completely uncovered shortly after starting work a half hour earlier. It appeared unexpectedly crude, as if constructed in a hurry, but the doorway had been reinforced with two slabs of limestone. The team worked on carefully removing the first, and he doubted they'd have it open before the night passed, especially with part of the crew off searching the jungle for some mysterious cavern opening.

Chris turned to the sound of approaching runners.

"Boss! We found it!"

Everyone at the site stopped work and stepped in the direction of Brandon and one of the male students, both panting for breath. Sweat ran down their faces and chests, and they were marked with cuts and leaf pieces as if they'd charged blindly through undergrowth.

Chris frowned at the sweet hint of blood in the air.

Nicole climbed the ladder in the excavation. "What—?"

"You won't believe this shit," Brandon said. Excitement in the young man's voice even brought Chris to his feet.

"What is it?" Nicole handed Brandon a water bottle. "The opening?"

Brandon gulped a healthy drink and then grinned. "Oh, it's a whole lot better than just the opening."

"What did you find?" Even Nicole's obvious annoyance didn't dim his expression.

"We found the citizens of this fair city." He exchanged meaningful looks with his assistant, who nodded, and then he smiled at Nicole again. "I think you're going to want to see this right away."

With a quick glance over her shoulder at the excavated doorway, Nicole grabbed her flashlight and nodded. "Let's go."

Everyone else in the group followed, trudging along like a herd of elephants through the darkness. Stones turned, and footsteps faltered as they searched for trails.

Chris fell behind, anxious to see the discovery, but reluctant to leave the excavation even for an hour. What if the talisman lay in the tomb they were uncovering? In spite of trying not to get his hopes up, they soared toward the heavens.

A quarter mile into the jungle, the group stopped and Brandon pointed to a small opening in a rock face, freshly uncovered and expanded, outlined in the night by bobbing headlamps from inside. "We had to dig it out. Malcolm discovered air coming from a hole about eight inches wide."

One by one, the group squeezed through the opening, following Nicole and Brandon. Chris entered last, squinting at the brightness of all the headlamps and flashlights.

The small entry opened into a large cavernous room that showed signs of human enlargement and adornments, with smoke-covered pictographs on the ceiling and glyphs carved into the walls. The ceiling art was older than that on the walls, which included many double rows of relatively modern Maya glyphs. Chris quickly scanned the interior, avoiding translations for the moment.

The students and Nicole had gathered in a spot twenty feet into the cave, so he joined them. Near the wall, a hole a foot deep and several feet wide in the otherwise smooth dirt floor revealed bones. On closer inspection, the largest bone protruding into the hole appeared to be a human femur, chewed long ago by a predatory intruder.

"Look at the outline." Brandon followed what could easily be the edges of the victim's grave with his flashlight. "And here." He followed another, and another. By stepping back, Chris could clearly see at least a hundred grave sites laid in neat rows throughout the cavern, all but the first apparently undisturbed.

"Hey!" The high-pitched voice of one of the undergraduates bounced through the room, causing Chris to wince. The young woman stood at the far end of the room, where she must have stepped from some kind of opening. "Wait 'til you see this."

Treading more lightly now, attempting to avoid the graves, the dozen or so people wound their way to the back of the main room and through a narrow shaft. They all squeezed into a small, square room, chiseled out of solid rock off the side of the shaft. In the center of the room stood a stone sarcophagus made of marble instead of limestone. Symbols had been carved into the sides and top, pictures instead of glyphs. Around the sides were humans and animals, hundreds of detailed carvings, each unique and depicting life in the ancient culture. The stone cover, skewed slightly on the base, held a field of stars with a quarter-moon in the center and leaves around the edges.

"Holy shit," Eric said, leaning forward to peer into a small corner space. "We've got to open it. There's something inside."

"No way." Nicole stepped forward, urging everyone back. "We follow procedure. I want everyone out except Brandon to take photographs. The rest of you work in the front room. I need measurements to everything and graphs, but don't disturb anything. No stakes. We don't have permission to be here."

Chris's chest tightened. "What about the priest's tomb? That's what we're here for."

Nicole spun around to face him, her eyes flashing anger and impatience, but also excitement that gripped him by the throat.

"I'm sure we can sacrifice one night on such a spectacular find, don't you think? If we get the basic information recorded, I can file a project plan to excavate this after the first dig is complete." She lowered her voice and stepped close to him. "You aren't going to try to forbid this, are you?"

Chris shook his head. After all, the site could be tied to the priest's tomb, and could easily contain more information about the talisman. For all they knew, the priest might even be the one in the crypt.

"Good." She sighed and straightened, glancing around. "Then you can help. Do you have your notebook?"

"No, but I'll get it." Chris hurried away and returned in record time, excited enough about the find to almost forget himself. He stopped outside the cavern entrance for several minutes, studying the darkness, and saw no hint of unwanted observers. Taking several deep breaths to make it look as if he'd run, he ducked into the cavern and hurried to the back room.

As Brandon photographed the sides, Nicole got very close to the small corner opening.

Brandon lowered his camera. "Who do you think this was?"

Nicole looked the sarcophagus over. "It's not fancy enough for a king, and I don't see Ahcaanan Uxmaal's name anywhere. But who knows? He must have at least been someone fairly important." She peered into the opening again. "The atmosphere has already done its damage. But this looks strange. I swear I see cloth."

"Shall we move the stone a little?" Chris asked.

Nicole looked up at him and laughed. "Yeah. It only weights about a ton."

Chris pressed his fingers to the edge of the slab. "True, but we don't want to lift it."

"We really shouldn't—"

Trying his best to look as though he were straining, Chris slid the stone sideways until a third of the sarcophagus was exposed.

"—move it."

Inside, a face stared up at them.

Dark, leathery skin surrounded empty eye sockets and a mouth without lips, but the head still bore long, straight black hair, and the body was clad in finely woven cloth that could have once been red. Gold bracelets hung from bony wrists below hands crossed over the chest.

"Mummified," Nicole whispered.

Chris leaned in for closer inspection. He found no scent of embalming herbs, just dusty hemp and ancient spices. "Naturally mummified."

"You think so?"

He glanced at Nicole. "Yes."

The skin on the mummy's face had wrinkled as muscles shrank, making it impossible to determine his or her age. The ears were pierced with jade rods, each two inches long, and the teeth appeared to be in amazingly good shape.

Chris moved to study as much as he could see. A flat, gold necklace encircled the mummy's neck, the skin of which was also leathery and wrinkled, but intact except for two small holes.

Chris straightened.

"What is it?"

His gaze snapped to Nicole's. "I, um, think we need to replace the cover so that nothing disappears."

"*Disappears*? Are you accusing my students of being looters? Grave robbers?"

Her anger helped calm him. As long as she stayed focused on him, she might not notice the obvious cause of death.

He shrugged.

"Well, they aren't."

"But there are thieves around, and I don't see any way to keep them out without a gate."

She huffed at the accuracy of his statement and motioned to Brandon. "Take as many pictures of the mummy as you can get, then we'll close this up for now."

"Yes, Boss." Brandon extracted another memory card from his pouch and slid it into the camera.

A new fear gripped Chris as he stood. At some point, a vampire had known everything this victim knew. Perhaps the talisman had long ago been stolen and put to the test. Since he'd never heard of a vampire walking in the light, he had to assume the test had failed, if it was conducted. That could mean the talisman wasn't in the priest's tomb.

Would this be just another dead end? Were they going to all this trouble for nothing?

Chris stopped in the passageway and listened. From his left came the many voices of archaeology students, whispering with excitement. But from his right, he heard soft, tinkling sounds.

Something dripped. Water? Was the source that had carved the cave still at work? If so, how many more secrets did this cave hold?

"Where are you going?"

He turned back to Nicole. "I hear water."

"So, you're just going to wander into a cave without a flashlight?"

It would have to get much darker before he couldn't see, but he certainly didn't want to admit that. "I, uh, was hoping you'd join me."

She didn't answer right away, but he heard her heart rate increase and for a moment he enjoyed the sweet melody of it. Then he purposely blocked it out.

"Why not," she said. "Might as well see what else is back here."

As she squeezed past him in the narrow passage, he worked to suppress a growl. Her wonderful scent and warmth were magnified by proximity, and his desire summoned the memory of holding her. Balling his shaking hand into a fist, he gripped his notebook in the other and followed several feet behind her, trying not to enjoy the view of her muscular thighs and rounded backside.

The passageway went on for quite a ways, winding left and right, getting narrower and shorter until they were practically crawling on hands and knees.

"I think this is about to pinch out."

Chris watched the bottoms of Nicole's booted feet so that he wouldn't focus on her amazing ass, and he told himself over and over to think about the business at hand. Still, he could smell her sweat and hint of feminine juices, and his fangs ached.

"I still hear water," he said. It was nearly a roar now to his sensitive ears.

"Are you sure? I don't think—"

They stopped. Nicole stretched out on her stomach, and stuck her head and one arm through a narrow horizontal slit. "Oh, my God!"

Then she scrambled forward until she'd completely disappeared through the opening.

Chris followed, sliding halfway through and then swinging down the three-foot drop to land on his feet.

They stood in an amazing room, covered completely with crystals. Nicole's flashlight beam on the thirty-foot ceiling shattered into pinks, blues, greens, and yellows, and bounced in all directions at once. When she moved the light around, it was as if they were standing inside a giant kaleidoscope.

"Wow," she breathed. "This is incredible. It's like being in the middle of a geode."

To their left, only visible after crossing half the room, a spring bubbled up into a pool and then flowed away, dropping out of sight through small submerged holes in the far wall. Unless they were missing something, those holes appeared to be the only other way out of the room.

Several inches of sand left by the stream covered the floor of the cave, and glistened with eroded crystals. Chris picked up a handful and examined it. "Gypsum," he said, "contaminated with sulfur and other minerals. Volcanic activity." Wiping his hands, he crouched at the edge of the pool and eased his fingers into the clear water. "Just cooler than bath temperature, I believe."

"Really?" Nicole knelt beside him and reached into the pool, shining her flashlight into the water as she did. From the bottom, several feet down, crystalline sand glittered through perfectly clear water. "This is unbelievable."

Chris studied her face as she admired the pool. All her anger and annoyance had been replaced by childlike wonder and joy. Her smile made his throat tighten with desire.

As much as the beast craved her, the part of him that was

man wanted her even more. A dangerous combination, and definitely hard to resist.

"It's a flowing stream, no signs of fish, and we aren't that far underground. Hardly a fragile environment." She turned her head and met his gaze, her smile intact. "What do you think? A quick dunk?"

He frowned, trying to understand her question.

She placed her flashlight on the ground pointed up and began unbuttoning her blouse. "I don't know about you, but I haven't had a real bath in weeks."

When she stood and unzipped her shorts, Chris looked away. The sight of her nearly naked body sent his senses into a tailspin, and his control promised to follow.

"Don't tell me you're shy."

Turning slowly, he watched her ease into the warm pool wearing only her undergarments.

All thoughts of the talisman, the mummified vampire victim, the hundreds of graves, and the dozen students working at the front of the cave faded. Every moment of wanting Nicole, craving her touch, wishing for her body pressed to his, rose begging for fulfillment as his cock did the same.

Nicole moved around to the far side of the small pool, sat, and spread her arms across the waterline. "Coming in? Promise I won't bite."

Chris barely suppressed the reply that he just might.

He knew better than to give in to the desire he felt for her and battled against it, but found himself losing the fight. If he were careful, he could enjoy a few stolen moments near her, touching her flesh, inhaling her scent. That was all this would be, just a few precious moments. Nothing more. He could hold the beast in check, he was sure of it. And what if he took a taste? He'd make sure she didn't remember with any certainty. Then he'd know her as just another woman, not this amazingly tempting creature he couldn't stop thinking about.

Yes, he could do it, if he were careful.

He drew off his boots and tossed them aside, stripped off his shirt, and, with some difficulty, removed his pants. Since he wore no undergarments, he stood before her bare, enjoying the color rising in her cheeks.

Nicole's gaze ran slowly over his body as he stepped into the water. Warmth crawled up his skin to envelope him in comfort, drawing a sigh from his throat as he sat on a limestone ledge directly across from the woman he hungered for.

They stared at each other. Water bubbled up through the sand, occasionally splashing at the surface with a *ga-lub*, and the overflow trickled down a smoothed chute of limestone toward the exit holes. The whole experience had a dream quality to it. Chris's concerns about being discovered as a vampire and about missing out on the talisman floated away.

"You're still interested in me."

He smiled at her statement. It would do him no good to deny it. "Yes."

"Then, why did you run away after . . . after—"

"You came in my arms?"

Nicole's cheeks reddened, but she didn't look away. "Yes."

He paused, trying to decide how much to tell her. Knowledge of his true identity could put them both at risk. Besides, one glimpse of the beast would terrify her and drive her away.

Strange. That fear had never concerned him before. He'd always been careful not to reveal the beast before feeding on his victims. Fear soured the blood. But once he'd had what he wanted, it hadn't mattered to him if they knew the truth. His only concern had always been that they not be able to describe him later. He found few humans willing to try to convince the authorities that vampires are real, and, so far, no authorities in recent times willing to believe it.

The memory of Eric and Megan's sighs of satisfaction, and their jokes as they held each other under the stars, carried a stab of regret. No matter what happened in this magical place, he'd never be able to hold Nicole in his arms after sex and joke about the future. Instead, he must worry that she simply survive the experience.

"I was afraid," he said.

"Of me?"

Chris shook his head. "Of myself."

After a long moment, Nicole leaned forward and floated across the pool until she knelt right in front of him. "What are you afraid of?"

Her green eyes drew him in to dizzying depths. He gripped his thighs to keep from reaching for her. "Hurting you," he whispered.

A fraction of a moment of fear registered in her eyes, but was quickly replaced by honest self-confidence. "I'm not exactly new to this stuff, you know. I've had lovers before."

Chris raised his eyebrows but clamped his mouth shut.

She grinned. "Let me guess. Not like you, right?"

He leaned forward, inhaling her scent over that of the mineral-laden pool. Water lapped against his bare chest as he approached her, and he heard her breathing grow shallow and quick.

He stopped with his mouth near her ear. "Right."

Nicole shivered in spite of the perfect water temperature.

With her eyes closed, she could feel Chris's presence although he didn't touch her. His mouth moved close to her jaw, across her cheek, and stopped in front of hers. She licked her suddenly dry lips and opened her eyes to find him staring at her mouth, his blue eyes dark as ink.

His gaze rose to hers and he frowned. She watched some internal struggle play out in his eyes, and then he reached forward, tilted her chin up with one finger, and leaned in to kiss her.

As soon as his lips met hers, the shivering stopped, replaced by a strange warmth that flowed over her like melted chocolate syrup. She pressed her palms to his bare chest, squeezing water out from between their skin, enjoying the feel of hard, lean muscles.

His mouth opened against hers, and his tongue traced her lips in a sensuous tickle that caused her to suck in a stuttered breath.

She felt his hands tentatively touch her bare waist under the water, and then slide around her to draw her close, pushing water ahead of the movement in a whispered stroke. She floated down to straddle his legs and encircled his wide shoulders with her arms. With her body pressed against his, her wet bra presented an annoying barrier.

The kiss deepened and intensified as his tongue stroked hers and circled her mouth, exploring, tasting, possessing. She surrendered in a way she'd never considered before. All her defenses shut down. Whatever he demanded of her she would do.

Even as she puzzled over that thought, it, too, faded.

His hands moved over her back, and her bra popped loose, floating up to her neck. She shrugged it off and tossed it onto the sand behind him. Then his fingers slipped into the back of her panties and ripped them away. She had no idea what happened to them, and she didn't care. The only thing that mattered was getting closer, offering everything she had to give.

His hands slid over her butt, then up her sides to her breasts. Her back arched so that her stomach lay against his and her nipples mashed into his chest. Water blurred lines where their bodies stopped touching, making the encounter all that much more erotic.

His hard-on rose against her crotch. Just the hint of it pressed to submerged flesh caused her belly to flip. She'd seen him partially erect when he undressed, and she'd tried not to stare. He was bigger than any man she'd ever known, not that her experience was all that vast. Still, with her recent bout of celibacy, she wondered if they'd have difficulty consummating this relationship.

God, she hoped not. The thought of mounting him did crazy things to her insides.

He lifted her until his prick pointed into her, nudging against her vulva, threatening to fill every bit of her. She tried to push down, to impale herself, but he held her up.

She pulled away from his mouth and frowned down at him. "What are you waiting for?"

"The right moment," he said.

"Isn't this it?"

He grinned and slowly shook his head. "Not even close."

She swallowed hard as her insides liquefied.

He raised her higher from the water and licked a long, slow line up the center of her chest. The velvety caress of his tongue brought back memories of the first part of her lewd dream. Closing her eyes, she let her head drop back and arched her back more.

His tongue moved left, rose up the inside of her breast, and slowly, torturously, circled her nipple again and again. The nipple tightened into a hard bud, wanting more direct attention.

The tips of his fingers traipsed up the base of her spine and back down, and her buttocks clenched at the delicious touch, just as his tongue flicked across her aching nipple.

She moaned.

His tongue crossed her chest and repeated the process on the other side, as his fingers feathered across her sensitized buttocks.

Dear God, the man knew exactly what he was doing. Her hands clenched on his shoulders.

When he sucked her tit into his mouth and squeezed her ass, liquid sparks shot up her spine and she cried out. His tongue thrashed her nipple back and forth as he sucked it to a hard peak. She ground her crotch shamelessly into his belly.

He released her breast and tenderly lathed the hard nipple, and moved to the other side.

Her entire body swelled with need. She sucked her bottom lip between her teeth to keep from screaming.

Chris moved up from her breast to her neck and eased her inches closer to the place she hungered to be. She felt the head of his rock-hard cock nudging into her vagina and tried to wriggle down.

Instead, he stood, holding her tightly to him and turned. Water flowed off her body, leaving her skin exposed to the cool cavern air, but the coolness provided no relief from the heat he'd produced.

Amazingly, when he placed her on the ground, she found his shirt spread under her. How had he done that?

The question wilted as he stretched out on top of her, pressing his hard, sinewy body to hers. Nicole raised her knees around him, trembling with anticipation, imagining his urgent thrusts.

Instead, he started down the front of her body, alternating between kisses, licks, and tender bites, finding every nerve bundle and hypersensitive spot. She squirmed. Her mind shut down beyond the moment, trying to understand the sensations rolling and sizzling through her.

Somewhere deep inside her, a spark lay on kindling, smoking and glowing white hot, promising a raging inferno. As his mouth moved down to the insides of her thighs, flames burst forth.

"Chris, what are you—?"

She sucked in a breath of surprise when his tongue stroked a wide swath up the length of her labia, ending at her clit.

Her hips rose off the ground.

He started at the bottom again, sliding his hands under her butt as he did, and flames crackled through her belly and up her torso.

At the top this time, he stroked her clit, slowly at first, side to side, up and down, then faster, cruelly shoving it in circles with his stiff tongue.

Her body moved as if attached to strings he controlled with ease, jerking and undulating.

Muscles twitched, and she knew she balanced on the verge of a wonderful climax. Cream welled inside, ready for release.

Chris stilled, his tongue blanketing her pussy, and she whimpered as release slipped away.

He started again, licking and sucking, and her skin bubbled with renewed heat.

Again, he stopped at the last moment.

She yelled her frustration through clenched teeth.

A sound of satisfaction vibrated through his mouth. He toyed with her, and he knew it.

"What the hell are you doing?" she asked.

He nipped the inside of her thigh as if chastising her for questioning him and she sucked in a breath of surprise.

Then he circled her seriously swollen clit with his tongue and sucked it into his mouth, squeezing it gently between his teeth as he licked.

She nearly rose completely off the ground and she cried out with joy. Her voice echoed back from the rock walls.

The promised inferno drafted over her, and every muscle in her body exploded at once. Heated waves of ecstasy pounded through her womb and scorched her flesh.

On and on they went, until the pleasure bordered on pain.

His tongue plunged into her and withdrew, and he lapped up the cream that must have been gushing from her pussy.

When the climax finally eased, she felt as if she'd been flung to the ground by a wrestling opponent, and she lay panting, her heart hammering against her ribs.

Chris rose over her on his hands and knees, and she felt warm droplets dance across her skin. When she opened her eyes, she found him staring down at her, his blue eyes glistening like ice crystals.

"Unbelievable," he whispered.

She smiled. "I think that's my line."

He didn't smile back. In fact, his eyes narrowed as if he were angry.

She reached up and touched the side of his face. His skin was cool and smooth, almost like satin.

"What's wrong?" She ran her hand slowly down across his neck.

He shuddered. "You tempt me to do things I shouldn't."

"I think we're a little late for that."

His eyebrows rose as they had before, as if he had something more to say but decided against it.

Nicole slid her hand down the front of his wet body and found his engorged cock. Watching his face, she wrapped her fingers around the shaft and gently squeezed.

Chris drew in a ragged breath and closed his eyes. "You're not making this any easier," he whispered.

Slipping her fingers up and down the length of him, she found him even larger than he had been, and a strange bud of excitement blossomed in her gut.

How could she possibly be turned on again, after what he'd just done to her?

But she was. Enjoying the agonizing pleasure transforming his expression, she drew down and pushed up, letting her hand slide from the head to the base.

Suddenly, he backed out of her grip and crouched over her

like a lion about to pounce. Then the corners of his mouth curved up into a wicked grin.

She caressed his shoulders, letting her fingers glide over bumps and valleys of tight muscles.

He turned his head and pressed his lips to her wrist and groaned. A strange prickling heat tripped up her arm.

What was it about this man that made just touching him such an unusual experience?

Then he lowered his mouth to her chest and snaked his way in a slow, dreamlike move up her body. He drew her knees up higher until she was completely open to him.

Still clutching his shoulders, she trembled. Again, she felt as though she were surrendering everything. Oddly enough, she didn't care.

As his tongue reached her neck, the head of his cock pressed against her pussy, and he stopped. She turned her head and froze, waiting for the next sensation.

He closed his mouth on her neck and sucked, and she clamped down on his shoulders. Nerve endings snapped and sizzled all through her.

He pushed then with a steady force against which her body first protested. Oh, God, she needed some kind of lubricant, something. He was too large, too hard. She dug her fingers into muscles, nearly piercing flesh.

He sucked harder and the air between them vibrated with a low growl, and liquid warmth flooded her pussy.

Suddenly, resistance disappeared and he entered her with one long thrust.

She drew in a breath of surprise.

He froze for a moment, and her body adjusted to him quickly, thrilling to the width and length of his cock filling her as no man ever had. She knew he wasn't fully sheathed, and that knowledge turned her backbone into Jell-O.

Chris turned his head to nuzzle her hair, his mouth near her ear. "So perfect," he whispered, his voice rough and low. "Such tight warmth. I've hungered for this moment, Nicole."

She whimpered. Burrowing her fingers in his soft hair, she grabbed a handful as she wrapped her left arm around his shoulders. All she could think about was wanting more of him. She tilted her hips up to him and heard him groan softly.

Tenderly kissing her cheeks, and lips, and forehead, he gripped her thigh and cradled the back of her neck. He started a slow, easy rhythm, withdrawing and returning, a little deeper each time.

True passion grew inside her, nurtured by his masterful tenderness, and tears burned behind her eyes. Even as her clit swelled and rubbed against his slick cock, she realized how much she'd craved the closeness she felt to Chris at that moment.

Each time he pushed, she thought she'd taken as much of him as she could. And then he pushed deeper. And deeper.

As her pussy stretched, the universe shrank down to the two of them, together, joined, merging into one. The scent of warm minerals mixed with the dust and earth in his hair, and the stream trickling away near their feet. His skin felt smooth under her fingers and his hair as soft as rabbit's fur.

Time stopped, suspending her in this perfect, sensual place, away from the rest of the world, holding her aloft.

He sucked in a breath as he buried his cock to the hilt.

Her internal muscles gripped him, refusing to release him, and he groaned again.

"Too perfect," he whispered.

Dark heat filtered through her senses, and need swelled like a flood behind a bulging dam. With one move, he would push her too far. She clung to him, not wanting the moment to end, but craving the bliss.

As if reading her mind, he withdrew almost completely and

thrust back in, sending her over the edge. She lost her grasp on the moment.

She rose up to his thrusts, muscles pounding, flesh on fire, fell back and rose again.

He held her close, matched her movements, reaching deeper.

Sensations replaced reason. Long waves, two bodies moving as one.

Slow, rolling pulses.

Pure liquid pleasure.

As she rose into the bliss, nothing else existed. Just raw ecstasy.

On and on it went, deep, slow thrusts, fulfillment, joy.

It seemed to continue for much too long, and ended too quickly.

Falling back to earth, she loosened her grip on his hair and back. Final pulses of pleasure shot through her as reminders of the phenomenal orgasm, and she smiled.

So, it hadn't been her fault after all, not reaching a climax with other men. She'd always assumed there was something wrong with her. Obviously, there'd been something wrong with them.

Chris lay still, his face buried in her hair, his cock hard inside her. His fingers moved tenderly along the length of her thigh, caressing her flesh.

Her smile faded as she realized he hadn't come. Was he worried about getting her pregnant?

God, she hadn't even thought about protection.

Well, she wouldn't get pregnant now, she knew that, and it was a little late to worry about anything else.

She stroked the back of his neck. "You don't have to stop."

He raised his head and smiled down at her. "Yes, I do."

"Why? It's not like—"

He stopped her words with a kiss, and then rose up again. "Please, don't ask me questions I can't answer."

"But—"

"You don't understand, and I can't explain."

She slid her hand down to his shoulder as confusion displaced afterglow. Here they'd just shared the most amazing experience of her life and he was pulling some kind of mysterious macho crap.

He kissed her, and she met him with tight lips. But he didn't give up. He nipped her lips and ran his tongue across them until the confusion began to slip away and she gave in. Opening her mouth, she drew him in, and he kissed her as if for the first time.

His exploration soon gave way to reignited passion, and he bruised her lips with urgency.

Then he tore his mouth away and turned his head to the side as he withdrew from her.

She sighed at the loss, immediately feeling a flood of grief. How could this just be over?

"We must go," he said. "It's getting late."

She propped herself up on her elbows. "What difference does it make? It's only daybreak."

Chris rose quickly, picked up his clothes, and began dressing.

This was too weird. Struggling with conflicting emotions she couldn't even define, Nicole gathered what she could find of her clothes and put them on, trying to shake sand out of the inside as she went.

She wanted to say something, but decided to wait and see how he reacted. Would he act like nothing had happened again?

If so, she might shoot him. Or at least, she'd want to. Frowning, she slipped the last button on her blouse through the buttonhole.

"Dr. Stephenson?" A blond head poked through from the darkness.

Nicole jumped and fear spiked through her as she realized how close they'd come to being discovered in a very compromising position. What the hell had she been thinking?

She hadn't been thinking.

Oh, God, had they heard her scream? Her face burned as she considered the possibility.

"Yes?"

"We're getting ready to shut down for the night. Brandon wants to know if we should wait for you."

Nicole shook her head. "No, you all go ahead. We'll be right behind you. See you tomorrow night."

"Okay." The student disappeared.

Nicole took a deep breath and blew it out, snatched the flashlight from the ground, and started toward the opening.

Chris grabbed her arm and turned her around.

She stared up into blue eyes glistening with jagged emotion.

"I hope you never regret what happened between us." He pushed her hair back and cupped her face with his soft palm. "I know I won't."

Then he tenderly kissed her forehead.

Her throat tightened. Could this be his way of telling her that what had passed between them would never be repeated? It certainly felt that way. The threat of tears burned behind her eyes.

He released her and stepped back.

Nicole hurried forward, blinking hard as she scrambled through the opening. As soon as he'd made it through, she led the way back down the winding passage, chastising herself for thinking they might have shared more than sex.

She should be happy; the last thing in the world she needed was an emotional quagmire in the middle of a project.

The crew had disappeared quickly. She stopped at the burial chamber and shone the flashlight in just long enough to make sure the top of the sarcophagus and been replaced, then started toward the sunrise lighting the cavern entrance.

"We didn't quite make it out before daylight."

She glanced over her shoulder, stopped and turned around. "Chris?"

Her voice echoed back.

He hadn't passed her, so he must have headed back into the depths of the cavern. What the hell was he doing?

5

Chris stood with his back pressed to the crystalline wall, trembling. He listened to Nicole call for him and hoped she had the good sense to give up and continue on to her cabin. The last thing he wanted was for her to see him like this. Not now, when there was so much at stake.

After more than an hour of agonizing restraint while touching her, listening to the pounding of her heart, reveling in the way her heat engulfed him, he'd had to get away before he lost control. As soon as he'd loosed the reins an inch, the beast had ripped its way out of his empty soul and taken command.

At least she was safe, guarded by daylight.

He'd never imagined he could feel so close to a mortal. The delight he'd taken in their discussions of Maya culture and archaeology in general had given way to attraction, much as it might have if he, too, had been mortal. But it was so much more dangerous for her than she knew, and the thought of hurting her terrified him.

If only he'd paid attention, he might have made it to the stash of blood in his Range Rover before dawn actually broke.

Now he'd suffer here in the darkness, fighting the fierce hunger until nightfall. He doubted he'd even be able to sleep, in spite of the daytime weariness settling into his bones.

He slid down the rock until he crouched with his arms locked around his knees. If he let his thoughts wander, he might be able to make time pass more quickly.

He recalled the first time he'd seen Nicole Stephenson when they finally met at the site a month and a half ago. She'd stood in dim lamplight wearing shorts and a sleeveless blouse, her hair pinned up. He'd admired her shape and the way she moved. Then the halogens had switched on and she'd stood like some angelic vision in dazzling white light, and he'd nearly fallen to his knees. Her eyes had sparkled like polished jade, and her skin held the glory of sunshine. From that moment, he'd thought about her every morning when he laid down to sleep, and those thoughts had grown more vividly sexual every day. Still, they hadn't compared to the joy he'd experienced seeing her face tighten with ecstasy.

The beast growled long and low.

Damn it all, this isn't helping.

Chris leaned his head back against cold rock, closed his eyes, and concentrated on the prize possibly waiting in the priest's tomb. If this were really the one thing he'd spent ages seeking, what would he do first? Sit and watch the sunrise? Maybe sit and watch a dozen sunrises, and a dozen sunsets.

When was the last time he'd thought they were close? Was it less than a century ago? It must have been the night Max had dragged him off to see a young doctor just as the Great War was ending . . .

"Fantastic strides were made in medicine during battle," Max said, clutching Chris's arm and walking fast. Their footsteps echoed off empty brick walls.

"You expect me to believe they had some reason to cure our condition during the war?"

"Of course not, dear boy." Max waved his arm and his cape billowed in the night air. "I'm just saying that they've made amazing advances. Some of these young doctors have found cures for things I never would have thought possible."

"And yet tens of thousands have died of influenza already this year."

Max tightened his grip. "I don't know that you're approaching this with the right attitude. Don't you want to see sunlight again?"

"Of course, but you're the reason I can't see it now."

Max huffed. "If not for me, you wouldn't have seen anything in the past two hundred years."

Chris couldn't argue with that. As trying as some days, or even years were, he had no desire to disappear in a puff of smoke.

Still, Max knew exactly how to annoy him.

They turned down a dark alley.

"The young Dr. Bowman has a laboratory back here, where we won't be disturbed. I've already visited him several times to donate fluids and such. He has created a vaccine that promises remarkable results." Max grinned. "You'll soon see."

"No doubt," Chris muttered. How many times had he built up false hopes over one of Max's discoveries? Yet, in spite of himself, he felt a degree of anticipation.

The alley reeked of urine, wet decaying garbage, and horse manure. Somewhere behind them, the putter of an engine followed a passing automobile and then died away to silence, save the skittering of rats along the curb. Chris drew his coat more tightly around himself.

Max didn't seem to notice the filth. He walked with a spring in his step, stopped suddenly, and glanced meaningfully at Chris before knocking twice on a wooden door. After a moment of scuffling inside, the door opened a crack, and then swung wide.

"Ah, gentlemen," an older woman said, grinning a toothless grin and pushing stray hairs into place, "come in. The doctor's expecting you."

Max handed the woman his hat and cloak. Chris grudgingly shrugged off his outer coat.

"Right through there," the woman said, pointing with Max's hat. "He'll be out in a minute."

Chris ducked through an ancient doorframe and followed Max into a semi-dark sitting room that didn't appear to have been touched—or cleaned—in the past hundred years. Oil lamps burned at each end, shedding little light, and photographs of people undoubtedly long dead adorned the walls. Max settled into a dingy Victorian spoon back chair, and Chris stood at the end of the room where he could see both the doorway they'd entered through and the one directly across from it.

After several long moments, a man wearing black pants and a white shirt open at the neck with sleeves rolled to his elbows stepped through the latter. His hair was a mass of wild black curls, and his light brown eyes glistened.

"Max, forgive me for keeping you waiting. I just had to complete one more trial."

"And?" Max straightened.

The young man nodded.

"Splendid!" Max jumped to his feet. "Then let us proceed."

"Dr. Joseph Bowman," the young man said, extending his hand toward Chris.

Chris accepted the warm, strong handshake, and immediately felt better about the doctor. "Christopher Strickland."

Bowman smiled. "This way."

He led them down a darker hallway and into a large room filled with laboratory equipment, candles, and lamps. Something yellow bubbled in a glass jar clamped over a blue flame, and a series of glass tubes ran to several other jars where liquid dripped. At one end of the room, a metal table suggested the doctor worked on the dead from time to time, and a hint of stale, clotted blood filled the room. Chris wrinkled his nose at the odor.

"Over here. Please make yourselves comfortable."

They followed Bowman to a corner containing two stuffed chairs and a sofa, all resting on a Persian rug. Chris took one of the chairs and Max chose the sofa.

"This has proven to be an interesting project." Bowman drew the remaining chair closer to them and sat, leaning forward with his elbows resting on his knees. "I have located elements in your blood that seem to cause your problem with sunlight. I believe these elements represent a kind of infestation, which causes many symptoms besides the light sensitivity. It slows your respiration and circulation, until you appear nearly dead. It is this slowing that gives you the ability to live a much longer life than others."

"You think we're alive?" Chris asked.

Bowman smiled patiently. "Of course. The idea of the walking dead is merely a superstitious belief that doesn't stand up to scrutiny by a scientific mind."

Chris glanced at Max, who acknowledged the look with a subtle nod. Apparently, they would go along with the doctor's theory, if it got them to the right result.

"The difficulty comes from the way the infestation manifests itself. Because you ingest blood to become infected, you must also ingest blood to fight that infection."

"You have blood you wish us to drink?" Max asked.

"Yes, in a manner of speaking. I found a compound that destroys these harmful elements without breaking down the rest, but it cannot be ingested directly. It needs a certain hormonal content that we have not yet been able to reproduce outside the human body." Bowman straightened, gripping his thighs. "I have a suitable donor, a young woman. I will inject her with the compound, and she will filter the substance for you."

"Donor?" Chris asked.

Bowman shrugged. "She has been well paid."

From Max's pocket, no doubt. Did she have any idea what she was being paid for?

"So you'll inject her and bring her in for us to . . ."

"Drink from," Bowman said.

Max had trusted the human with more information than was customary. Chris glanced at the older vampire again and saw a twinkle in his eye that worried him. The good doctor could be in mortal danger, no matter what the outcome.

"There is one catch," Bowman said, rising. "The woman must be sexually stimulated in order for her hormone levels to be sufficiently high. Otherwise, the vaccine will not work." He rubbed his hands together. "Are we ready to begin?"

Max nodded. "Quite ready."

Bowman hurried across the room and disappeared behind a door.

Max shrugged off his coat and slung it over the arm of the sofa. Then he removed his cravat and looked at Chris. "Don't you want to be more comfortable?"

Chris sighed, resigned himself to what was to come, and slipped off his coat, tossing it onto the chair Bowman had abandoned. He slipped loose the top button on his shirt, then sat back and glared at Max.

"Look at it this way," Max said. "Even if it doesn't work, it shouldn't be an unpleasant experience, unless, of course, the female is unusually distasteful."

Memories of spending a day stuffed under a pirogue with Max swam through his brain. "Shouldn't be."

They turned at the sound of the door opening again, and rose as Bowman led a young woman by the hand into the room. The woman was tall with blond hair and blue eyes, and would have been beautiful with a few more pounds under her flesh.

Still, she was attractive enough that Chris began to warm to the plan.

"May I present Elsa?" Bowman urged the woman toward Chris and Max.

Max took her hand first and raised it to his lips. "Lovely," he said.

Elsa curtsied, and her cheeks reddened.

Chris bowed formally.

"My friend is a little unsure about this arrangement," Max said. "Do you understand what is expected of you, my dear?"

Elsa nodded. "Yes, sir, I believe I do. I'm to get an injection, and then you'll . . . take blood from me."

"Yes." Max grinned. "Shall we get started?"

Elsa nodded again, and stood with her arms at her sides, watching Max. She wore a red silk Chinese robe, and appeared to have nothing else on. The fabric clung to her curves.

Bowman produced a large syringe, raised it into the air and sprayed out a little of the yellow liquid, then lifted the sleeve on Elsa's robe and jabbed it into her arm. The woman winced, but didn't break her hold on Max's gaze.

The older vampire studied her face and seemed to find it pleasing. He circled her, sliding his fingers along the top of her back.

"Will you be watching the entire time?" he asked of Bowman.

"Naturally, I must observe, but I will withdraw as much as possible."

Max returned to stand in front of Elsa, and eased the collar of the robe down to expose her milky shoulders. Chris admired the firm rise of her cleavage, wondering exactly what lay hidden beneath the silk. As Max traced a line from her shoulder to the side of her neck and stopped with two fingers touching her pulse, Chris's pants tightened and a subtle tingle started where his fangs would soon appear.

"Come, Christopher," Max said, in a voice too soft for the others to hear. "You may have one side while I take the other."

They'd shared women before, but not with someone watching. Chris glanced at Bowman, who sat at his workbench furtively studying them and making notes.

Keeping the young doctor in view, Chris moved to stand behind Elsa.

The woman was only a few inches shorter than his own six feet, and had wide, strong shoulders that yet whispered of feminine passion. He brushed her hair to one side, and then skimmed his hand over her pale skin to where wispy hairs tickled his palm. Leaning closer, he caught her scent: soap, female sweat, and a hint of something tantalizing underneath. At first he thought it was perfume, but realized the smell rose from her skin, and seemed to be getting stronger. Could it be something in the vaccine?

He glanced up to meet Max's golden gaze and realized he smelled it, too. Max smiled to reveal lengthening fangs.

Chris returned his attention to Elsa, who didn't move a muscle.

The woman had no idea what kind of danger she faced with such an enticing aroma, standing between two vampires.

Max stepped closer to her, easing her robe away from her arms, and Chris watched the silk flow down her back and over her buttocks to pool on the floor at her feet. As he'd suspected, she was bare beneath the robe, and now stood temptingly naked between them.

Max kissed her, cupping her jaw tenderly.

Chris spread his hands over her shoulders, not quite touching her. He felt the air under his palms shimmer with her warmth.

She raised her arms to encircle Max's neck, and Chris slid his hands down to the sides of her breasts and feathered his touch across her smooth skin. She shuddered in response, and his body answered with instant excitement. He heard the steady beat of her heart now, just above a whisper.

He also heard the hum of his master's pleasure in his head.

Max had made the connection he only used when they were sharing—a connection that allowed emotion and discovery to pass between them. Chris had never learned to initiate the connection, but he knew how to use it, and drew on the anticipation of joy now traveling the thread.

"Arouse her," Max silently commanded.

Chris leaned forward and pressed his lips to her shoulder. Her skin tasted as tempting as it smelled—ambrosia. He licked a wide swath to gather it all in.

With his senses inflamed, he moved his hands down to her waist, and then followed the movement along her spine with his mouth and tongue.

Elsa shook and released soft sounds of longing.

Chris's fangs lengthened in a rush, and he knelt to nip at the small rounds of her smooth ass. Her hips jerked forward and back, and he slid one hand up the inside of her thighs.

He knew the delight Max took in exploring her firm breasts with his hands and tongue, and the way it felt to have her hand fisted in his hair. Pleasant sensations vibrated along the connection, pushing him closer to releasing the beast.

His fingers found wet warmth between her folds, and touched her small budding clitoris. She jerked more violently, nearly causing him to accidentally pierce her flesh with his fangs.

Growling at the urgency spreading through him, he rose and drew Elsa slowly backward until he sat on the sofa and could ease her down into his lap. Reaching between them, he freed his cock, and it sprang up against her heated cunt.

She sucked in a soft breath.

Max now knelt in front of her, caressing her flesh and kissing her neck. His eyes opened and he met Chris's gaze. Gold irises flickered with blood-red desire, and Chris knew the beast was close for both of them. It must be the vaccine drawing them forward, because Max usually maintained control long after he'd lost it.

Aching with hunger and need, Chris reached around Elsa's wide hips and slipped his finger along her crease, reaching once again for her clit and finding it growing. He nipped at the heated flesh on her back, careful not to break the skin. She whimpered and rocked her hips back and forth as she turned her head.

He felt Max's hunger surging forth, and also his measure of restraint as he rested his lips above her sweet pulse.

Elsa reached down between her legs and hesitantly touched the head of Chris's cock. He grunted at the sensations shooting through his body, fanning the flames of human desire that accompanied the hunger. He pressed his palm to the middle of Elsa's lower back and eased her forward, positioning her hips for him.

Needing only his fingers stroking her clit, he guided himself into her tight warmth, following his own progress as he eased in. He felt her cunt stretch to accommodate his swollen cock, and growled when she rolled forward, bending him nearly to the point of pain. Her breath stuttered from her chest as she leaned back into him. Chris wrapped his arm around her waist and continued to stroke her clit, now working the bud side to side. Her tight inner muscles twitched around him.

Then he felt Max's desire melt over him as the older vampire's prick pushed against the base of his own.

"Together," Max commanded.

Chris withdrew just enough to allow Elsa's precious juices to cover his fingers, and then he spread them onto the head of Max's stiff cock. As Max pushed, the wet friction against sensitive skin and tightness squeezing his hardened shaft sent Chris's head back to the sofa, his mouth open to leave his fangs exposed.

Max thrust in and Elsa groaned. Chris fought to hold still as Max withdrew and thrust again and again, faster now.

Delight and desire quivered along the connection in both directions, intensifying into waves.

The beast reached the end of its tether and bounced the chain as it lunged forward. Chris opened his eyes. He watched as Max studied Elsa's pounding pulse and drew his lips back. Fangs shimmered in the light, poised to strike, and then Max penetrated the woman's flesh with perfect precision.

Chris felt the blast of white light in his own head as Max did, and he drank in the strength and satisfaction. Emotions spilled out in a rush, promising rejuvenation when his turn came.

Elsa cried out as her cunt squeezed their cocks together in pounding pulses, and her cream slid down between them.

Hunger sliced through Chris's insides and he drew her closer to him, prepared to take what he could from her shoulder.

An explosion of ghastly pain incapacitated Chris and he fell back.

Max pushed himself away from them, collapsing to the floor, and the connection snapped.

Elsa screamed.

All sensation stopped, and Chris shoved the woman away. She huddled into the arm of the sofa, still screaming.

Max looked up, his face transformed into that of a hideous beast, something emerging from hell. Pain radiated from him as if he were being torn in two, and he clawed at his own chest, shredding his shirt.

Chris dropped to his knees in front of Max, uncertain what to do. He glanced at Bowman and found him staring, wide-eyed, pen in hand.

Rage drove Chris to his feet. "What have you done?"

Bowman backed into his chair and sent it skidding across the floor.

Chris stalked toward him, determined to get answers. As he stepped within reach of the man, he was suddenly flung aside where he crashed into a wall.

Max moved as a blur, grabbing the man by the shoulders,

whipping him around, and ripping open his throat. He latched onto the open wound, sucking in nourishment with animal-like slurping sounds.

Bowman struggled for only a moment, then hung limp in Max's arms, his skin visibly whitening.

Max dropped the lifeless body to the floor and stared at Chris with beastly yellow eyes, his face still hideous. "He tricked us," he hissed. "He meant to kill us both."

Chris frowned at Elsa, who lay curled in a ball on the sofa, trembling and weeping. Had she expected them to bite her and die before her eyes? Had that really been the plan? Or had the doctor simply been wrong?

His own beastly transformation began to fade as he pushed himself to his feet and straightened his clothing. Hunger still clawed inside him, demanding satisfaction. He would have to hunt in the shadows of the streets.

"Chris? Are you in here?" Nicole leaned through the narrow opening and shone her flashlight around the glittering cavern. Fresh batteries provided new intensity to the beam, and the entire room seemed to glow.

He had to be here. She'd searched everywhere else. He couldn't have slipped past her, she was sure of that. And there weren't any other passages.

"Chris?"

She walked slowly across the sand, aware of some kind of strange sound just audible over the trickling water. It almost sounded like a distant motor, or the purr of a lion. She waved the light across the wall, checking all the indentations and ledges of rock. Was he hiding back here for some reason?

Her beam fell across a beastly figure and she screamed as she stumbled backward and dropped the flashlight.

It took her mind several long moments to process what she

saw, and she still wasn't sure she was right. This monster that crouched in the corner, now covering its face with its arm, wore Chris's clothes and was roughly the size of a man.

"What the hell?" She snatched the flashlight and directed it at his face as she scrambled to her feet. "Chris?"

He hissed, opening his mouth to reveal beastly fangs, and she took a step back.

"The light," he said, in a voice that she definitely didn't recognize.

She lowered the light beam. "What the fuck . . . ?"

He moved his arm away and she knew for sure it was Chris, but something horrible had happened to him. His face looked like a cross between an animal and a man, and his eyes were a strange gold and red color.

"Go away," he said.

"What's going on?"

"Leave here. Now!" A roar punctuated his command.

Nicole gulped at the fear tightening her throat.

None of this made any sense. Moments ago, she'd been in the arms of the most amazing man she'd ever met, reaching heights of sexual pleasure she hadn't even known existed. Now that same man cowered before her partially transformed into some kind of animal, and apparently in pain.

Her whole body shook, and her brain told her to run, but she couldn't. She couldn't leave until she understood what was going on and knew there was nothing she could do to help.

"Chris—"

She screamed for the second time when he suddenly appeared before her, looming over her, his face mere inches from her own. His gaze bore into her.

Her heart jumped into her throat and she struggled for breath.

He wrapped one arm around her waist and crushed her body to his.

"So," he said, his voice a deadly whisper, "you don't want to leave? How perfect."

"Chris, please." She pushed against his chest, but all her strength had no effect. "You're hurting me."

"Am I?" He leaned close, sniffing her neck, growling softly.

Even in her fear and pain, excitement sizzled in her belly.

"You want me," he whispered. "I smell your desire."

Her arms and knees buckled and she crumpled against him.

He held her up as if he hadn't noticed. "I smell your blood, so sweet and pure." His cool lips brushed along the side of her neck. Instinctively, she moved her head, surrendering once again, only this time she didn't know what she surrendered to.

"I will make you tremble with longing before I take you again."

She did tremble, from the inside out. Every cell in her body seemed to suddenly come to life.

"Nice," he said. His voice vibrated against her skin.

She whimpered. "Chris." His name rose softly from her heart.

He froze.

And then he slowly released her, letting her find her footing before backing away. When he hit the rock wall, he stopped and stared at her.

She saw something strange in his expression. Fear? Vulnerability maybe? Or heartfelt sadness? Whatever it was made her want to cry.

She took a deep breath and blew it out. "Chris, what is this? What's going on?"

"*This*," he said, "is me."

She frowned.

"I'm a vampire."

"Vampires aren't . . . real?"

He didn't respond, but she saw by the way he watched her that he'd shared a secret he didn't often share.

Working at night, seeing in the dark of the cave, making love to her unlike any man ever had . . .

Holy crap, he was a vampire! Or something.

Unable to stand, she sat suddenly in the sand.

He crouched so that they remained at eye level.

Her thoughts seemed to be moving through molasses. "You're trapped in here by the daylight?"

He nodded.

"And you're . . . hungry?"

He nodded again, more slowly, one corner of his mouth curving up.

She swallowed hard. "Do you plan to kill me?"

His expression hardened. "I don't plan to, but you must leave before I no longer have a choice."

"I can't leave you like this."

He growled and looked away as if studying the wall. Then his gaze snapped back to hers. "There's a cooler in my vehicle."

"Is it locked?"

He rose to his feet, drew keys from his pocket, and held them out.

Nicole struggled to stand, her senses returning, picked up the flashlight, and tried to walk toward him, but her feet wouldn't move.

Chris stepped slowly forward until he held the keys over her palm, and then dropped them, careful not to touch her. She closed her hand around the keys, and he stepped back and slid down the rock face.

"I'll be back in a few minutes," she said.

As she turned, she heard him answer softly, "I'm not going anywhere."

Once she'd crawled out into the sunshine, she stopped and glanced back at the cave opening, wondering if she'd just hallucinated the whole thing.

Cold keys poking into her palm suggested she hadn't. She opened her hand and stared at them.

They were plain, ordinary keys on a plain silver ring. Nothing special. Nothing strange. Except that they belonged to a vampire.

This was her chance to escape. He'd admitted he couldn't leave the cave because of the sunlight. She was safe out here. All she had to do was walk away.

And then what?

What would she do, wear a crucifix to work tonight and hope it protected her? Go gnaw on a clove of garlic? Or should she run out and find someone to tell that she knew a vampire, that vampires were real, and that they were all at risk?

Or were they at risk?

"Boss?"

Nicole jumped.

Brandon grabbed her arm. "Are you okay?"

"Yes, I'm fine."

"Where's Marsh?"

Surprised by Brandon's obvious anger, she frowned at her reflection in his eyes and realized what she must have looked like with puffy lips and wrecked hair. Trying to hide her confusion and concern, she smiled as much as she could. "Really, I'm fine."

"Where is he?"

"Brandon, everything's okay and this is none of your business. Please, go get some rest. I'll see you tonight."

For a moment, she wasn't sure he'd leave. He studied her eyes intently, then swung his gaze to the cave opening and nodded. "All right."

She watched him, wondering if she'd made the right decision by sending him away. Was his concern for her welfare justified?

Chris had held her against him, obviously in charge, and his fangs had been millimeters from her neck. Yet, he'd backed away. He was some kind of creature, but he was also Chris Marsh, the man she'd fantasized about for a month and a half. She'd worked beside him all that time without knowing anything about him except that the air crackled when he was near.

Strangely enough, she felt as though he'd touched her heart when he touched her body. Was that just the nature of the beast, so to speak? Had he deceived her?

With questions screaming in her head, she walked to his Land Rover, removed the two bags of dark red blood from the ice chest, and carried them back to the cave.

6

He'd almost hoped she wouldn't return. Temptation brought the beast too close to the surface.

Chris listened to Nicole's footsteps as she made her way to the back room, surprised to find them so sure. He'd expected her to at least hesitate.

Within moments, she knelt before him, offering the bags.

He snatched them from her, pierced the plastic, and drained them both in a matter of seconds. Then he closed his eyes and let the nectar work its magic.

Nerves snapped and fired, emotions flowed through his brain, and he felt alive for a few glorious moments. Then the feelings settled into simple satisfaction and he relaxed, the beast firmly in check—for the moment.

Chris opened his eyes to find Nicole watching him. "You're staring."

She glanced down. "Sorry, I'm just . . ."

"Curious?"

She shrugged. "I guess that's as good a term as any."

"Yes." He rose and stretched his back. "You are, after all, a scientist." He crossed to the warm pool, where he crouched, took a handful of water, and splashed it on his face. As the pool settled, he studied his reflection. With his fangs gone and his eyes back to normal, he looked like himself again.

What, exactly, had she seen when she found him? Had he looked as horrifying as Max had the night he drank from Elsa?

If so, Nicole had nerves of steel.

He stood and returned to where she sat cross-legged, apparently waiting for an explanation. As he sat in front of her, his gaze drifted down to where her shorts rose on her tender inner thighs, and he gulped. More than anything, he wanted to hold her again.

But that wouldn't happen, now that she knew what he was.

"I'm a vampire," he said.

She nodded. "Yes, I got that. How? When?"

Had she truly already accepted the truth?

"I was brought into the Darkness by another of my kind in 1691."

She blinked several times and her eyes widened a bit, undoubtedly as she calculated his age. "That's impossible."

He shrugged. "It's important that mortals believe that. Otherwise, we would be hunted."

Did she see the difference, the clear line that separated them? He watched lightning-quick thoughts flash changing emotions in her eyes.

"You've lived more than three hundred years?"

"Not lived, exactly. I've experienced three centuries."

"I just . . . I can't—"

He waited, studying her beautiful face, letting her mind adjust to him as her body had before.

"Cars, electricity, our whole country," she whispered. Her gaze rose to his face. "Where? Where were you when it happened?"

"On a quiet street in Boston."

"Boston. Holy crap." She shook her head slowly.

"Yes," he said, "much has changed. We were colonials back then, still under the King's rule."

Several long moments ticked by.

"So, did you know George Washington?"

"Not personally." Chris smiled. "I did hear him speak a few times, though."

"Oh, shit. That's incredible." Her eyes narrowed, as belief brought on the harder questions. "You really live off of human blood?"

"Most of the time. Few animals offer the same satisfaction as humans." Somehow, he felt a great sense of relief at being able to answer her questions honestly. He couldn't remember when he'd been so open with a mortal, and almost laughed at the joy of it.

"I don't understand."

He fought the growing drowsiness threatening to dull him. "When we feed, we take in more than just blood. We take in emotions, memories, everything that makes you unique. We connect with you in a way I can't explain."

"We? How many others are there?"

Chris shrugged. "We're generally loners. It's difficult enough for one of us to feed without being noticed, and nearly impossible for a group."

"How do you . . . I mean, how much do you take? Does your victim die?"

He sighed. "Hopefully, the *victim* barely notices. It can be quite an erotic experience. Unless I lose control of the situation."

Her hand rose to the side of her neck. "You didn't—"

He shook his head. "No. I find you a little too attractive, Nicole."

She swallowed hard, as if she understood his meaning. He hoped like hell she did. In spite of the two pints he'd just drained, her heartbeat whispered to him.

"When we were together earlier," she said, hesitancy appearing in her voice, "why didn't you, you know, climax?"

He suddenly regretted the honesty and considered how to respond. Unfortunately, he had no stomach for lying to her anymore. He'd gone too far to return.

"What you saw when you came back for me, that was the true nature of the vampire. It's always just below the surface, even when I'm in control. But when I lose control, it takes over. The vampire doesn't care what happens to you."

"So, if you lose control . . . sexually, I mean, the vampire takes over?"

"It can."

"But it doesn't always."

Horror filled him as he realized where she might be headed with this. He rose to his feet. "Nicole, you should go."

She looked up, stood, and brushed off her hands and backside. "And just leave you here? What if something happens? What if someone else comes in here, like one of my students?"

He moved around her and crossed the room to peer through the lens-shaped opening. A hint of light brightened the winding passageway.

He hadn't considered the prospect of someone else coming back before nightfall. With any luck, he'd be able to keep himself awake. Asleep, he was vulnerable, as was anyone who woke him.

"You should go," he repeated.

"Is this why you're looking for the talisman?"

He sighed, realizing she wasn't planning to do as he suggested, and returned to stand in front of her, leaning against the wall.

"The keeper 'walks in the light,' " she said, and then looked up with wide eyes. "That's it! This has nothing to do with a deity. It's literal. You'd be able to walk in the daylight."

He nodded. "Perhaps."

"That's what you're hoping for, isn't it?"

"Yes."

"Does it mean you'd no longer be a vampire, or you'd be a vampire who can walk in daylight?"

"It could mean nothing at all."

She drew up one knee, rested her arm on it, and raked her fingers through her hair.

Something about the movement sent a shiver through him. He definitely wanted more of her.

He wanted all of her.

Groaning in frustration, he pushed himself away from the wall and ambled across the room.

"I have so many questions."

He spun around to find her standing close. "Ask what you will, but not now. You must leave."

"Why?"

Chris sighed. "Because daytime strains my defenses. And I want you too much."

"Meaning what?"

He opened his mouth just enough for her to see the tips of his fangs.

Her eyes widened again, but she didn't move. She just studied his face for a long time with her beautiful green eyes.

Then she stepped forward, raising one palm to his chest. "How erotic?"

"What?" He covered her hand with his own, enjoying the warm magic of her touch.

"You said it could be an erotic experience for me, taking my blood."

"*If* I don't lose control."

She stepped closer until her face was only inches from his. "You didn't lose control last time."

Damn. He didn't really want her to leave. He wanted to take her, both as a man and as a vampire. He wanted all she had to give.

Burying his fingers in her soft hair, he drew her face to his and kissed her, careful not to injure her tender mouth with his fangs. Delight surged through him as he tasted her again, and he encircled her with his arms.

She returned his kiss, her tongue sliding dangerously and deliciously into his mouth. He groaned as he drew her up against him so that the full length of her body met his.

She began to unbutton his shirt. He tore his mouth from hers and gazed down at her, finding a hunger to mirror his own blazing in her eyes. Holding her gaze, he removed her clothes as carefully as he could, losing only a button or two in the process, and then helped her finish removing his. As he thought of having her warm skin against him again, his fangs lengthened and his cock swelled.

He hadn't had nearly enough of her.

Slipping one arm around his neck, she drew him back down to her. He took her mouth, lifting her from the ground.

She wrapped her legs around his hips, gripping him with her limbs, her heat, and her heart, and he knew his existence would never be the same.

No matter what happened, Nicole changed him with her simple embrace, her acceptance, her ability to care for him no matter what the truth revealed. He ached to touch her in the same way, and only hoped that by doing so, he didn't end her desire to accept him. Or her life.

Moving his mouth to her ear, he growled softly as he eased her onto his waiting cock, returning to where they'd left off. A shiver ran though her, and she made soft sounds of pleasure as her warm, wet body took him in, a little at a time, biting and releasing.

"I've never known such perfection," he whispered. "You were made for me."

She groaned and held him tighter.

Her clit furrowed his hard shaft as she slid down, swallowing more of him with her velvety grip.

Oddly enough, the hunger swelled in him without the cruelty of the beast. He thirsted for her, but only her, not simply blood. He needed to know her dreams and desires, her strengths and weaknesses. He needed to understand her fantasies.

Her cunt tightened as he buried himself to the hilt and his human desire rose to match the hunger.

How could this be? He wasn't mortal. Yet, joined with her, he felt as if he were. His seed churned and demanded release.

"Give yourself to me, Nicole," he said.

Her fingers dug into his shoulders and her heels into his buttocks, and she slowly, purposely raised her chin and turned her head.

He nearly dropped to his knees as the promise of bliss sang in his chest.

Chris tasted the feminine saltiness of her neck and held his lips to her pulse. The whisper of her heartbeat rose to a roar.

Drawing back his lips, he pressed the points of his fangs to her tender flesh, which he could pierce with the slightest pressure. Everything she was would be his to savor.

He spread his fingers to touch more of her, and widened his stance.

With a growl, he bit down.

Her coppery warmth flooded his mouth.

She cried out as her cunt began to pulse around him, biting into his rigid cock.

And then her amazing essence exploded in his brain.

In an instant, he knew her from the inside out. He knew

every moment of her life—the death of her father, the joy of graduation, the loneliness and isolation her career demanded. He knew how much she wanted him, and felt her orgasm as if it were his own.

His seed flowed in a volcanic eruption, mixing with her gushing cream to run as liquid heat down his thighs.

He drew harder, taking more, desperate.

She cried out again, and her cunt pounded harder. She clung to his shoulder and gripped a handful of his hair.

Emotions rolled through him with a power he couldn't have imagined. He felt her tie to the past, her insatiable desire for knowledge, her need for more than life had yet offered. He knew her fearful delight at having discovered what he was.

He tasted her total trust.

Fighting his own depraved desire to drink more, to steal more of her emotions, he withdrew his fangs and held his mouth to the wounds. He felt the holes close under his lips.

Her life continued to swirl though him, offering tenderness and acceptance. He relished the beauty of it all as he held her.

She turned her head and rested it against his chest, and stroked the back of his neck.

The aftereffects of their orgasms passed between them as small contractions and peace-filled sighs, and he smiled as he marveled at her inner strength still rushing through his veins.

At that moment, he knew that if the talisman were to ever be found, Nicole would be the one to find it.

He'd held her as if she weighed nothing until Nicole had become uncomfortable, and then released her gently, kissing her temples and cheeks as he placed her on her feet. Her knees had trembled and she'd felt generally weak, but satisfied in a way she'd never imagined.

Erotic wasn't the word. It was so much more. With his cock filling her completely, he'd penetrated the rest of her body with his bite. Strange. She'd sensed him in her head. She'd felt him in her soul and heart. Until today, she hadn't even believed she had a soul.

As soon as his fangs had pierced her skin, she'd tensed, but then the sting had morphed into something else, and he'd sucked hard, pushing her into an orgasmic haze. And just as she thought she'd made it through in one piece, he'd done it again. The weird part was that she'd felt him riding the second wave with her, which had made it all that much more intense.

Now she sat on the ground leaning against the rock wall, her clothes worse for wear, stroking his soft blond hair. Chris lay on his back with his head in her lap, asleep.

No, he wasn't asleep. He was dead.

The last thing he'd told her was not to worry, that he would wake again when the sun set, and he'd kissed her.

His taste lingered on her lips.

How could she possibly be sitting in a cave, watching over a sleeping vampire, when just a day earlier her life had been normal? Everything had changed as quickly as someone switching off the lights.

A vampire. Jesus Christ!

The worse part was the fear that she was in love with him. Her body still sizzled at the memory of his touch, but there was so much more. Certainly part of it was fascination. How could she not be fascinated by someone who'd lived through so much of the history she could only study? Imagine the stories he could tell her! But there was more. She saw something of herself in his eyes. She saw the solitude, loneliness, and isolation.

After her father's death, she'd never found anyone who truly understood her. Even to her mother, whom she loved dearly, she'd always been a mystery. "Why would you want to spend all summer out in some godforsaken place, digging in the dirt?" she asked every year.

Chris understood her curiosity.

Nicole sighed.

What the hell was she going to do now? She was in love with a vampire. She couldn't exactly take him home to her mother. "Hi, Mom. This is Chris Marsh. No, we can't have dinner with you because he prefers his straight from a vein. Yes, we would have been here earlier, but he can't walk around in the sunlight."

Sunlight.

The talisman.

The easiest way to have Chris in her life, assuming he wanted to be there, was to find the talisman and have it work. It was the bridge between their worlds.

A chill ran up her spine. What if that bridge wasn't supposed to be built? What if, instead of the caring, tender man she thought she knew, Chris was really the bloodthirsty beast she'd found that morning, looking for a way to rule the human race? He'd admitted there were other vampires out there. Mortals could be nothing more than chattel to be chained and fed.

Once he could walk among them, what would stop him?

Something about that thought led her to a picture of the graves at the front of the cave.

Chris opened his eyes to empty rock above him and felt cool sand below. As usual, he was alone.

No, wait. He heard her heartbeat, gentle and pure. He knew it as well as he knew her scent and taste. He sat up and looked around for Nicole.

She stood with her back to him, studying the water in the warm pool, appearing to be lost in thought.

"Nicole," he said, reaching out to touch her back.

She jumped and swung around. "Shit! Don't sneak up on me like that."

What he saw in her eyes physically hurt. The tenderness and joy he'd seen before sunrise now gave way to suspicion and fear.

"What is it?"

She shook her head and frowned down at her hands.

Chris cupped her jaw and drew her gaze back to his. "What is it, Nicole? I've trusted you with everything. Tell me what's wrong."

"Everything?"

"What?"

Her green eyes searched his. "Have you told me everything? What about your reason for wanting the talisman?"

He smiled and shook his head, then turned away from her, looking out at the slit of fading light. "You can't imagine what it's like not to see the sun for three hundred years. I see paintings of sunsets, and photographs, and I don't know if the colors are real or not. I can't quite remember. I want to watch the sun rise from a white sand beach, see the yellow rays glisten off blue water. I want to feel its warmth on my face and neck, and hear the sounds of the world waking." He turned back to find her studying him. "I can't begin to explain it."

There was even more that he couldn't say. He felt things for Nicole that he shouldn't be able to feel—tenderness, joy at the sight of her, the desire to wake in her arms, and he truly cared what she thought of him.

Vampires couldn't love mortals. Max had drilled that fact into him in his early years. But these feelings he had for Nicole had to be as close as it got.

Her eyes still darkened.

"What is it you suspect?"

She swallowed hard.

And then he knew. He knew how her mind worked, and followed her logical train of thought. She'd been safe outside in the sunlight. Once she no longer had that protection, would she still be safe from what she knew he could become? Would anyone?

"You're right to be afraid," he said, "but not of me. There are others who could use the talisman exactly as you fear. Once I discovered it might actually exist, I knew I had to find it before anyone else did."

"And do what, become the guardian of the talisman?"

"Yes, I suppose."

"So, will you try it to see if it works?"

He huffed. "If I had a chance to watch that sunrise, or to walk through a sunlit field with you, how could I resist?"

"With me?"

How had he let that slip? He knew better than to expect too much from this mortal woman, in spite of what she meant to him. She hadn't learned all the lessons only centuries could teach, and she knew what he was.

They stared at each other for several long moments. He was tempted to say more, but he couldn't.

"The sun has set. We should go." He motioned for her to precede him from the cavern.

She hesitated, then nodded and started forward, following her bouncing beam of light.

When they stepped out into the early night, he took a deep breath of the cool air and froze. He grabbed Nicole's arm to stop her.

She spun around. "What?"

Chris raised his nose and inhaled deeper, sorting out scents both familiar and alien. Animals, plants, flowers, car exhaust, warm rock, and something else. Was it . . . ?

No, there was nothing else. He sniffed again and again. Still nothing.

He shook his head as he released her arm. "Nothing."

She started forward and he followed, scanning the shadows as they walked.

For a moment, he would have sworn he smelled someone he knew better than any other, but it could have just been paranoia producing the scent.

Was Max really in the vicinity?

His chest clenched at the possibility as he thought about the last time he had seen his master, shortly after leaving Dr. Bowman's laboratory. That was when he'd discovered the truth . . .

Chris followed Max's scent down alleys and along streets for a good hour before finally catching up to him. He found him in a narrow alley between two brick buildings, pinning one woman to a wall as he drank from her neck where he'd ripped open her dress. A young redhead lay at his feet.

Chris crouched to check for the redhead's pulse and found none. Then he stood as close as he dared. "Max?"

The older vampire raised his head to glare at Chris through blood-red eyes. "What do you want?"

"What are you doing?" he asked, motioning toward the redhead. "You're killing them."

Max hissed. "They mean nothing. I must rid myself of this vile poison."

Chris tried to push Max away from the young woman he still held against the wall, but the older vampire didn't budge. His glare turned lethal.

"They're innocent," Chris said, trying again to get through. "You're murdering them."

Max threw back his head and released a madman's laugh. Then he smiled at Chris. "Murder? They are nothing more than food, Christopher. Sustenance. What you do with them beyond that is for your own entertainment, nothing more." He tossed aside the woman he'd held against the wall without even looking back, then wrapped one arm around Chris's shoulders and guided him toward the street. "Have you forgotten what you are? You're immortal. We could rule these puny mortals if we wished. Imagine, having the most beautiful women sitting at our feet, waiting for the command to bear their breasts and necks to us. And the most delicious young men."

"You've always been careful not to take their lives."

"For self-preservation. We don't want to leave a trail of bodies like breadcrumbs for angry mortals to follow."

"But you were once mortal. Don't you feel any guilt?"

Max laughed again, more quietly this time as he eyed a couple passing them. "It doesn't take long to shed the chains of mortality if you try, dear boy." He slowed, then stopped and watched a woman hurrying along the opposite side of the street, clutching the hand of a young girl.

"This drug has driven you mad."

"No, it has freed me. I no longer need to waste the energy on a human mask." Releasing Chris's shoulders, Max stepped into the street, then stopped and glanced back. "Coming?"

Chris shook his head and watched Max stroll across the street and fall into place ten feet behind the pair.

He considered running after him, trying to stop him from hurting the mother and daughter, but he knew he stood no chance against Max's strength. And now he realized he stood no chance against Max's madness, either.

His gut churned as he spun around and headed for the red-light district. Hunger still burned the inside of his skin, but he would not take the life of an innocent to appease it. Not if he could keep the beast in check.

Had Max thought this way all along? Had it been only the mask Chris had known?

As he walked, his boots thudding on the empty sidewalk, he wondered how many more like Max were out there.

* * *

"Hey, boss. We started without you." Megan wiped her forehead on her shirt sleeve as she straightened. She'd just pulled a bucket of debris up from the widening pit, exposing the opening to the priest's tomb.

"Sorry I'm late. How's it looking?"

Brandon met her gaze, glanced at Chris, and then tried to hide the jealousy that flashed in his eyes. "Great. We've already moved the second limestone slab, and the door's exposed."

"Has it been breeched?" Nicole crouched at the edge of the hole.

"Doesn't look like it." Brandon crossed to the side of the pit and gazed up at her.

Excitement blossomed in her, nearly driving her to her feet. It was all she could do to keep from squealing. "Well," she said, standing and wiping her palms on her shorts, "let's get busy. I expect to be in the tomb before sunrise."

"What about the cave?" Brandon asked.

"Once we get this open and photographed, you can take a crew over to get some more data. I want a proposal for next year that can't be turned down. And see if you can figure out how we might block it off."

"You got it," Brandon said. Before turning, he tossed one more glare over at Chris.

Crap. Had he told anyone else about the state she'd been in that morning? Did everyone know?

Trying to ignore the concern, Nicole headed to the folding table where she'd left her tools the night before. Fortunately, no one had swiped them. As she slung the canvas bag over one shoulder, she studied Chris, already bending over his notes.

He raised his steady blue-eyed gaze to her eyes, and she felt the air crackle around her again. It took every ounce of restraint she had not to lean over and kiss him.

And yet he was a monster.

How could everything suddenly be so absurdly complicated?

If they hadn't gone exploring together in the cave, she would still think of him as just some gorgeous guy she was ready to hop into bed with.

The weird part was that knowing the truth hadn't lessened her desire for him. The memory of his mouth on her neck, his arms around her, and his cock buried inside her weakened her knees and glued her tongue to the roof of her mouth.

Taking a deep breath and blowing it out silently, she purposely walked to the pit and descended the ladder.

Within moments, she was completely submersed in the process of solving the most amazing archaeological mystery of her career.

Two hours later, every "i" had been dotted and every "t" crossed; they were ready to remove the first part of the door, actually three limestone slabs stacked and fitted into the opening.

"Everyone knows what to do?" Nicole glanced around at her crew, both in the pit with her and above them on the ropes, and everyone nodded. Chris stood behind the crowd, watching.

Ropes had been set through drilled holes at the top and bottom of the top slab, and would be used to keep the block from falling when pried from its resting place. Moving to the side, she gently tapped the chisel into place at the edge of the block and then twisted it and pulled, easing the block toward her a little at a time. Eric and Brandon braced themselves against the front to keep it from swinging across the pit.

As the block finally slipped free, it fell several inches to tighten the ropes, and students at the top of the pit grunted. But the block continued to slide down when it should have stopped.

"Shit," one of the students said as his footing slipped and he dropped to the ground. The one behind him tripped over his legs and the rope started to slip faster.

Nicole jumped out of the way of the slowly falling slab. "Watch out!"

Suddenly the stone stopped falling, and she looked up to find Chris holding the end of the rope alone. The other two men scrambled to their feet and returned to their spots on the line, and they all worked together to bring the slab to the surface. Once it was secure, Chris approached the edge and looked down at Nicole. Had he been worried about her?

He couldn't truly care about her, not like she cared about him. It had to have been a mistake on his part when he talked about walking in the sunlight with her. When she'd called him on it, he'd ignored her question.

She must get past the irrational desire to make him into something he wasn't. He wasn't some eccentric millionaire who would fall in love with her, carry her off to his Malibu beach house, and shower her with ancient Egyptian jewelry. He wasn't even a wannabe archaeologist with a house in the suburbs of Boston who planned to ask her to move in with him.

He was a vampire.

No matter how many times she thought it, it always came as a shock.

Mentally shaking herself, she turned to peer into the newly formed opening—the first to see something hidden for more than a thousand years. Air emerging from the darkness carried scents of rock, dust, and some kind of ancient spice.

With a trembling hand, she raised her flashlight, letting the beam slice across the middle of the room. It couldn't be more than five meters across, as indicated by GPR, but it glistened as if the walls were covered with glitter.

Steadying her hand, she moved the light left and then right, and found the room empty except for a stone altar at one end, covered with glyphs. When she shone it directly on the wall to her right, she realized the wall had been coated with gold, as though thin sheets of the precious metal had been hammered into the rock's surface.

"It's beautiful," she breathed.

Brandon and Eric looked over her shoulders.

"Holy shit," Brandon said. "That looks like gold. And look at the glyphs!"

Nicole turned around to speak to everyone at once. "Okay, everyone gets a chance to look in, then we all back off while Brandon takes photos. Whatever you do, don't even breathe into the chamber until the pictures have been taken. Got it?"

Everyone nodded and hurried to line up at the ladder.

Nicole climbed out and stood beside Chris as the first students started down.

He waited patiently for her to speak.

"The chamber's empty except for a rock altar covered with glyphs. And the walls are covered with gold."

"Nothing else? No sarcophagus?"

She swigged on her water bottle and then shrugged. "Not that I can see."

"Could you read the glyphs?"

"No, not from that distance."

She knew exactly how far his arm was from hers as they stood there, and that awareness angered her. Why had she let him touch her? Why did he have to tell her the truth while they were in the middle of a dig? Especially one so important. Damn.

"Nicole—"

She stepped away as if she hadn't heard him, but his voice softly speaking her name scrambled her senses.

"Ah, you're awake." Max crouched in front of the creature, studying her face. "Let me see your fangs."

She drew back her lips and hissed.

"Excellent. I do believe the transition is complete." He unlocked the cuff from her ankle and rose.

She rubbed her bare leg as she glared up at him, hatred burning in her eyes. Her dark knotted hair and blood-smeared mouth gave her the appearance of a wild animal, freshly returned from the kill.

Max sighed. "I must clean you up, my dear."

In a flash, she sprang from the floor and attacked, her fangs slashing at his throat.

He slammed her against the wall, holding her there with his weight. She growled and clawed at his face, but he managed to avoid much damage.

"Full of energy, are we?" Pinning her with one hand around her throat, he tore off her tattered clothing and freed himself from his pants. "Let's focus a little of that energy."

When he stepped close again, she attached herself to him like a savage monkey and sank her fangs into his chest. He gasped at the pleasure as he quickly buried his erect cock in her unprotected cunt.

She sucked in a breath of surprise, but didn't release him.

"Yes," he whispered, withdrawing and thrusting again, pressing her back to the wall, "quite pleasant."

As he continued, her growl quieted to one of contentment. Grabbing a handful of matted hair, he pulled her mouth from his chest, drew her head back, and sank his fangs into her neck.

She cried out at the pleasure and clutched his shoulders.

He drank his fill as he continued to fuck her until he'd had enough, and then he leaned against her as he smiled down into her dark eyes. "Better?"

She licked her lips and nodded.

"Good." He withdrew and stepped away from her, straightened his clothing, and offered her his hand.

She placed her hand in his and he patted it as he studied her face. "Nothing a little soap and water won't cure, my dear. And I have a lovely gown for you to wear when we go out. Perhaps you'll even see some of your old friends from the university. It's always nice to renew lost friendships, don't you think?"

There was at least one friendship of his own he was anxious to renew.

7

Careful not to expose his true strength, Chris helped lift the other two pieces of the door out of the excavation pit, and watched as Brandon photographed the room from the opening. Brandon and Nicole then donned paper booties over their shoes and stepped carefully into the room.

He now knew that Brandon had expressed his affection for Nicole in the past, and fought a renewed wave of jealousy as the two disappeared through the doorway together.

Sighing, Chris walked away from the excavation and the lights, and stood in the starlight to focus his thoughts.

The longer the night stretched on, the more he wanted Nicole back in his arms. His entire body ached with need that wouldn't be cured by donated platelets. He needed to feel her lips pressed to his shoulder, her fingers fanning the hairs on the back of his neck, her body writhing under his. He felt as though he were on the verge of insanity.

Suddenly, something skipped up his spine.

An awareness.

He stood perfectly still and listened.

He heard the students talking, night creatures moving about on the ground and in the air, leaves on trees rustling in the breeze, and even distant traffic noise, although the site was miles from a road. But he heard nothing else. No footsteps, no familiar voice calling his name.

Max couldn't have found him. He'd been careful to cover his tracks since leaving New York in 1918. He'd changed his name from Strickland to Johnson for several decades, and then to Marsh, created new records himself instead of relying on others to do it for him, and he'd broken the few contacts he'd maintained with the loose-knit vampire community. He'd even insisted this project not be advertised.

When the strange feeling didn't return, he decided it must be nothing. He'd lived with the dread of Max finding the talisman for so long, he was starting to imagine it happening. If anyone would use the talisman as Nicole feared, it would be Max.

Chris waited until the team left for the cavern before returning to the excavation. Since no one was watching, he hopped down into the hole where he pulled a pair of booties from the box, slipped them on, then ducked through the doorway.

Across the room, Brandon and Nicole crouched in front of the altar, bagging dust from the stone and the surrounding floor. According to Nicole, one major university project was analyzing dust like this for information about the atmosphere and vegetation a thousand years ago.

"What's the black stain?" Brandon asked.

Chris knew the answer before he heard it.

"Blood," Nicole said. "Something or someone was sacrificed here."

"You want me to swab it?"

"Yes, please. And take an extra set of samples. I want every piece of information we can get out of this."

Chris crossed the room quietly. As his booties crinkled under his footstep, Nicole jumped and spun around.

"You scared the crap out of me," she said.

"Sorry." He crouched behind her where he could get a look at the glyphs.

Nicole moved aside and they stared in silence at the symbols as Brandon swabbed ancient blood stains. There wasn't enough blood to suggest more than one sacrifice, perhaps to cleanse the altar.

"Here's his name again," said Nicole, pointing.

"Ahcaanan Uxmaal," Chris said, nodding. He spoke the language in his head, reading down and moving across. "This is his altar."

"Where's his tomb?" she asked.

Chris concentrated on the words forming before him.

Brandon placed the last swab in the sample bottle, screwed on the top, and stood. "I'll go put these away."

Nicole looked up at him. "Then you can head up the crew at the cave while we work through the glyphs."

The young man hesitated for several seconds, and then he turned and left.

Chris listened to his departing footsteps.

"He created this wand of power?" Nicole asked, whispering.

He had interpreted the phrase the same way and nodded.

"Does that mean it's supposed to be here?"

"I don't know." Chris moved over to study the next set. "These look like instructions."

Nicole leaned closer. Her breath warmed the air around him. He closed his eyes to savor her essence. Then, clenching his jaw, he forced a picture of her lying naked under him out of his mind and concentrated on the glyphs.

"Does this really say that a woman must be sacrificed?" she asked.

"It could mean that." Silently, he turned the words over and interpreted them. "A woman with heart of stone and eyes reflecting great waters will be made a sacrifice to walk in the light."

"What is this, some kind of riddle?"

Chris frowned. "My interpretation could be wrong."

"But where's the talisman?"

His hopes began to wane as they studied the rest of the glyphs. Work of ancient hands told of the seasons, of harvest, of planting, of the changing nature of the gods. Some glyphs related specifically to Ahcaanan Uxmaal, told of his unusual birth from earth and fire, and his abilities to please gods and heal the sick.

There was no other reference to the talisman beyond the one at the center of the altar.

Chris sat back on his heels. Were they too late? Had some ancient vampire discovered the talisman a thousand years ago, tried it, and found it to be as useless as all the other purported remedies?

The sound of Nicole's heavy breath and pounding heart suggested her shared disappointment as she knelt beside the altar, rereading the glyphs. Her skin glistened with moisture, and fine hairs escaped the clip at the back of her head. She glanced up at him with her emerald gaze.

Her beauty only made the loss more potent.

"So, it wasn't a tomb." Eric handed the bottle to Nicole.

She took a swig. In spite of it being warm, she enjoyed the taste of the hearty red wine and the way it prickled her taste buds. "No," she said. "It was his altar."

The group, including her grad students and a few of the undergraduates, sat on the ground in a circle around a lantern, twenty yards from the excavation. Chris sat across the circle from her, watching her with an unreadable expression. Every time their gazes met, her heart seemed to trip up and miss a beat.

Damn him for affecting her like this.

She passed the bottle on to Brandon, to her right.

Cindy, one of the perkier undergrads, started to raise her hand, and then dropped it as if suddenly remembering where she was. "Aren't most of the altars at the tops of pyramids?"

"Some are," Nicole answered, "those used for sacrifice to promote a good harvest, or more rain. To reach the gods living above, they raised their altars as high as possible."

"What was this one designed for?"

She shrugged. "We don't know, exactly. The glyphs say that Ahcaanan Uxmaal was born of earth and fire. Perhaps the people believed he had clout with the aged gods of Xibalbá, the underworld."

"What about the talisman?" Megan asked. She sat with her hand resting on Eric's thigh, their relationship apparently no longer a secret, although it had never been a very well-kept one. "You still think it's here?"

"I don't know yet. Maybe it's hidden somewhere in the ruins."

"Maybe it's in Brandon's trash pit," Eric said. "What better hiding place than one covered by crap?"

The group chuckled and Brandon shot his fellow grad student a nasty glare. Then he turned his attention to Nicole. "We've worked on some of the glyphs in the cave. I'm not sure we've really got this right, but they seem to talk about the people being held captive and killed one at a time. Then, toward the end of the glyphs, they talk about mass sacrifices to Ah Puch and K'in, as though they were sacrificing themselves. It's kind of weird."

"Who are Ah Puch and K'in?" Cindy asked.

"Gods of death and the sun," Megan answered.

Nicole glanced at Chris and found him listening intently.

Brandon continued, "There's one big section we can't figure out at all. I think I found Ahcaanan Uxmaal's name, but the rest doesn't make sense."

Nicole nodded. "We'll look at it tomorrow."

Chris suddenly rose and nodded in her direction. "Tomorrow." Then he turned and disappeared into the fading darkness.

The group began to disband, rising and brushing off backsides and flicking on flashlights. Eric drew Megan to her feet.

"There's something wrong with him," Brandon said softly.

Nicole looked at him. "Eric?"

"No. Marsh."

"Brandon—"

"I mean it, Boss. This has nothing to do with . . . us. I'm worried. There's something, I don't know, evil about him. I know that sounds goofy, but those are the vibes I'm getting. I just—"

"Look, I know him better than you do. He's different, but he's not evil." She tried not to wonder how accurate her statement was. Wasn't a vampire by definition evil? But how could she care so much about him if he was?

The head doesn't always control the heart, she reminded herself.

"Just be careful, boss. That's all I'm saying."

Nicole reached out and patted the young man's shoulder, trying to reassure him. "Don't worry."

Judging by his expression, he wasn't reassured.

"Are you okay?" Nicole spoke softly. "You don't look too good."

Chris decided he probably felt worse than he looked. How long had it been since he'd had insomnia? Since he was mortal, maybe?

Nicole had haunted his bed all day. He'd consumed enough cold, donated blood to leave him nearly drunk, and still when he closed his eyes he saw her face, smelled her scent, felt her warm skin under his palms. It had been all he could do to wait for the sun to set to return to her.

"I'm fine." He held up the lantern and moved closer to her, trying to ignore her sweet heartbeat. "Where is everyone?"

"Brandon and two of the undergrads are mapping the crypt, and everyone else is back at the dig."

He nodded.

"I was working on this part," she said, pointing to two double columns of glyphs. "It seems to be the oldest, or at least done by a different hand than the rest." She glanced around. "None of this is like anything I've ever seen before. We don't usually find glyphs on cave walls like this. Makes them hard to read."

The rugged rock gave some of the glyphs a smeared look, and others near the ground had been erased completely, perhaps worn smooth by the same animals that had unearthed at least one of the bodies. Where the limestone wasn't fractured, the writing was easier to read, and probably hadn't been too difficult to produce in such soft rock.

The part they studied had been carved into fractured rock.

"I've noted the ones I can read, but it really doesn't make much sense." She offered Chris her notebook.

Using her notes and his preternatural vision, he sounded out the words and translated as they moved together down the columns until they both knelt.

"The wand of power . . . moved from the altar of Ahcaanan Uxmaal's . . . something here I can't make out . . . under protection of the heavens."

"You got a lot more than I did. How'd you do that?"

He met her question with a smile. "I can see fairly well in here."

"Oh." She turned her attention back to the wall.

"'Under protection of the heavens,'" he repeated. "The heavens could be God, or the moon and . . . the stars." He jumped to his feet. "I know where it is."

"Where?" Nicole rose beside him.

"Under the moon and the stars—"

Her green eyes widened. "The cover stone, the moon and the stars. It's in the sarcophagus!"

Chris nodded. As Nicole turned toward the crypt, he grabbed her arm.

She spun around. "What?"

He lowered his voice so that only she could hear. "The talisman. It can't go through proper channels. If it's here, I must take it."

Nicole pulled her arm free. "You're asking me to go against my principles and break the law," she whispered.

"I'm trying to protect you. If someone else finds out about it—"

"Some other vampire, you mean."

"Yes."

She studied his eyes for a long time as if looking for some sign of his true intentions, and then sighed heavily. "First let's see if it's even there. The crypt wasn't sealed."

"What about your students?"

She turned toward the doorway again. "I doubt they'll protest a few hours off."

"You sure I shouldn't stay and help?" Brandon glanced over at Chris as he asked. "I don't mind."

"No." Nicole squeezed his arm. "You deserve some time off, even more than the others. I'll close down the site tonight. You keep an eye on the undergrads. I don't want any of them to get lost. Okay?"

"Okay, boss, whatever you want." He turned and stalked toward the mouth of the cave, looking back before ducking through the opening. She hated sending him away without a real explanation, but at the moment she had more important things to worry about.

A war raged inside her. She knew better than to touch a site that hadn't been thoroughly documented. They didn't even have permission to be in the cave, much less disturb the contents. And what they were talking about was the most despicable kind of theft.

Chris stood still, his head cocked as if listening. Then he straightened and hurried to the burial chamber. She followed, her flashlight beam bouncing between them.

At the sarcophagus, he gripped the cover stone gently and lifted it off with ease, placing it carefully on the floor. The stone had to weigh several hundred pounds.

Nicole gulped. She hadn't realized just how strong he was.

Shaking off the surprise, she stood across the sarcophagus from him and they gazed down at the body.

"You think this is Ahcaanan Uxmaal?" she asked.

"I hope not."

"Why?"

Chris pointed to the mummy's neck, and Nicole leaned close to examine the place he indicated. Two round holes marred the otherwise smooth leathery skin.

Her gaze jumped to his and she straightened.

"If this was the priest," he said, "the talisman is gone."

"Why?"

"The one who killed him knew everything he knew. The connection I told you about."

She took a deep breath and blew it out. She had to know if the talisman had been taken or not. "Okay, we start at the top and work down."

She started around the inside of the sarcophagus, searching with her fingers and her eyes. The stone had been worked smooth by ancient carvers.

Chris matched her movements and they circled the sarcophagus.

When they reached the bottom, they stopped.

"We have to look under the body," Chris said.

Nicole rubbed her forehead, wishing away the headache starting. Was she really willing to move the mummy from its thousand-year-old resting place to look for some magic stick? It wasn't as if magic really worked.

She looked at Chris. Her neck tingled where he'd bitten her, and a strange thought fought its way into her brain. If vampires were real, maybe magic was, too.

Her headache instantly worsened.

"We need a sheet of some kind to lift him out," he said. "I'll get it."

In a blur of movement, he disappeared.

Nicole stared down into the grotesquely grinning face. Had this man really been killed—murdered—by a vampire a thousand years ago? And what about the others buried in the front part of the cave? Had they also been murdered by a vampire? Or vampires? Or had they sacrificed themselves in an attempt to rid themselves of demons from the underworld?

What the hell had she gotten herself into?

Before she could carry the thoughts any further, Chris returned with a blue tarp folded to roughly the size of a person.

They worked carefully, sliding the tarp a centimeter at a time, until they'd placed it under the body. She stood at the head, and Chris took the feet.

She looked up. "Ready?"

He nodded and they lifted, easily raising the dried body from its resting place and placing it on the floor of the chamber. As the mummy settled onto stone, the head rolled to one side, snapping from the neck.

"Shit." Nicole rose and raked her fingers through her hair, trying not to picture the shameful end to her career she had just caused.

Definitely committed now, she returned to the sarcophagus. Dirt and dried vegetation of some kind littered the bottom. "Must have been a mat under him." She brushed the debris gently to one side, revealing a series of carved channels, and ran her fingers along the channels, tugging as she went.

A piece moved and she froze.

Using both hands, she traced the loose piece, about eight inches by three, and carefully pulled. The thin slice of stone rose to reveal a small chamber, holding a long, blue crystal.

Her breath caught in her throat.

They'd found it.

The talisman was real, and they'd found it.

"Oh, my God," she breathed. "It's really here."

Chris reached out and touched the crystal, which seemed to glow as if from its own light source.

"It's phosphorescent," she said. "But—"

"It hasn't been exposed to light in a millennium," he said, completing her thought. "Perhaps its light source is from a realm we don't understand."

Magic whispered in her thoughts.

"This is insane." She shook her head. "And to make it work, someone has to die?"

"A woman with a heart of stone," a voice said from the doorway.

Nicole jumped and Chris spun around.

The man who stood just inside the doorway was nearly six and a half feet tall, as pale as bleached cotton, and had black shoulder-length hair. His eyes were an indefinable color and sparkled in the darkness.

"Excellent job, Christopher," the man said. "I knew you'd find it."

Nicole's heart pounded and a sour knot of fear coiled in her gut.

"Aren't you going to introduce me to your friend?" He walked forward, so smoothly he could have been gliding across the floor, until he stood beside her. He brushed his fingers along her shoulder.

Chris stood watching, his face completely expressionless, his blue eyes cold and heartless.

Had she been wrong about him?

"Vampire?" she managed to get out.

Chris nodded once.

"Ah, so she knows." The man raised her hand in his. "Allow me to introduce myself. Gaius Fabius Maximus, at your service. You may call me Max." He bent forward and pressed his cold lips to the back of her hand, and a shudder ran through her.

Max smiled, revealing the tips of fangs. "She's lovely, Christopher. And perfect. You couldn't have chosen better."

Nicole pulled her hand away and Max's smile broadened.

"What's he talking about?"

When Chris didn't answer, she looked over to find him still expressionless, still watching.

"Chris?"

His eyes met hers, and his lips curved slowly into a smile to match that of the beast standing beside her.

"Son of a bitch," she muttered, instantly realizing she'd made a huge mistake trusting a monster disguised as a man.

Her only hope was to escape.

Before she could do more than think to move, she was snatched off her feet. Max swept her into his arms with ease.

"Let go of me!" She kicked and struggled to get free.

He tightened his grip and put his face close to hers. "If you resist, I'll break your pretty little neck."

Terror flooded her body, and her arms fell to her sides. She wanted to call out for Chris, but no sound escaped her throat. It wouldn't have mattered; he obviously wasn't going to help her.

Max spoke over his shoulder as he made his way from the crypt. "Grab the talisman, dear boy, and let's see if this one works."

Nicole realized she was probably about to die, and all she

could think about was that Chris had deceived her. How could she have been so naive? Of course, what could she expect since she'd been duped in the past by a simple musician? Still, her heart physically hurt as if it were breaking, and tears burned in her eyes.

She stared up at the face of the monster carrying her, silhouetted against the night sky. He moved through the darkness without so much as stumbling.

At the excavation, he simply hopped into the hole and ducked through the doorway, then carried her to the altar as Chris followed with a lantern. He placed her on the cool rock surface on her back and smiled down at her.

"There," he said. "See how perfectly she fits?"

Words finally formed as she raised herself onto her elbows. "What are you doing?"

Acting as if he hadn't heard her, Max extended an open hand toward the doorway. "My dear?"

A woman walked in wearing a flowing white robe, her hand reaching for Max's. Her pale skin practically glowed in the dim light, and her eyes seemed to be metallic colors. Dark hair framed her face, and her lips looked blood red.

A chill shot through Nicole as she recognized the woman. She'd assumed her safely home long ago. "Rachel?"

The former student looked at Nicole and smiled, flashing a set of fangs.

The bottom fell out of Nicole's world.

As horrifying as it was to face two creatures who shouldn't exist, to see someone she knew, taught, and worked alongside turned into one of them kicked the whole experience up a notch. "What have you done to her?"

The three vampires ignored her question.

"I want to introduce you to your sister, Christopher. Greet her as you should." Max led Rachel to Chris and relinquished her hand. Chris took it, bowed, and pressed his lips to it.

Rachel feathered her fingers through his hair in a loving gesture.

Chris stood and studied the woman for several long moments, then reached out, slid his hand behind her neck, and drew her mouth up to his. He kissed her roughly, and the air in the room suddenly vibrated.

Nicole's gut clenched as she watched the two embrace. Chris held Rachel close, and her fingers curled into fists on the sleeves of his shirt.

Christ. How could she possibly be jealous? Here she was in the hands of a bunch of blood-sucking monsters, and she wanted to be the one Chris held. Could she be any more pathetic?

Max crouched beside the altar. "Aren't they a lovely couple? I have such good taste. They'll be perfect together."

Chris suddenly spun Rachel around in his arms and held her close, staring at Max. He looked much as he had when Nicole had found him in the cave, but this time he wasn't trying to hide from her. Gripping the talisman, he wrapped his arm around Rachel's waist and used the other hand to urge her head slowly to one side.

Time slowed to a crawl.

"Yes," Max whispered.

Chris opened his mouth and drew back his lips so that monstrous fangs glistened in the dim light. Then, continuing to hold Max's gaze, he lowered his mouth to Rachel's neck, easily puncturing her skin. As his mouth closed over the bite, his eyes rolled shut and he groaned.

Rachel gasped in obvious delight, gripping Chris's arm.

Nicole's tits hardened and muscles twitched between her legs. She could feel his mouth on her own flesh, and remembered the sensation of him drawing out more than just her blood. She recalled the exact moment his teeth had penetrated her outer shell, allowing him to reach inside and touch her in a way no one ever had. Or would.

Try as she might, she couldn't look away.

Rachel writhed in his arms, her own fangs flashing, and tried to reach back to return the bite, but couldn't.

"Christopher," Max said, apparently in warning.

Chris raised his head and licked blood from his lips before finally opening his eyes.

Nicole knew she should have been horrified, but she wasn't. Heat of excitement flashed across her skin.

Rachel spun around and reached for Chris's shoulders, but he pushed her away with a nasty grin. "Later," he said, "when we're alone. You can have as much as you want."

If Nicole had had a weapon in her hand, she would have tried to use it against the bitch.

Max rose. "Well, now that the introductions are over, we should move along. Time for the sacrifice."

"The what?" Terror flooded Nicole's chest as Max smiled down at her. "Why are you doing this?"

Max shook his head as if disappointed. "Weren't you listening? The instructions say that a woman must be sacrificed for the talisman to work—"a woman with a heart of stone and eyes reflecting great waters." It's quite simple, my dear. Your bravery proves your heart to be as strong as granite. Christopher told you of his nature, and you didn't run away. And your eyes are definitely sea-green. I'd say that makes you the perfect candidate. Wouldn't you say so?" He glanced at Chris, who nodded. Rachel stood a step behind Chris wearing an expression Nicole could only describe as feral.

The terror settled over Nicole like a chill.

Max reached into his coat and produced a long, gold knife, ornately decorated with stones and shaped unlike anything she'd seen before. It vaguely resembled a scimitar, only smaller.

He held it up as if inspecting it. "Isn't it lovely? I found it on this very altar shortly after the room was first sealed."

"You were here?" she asked.

He shrugged, as if embarrassed to admit his achievements. "Yes."

"You killed the priest?"

"He wasn't the priest." Max frowned in disgust. "He was only a stone carver dressed up to deceive us. He was the one who carved these hieroglyphics, by the way." He waved the knife at the altar. "Unfortunately, he didn't know anything about the talisman, and couldn't even read what he'd carved. And the rest of the population was no help. Turned out the priest had left days before we arrived. What a waste of time."

"*We?*"

He ignored her question.

"Now," he said, crouching, "let's see if this thing works." Max looked up at Chris. "Will you do the honors, or shall I? After all, you're the one who found the secret. I hadn't thought it possible after all this time. And you will be my second in command when we take over."

"I'll do it." Chris held out his hand for the knife.

Max smiled and placed the handle in his palm, then rose and stepped aside. Rachel looped her arm through Max's.

Chris dropped to one knee beside Nicole, gripping the knife in one hand and the glowing talisman in the other.

"Don't," she whispered.

"You don't understand," he said. "Max is the one who made me. I can't disobey."

"I don't see you trying too hard."

Chris studied first the knife, and then the talisman. "To walk in the light . . . "

He leaned forward, his face only inches from hers, and he sniffed, as if taking in her scent. Then he studied her face.

Nicole lay back, unable to stop the tears now. His gorgeous face blurred in her vision.

Cold metal rested against her neck and she braced herself for the pain.

"Chris," she whispered. "Please—" Her voice faltered, and she tried to close her eyes, but she couldn't.

She flinched as the knife nicked the side of her neck.

Chris leaned forward and pressed his cool lips to the wound.

Oh, crap, even now, as he was about to slit her throat, his touch produced insane reactions. Her tits hardened again, and tingles of excitement rolled up her back. Moving up, he kissed her mouth, and she tasted a coppery hint of blood.

Her own blood.

"I'm sorry," he whispered.

She wanted to scream at him, call him every bad name she could think of, but nothing came out.

This was it, her last few moments on Earth. Her heart pounded so hard, she was sure a blood vessel was about to burst.

In a sudden rush of movement, Chris jumped straight up.

Rachel fell to the ground like a toppled stone, a red line forming at her throat, and Max staggered back a step staring down at the knife protruding from his chest. He took another step backward and dropped to his knees.

And then they were moving.

Chris held Nicole against him as he ran, and she clung to his neck. He must have cleared the excavation in one leap because before her mind could adjust, they were headed for his Land Rover, moving so fast everything around them was no more than distorted shadows.

He placed her on her feet as he drew his keys from his pocket and unlocked the door, then urged her in with his hand on her back. She scrambled into the passenger's seat, bruising her shins on the shift and the console as she did. Before she could even get turned around, Chris had spun the Land Rover a full circle in the parking lot and was racing down the dirt road.

Fighting the bumping and jarring, Nicole managed to grab the seat belt and click it into place. Then, holding the door handle and the console, she looked at Chris. "What the hell just happened?"

"I put the knife through his heart."

"You killed him, or whatever you call it?"

Chris glanced at her, briefly meeting her gaze. "No."

"Rachel?"

He looked away. "She was young. She may be gone."

Nicole stared out as they whizzed past trees and tall grass, bouncing through some potholes and dodging others. They must have been doing eighty.

"Is he following us?"

Chris handed her the talisman. "I hope not."

She wrapped her hand around the crystal and held it to her chest so that it wouldn't smash against anything. It warmed her palm and tingled strangely.

They skidded onto the highway, and Nicole winced, waiting for an impact, but none came. Chris stomped on the accelerator and they picked up speed.

Shortly before reaching the outskirts of Mérida he turned north, headed for the Gulf. They passed through small towns at unbelievable speeds. If it hadn't been the middle of the night, they'd have left hundreds of bodies in their wake. On the open road, he raced even faster.

Without warning, Chris slammed on the brakes, skidded off the road, and turned onto a two-track that wound through trees and heavy vegetation. The seat belt dug into Nicole's shoulder, but she wasn't about to complain. Anything was better than facing Max again.

When they slid to a stop, they were under a carport in front of a cold, dark house without even a hint of light. Following Chris's lead, she climbed out.

"Where are we?"

"My place." He led the way to a door that he unlocked and

held open for her, and then he took her arm and guided her through the darkness.

"Stairs," he said, "down."

With one hand on the wall and the other wrapped around the talisman, she descended a flight of stairs and stopped.

From the sound of it, Chris opened a heavy metal door that he closed and locked behind them. He turned on a small lamp and she squinted at the sudden light.

They stood in a windowless room, nicely furnished and comfortably modern. A stone fireplace at one end looked too clean to have ever been used, and the other end of the room opened into a dark hallway.

"You live down here?"

"Yes, for now." Still holding her arm, he led her to a sofa near the fireplace and urged her to sit.

She did, dropping onto the black leather sofa and taking the first big breath she'd managed since Max had appeared in the crypt. She released the talisman, placing it beside her on the sofa.

Chris hurried away down the hall and returned with a glass of water. Perched on the edge of the sofa, he offered her the glass.

She took it, draining the entire thing in one long drink, then handed it back with a nod. "Thanks."

He studied her, his expression tight with concern. "Are you all right?"

Interesting question. Moments ago, she'd lain on an ancient altar, a knife at her throat, staring up at three vampires. Now she sat in a basement shelter with one of those vampires, waiting for the others to show up.

"You were about to slit my throat." She touched the spot where he'd drawn blood with the gold knife.

He shook his head.

As her thoughts and events clicked into place, anger replaced fear—anger at him, and anger at herself. How could she have let her defenses down when she knew better? Why had she opened herself up to him?

"You kissed her," she said, surprised by her own words, "and drank from her."

"I had to. I had to know what Max planned." He sighed and looked away. "And I had to make sure she was weak."

"Damn you," she muttered. "Which one are you, my savior or a nightmare? How the hell am I supposed to trust you?"

Chris winced and rose. "You shouldn't trust me." He paced back and forth across the room in front of her, rubbing the back of his neck and scowling at the floor. He muttered something she couldn't understand. Then, as if he'd made a vital decision, he stopped, walked to the sofa, and fell to his knees in front of her.

Holding her gaze, he grabbed her hand and held it tightly in his.

"I care about you very deeply, Nicole. I don't know how. I didn't believe I was capable of such feelings, but I must be. When I saw you in danger, I felt as if my heart were being ripped out. I no longer cared about the talisman, or the future, or even my own existence. I even cut you accidentally because my hands were shaking so badly.

"You're right to be afraid of me. You've seen what I am." He cringed, as if the memory hurt. "I don't deserve you."

Then he stared into her eyes as he picked up the talisman and placed it in her palm. "Take this and the Land Rover and get out of here. Go into the city. You'll be safer there."

"The talisman—"

"Take it to a museum, or throw it into the ocean. I don't care. Just get rid of it before he comes after you." Chris lowered his voice to a whisper. "Sunlight holds no promise for me without you."

Disbelief stunned her into immobility.

He was ready to just give her the talisman? To give up on his dream of seeing daylight again? This man who had both stolen and broken her heart in the course of two days now knelt before her professing his love? He hadn't used the word, but certainly the meaning.

He wasn't even human.

The crazy thing was that her heart didn't seem to care. It sang with joy.

She reached for him and encircled him in her arms.

At first, he remained rigid, as if trying to resist giving in. Then he wrapped his arms around her and drew her closer. She slid off the sofa and they held each other, both on their knees. She trembled as he tenderly embraced her in arms that could crush stone.

Nicole opened her eyes to the talisman, still clutched in her fist. It pulsed blue and purple with the hint of a heartbeat.

"Chris, look."

He eased away from her just far enough to see the crystal.

"What's it doing?"

"I don't know." He took it from her and studied it for a long moment, then placed it on a nearby end table. He caressed her face. "And I don't care." He leaned forward and drew her mouth to his.

His kiss captured every bit of her attention as his mouth covered hers, his lips parted hers. With that simple move, he claimed her. She felt love in the way he held her, and she melted against him.

Clinging to his shoulders, she tilted her head and offered more, and he took it.

Everything that had come before that moment melted away.

8

Chris spread his hands across Nicole's back and pulled her closer, thrilling to the heat of her body against his. Hunger surged, but tempered by the amazing feelings growing in the soul he'd lost long before meeting her. Somehow, she seemed to be restoring him, making him whole again.

She groaned and her ribs vibrated under his palms.

Moving his mouth from hers, he held her. Was it possible that she shared these feelings? Would he wake from this dream to find himself alone again?

No, she was real. Her breasts pressed against his chest as he held her, and her heartbeat filled his head.

A strange sensation tingled in his right hand where he'd held the talisman moments earlier. As he focused on it, the sensation ran up his arm and seemed to radiate through his whole body, warming muscles and flesh as it did.

And it wasn't just physical warmth, but a mental one as well. He was filled with a sense of peace unlike anything he'd ever experienced before. Suddenly, he didn't care what happened around him, as long as he could hold Nicole close, feel her body quivering with delight, hear her soft sounds of surrender. He nuzzled her hair.

"Chris." She pushed back to look up at him, her eyes dark with concern. "This is crazy. We only met six weeks ago. How can you care so much? We don't even know each other, not really."

He leaned against her heated palms. He couldn't get enough of her scent, or any other part of her.

"I know everything about you," he whispered.

She gulped.

His fangs dropped into place as he moved his mouth to her ear. "I know exactly what excites you."

Nicole closed her eyes and flattened her hands to Chris's chest. The rest of his body was so close that mere molecules vibrated in the space between them. In a deep, soft voice, wild and dangerous, he said, "I know where to touch you. And I know where to *bite*."

His lips brushed the side of her neck. She shivered and raised her chin.

He lifted her to the sofa with ease and moved her knees apart to slide between them. Her hands rose over his chest and to his shoulders where lean muscles roped under cool cotton.

He covered her face with tender, teasing kisses as he unbuttoned her blouse. His hands slid around her waist and up her sides to caress her breasts through her bra.

"I need all of you," he whispered against her cheek. "I can't get enough."

Just his words drew a liquid gush from her womb. Did he really know what she wanted? Could he have uncovered her darkest fantasies? The possibility excited her.

"Yes," he breathed, as if reading her thoughts.

Leaning back and glancing up into her eyes, he slid her

blouse over her shoulders, but left it halfway down her arms, binding her elbows together. Then he raised her bra, freeing her breasts to his ravenous gaze.

Holding her sides, he ran his thumbs across the nipples until they beaded, and he pushed the sensitive buds in circles.

His eyes began to glow, and when his mouth opened, she saw the tips of fangs. He licked his lips as if eyeing a feast.

Wrapping one arm around her hips, he drew her forward until her crotch pressed firmly against his lean, hard stomach. She started to reach for him, but her shirt held her arms back.

He grinned. "You are mine to do with as I will."

She'd always fantasized about a man taking charge during sex, but never found one who did so. Maybe she'd intimidated the men she knew.

She sure as hell didn't intimidate Chris. She'd seen his strength in action, and that thrilled her even more.

He drew back his lips to expose his fangs and lowered his mouth to her left tit. Cool enamel pressed against her skin as he licked circles around her swollen nipple, and then lashed across it.

Her breath caught in her throat and she arched her back.

He grunted approval and drew her closer. With amazing care, he sipped her hard nipple between his lips and sucked.

Her head went back, and tendrils of excitement snaked down her spine to her hips. Her clit swelled to rub against her panties as if they were sandpaper.

He continued, moving from one side to the other, sucking and licking. Her hips rocked on their own, pushing her clit up and down against him.

Chris turned his head until his cheek lay against the middle of her chest. "I smell your arousal, that wonderful rich cream pooling in your cunt."

Oh, God, was it ever! He leaned over her, practically wrapping himself around her.

He pulled her up and removed her blouse, then ripped off her bra and went to work on her shorts. He seemed to be moving faster than was humanly possible, and had her stripped in no time.

She wrapped her freed arms around his neck. As soft as his shirt was, she wanted skin. "Your clothes," she breathed.

"When I'm ready."

He slid from her grasp as he moved down the front of her body. Every time he nipped her, she expected his razor-sharp fangs to break the skin, but they never did. By the time he had her legs spread and his mouth moving up the inside of her thigh, she was trembling with need. All she could think about was his hard cock filling her as completely as it had before.

He licked slow laps up the length of her swollen labia, swabbing her clit and causing her hips to lift into the air with each exquisite pass. It didn't take long to feel the tightness start as her body prepared for release.

He turned his head and nipped the inside of her thigh hard enough to make her jump. "Not yet," he said, his mouth pressed to her tender flesh.

She whimpered and curled her hands into fists.

Every move he made, every touch seemed perfectly tuned to her need. Sweat beaded on her upper lip and chest, in spite of the cool air in the subterranean room.

He rose to his knees, drawing her right leg up in front of him.

She looked up and found him gazing down at her with hunger burning in his eyes. A new level of excitement sizzled in her belly.

Holding her gaze, he kissed the inside of her knee as he leaned forward.

His prick nudging against her pussy took her by surprise. She had no way to control his entry, nothing she could do.

He grinned.

Damn, he could read her mind. He must be able to. How else could he know what he was doing to her?

He pushed, parting her dripping folds just enough to tease. She tried to wriggle toward him, but couldn't budge.

He leaned further, entering her, filling her slowly until he reached her limit.

"Take all of me, Nicole," he said, his voice low and dangerous. He slid his arm under her and drew her up so that her back arched, and he pushed deeper.

There must be even more of him than before, and she sucked in a breath of surprise as the move assaulted her aching clit, but he waited until her body adjusted and the threatening orgasm waned.

Then he withdrew and thrust in deeper.

"Oh, God," she breathed. Promise of release clawed its way up the backs of her thighs.

He gripped her leg as he withdrew and thrust again and again.

Her inner muscles began to contract around his massive erection, trying to pull him deeper.

Her world exploded.

He thrust in time with her pounding waves of ecstasy, drawing the orgasm out until it bordered on pain. Her left leg shook as it locked around his thigh.

Then he stopped, and she felt the last of her orgasm pulse along the length of him.

Panting for breath, she collapsed.

After a moment, she opened her eyes and found him watching her, his lips pressed to her knee again.

"Holy crap."

The corners of his mouth drew up slowly into a grin.

"What?"

He eased her leg down and leaned forward until his face was inches above hers. "I'm not nearly done with you."

"But that—"

He quieted her with one finger to her lips. "Was a warm-up."

She groaned as he withdrew, feeling deserted as she had before.

Chris stood, reached for her hand, and drew her up to him. She balanced on shaky legs. His erection, now slick with her juices, poked her in the belly.

She wrapped her hand around his penis, shocked again at the girth, and pushed. He rewarded her by drawing in a slow breath between his teeth. Then he grabbed her wrist, raised it to his mouth, and threatened to bite.

She tensed, ready for pain. Instead, he kissed the tender underside of her wrist, just at her pulse.

He lowered his mouth to hers and kissed her, sliding his tongue along her lips, and she tasted herself on him. Then he lifted her, walked with her feet dangling against his shins to the closest wall, and put her down.

Raising her hand, he turned her as if she were pirouetting. When she stood with her back to him, he stopped her and wrapped his arms around her. His cock slid along her ass and across her puffy labia.

With his mouth to her ear, he spoke in a seductive growl.

"You are mine. I'll fill that hot cunt and fuck you until I've had enough. Do you understand?"

She nodded, her body already responding to his promise. Juices welled in her pussy and dripped down her thighs.

"Lift that lovely ass against me."

She did, bracing herself with her hands against the wall, and felt him draw back to enter her. Her pussy began to twitch in anticipation.

Instead, he ran the head of his hard prick back and forth over her clit, spreading her cream and causing her to jump and squirm. Her clit swelled and her vision blurred.

Chris covered her right hand with his, drew it from the wall, and placed it on her abdomen.

He started in easily, slipping in her wetness, until she felt him nudge against her palm. God, he was amazingly hard, and he held her hand firmly in place with his own.

The bulge of his prick disappeared and returned, deeper. Her muscles stretched to take him.

He kissed the side of her neck, and then licked it. She remembered the sensation of him drinking from her and her pussy clamped down hard on his prick.

He groaned.

With his fingers laced between hers, he moved her hand down until they both touched her clit, and further to where she felt his wet cock sliding slowly in and out.

"We fit together perfectly," he whispered.

As she explored, he returned to her clit, stroking in time with his thrusts, and pushed deeper and faster.

Nicole flattened both hands on the wall and arched her back as her body stiffened, undulating to his rhythm.

He held her around the waist, tightening his grip with each stroke, and a strange darkness seemed to be filling her from the inside out. He wanted her, she felt his urgency. His cock thrust deeper, as if searching for her center. And she sensed his mouth near her neck.

As the darkness thickened, threatening to fill her lungs, she turned her head, bearing herself to him. Only he could save her.

His body vibrated against hers.

"You are mine and mine alone," he whispered.

She moved her head farther to the side.

Sharp points pressed against her skin.

Then he almost completely withdrew his cock, grabbed her clit between his finger and thumb, and carefully squeezed as he thrust all the way in, sheathing his entire length.

She gasped as her body screamed with delight.

Light swept away darkness. An orgasm unlike any other flooded her with pounding bliss.

With no control over her movements, she slammed her ass back against him, rocked forward, and slammed it back again.

Blinding pulses of pleasure burned through her muscles and she fisted her hands against the wall.

And then he penetrated her flesh.

She screamed as a second orgasm started before the first was done. White-hot waves surged through her, scorching away her past and future. Nothing left but the moment.

He held her to him, filling her as he drank, sucking hard.

She felt him inside her body, soul, and heart, and ached with the beauty of it. All she could think was *more*.

Chris raised his head and groaned with each long thrust.

Her orgasm slowed to pure, lazy pleasure.

And then they stood together as she panted, palms again flattened to the wall. She'd dreamed of an encounter just like this, although she'd never imagined it could be so incredible.

He knew.

A bead of sweat slipped between her breasts, and she dropped her forehead to her arm. How was she ever going to enjoy sex with a mortal again?

Oh, shit. She wasn't. She truly was his and his alone.

He withdrew from her, turned her around, and wrapped her in his arms, pressing his mouth to the spot on her neck still raw from his bite. She stood on her toes to embrace him.

"Next time, we take your clothes off, too," she said.

He grinned against her skin.

Releasing her slowly, he cupped her face and gazed down at her. "You are delicious enough to be dangerous."

She swallowed hard. "Is that a good thing?"

"I don't know." His eyes sparkling like blue diamonds accented his unexpectedly serious expression.

As she stood looking up at him, her body still twitching in

strange places, the past inched its way back in. "What are we going to do about the talisman?"

He glanced over his shoulder to where the crystal rested on the end table and sighed.

He placed the glowing talisman on the dining room table and they sat across from each other, studying it. The strange heartbeat-like pulse of light that had started after they arrived at his house still radiated from its core.

"You know the Maya also practiced blood-letting sacrifices that didn't involve death," she said.

"Yes, I know."

"Maybe we should go back to the crypt and—"

"No."

"Why not?"

A knot of fear tightened in his gut. "I will not risk your life."

"Might as well." She propped one elbow on the table and rested her head against her fist. "I've completely screwed my career."

"If so, I'll fix it."

Her gaze rose to his, her eyebrows arched in disbelief. "How?"

"All you have to do is tell the authorities I held you prisoner and forced you to act against your will."

She straightened. "But they'll come looking for you."

He shrugged. "They won't find me."

After studying his eyes for a long time, she looked away. "You're leaving, just like that?"

He couldn't tell her that leaving her behind was the worst thing he could imagine doing. If not for the threat Max posed, he would try anything to make the talisman work.

He'd never know the joy of walking beside her in the sunshine.

"Yes."

Her gaze snapped to his, and unshed tears glistened in her eyes.

Maybe he was wrong. Maybe the best thing he could do was tell her the truth. "Nicole, I—"

Awareness prickled at the back of his neck, stealing his voice. He grabbed the talisman and rose.

Nicole looked up at him. "What is it?"

Upstairs, wood splintered as the exterior door separated from its hinges.

"He's here."

"Max?"

He nodded, then grabbed her hand and drew her to her feet. "Listen to me. Go up the stairs at the end of the hall as quietly as you can. There's a trap door that comes out at the back of the library."

"But—"

He stopped her with a kiss, savoring his last taste of her. Then he straightened. "You'll have to make it through the house in the dark, but don't stop. Take the Land Rover and drive into town. No matter what, don't come back here."

"Chris, I can't just leave you."

"You must."

The metal door shuddered under an impact.

"Hurry, Nicole. Grab the keys and go." He pointed her toward the end table and pushed gently.

Another impact left the metal doorframe quivering.

He pushed her again, and she picked up the keys and trotted down the hall.

On the third try, the door swung open and slammed against the wall.

Max loomed in the doorway with eyes flashing murder. He held the knife in his hand, and blood darkened his pale blue shirt.

"What the hell did you think you were doing?" he roared.

Chris squared his shoulders, listening to Nicole's quiet footsteps on the back stairs.

Max stalked forward, one slow step at a time. "I give you eternity and you treat me like this?"

"I had no choice."

Standing less than an arm's length away, Max glared. "No choice?"

"I couldn't let you kill her."

"Her?" His brow furrowed. "You mean the mortal?"

"Yes."

Max glanced greedily at the talisman in Chris's fist, then reached out, dropped his hand to Chris's shoulder, and lowered his voice to a civilized volume. "Dear boy, we're talking about a mortal. Entertainment, at best. I even brought you sweet Rachel as a gift, and you left her turning to dust. Completely unappreciative." He shook his head and sighed, then raised the knife in the air. "I'm willing to forget this. Let's start from the beginning, shall we? We still have a half hour before dawn, plenty of time to make it back to the altar. Where have you hidden her?"

"No, Max." He winced as the older vampire clamped down hard on his shoulder, but he refused to bend. "You can't have her."

"*Can't*? I don't think I like your tone. You've always cared too much about these mortals." Gold and red sparkled in his narrowing eyes and his gaze slid to the talisman once more. "I may take back my offer to forget our misunderstanding."

There wasn't even a possibility that this would end well, not with Max so angry. His calm demeanor and offer of reconciliation didn't fool Chris; he'd known Max too long. As long as the talisman existed, Nicole would die.

Chris listened for the Land Rover's engine, but heard nothing.

The irony wasn't lost in the moment. He now valued the talisman more than he ever had. If by some miracle they could unlock its secret, he'd be able to share in Nicole's life. They could exist together in the daylight, leading a relatively normal life as if he were simply a man in love with a woman and not a creature damned to the shadows.

But there was only one chance to save her.

Max's gaze rose back to Chris's, and Chris saw the intention. The moment of consideration had passed.

Moving as fast as he could, he threw the talisman to the stone fireplace behind him where it shattered, showering the floor with splinters of glowing crystals.

Max stared at the remnants, and a groan rose from his chest. As the groan deepened to a growl, he turned to Chris, raised his hand, and thrust the knife into Chris's chest.

Normally, a knife wound wouldn't have been all that painful, but he felt the metal slide into his heart. Chris grabbed the handle as he cried out and dropped to his knees.

"Hurts a bit, doesn't it?" Max loomed over him. "Good. I want you to suffer before I end your miserable existence." He stepped closer. "You can watch while I drain the life from your pretty little mortal. Where is she?"

Chris spoke through clenched teeth. "Gone." He could only hope it was true. He still hadn't heard her drive away.

"Oh?" Max raised his head and sniffed, then sneered. "She couldn't have gone far. I'm sure she wouldn't want to miss this party."

In a blur, he disappeared.

Chris fell onto his back.

He couldn't let Max track down Nicole. He couldn't let his sacrifice be for nothing.

Closing his eyes, gritting his teeth, and yelling, he gripped the knife handle with both hands and drew it out. Searing pain shot through him, radiating down both arms and back up.

He rolled to his side and shook until the pain finally began to subside, then he staggered to his feet. He rushed to the desk, snatched the stake from the drawer, and ran as fast as he could up the stairs and outside.

The Land Rover hadn't moved.

Damn. She was still there somewhere.

He leaned against one of the carport posts and whispered. "Nicole?"

She didn't answer.

He stood perfectly still and listened.

At first, all he heard was the surf, a truck on the highway, two dogs barking, and an owl. Then he heard a faint sound, distinctly that of a woman's muffled cry.

"Nicole." He ran around to the front of the house and paused in the yard where he could see the land around for a quarter mile. Halfway down a trail to the beach, he saw Max holding Nicole with one arm around her waist and the other hand clamped over her mouth. He spoke softly as he carried her back up the trail. Nicole's eyes were clearly wide with fright.

At least she was alive.

Chris started toward them moving as fast as he could, but felt as if he were crawling. He gripped the ancient stake tightly enough to crush the wood fibers.

Max swung Nicole around between them.

Chris skidded to a stop. "Release her."

"Or, what?" Max uncovered Nicole's mouth as he drew her up closer.

Nicole focused her terrified emerald gaze on Chris, but didn't cry out.

Max lowered his cheek to hers. His nostrils flared as he took in her scent, and gold glittered in his eyes. "She's really quite magnificent, Christopher. It's a shame to have to snuff out her life force. But don't worry." He turned his head and drew the tip of one fang across the side of Nicole's neck, then smiled. "I won't waste a drop."

A red line swelled across her tender skin, and her eyes sharpened with pain. Wind blowing off the beach wound her wonderful scent around Chris so that his own vision reddened, but abject fear soured his desire. Max wouldn't hesitate to kill her, and he'd make it as painful for both of them as possible.

The older vampire's eyes rolled shut as his tongue ran slowly across the line, wiping away just enough to taste her essence. A low rumbling growl filled the predawn air.

As Chris watched, he realized with horror that he was peering into a mirror, watching a beast like himself feed off the woman who filled his every thought and defined his desire. How could he be so deluded as to believe himself worthy of her?

"Nicole," he whispered.

Tears rolled out of the corners of her eyes and down the sides of her face. He caught the acrid scent of her fear, and realized he hadn't smelled it when she'd first encountered him as a vampire in the cave. She hadn't been truly afraid then. Now she was, and with good reason.

Max looked up, his eyes reddish gold. "Delicious," he hissed. Pulling Nicole's head further to the side, he opened his mouth.

Fangs glistened, poised to strike.

In one lighting-fast move, Chris ripped Max's arm from around Nicole's waist and shoved her aside with his shoulder as he charged forward. He wedged the stake between himself and Max, cringing at the pain shooting through his still-healing chest.

Max glared at him as he held Chris off with ease. "Did you really expect to square off with me? Don't you know I can tear you to pieces in the blink of an eye?"

"I won't let you hurt her."

"Oh?" Max leaned close, his chest pressed teasingly to the point of the stake. "How, exactly, do you plan to stop me?" He glanced down at the piece of wood between them. "With this?"

Suddenly the stake spun from Chris's grip so that the point

pressed against the left side of his own chest, and he struggled to hold Max back. His master leaned forward an inch and the wood broke through Chris's skin.

"Chris," Nicole said, grabbing the back of his shirt.

"Run," he told her.

"It's too late," she said, her voice choked with tears.

He wrestled with her meaning for a moment, until he glanced over Max's shoulder and noticed the lightening horizon.

"She's right," Max said. "I'll have her before she gets ten feet away. And as you lay watching in your final moments, I'll draw the blood from her body. Don't worry, though, she'll enjoy it. At first."

Chris tried with every ounce of his strength to turn the stake back, but it didn't budge. As blood blossomed in his shirt around the point, he refocused his energy on pushing Max away. Nothing he did made a bit of difference.

"Why are you forcing me to do this?" Max whispered. "Why now?"

"Because I love her."

Max's eyebrows rose slowly. "*Love*? You think you love her?" He glanced over Chris's shoulder at Nicole, and then smiled at him. "You, dear Christopher, are forgetting what you are. You can't love." He shook his head slowly, as if they were simply standing in casual conversation and not clinched in a death struggle. "I can see it now. You'd spend her meager life trying to please her, and then pine away over this mortal female for centuries after she withered up and turned to dust. It's a much better payment for what you've done to me than anything I could devise." His eyes crinkled with false merriment. "Too bad you won't survive long enough to find out that I'm right."

Max pushed forward, but Chris managed to hold him back so that the stake didn't move.

"We made a good pair," Max said. "We are so alike, the two of us."

Chris shook his head. "I'm nothing like you."

Nicole tugged on his shirt again. "Please."

The sky paled to powder blue, taking on a yellow hue at the horizon behind Max. Chris's only hope was to keep the older vampire focused on him until it was too late. Nicole would only survive if the two vampires went up in flames together.

"Ah, but you are," Max said. "It's only your modern sensibilities that allow you to believe otherwise."

"I'm not the killer you are."

"You mean, that I admit to being. I've watched you take lives when you thought it justifiable. I simply don't pretend. In my day, we understood the divine truth."

"What divine truth?"

Max flashed his fangs in a grin. "That we are all animals and that the strongest survive longer than the rest." He drew Chris an inch closer, as if to embrace him.

The stake pushed deeper, impaling muscle tissue. A whimper of pain escaped from Chris's throat, and he felt his knees weaken. He gripped the front of Max's shirt tighter and pushed harder.

"We could have ruled the world together, Christopher." Max's expression lost all hint of playfulness. "Now I'll have to start over and look for a new protégé."

Chris shook his head. "No. I can't let you go."

Max frowned, confused.

As realization dawned and smoke began to rise from Max's head, his eyes widened.

Shoving Chris to the ground, he spun around to face his enemy.

Chris had only a split second to react, but he'd known the moment was coming and Max hadn't. Springing forward, spinning the stake around as he leapt, he wrapped his right arm around Max's neck as he thrust the stake in from the back and leaned into it with his whole body.

They dropped to their knees.

Thin rays of light shot up from the horizon, brightening the sky to pink and yellow, and Max howled. Smoke rising from his writhing body blocked Chris's vision and he regretted missing the sunrise, but couldn't risk releasing his master at this moment. He had to be certain there would be no escape.

When the vampire's solid body dissolved into flames and smoke, Chris fell backward to the ground, pinned by a hand on his shoulder. He looked up into Nicole's face as she leaned over him, and he regretted that it would be the last time he'd see her. An amazing orange shaft of light reflected in her eyes.

He had to see it, just once before the end. The sunrise. Just one quick glance.

Rolling over, he raised up on one elbow.

He'd forgotten how intense it was, how perfect the colors were as they streaked across the sky. Pale yellow arched up over the eastern horizon, followed by deep orange and wild pink, all covering a purple-blue haze. A lone wispy cloud above the horizon glowed red and silver.

"It's so beautiful," he whispered, drawn to his knees by the wonder of it, no longer caring that this was his last moment.

And then a slice of the magnificent sphere eased up over the sandy land, and he squinted at the brilliance. The skin on his face warmed as if from the faint hint of an oven. Higher and higher the sphere rose, filling him with peace.

"What's supposed to happen to you?"

He glanced at Nicole, now kneeling beside him, studying his face.

He looked down at his hands, bathed in soft morning light, and then at the smoldering pile of ashes that had once been

Max. "I should be turning to dust about now. Strangely, I'm not even tired." His gaze snapped back to hers as the answer became clear, and confusion blossomed into delight.

Overwhelmed, he drew her into his arms and whispered her name.

She pressed her face to his. "The talisman?"

He nodded. "It must be."

She pushed back out of his arms. "Max said you'd destroyed his chance to walk in the light. I assumed that meant you'd destroyed the talisman."

"I did."

"Then how could it have worked? No one was sacrificed."

"I don't know." He looked out at the rising sun again and smiled as a possibility occurred to him. Taking Nicole's hand, he rose to his feet and drew her up beside him. "You know, there is another way to interpret the glyphs. It could be, a woman with heart of stone and eyes reflecting great waters will be sacrificed *to*, instead of sacrificed."

Her eyebrows knitted.

"Do you remember when the crystal started glowing with that strange beat?"

Nicole rubbed her forehead in thought. "I noticed it right after . . . you told me how you felt about me. That's it, isn't it?"

He shrugged and gazed back out at the sun, now nearly a half circle of fiercely burning light. "Perhaps."

There was no perhaps about it. It had taken every bit of courage he'd ever had to tell her how much she meant to him. He'd been ready to end his existence rather than face life without her.

His long-dead heart soared with joy, and he drew her hand to his lips and kissed it as he marveled at sunlight dancing on the water.

"You're hurt."

He glanced down at his bloodstained shirt and shook his head. "It's already healing. There are some advantages to being a vampire."

"What now?" she asked.

He studied the beauty of her face, appreciating the way her green eyes glistened. "That depends on you."

She looked out at the Gulf. "My career's in the toilet and I'm in love with a vampire. I'm not sure I'm ready to determine my own future, let alone anyone else's."

"Are you certain?"

Her gaze moved back to his. "About what?"

"That you're in love with me."

She nodded.

"Good." He drew her trembling hand up around his arm. "I propose a walk on the beach in the sunrise. Then we'll worry about the rest of it."

Everything about the morning mesmerized him—colors trapped in the sand and water, sounds of the waking Earth, warmth in the air. He longed for a way to share the wonder of it with her, but found nothing.

Nicole sighed.

"Don't worry about your career," he said.

"How can I not? My credentials are shot."

He patted her hand. "If you could work anywhere in the world, where would it be?"

"Egypt, of course. But who's going to let Dr. Nicole Stephenson dig in Egypt?"

"You mean Dr. Nicole Summerset, world-renowned Egyptologist?" He glanced down to find her gaping at him.

"A new identity? You know how to do that?"

He chuckled. "My dear, I'm an expert."

"What about my crew? They're good kids. Some of them could even be great archeologists. I feel terrible abandoning them."

"Do you think perhaps the famous Dr. Summerset will write them glowing recommendations?"

She laughed. "Excellent idea."

They stepped out onto the wide beach and turned south. Waves crawled up wet sand, reaching for their feet.

"And who will you be," she asked, "Christopher Summerset?"

He stopped and drew her around to face him. "If you'll allow me."

Her beautiful eyes widened and filled with tears. She nodded and whispered, "Yes."

Chris swept her up and she encircled his neck. How could he possibly deserve to be so happy?

"You feel warm," she said, her voice soft in his ear over the crash of waves. "Are you still a vampire?"

He nuzzled her hair and felt the familiar surge of hunger, but noted the softened edges. Had he really changed, or was it the excitement of the moment?

"I don't know what I am," he whispered into her ear.

She leaned back, holding his shoulders, and grinned up at him. "But you still . . . bite?"

He smiled down at her, enjoying the wicked glint in her eyes, and his gums began to tingle. "Definitely."

She laughed. "Good."